To those who...
have never felt like the main characters in their own lives,
have been hopelessly lost in the dark,
have experienced failure more times than they can count
and continue to rise every day.
This book is for you. Just remember,

You are more powerful than you
could ever imagine.

AMANDA CARNAHAN

Rising
OUT OF THE
Darkness

DIVINE GUARDIANS DUOLOGY: BOOK 1

RISING OUT OF THE DARKNESS

DIVINE GUARDIANS DUOLOGY
BOOK ONE

AMANDA CARNAHAN

Ebook ISBN: 979-8-991532-1-0

Paperback ISBN: 979-8-9991532-0-3

Hardcover ISBN: 979-8-9991532-2-7

Editing by Eleanor Boyall

Cover art by Miblart Art

Formatting by Megan Bowen

AUTHOR'S NOTE

Rising Out of the Darkness contains darker themes and topics that may not be suitable for all readers. Before reading, please note that this book contains mentions of the following: Emotional and mental abuse, explicit language, physical abuse, non-consensual touch, threats of SA, loss of parents through murder, mention of death of children-not shown on page, explicit sexual content, panic attacks, anxiety, thoughts and attempt of self-harm, brief moment of suicide, scenes involving murder, torture and violence.

Your mental health matters.

PROLOGUE

W hen death stares you in the face, your reaction can go one of two ways. One, you choose to spend your final moments full of regret over the risks not taken, life not lived. Or two, you decide to embrace what few moments you have left, making every last one of them count.

Those are the moments in which we truly learn what it means to *live*.

Unfortunately, time was not a luxury that Queen Lenora and Prince Keir could waste any longer. They'd decided to meet their fate head on, meaning they would need every precious moment to secure the future of their kingdom and all those who lived within it.

Shadows from candlelight flickered against the cold stone walls of the room as a fog of dread loomed over the two souls inside.

Almost as if time itself had stilled, each shallow breath that Queen Lenora took became increasingly difficult. Heavy footsteps paced back and forth across the wood floor behind her and rang in Lenora's ears as she waited for the hot wax seal to cool. A bead of sweat rolled down her cheek as she released a precious breath over the wax to help expedite the process.

After a few moments, the queen turned in her chair, meeting the tormented gaze of her older son. Keir extended a hand to help his mother up from the blue velvet chair at her desk. Clutching the letters and satchel, Lenora stood, and they both walked towards the living room of the royal suite.

As she lingered near a small, ornately carved side table, her eyes were drawn to the crystal vase holding her favorite flower, peonies. As she caressed the petals, it awoke memories of happier times.

Being an Empath, Lenora had lived her life deeply feeling every emotion around her, including her own. She'd learned that nature was the best way to keep her soul grounded, calm, and most of all in control of her dynamis. Inhaling deeply, she sighed as her hand drifted to her side. *If only I could walk through the gardens one more time.*

Meanwhile, Keir resumed pacing.

A rattle against the door disturbed them. Lenora's heart thrummed inside her chest as Keir made haste towards it. His fingertips curled around the handle, and he opened the door just slightly to see Queen Lenora's lady-in-waiting peeking through the crack.

"Your Highness." Eloise gently bowed as she slid into the candlelit room.

Keir closed the door behind her as Eloise rubbed her delicate hand over her chest. Lenora sensed the endeavor that lay before them all weighed heavily on Eloise's heart.

"Good evening, Eloise." Lenora spoke gently as she handed two pieces of parchment and the small satchel over. "I know that I need not remind you of the precious cargo and task that I am entrusting you with."

Eloise slid the objects into one of the deep pockets of her dress. The usual brightness and warmth of her features had been replaced with somberness and creases of worry between her brows. "I will guard them with my life and ensure that they are delivered safely, my queen. You have my promise."

Lenora's heart ached as Eloise brushed soft, brown curls behind her ear. Eloise bowed her head. "You don't have much time, my queen, Your Highness. He is coming."

"Eloise, I..." The normally composed queen stuttered, trying to free the words from her mouth. "There are no words to express the love and gratitude that I have for you. You are more than just my lady-in-waiting, you're my greatest friend." Lenora tried her best to withhold the sob in her throat and wrapped her arms around Eloise. "But you'll always be like family to me."

A trail of tears slid down the sides of Lenora's cheeks as she murmured into Eloise's hair. "May the light always guide you, and the gods surround you."

Eloise turned on her heel towards the door. Lenora saw the determination in her face as her friend tried with all her might to hold back the tears. Keir extended his hand to her shoulder, causing her to pause by the door. He retrieved a small silver dagger from his side and placed it in the pocket of her apron.

"Just in case." Prince Keir whispered, brushing his knuckles across her cheek. Tears trailed over her flushed cheeks. Eloise took one more longing look, then exited.

Keir closed the door, staring at the space that Eloise had just vacated, running his palm through his thick, chestnut locks. It slid to his neck to rub the tension creeping behind it.

"I hope those letters find their homes swiftly...and safely." Keir's throat bobbed as he gazed at the empty space where Eloise had once stood. "Yesterday's assassinations have sent the city into panic, especially now that Father has put the blame on rebels. We both know that isn't the truth, and they do as well." He gestured toward the roars of protest and the clash of metal that rattled through the open window. "They're tired of being lied to, just as we were."

Lenora nodded in agreement. The High Priest had been attacked in his carriage yesterday morning. He'd perished alongside his wife and son-in-law. Finn had been well known for his views on how Lenora's husband had begun to treat the humans in their realm. Finn hadn't agreed with the brutal campaign that had been launched against them, just for inheriting small traces of dynamis without going through Ascension. Many Elysians had begun to believe that he had been murdered for his views, and possibly even for his closeness to the king.

Keir smoothed his hand over his face. "If anything happens to us here today, and they never receive those letters, or..."

"We must hold faith that Eloise will get them delivered safely," she interrupted as Keir nodded solemnly.

"I wish you'd gone with them. However, I'm glad to not be alone. I love you so much, my sweet son." Reaching up, she brushed back the pieces of hair that had fallen into the prince's face. "No matter what happens tonight, I hope that you know how proud I am of the man you've become."

His eyes fluttered with a hint of warmth once again. "You know that I wouldn't be the man I am today without you." He leaned in to give his mother an embrace.

"Gods, Keir," she whispered into his shoulder, "I just hope we've done enough to set everything in motion. Our people deserve a chance for a better life."

"This all started as a response to the violence. They're tired of being lied to. Tired of being suppressed." More angry yells seeped into the from the courtyard below.

"We'll do this together, like always. I'll be right beside you, no matter what happens when he walks through that door."

Lenora clutched the amethyst stone that dangled from the golden chain around her neck, a necklace her sons had given her over a century ago. She caught the solemn gaze of Keir knowing he knew where her mind had wandered. The queen couldn't help but worry about her youngest son, Declan.

"I hope he will understand why I want him to try ..." Lenora's lip trembled. "Maybe he'll be able to break through to Alaric where I could not."

"Declan is the strongest man I know. If this is the end for us..." he paused, exhaling a deep breath, "Then I can think of no one better to help our people rise once more."

A hiss sizzled its way into the room, and their heads snapped to the opening.

Time had run out.

The massive wooden doors that guarded the suite shattered into thousands of pieces. Keir unsheathed his sword from his waist as the queen pulled her own dagger into her hand.

With a flick of his wrist, Keir let his shadows spill out from his free hand. Darkness filled the room, trailing towards the now gaping hole. A deep, sinister laugh could be heard before the man it resonated from set foot inside.

Hair rose on the back of Lenora's neck, sending shivers down her spine. Steady footsteps now replaced the laugh as the new advisor to the king, Alastor Grimshaw, presented himself in the doorway. His black cloak swirled around him as amusement danced across his face.

"Did you really think I was naive enough to not discover what you two were up to?" Alastor purred. "You've both been *very* busy."

A flash of light illuminated the room as he projected his lightning dynamis towards Keir before the prince's shadows could wrap around him.

Keir staggered back, but not before he pulled Lenora behind him. He launched another wave of shadows from his fingertips. They thrust the king's advisor backwards into the stone wall. Keir's shadows tightened around Alastor, whose face reddened. Lenora could feel Alastor's fury ripple off him like steam.

One of Alastor's arms broke free, and he launched a bolt of lightning across the room. The flash seared Lenora's eyes, and she missed its impact as it made contact with her son.

Keir's body shot through the air. Lenora's breath stopped as she extended her arms towards him to catch him. Nothing but air flew through her fingertips as Keir, crashed against the far wall. His body slumped to the floor as blood trickled from his nose.

An eerie feeling crawled over Lenora's skin. Realization struck her just as forcefully as his dynamis. They had severely underestimated their opponent.

Lenora's knees buckled and she fell back into the coffee table, sending her beloved peonies crashing to the floor. The glass vase shattered. Shards of glass and petals tumbled in waves, covering the floor.

A deadly grin illuminated Alastor's face. At first glance, you would never be aware of the evil that lurked below. His fair complexion was a contrast to not only his closely cut locks of thick onyx hair, but his nearly silver-blue eyes. He had used his charm and looks to work his way into the castle, and as of late, he was the only one to whom her husband listened.

Over time, Alastor had let his darker side slip out, but Lenora always sensed a deep sorrow within him. It hovered over him like a haze, and she couldn't help but feel a tinge remorseful for whatever had made this man be so consumed by sadness daily.

Holding her dagger tightly, she prepared her stance, remembering how her younger son Declan had trained her.

"This isn't the end, Alastor. You may try to break it, but hope always finds a way," she declared boldly, launching her dagger into the air.

A blast of his dynamis launched the dagger back towards Lenora. She dodged with just enough time for the dagger to miss her forehead, but not enough to avoid it slicing her cheek. Blood leaked from the wound as malevolent laughter crowded the room.

"Such a shame to have to cut down such a delicate flower, but you've given me no choice." Alastor unleashed his lightning again with a lazy movement of his wrist.

Lenora shrieked as she crumpled to the ground. Ringing echoed inside her head, her dagger far from her reach. Shards of glass clawed into her knees as Alastor continued to hold her with his power. As blood began to pool beneath her, the queen's vision darkened.

Throwing her shoulders back, fighting against the grip of the lightning, she pushed her dynamis towards him.

"Don't think that I'm not aware of how you're trying to turn my emotions against me, Lenora." He stepped towards her. Towering over her, he leaned down close enough to invade the air she gasped desperately to breathe. "I know your secret. Emotions are truly powerful little things, aren't they?"

Lenora's eyes widened as she found the terror within his words. His dynamis became more intense, radiating pain throughout her entire body. How could they have misjudged Alastor so disastrously? So much planning, preparing, coordinating, and he could be the undoing of it all. Tears streamed as she began to realize what evil stood before her.

"Goodbye, dear Lenora. It's truly such a shame to waste such beauty. To think your king never took advantage of your full potential." He ticked the roof of his mouth once more, silencing her with a malicious grin.

Raising his hands in front of him like a viper ready to strike, he prepared for Lenora's demise.

Out of the corner, Keir leaped in the air, his sword extended, aiming for a fatal blow.

Alastor wasn't fast enough to block the attack, and Keir's sword slid deep inside his side. Keir grinned wildly as the advisor groaned in agony. As he released the bloody sword, Alastor vanished before their eyes.

For a split-second Lenora caught her son's shocked expression, the same one that she mirrored. No one had ever had multiple abilities except her younger son, Declan. The kingdom believed it to be a blessing from the gods and the Light Phoenix to the Stallard line, but the secret ran far deeper than they really knew. If Alastor had zephyred, that meant he knew the truth and must have for some time.

Neither of them saw Alastor appear before he shoved his own sword deep into Keir's back, through his chest, right next to his heart.

Elysians might be able to heal themselves and live for centuries, but some wounds they could not return from. This was one of them. Prince Keir's eyes widened as he slumped down, sliding off the sword onto the stone floor. Panic danced across his features as he clutched his chest to stop the blood from flooding out of the wound.

Lenora released a scream of pure agony. "Gods, not my son! How could you!"

Keir's body slid towards his mother, coughing blood from the side of his mouth. His gaze shifted up towards his mother's deep blue eyes. "I'm—" His breathing slowed as he whispered, "I'm so sorry I couldn't protect you."

Lenora tried to reach out for her son. Fighting against the intensity of the lightning that still radiated electric fire throughout her body, she rasped out her final words to her eldest. "I love you," she gritted her teeth as the lightning pulsed through her. "Don't you dare ever be sorry for anything. May the light always guide you, and the gods always surround you."

The remaining air in Keir's chest gurgled as one last raspy breath passed through his lips. Every one of his last moments he had used to protect the people he loved. His eyes slid shut, and Lenora's scream matched the feeling of her heart shattering into a million pieces.

Reaching down to the depths of her body where her dynamis resided, she unleashed every painful emotion she had towards Alastor. A gust of wind blew around them from her dynamis, only causing a slight hitch in his stance. She continued to launch wave after wave until the well of her dynamis ran dry. Alastor barely flinched.

The queen shuddered as he finally released her from his dynamis. Burning with rage, she glared at the man still towering before her.

"You may kill us, Alastor, but the gods will never let your evil win. Our people will continue to rise up against you, just like they are right now." Her gaze drifted to the open window, to the sounds of chaos outside.

A deep rumble of laughter thundered throughout the room, low and raspy enough to make the queen's stomach seize with fear. Blood continued to soak the wound in Alastor's side as he lifted his sword to align it above the queen's chest, piercing through the delicate edge of her velvet gown, straight below to her heart. He hummed with satisfaction, like a predator ready to pounce on his prey.

"Oh, Lenora. I've already won."

He slammed the sword deep into Lenora's heart.

One gasp of air, and life faded from her eyes. Alastor wiped the sweat off his brow with the back of his hand. He bent down and picked up a peony from the floor, placed it over Lenora's lifeless body. After sheathing his sword, he stormed out of the room, shaking his head.

"Such a waste."

CHAPTER I

ELENA

TWENTY-THREE YEARS LATER

S hattered pieces of glass lay askew on the wooden floor as I wrapped my palm with cloth to stop the bleeding. I rose on shaking legs to survey the damage. All the elixirs I'd worked on until the early hours of the morning now dripped between the cracks of the floorboards.

Sweeping my palm over my face, I brushed aside tangled hair slicked with sweat. Tears prickled behind the back of my eyes as my head sank deep into my hands. Another panic attack, another nightmare.

For twenty-three years, I'd endured restless sleep, purple, puffy eyes, and a constant state of anxiousness. You would think, after all these years, it wouldn't affect me so dramatically.

Unfortunately, the gods hadn't blessed me with luck.

Today was going to be a long day.

Every muscle cried out as I bent down to begin picking up the shards of glass. A week's worth of fretting over today's Ascension ceremony had led to this morning's panic. Add in the nightmares that haunted my nightly slumber, and we had a recipe for disaster.

I had already been running behind and this setback had only made matters worse.

Even though we were midway into the spring, mornings in this cabin were always unbearably frigid. Throwing my heavy sweater over my shoulders, I rushed towards the only other room in our house, the bathroom.

Squeezing inside the small space, I closed the door behind me and felt the handle bump against my lower back. Wasting precious moments, I peered at myself through the cracked mirror, assessing the damage and planning how to fix it before I had to face the rest of society this morning.

In return for my father's service as leader of our town guard, and my mother's expertise as a Healer, this house had been given to my parents by the town council of Lostburrow. A small corner of our cabin had been dedicated to healing the members of our community with her dynamis. Like others, the strength of her dynamis had dwindled compared to those who lived in the cities. Over the years she'd learned to find other ways to assist her dynamis.

When I was a child, she began to teach me ways of using different herbs and plants to create elixirs. When I became old enough, I assisted her with her healing duties. My mother brought love and life to all those around her, until the Nightshades took her soul from us four years ago.

Using the freezing water in the basin, I splashed my face. It shocked my senses, helping me shove the horrid memories of my mother's death back to the depths of my mind. Hidden in those shadows were the darkest parts of me that I kept locked away. Nothing could keep them from haunting me while I slept, however.

Tossing my unruly hair to the side, I arranged it in a simple braid. Pieces of my wavy auburn hair slipped free. No amount of fussing could tame the wild beast that was my hair, so with a shrug I let it be and closed the door behind me.

A clatter rumbled behind me, and I turned to see the door had fallen off its hinges.

"Hells! Anything else?"

Glaring at the ceiling, I groused at the gods above. There was no time to fix it now. With a little effort, and a few curse words, I leaned it up against the wall. Once confident it wouldn't come crashing back down, I shoved what I needed for the day inside my satchel, while cursing the king for causing us to flee here in the first place.

Anger towards our ruler had surged shortly after our beloved High Priest had been murdered alongside his family, just days after announcing he could not condone atrocities the king committed against the humans in our kingdom. Two days later, the kingdom endured another loss, the queen and her elder son.

The king blamed it on rebels, but those who had suffered under the king's tyranny and had witnessed targeted attacks also knew that these so-called "rebels" would never harm the only people who seemed to be actively trying to help the kingdom.

Tired of all the lies, a true Rebellion had arisen. Thousands had flocked deep into the forests surrounding the cities. With limited supplies to work with, many towns were constructed quickly and haphazardly.

In the earlier stages of the Rebellion, many of these towns were destroyed in a night, thanks to the vicious group of Flames we had come to name the "Nightshades." Cloaked by the dark of night, shielded by black hooded robes and masks that covered everything but their eyes, they left nothing but death in their wake.

Elysians with extreme dynamis abilities could only be found living inside the walls of the cities. There were four cities in the realm of Ehora: Vragos, the City of Ash; Grinwood, the City of Life; Atheling, the City of Luminance; and finally, the capital of the kingdom, Vrine, the City of Shadows. King Alaric Stallard liked to call those within these cities "the Blessed," because they had maintained the full strength of their dynamis.

As for the rest of us on the outside, our dynamis had only weakened and dwindled the further we were away from the cities. Every new Ascension ceremony left each Elysian with weaker dynamis.

We were considered inferior, low-class, and mundane. The kingdom believed us to be just a step above the humans, whom the king hated even more. In the past few years, some Elysians who had initially fled had made their way back to the cities in hopes that they would regain the strength of their dynamis.

Out here, we were far opposite of the Blessed. I suppose you could even say we were the Cursed, evidenced by the events of this morning and the door that lay broken behind me.

I headed to the short wooden dresser that my mother and I used to share. Socks were my priority. Once a protective layer of wool cocooned my frozen toes, I began to pull out clothes for the day. It wasn't until I bundled up in one of my mother's tunics, leggings, and heavy boots and pulled my heavy sweater back on that my teeth stopped chattering.

Raising the collar to my nose, I momentarily stopped to bask in the scent that still lingered. Somehow, the fabric maintained the faintest hint of her scent, sweet flora and herbs. Reaching behind my pillow, I grabbed my dagger and slipped it into my boot as I sauntered towards the door.

The beautiful dagger had been a gift to me on my nineteenth birthday, and it was one of my most cherished possessions. The onyx hilt looked as dark as night. Stars of all shapes and sizes had been carved into it by my father. My parents knew how much the night sky mesmerized me, making this gift even more meaningful.

That day would always have a spot in the happiest parts of my soul. Especially when two days later my mother was killed. Ever since, I'd carried it with me everywhere I went, along with the memory of a happier time.

I wrapped my fingers around the door handle and swung it open, met with a blast of frigid morning air and the scowl of the woman the elixirs had been for.

O phelia glared at me with her arms crossed over her chest. "We expected you an hour ago."

All night I'd struggled to find the perfect mix of herbs and other ingredients to make those elixirs. Ophelia's husband had been bedridden for weeks with a sickness in his chest. I'd tried over twenty different elixirs without any success. With every failed attempt Ophelia had grown more impatient with me, and I'd grown more anxious that I wouldn't be able to help him.

If only I could make more sense of what went on inside his body, like my mother had always been able to, then maybe my attempts to heal him would have come easier.

For four years, I'd been creating healing elixirs based on pure instinct and what I'd learned from my mother. Most of the time I was successful, but there had been several patients I'd lost when they needed me the most—failures that haunted me. Further chipping away at what little confidence I have left.

Sighing, I pushed those unwanted thoughts out of my head. Out of all days, today, I needed to remain calm and in control.

I wasn't off to a great start.

"I'm sorry, I fell asleep for a few hours after being up—"

Ophelia's hand shot up, silencing me. "I'm not here for your excuses. I'm here for the elixirs, Elena." Her eyebrows lowered as she motioned me to hand them over. Fear took hold of my body, and I could feel my muscles begin to tighten.

"Ophelia … I—I…" The words trembled out of me, and I took a deep breath to regain composure. "The vials broke this morning, so I'll—"

Her groan cut me off as she scrubbed her hands over her face and through her hair. "I should have known better than to trust you."

My teeth crashed into my bottom lip. Shame flooded my body, and it took everything inside of me to not drown inside of it.

"We came to you out of respect for your mother, gods rest her soul." She placed a hand over her heart. "Althea would be so ashamed of you."

I stood frozen in the doorway as Ophelia stormed off back to her house. A tear slipped free, and I swiped it away, forcing myself to close the door and keep moving.

Her words pierced through me. My heart knew that her words

came out of anger and fear for her husband. However, my brain told me that there was truth within each word.

This would be just another scar to add to my collection, reminders of the fact that no matter how hard I tried, I would never be enough.

My gaze washed over the garden that I'd taken over tending after my mother passed. Closing my eyes, I inhaled deeply, allowing the calming scents of herbs and plants to flow over me.

There had always been something soothing about being outside and being with nature. It was one of the reasons I loved going on walks in the morning. It's the only time I found peace within the turbulence of my mind. Whenever my feelings became too over-whelming, it was nature where I escaped to regain my balance.

"I'm sorry," I breathed, bending down to brush my fingers through Mother's favorite flowers, verbenas. As I began to rise, a white butterfly fluttered into view, landing on my wrist. Its delicate wings flittered once more before it took off back into the sky.

The sun warmed me with each step I took towards the training ring where my father waited. I couldn't help but hope that butterfly had been a sign of my mother's forgiveness.

CHAPTER 2
ELENA

My father paced as I approached the training ring. I shrugged the satchel off my shoulders and tossed it into the dirt, then pulled out my gambeson and threw it on over my tunic. I hastened over to my father.

He shoved a sword into my open palms. I almost dropped it but recovered my grip just in time to meet his disheartened gaze. "Sorry, I—"

Dismissing me with his hand, he turned towards the center of the ring. My fingers tightened around the hilt as I followed behind him.

Father stopped in the center of the ring and nodded towards me to take my stance. I'd witnessed Warren Morrigan's many moods, but today he seemed completely out of character.

Straight to training it is, then.

Rolling the tension from my shoulders, I readied my stance. He lifted my arms to where they should have been and nudged my feet with his own to give me a more balanced stance.

With a nod, he stepped back to take his position, and his deep voice echoed between us. "Begin."

Father lunged towards me, sword swinging. I parried the attack just in time. The weight of our swords clashing together radiated through my already sore muscles.

Before he could launch another triad of attacks, I twisted out of reach. We circled each other as I adjusted my slipping grip on the hilt of my sword. No matter how much I'd trained with swords, I could never quite seem to get it right. Honestly, the only thing I was decent with was my dagger.

Father advanced forward, and I parried his high attack once more and shoved back with all my weight. We both stumbled backward as I struggled to calm my breaths. My heart thundered against my chest. So many thoughts ran rampant inside my head that, though I tried to regain my focus, I failed miserably.

Lost in thought, I barely noticed his next move. I blocked his attack just in time, but my hold on the sword slipped and it crashed into the dirt behind me.

A growl erupted from my father as he dropped his own sword, running both palms through his dark chocolate hair. "Elena, where is your head at?"

"I—"

"You need to focus, Lena! I won't always be able to protect you. It's about damn time you start figuring out how to do it yourself."

A sharp gasp escaped my lungs. My father's face fell, regret written all over it. Shame swallowed me whole, and I wrapped my arms around myself.

It was barely midday and I'd already failed multiple people. Something told me that I shouldn't even attempt to follow through with my Ascension ceremony today.

As I took a step back, my father reached out and pulled me into an embrace. Resting his head over mine, he whispered into my hair. "Gods...I'm so sorry, Sunshine."

I buried my head deeper within in his chest as I mumbled, "You don't need to be sorry. I wasn't focused like I should have been."

He pulled me back so he could see my eyes. "No, Sunshine. You have nothing to apologize for, I do."

He guided me over to one of the pine trees that lined the outer edge of the training ring. Once we were both seated on the ground, leaning against the tree, Father broke the silence.

"A group of the Royal Guard rode in early this morning for the ceremony, and they've been causing chaos since." He sighed, running his hand over his face.

The worry lines across his forehead seemed even deeper than usual. I placed my palm over his hand in the grass between us and gave it a squeeze. "However, that's no excuse for the way that I spoke to you. I apologize for hurting you, and I didn't mean any of those words."

He let go of my hand and pulled me into his side, wrapping his arm around my shoulders. This was the version of my father I knew and loved—the supportive, calming man, the one who had always been there for me.

We'd had guards come through our town several times before, each time creating trouble. My father's demeanor would always shift, but never to this extent. It made me wonder if there was more that he wasn't telling me.

"I should have noticed that you had already had a rough morning and not pushed you so hard." He smiled sadly. "Another attack?"

I nodded. "I let myself sleep for just a couple of hours, then the nightmare came and…" A heavy sigh rolled through me. "I broke all of the elixirs for Ophelia."

"Oh Lena, you'll make more tomorrow. It'll be okay, you'll see."

I wished I could be as optimistic, but I truly couldn't see the light at the end of this tunnel.

"You're still worried about the Ascension ceremony, aren't you?"

I groaned into his shoulder. "When do I not worry?"

A small laugh fled his lips, releasing some of the anxiousness inside my chest. Pushing myself back up, I tilted my head back against the bark of the tree trunk.

"Someone like me shouldn't be allowed dynamis," I breathed. "Maybe I should just stay home today?"

"Elena, I wish you could see how strong you truly are." I scoffed at his words and gestured to the training ring.

"Strength comes in multiple forms, Elena. Everything we've been through, everything that life has thrown your way, you've always risen above it. Today will be no different. It's true, I do worry about you… all the time." His eyes flickered down for a second before returning to mine. "Sometimes so much that I'm hard on you."

Silence passed between us for a few moments.

"I'm so proud of you, and I know your mother is looking down at you with a smile today as well. Remember, when you feel like the darkness is threatening to pull you under, just look for the light and hold onto it. The light will always find a way to guide you through."

"Do you think I'll end up with your Tempest dynamis, or Healing like Mother's?" I said timidly.

Instead of answering, he stood and pulled me up to stand. "The gods will choose your fate by looking at what's inside here." He tapped my chest, just above my heart. "They know exactly what you can handle but will also push you to grow into the Elysian you were always meant to be. I'll love you no matter what dynamis you come home with."

A small smile grew on my lips. He reached down into his pocket and pulled out something I'd thought had been lost for four years.

Time stood still and words failed me as he placed the necklace over my head. The rough twine tickled the side of my neck. I traced over the smooth white stone and rubbed the wavy edges of the carved feather charm.

"Found it wedged between the floorboards after that night." My father's throat bobbed. "I knew she would have wanted you to have it one day, so I cleaned it up and saved it for today." Our eyes glossed over with unshed tears.

"Let it give you some comfort during your ceremony today, a reminder that she will always be with you to light your path."

Just as he pulled back, yells arose from behind me. I spun around to see what had caught my father's eye.

One of the Royal Guards indulged in a fresh loaf of bread from a baker's cart. The other soldier had his sword out, blocking the baker from interfering.

"You need to pay for that," someone else shouted, as a few more voices rang out in agreement. The smile on my father's lips vanished.

"I've got to—"

"Go, it's okay. They need your help. I'll see you later tonight." I pushed out my most convincing smile.

He hesitated, reading the anxiousness behind it.

"I'll be okay, promise. Now, go." I waved him away. He gave me a nod and jogged towards the commotion at the baker's cart. Nerves swirled in the pit of my stomach as I watched him go. The weight of my worry for him was likely just as heavy as the one he held for me.

Closing my eyes, I exhaled a deep breath, forcing myself to turn in the opposite direction to meet Brietta in the temple.

CHAPTER 3
ELENA

Children ran out into the street as I dodged out of their way while they played a game of chase around me. Ascension Day meant no school, so the streets were more lively than usual during this hour. Their laughter fluttered through the air, and it helped ease the tension that was building as I walked towards the Temple to meet Bri.

Brietta Kantor was the priestess of our small town and had been my mother's best friend. Father had worked as a guard for her family, and my mother had worked in her home as her lady-in-waiting. After Brietta's family was killed in the capital city, she chose to flee with my mother and father to come live in this town. She was the only other true friend I had here, besides Father and Will.

Since she had lived in the City of Shadows for a time, her dynamis was like my father's, stronger than all of ours. Bri had Empath dynamis and could not only feel emotions around her but manipulate them as well. Empaths could bring anyone to a state of calm.

My parents had me start regular meditation lessons with her once my panic attacks began to spiral out of control. She'd been with me through the darkest of times. Without her help, I didn't know if I would be where I was today.

These past few years I'd been working on myself, struggling to embody this "strength" that both Bri and my father seemed to believe dwelled within me. However, it had been hard to fight against the most brutal tormentor I had ever faced—my own mind. It often left me feeling like I'd fought a century-long battle.

Some days I could push past the darkness that plagued my thoughts and filled me with anxiousness. Other days, I'd scream, kick, and fight just to break free. Masking my weakness with a smile and laughter had become a habit as every day I strove to just make it through.

An ache in my chest blossomed. Concentrating on my breathing, I paused and placed a hand over my chest to alleviate the anxiety welling beneath.

This ceremony today was more than just about coming into my dynamis. It was a way for me to repay them for all the kindness and love that they had shown me, for supporting me every time I failed. There was no way I could let them down today.

Ascension days were the busiest days that the temple ever saw. Elysians strolled in and out to give blessings to the gods, asking them to guide their children or friends towards the dynamis that was meant for them. Countless members of the town pulled together to make sure that the stone temple was decorated and prepared for the ceremony.

Lost in thought, I barely noticed the man trying to squeeze around me with arms full of bundles of flowers. He shoved past me with a grunt, as he shook his head. Rolling my eyes, I shifted course, heading left down the hallway towards Bri's room.

My panic attacks had begun plaguing me at a very young age, some so bad that they would take over my entire body, rendering me useless until the wave of anxiety passed. They were uncontrollable, and they didn't happen only within the safe boundaries of my home, no matter how hard I tried to keep them concealed. As a result, many of the villagers had witnessed my attacks, causing me to be a bit of an anomaly around town.

As I walked towards Bri's chambers, I gave myself a once-over and cringed. Dirt crusted underneath my fingernails and dusted my clothes from training. My hair felt frazzled and wild.

Gods bless Brietta and give her strength for what she's about to do.

She must have heard my steps in the hallway, because before I could knock on the wooden door, she opened it to throw her arms around me in a hug.

Brietta was truly beautiful, the only person who could ever compete with the beauty of my own mother. Perhaps that was one of the many reasons that they'd gotten along so well—they were beautiful not only in appearance, but within their souls as well.

Bri's white-blonde waves framed her petite face and curled in waves down her back. Striking amber eyes shone against her fair complexion, and her cheeks always appeared painted with the softest shade of rose.

She herded me towards the basin in the corner as I tossed my sweaty clothes aside. One toe in the water was enough to take my breath away. When I pulled it out abruptly, I was surprised to not find it encased in ice. I opened my mouth to complain when a sponge collided against my forehead.

"If you hadn't taken so long at training, it would have been warmer. I told Warren to let you skip training today. He's a stubborn ass, like someone else I know."

She snorted as I gritted my teeth and plunged into the freezing water to wash away the sweat of the morning.

Moments later, she hummed happily towards me, tossed me a fluffy towel and motioned towards a robe hanging over the chair. After tying the sash around my waist, I joined her by her desk.

An arrangement of tools lay neatly on top of it. Something about it made me grimace in fear. Perhaps I should pray to the gods for divine intervention? My face must have looked amusing, because Bri laughed, politely shoving me onto the wooden stool in front of her.

"Stop your fretting, Elena." She picked up a comb. "You have no idea how long your mother and I have been wanting to do this to you."

As my heart plummeted to my stomach, I watched in the mirror as her smile fell. This would be another memory I wouldn't be able to share with my mother. Sadness began to weave its way in once more. Ever observant, Bri grabbed a cloth from the table and swiped the tear that managed to escape.

"I'm so sorry, Lena," she spoke softly, "I know how hard today is for you. Your mother loved you so much. She would be so proud of what a wonderful woman you've become." Bri placed a kiss on top of my head. My heart swelled from her words, but no matter how hard I tried, there was no avoiding the dark voice in my mind, the one that relished in reminding me that it was because of me that we only spoke of my mother in the past tense.

Bri began to comb out the endless tangles of my long, auburn hair. I glanced towards her reflection in the mirror, meeting her eyes.

"So, what do you think you can do with all of ... this?" I gestured a circle over all of me.

Her infectious laughter filled the room. I tried not to take offense, but I could feel the heat of embarrassment burning on my cheeks.

"Elena!" she scolded. "How can you not see how gorgeous you are? Why do you always dismiss your beauty? You're every bit as beautiful as Althea. Your eyes are the most fascinating combination of your mother's ocean blues and your father's sage greens. Sometimes, I swear they sparkle like the jewels they are." She tilted the mirror closer towards me. Her eyes begged me to take a second look.

I'd never been one to linger while using a mirror. It was hard to focus too long when you were ashamed of the reflection that stared back at you. Not wanting to frustrate Bri any further, I did as she asked.

As I peered into the mirror, hints of my mother's beauty misted through. Her hair had been lighter, more of a copper tone than my deep reddish-brown locks. Her hair had fallen around her in delicate waves, as opposed to my boundless, unruly waves, but once the sun reflected onto them, the same flecks of gold flickered through like embers of fire.

Compared to my mother's, my complexion was fairer. No matter how long I spent outside, my complexion never deepened in shade. Millions of speckled spots kissed the tip of my nose and the tops of my cheeks, and I couldn't help but roll my eyes. Another thing I didn't share with either of my parents, just like my anxiety.

Deeper into the mirror I fell, until the only part of my face that I really liked flashed in front of me. My eyes. Not the puffy, purple patches of skin underneath them, but the collision of blues and greens. It was like looking into the deepest most turbulent parts of the ocean. The two colors crashed into each other, spilling into the endless voids of my pupils, a beautiful illusion for the turmoil behind them.

"Alright, I think that's enough introspection for now." Bri laid the mirror flat on the desk. "We'll save that for the grand reveal." She hummed away as she began to fuss over my hair. Bri settled on leaving most of my long waves to fall down my back, pulling up pieces from the sides of my head into intricate braids that she fastened together with pins at the back of my head. Her fingers tickled against my cheek as she tugged a few strands out, letting them fall to frame my face.

Fear began to build pressure in my chest as she perused the small jars of different-colored pastes. We didn't have access to delicate powders for our faces, like in the city, so my mother and Bri used to make their own from a variety of ingredients we grew, like flowers and berries. Neither of them wore makeup often, but I did remember a few special nights where they would apply them, and I would watch excitedly.

Brushes swirled over the tops of my cheeks and swept over my eyelids. My posture was enough to make any proper lady shudder as I slouched down into the chair. Truly, I was amazed by the patience of women who did this regularly.

Finally, Bri picked up a smaller brush and dipped it into the softest shade of peach I had ever seen. A thin layer of the paint was smoothed over my lips. The shade reminded me of the gerberas my father had once bought for my mother, after coming home from a long trip helping the surrounding villages. They had taken her breath away. A smile warmed my face as I recalled her determination to keep them alive for as long as she possibly could.

Rustling brought me back to the present, and I opened my eyes to notice that Bri had placed the mirror before me. *Gods.* My mouth hung open as I stared at the stranger in the reflection. Gone were the puffy, discolored circles under my eyes. There were no more crease lines or discolored pigments in my face. Each freckle remained but covered so delicately that they complemented the rest of my features more than ever before. Charcoal lined the tops of my eyes, making them look larger and more striking. Brietta should really be a High Priestess, because this woman could turn a mule into a stallion if she wanted to.

"You look beautiful, Lena." She set down the brush she'd been using on the desk.

Even though she smiled, there was no hiding the tears that welled in her eyes. Rising from my chair, I pulled her into my arms, squeezing tight.

"Thank you so much, Brietta." I tugged on the necklace around my neck as I struggled to find the right words. "You've always been there for me, especially after Mother—" I paused, swallowing down the sob that threatened to break free. "There's not a day that passes that I don't wonder if I would have made it through without your guiding light."

Her embrace tightened as she sniffled. "I would do anything and everything for you and your family. You and your father are all I have left."

Before we both melted into a sobbing mess, Bri herded me towards the door. "Okay, no more of this. We mustn't ruin all my efforts before anyone gets a chance to see."

I reached for the door, but with a squeal she slapped her hand over her forehead. "Oh, gracious me, how could I forget the most important part! Sorry Elena, my mind has been everywhere else but where it needs to be today."

She made her way to a simple wooden chest and pulled out a plain white corset dress from inside. As was tradition in sacred ceremonies like the Ascension, we must wear white. It was believed that we should stand in front of the gods, clean and pure.

She placed the dress into my hands and helped me into it. The hem tickled the top of my knees. I was a lot taller than everyone in my town, even some of the men. Where this dress covered most of Bri's calves, it was considerably shorter on my long legs. Fortunately, it was still modest enough for today's ceremony.

She finished lacing the back of the corset and ran her fingers over my hair. As I thanked her once more, my body trembled. It was like it knew the ceremony was approaching.

Brietta's voice echoed after me as I walked through her door. "Promise me, no matter what happens later this afternoon, you will never forget how truly strong you are."

"Of course, Bri. I'll try the best that I can." When I turned back for one last glance, her smile was bright, but her eyes were still full of worry. With a heavy sigh, I let my feet carry me outside to wait for Will.

CHAPTER 4
ELENA

O utside, the frigid air had begun to warm, and I paused to let the sunlight melt through me. The warmth of the sun against my face could wash away even the darkest of worries.

As I made my way around the back of the temple to wait for Will, muttered whispers and laughter followed from a group of men behind me. Once hidden behind the back wall, I leaned against the cool white stone and ran my hand over my reddened cheeks.

Wilton Stewart, Will to those closest to him, had been my friend since he'd come to our town when I was fourteen. Will had arrived with his mother and sister after their encampment had been attacked and his father had died during a Nightshade raid.

He was the first boy in my town to be kind to me and not treat me like some sort of oddity. If I was being honest, Will was the only friend I'd ever really had.

Our bond grew closer a few years ago after he found me sobbing in a pathetic heap on the ground after school one day. The same group of boys I'd passed by just a few moments ago had decided that their wicked taunts weren't enough to embarrass me, so they added rocks to their brutality.

Thankfully, Will happened to turn around the corner just as

they hammered against my flesh. Observing the bruises and cuts forming, he had made quick work of providing the rest of the boys with matching marks. All boys in the town stayed at least ten paces away from me from then on, which honestly, I didn't mind.

Shortly after that, the two of us became inseparable, wreaking havoc throughout the town everywhere we went. Eventually, I insisted that my father let him train with us a few mornings each week.

Father had been training me since I was young, always saying that he wanted me to know how to protect myself from the darkness of the world. Girls did not receive training in combat, and it was frowned upon to allow them to own weapons. It wasn't considered proper.

Naturally, that meant we had to train early in the morning before the rest of the town awoke. I was already a pariah in my town, and people knowing I was training in combat would only further ignite their distaste for me.

Heavy booted footsteps and the clang of metal arose from behind me, jarring me out of my thoughts. The Royal Guards.

They came every Ascension to make sure that all Elysians who were of age went through the ceremony. It was also an opportunity to keep an eye on those of us outside of the capital city's walls.

Years ago, the king had deemed our town "Rebellion-free," and had this small stone temple built for us. Though we appreciated this sacred place, it was also a constant reminder that no matter how far away we lived, we couldn't escape the eye of the king.

One of the guards peered around the corner, and my heart began to pound inside of my chest.

"You," He scowled and took another step towards me until he was hovering right next to me. "Why are you behind the temple? You should be waiting out front with everyone else."

It took everything in me not to roll my eyes. "Sir, I'm waiting for my friend. As soon as he arrives, I promise we will make our way back to the front entrance."

His eyes narrowed into slits. Mine wandered down to the metal chest plate of his armor, where the kingdom's crest was etched.

Five twisting knots, tangled into each other, represented the gods trees and the strength within connections with one another. My gaze lingered on the single, soft feather floating above it.

After the Light Phoenix had sacrificed herself to bring peace to the entire realm of Ehora, our lands had become a kingdom under the Stallard rule. They'd added the feather to the crest as a tribute for all that she had given.

"Fine." the guard huffed. "If we don't see you out front soon, we'll come back and make sure you do."

He turned and stormed off. Once alone, I let out a deep breath. My gaze roamed over the row of small wooden cabins in front of me. Still no Will.

Worry overtook my movements, and in no time, I found myself walking around the corner of the temple in search of him. After everything I'd gone through today, I wasn't surprised to feel the dull ache that began to form in my head. Massaging the sides of my temples, I let my eyelids fall closed for a moment. Just enough time to run right into the wall of a man in front of me.

"Gods, Lena!" Will stepped back into my view, pouting like a child as he rubbed his chest. "You think you could run into me a little harder next time?"

Even though my heart fluttered at the mere proximity of him, I punched him in the shoulder. He stumbled back dramatically, pretending that I had wounded him.

"Where have you been?" I grumbled as I pushed past him.

"There was something that I had to finish." He tugged me into his side. "Always over-retaliating," he teased, then proceeded to rub his knuckles back and forth over the top of my head.

"Hells!" I gasped, shoving my way out of his grip. "Bri is going to get so mad at you for messing up her work. You better watch yourself, Wilton Stewart," my pointer finger sharply stabbed into his chest. "— before I use said skill in the training ring tomorrow."

I shot him a vulgar gesture with my finger. His eyebrows shot up to his hairline. "Such a wild thing you are, Lena." He leaned in closer to my face, forcing me to lock onto his bright blue eyes, and whispered. "There's nothing I enjoy more than watching your little attempts at retaliation in the ring."

A huff of frustration flew out of me as I stormed ahead before he could see the heat that was blossoming on my cheeks.

Not quite ready to make my way to the front of the temple, I turned and walked towards the back side of the seamstress's cabin. Will followed, chuckling.

Pausing, I slumped against the log wall. My palm ran over my ruffled hair as I tried to smooth it back to its place, at the same time trying to cool the heat that I could still feel in my cheeks.

"You still worried about today?" He paused, his words softer than before. I nodded.

Will's movement caught my attention, and I turned to see he had pulled out a little burlap package from his pocket. "Well, maybe this will help alleviate some of that." He smiled sweetly, lifting my hand to place the package inside of it.

"For me?" I teased, fluttering my lashes as I pretended to swoon like all the other girls in town did in proximity to Will.

It was no secret he held the affection of several of their hearts and had acted upon those affections on more than one occasion. Honestly, I knew way more than I wanted to know about Will's social life, which was difficult, since over the past few years I'd started to develop an attraction to him myself.

Unfortunately, that attraction had always been one-sided.

"Smartass. Of course it's for you, Lena." His lips curled up as he shook his head.

"I just...I mean...we've never given each other gifts before." Tossing my shoulders up in a shrug, I feigned indifference. Buried behind that mask however, my thoughts were a swirling tornado of curiosity and anxiousness. "Now I feel horrible that I didn't make anything for you."

"Lena." His voice lowered, wrapping around me like a breeze. "Stop overthinking and just open it." He tapped the center of my forehead, then feathered his finger down the side of my cheek until he pulled it back. The stubborn organ inside my chest began to beat erratically.

I carefully pulled apart the rough fabric. My eyes landed on what was enclosed, and I swore my heart stopped beating altogether.

Will had always been especially skilled at working with leather and metals, which he had been practicing as a trade until we received our dynamis on our Ascension day.

Inside the package was a brand-new leather sheath for my dagger. My other one had broken while we were sparring a couple weeks ago, which had forced me to use a torn piece of fabric to secure it to my thigh in the meantime.

"This is too much—this is new leather." My hands trembled. "It's beautiful, but I can't accept this. You should sell it. I know it's been difficult lately, and you need the coin more than I need a new sheath."

When Will had arrived in our town alongside his mother and younger sister, they were given a tiny cabin, and luckily both he and his mom were able to secure jobs in town.

However, a few years ago, his mother had fallen ill. Without my mother's ability to sense inside and find what was ailing others, I'd done the best I could to help, but Lila had never fully regained her strength. Most days it was an effort for her to even get out of bed. Will had been the sole provider for his family ever since.

He placed his warm hand on my shoulder, brushing circles across it with his thumb. "This piece was too small of a scrap to be used for anything else but this. Theo allowed me to have it in exchange for helping him with small projects around his home he needed to get done. Please take it, Lena. I'll be forever offended if you don't." He mimicked my fluttering lashes from earlier, and the smile that cracked my lips couldn't be helped.

I tossed the wrapping aside and went to strap the sheath straight onto my thigh. However, he stopped me from bending down.

Mischief sparkled in his bright blue eyes as he retrieved my dagger from its current residence, my satchel. Tendrils of his honey-gold hair fell into his face as he bent down on one knee in front of me. My fingertips twitched by my sides, and it took everything in me not to glide my hands through those glistening locks.

As his hands wandered up my leg to my thigh, my breathing stopped altogether. I tried to calm my body as his fingertips traced over my bare legs. He paused, his eyes roaming over me like he was taking in the view, then secured the sheath tightly around my thigh.

After what felt like ages, he placed a hand around the back of my thigh and placed the dagger inside the sheath with the other. Small shivers rained down my spine, and I tried desperately to regain my composure.

His warm palms lingered almost unbearably too long before he pulled them back to his sides as he rose. The whole interaction was only a few seconds, but gods, did it do some damage. I wobbled, my knees feeling weak. Realizing I had yet to breathe, I exhaled quickly.

This man is going to be the death of me.

Will smirked to himself, proud of the rose color that he had made bloom upon my cheeks.

My breath hitched as he stood there letting his eyes glaze over my entire body once more. The lightness of his eyes darkened as he stared at me like I was something he was about to devour. His tongue wet his bottom lips, causing my eyes to shift down to them. The shift made his lips twitch into a smirk.

I'd never felt so vulnerable as I did right now. My skin felt aflame, like his gaze could see straight through the thin fabric of my dress. Inside my chest, my heart clamored, and I bit my lower lip trying my hardest to look away from the intensity I could feel burning behind his eyes. *Gods.* He really needed to say something before I melted into the ground right in front of him.

As if he could read my mind, he closed the gap between us. "Elena, you are—" He licked his lips, as if trying to find the strength to say the next word. "Breathtaking."

Did he just call me breathtaking? There was no way those words could have left his lips. That was when I knew I must have been hallucinating. I hadn't eaten anything since this morning, and lack of food always made mind a little hazy. Now I was standing here blushing at absolutely nothing like an idiot.

Reading the turmoil written all over my face, the man in front of me decided to take matters into his own hands. He wrapped one arm around my waist sliding me closer into him, as he cupped my face with his other hand. Burning heat flooded my entire body, and again I squeezed my eyes shut as he tilted my chin up to look at him.

Is this happening?

"Elena, did you hear what I said?" His voice rumbled over me in a slow cadence that vibrated against my bones. "Come on, please open those beautiful eyes for me, Lena."

I took a deep breath and glanced into the smoldering eyes gazing down at me.

"Why do you do that, Elena?" His fingers brushed against the side of my cheek, sending delicious shivers running down my spine.

"What do you mean?" I asked innocently, knowing he knew full well I was avoiding answering. Compliments were something that I had never been comfortable with. It was hard to accept words that your head constantly told you weren't truth.

"Why do you always dismiss anyone who mentions anything about your beauty, or shows you affection? Gods Lena, you've got to know how truly gorgeous you are. If you don't know, then I'm definitely not doing a good job of showing you that you are."

He lifted my shaking hand and placed my palm flat over his chest. Will's hand enveloped mine as the other hand smoothed back and forth against my back. Even through his solid rock of a chest, I could feel how his heart was racing, proof my affections weren't one-sided.

"Lena." His voice became even more raspy. "Do you even know how long I've been waiting for you to notice my affections?" His eyes locked on my own, pleading for me to give him some kind of confirmation.

My mouth had become so dry I was unsure if I'd even be able to respond. "Will, I—" I took another deep breath. "You are incredibly flirtatious with everyone, and I'm definitely not anywhere near as beautiful as the rest of the girls whom you've—" He stopped me by tracing his thumb over my lips as he lowered his head closer. I could feel his warmth as he whispered inches away from my lips, "Not one more word about you not being beautiful. I won't allow it any longer."

His hand slid down to cup the side of my face as the other now gripped my back. His eyes darkened. Sharp tingles radiated throughout my entire body, heating me from the inside out. Will's lips curled up in a satisfied smile.

"From this moment on, Elena, I'll never let you forget how stunningly beautiful you are. I plan to show you every day just how enamored I am by you."

My breath hitched just as his lips plunged onto my own. The kiss was hungry and longing, like he had been waiting for this moment for an eternity. Mine was just as needy as I parted my lips to allow our kiss to deepen.

Will's experienced lips devoured my own, both of us gasping for breaths in between. He twisted his fists through the waves of my hair, pulling me even further into his embrace. Our hands roamed, mine around his neck and hair, and his *everywhere* else, tugging each other closer and closer until there was no space left between our bodies.

Just when I thought I couldn't take it anymore, he left my mouth to explore the curve of my neck. The sensation of his lips sizzled against my skin. He walked me back towards the side of the cabin behind me, pushed me up against it and pinned me.

One hand drifted down, lifting my leg wrapping it around his hip as he pushed his chest against mine. My body trembled beneath his grasp. His hand slid up over my knee, stopping to caress my skin along the way. With each caress, a moan escaped from my mouth into his.

He continued his tortuous path higher and higher until I felt him pull away just a breath, pulling my lip between his teeth before releasing. The loss of his lips made a small whimper of frustration escape.

With a husky laugh, he pressed his nose into mine until we were eye to eye. The only sounds were our heavy breaths. The rest of the world had already faded away.

"Lena," he rasped, "that was better than anything I've ever imagined."

Shocked, my teeth slid against my bottom lip. "You've imagined us—?"

A wicked smirk tugged at his lips. "Several times."

My eyes widened, and he devoured my lips once more.

The clatter of armor rattled next to us, followed by a familiar booming voice. My out-of-body experience ended, and I was slammed back into reality.

Guards.

Ascension.

CHAPTER 5
ELENA

"I see you've found who you were looking for."

The guard's glare flickered between the two of us as Will lowered me back to the ground then stepped in front of me.

A dark chuckle rolled through the guard's chest as he shifted his gaze towards mine. "If I'd known that was all you wanted sweetheart, I could have helped you out. All you needed to do was ask."

Laughter rang out from the two other guards behind him, and Will's body jolted towards them. I wrapped my hand around his biceps, tugging him back towards me. A frustrated growl rumbled inside of him. I shook my head, motioning that the fight wasn't worth it.

"I'd listen to her if I were you." The first guard snickered. "You haven't even received your dynamis, you'd be no challenge to us, boy."

This time, the guard was met with both our seething glares, causing them all to laugh again.

"Move it. It's time for your Ascension. We wouldn't want to you to miss getting your sympathy gifts from the gods." The guard tilted his head towards the temple behind him.

As we passed, he gripped my wrist, causing me to turn back. The guard tugged me closer, the other two placing their hands on Will's shoulders holding him back from me. A snarl rang out from Will.

"Take your hands off of her!"

Anger swelled within me as the guard inched closer to my face. "If you change your mind, sweetheart, I wouldn't mind slumming it for you. Maybe then you could find out what real power feels like."

Nausea rose within me as I tugged out of his grip and leapt towards Will. Laughter surrounded us. We pushed past them all and made our way to the front of the temple.

Fury raged within me. Sometimes, I truly wondered how Elysians like that were even blessed with dynamis in the first place. Wrapping my arms tightly around myself, I paced back and forth in the dirt in front of the temple.

Will pulled me back towards him, jarring me free from my spiraling thoughts. He twirled me around to face him. "You alright?" He brushed his palms up and down over my arms in a calming motion.

My shoulders sagged along with my fury. "No." I sighed deeply. "But I will be."

He pulled me into him and rubbed my back tenderly. The brass bell on top of the temple began to thrum, but I wanted nothing but to lose myself in this moment with Will. Reluctantly, I peeled myself away. A few others passed around us, making their way into the temple through the now open navy-blue doors.

"Come on, Lena, let's get inside." Will brushed his palm against my cheek one more time. "The sooner we get in, the faster we can get out, right?"

I nodded slowly. "Right."

A s we walked into the temple, I trailed my fingertips over the cold stone wall of the hallway that led towards the main gathering hall, trying to ease the wave of nerves.

We approached the wide archway of the great room, and I

marveled over the view as we stepped inside. Curtains covered the windows, creating a dim, but intimate mood.

Everywhere my eyes wandered, an array of beautiful flowers and plants consumed my sight. Candles fluttered warm light within the dim room, covering every empty space that wasn't touched by flora. Even the scent of the space was intoxicating. Hints of lavender and sage tried to coax me into a state of calm. The entire room felt serene, quite the opposite of the emotions that lingered within me. I let my eyes flutter closed, taking a moment to collect myself before I opened them once more.

We made our way towards the center of the room, where the rest of the Elysians had begun to huddle around the sacred ring. This open circle in the middle of the temple mimicked the smaller circles that we would step into during our individual ceremonies. Smooth white stones bordered a large circle filled with soft sand. It was meant to connect us to the gods, a way to give back to them for all the blessings that they bestowed upon us.

Will placed his palm against my back, its presence grounding me as he ushered us towards the rest of the group. Only ten participants this time—quite a few less than in the past years. However, this didn't surprise me, considering Elysians struggle with fertility. Sadly, some never got the chance to experience being a parent. Others were only able to have one or two children. It was extremely rare for an Elysian to have any more than that.

My boots touched the edge of the marble stone of the sacred circle, and I paused, catching Bri's troubled gaze. She had always been the portrait of calm, but deep wrinkles creased her forehead. Something seemed off about her and my father today. Both almost seemed full of … fear. The question that swirled inside my head was why.

Brietta cleared her throat, alerting our attention back to her. The guard stormed away towards the entrance of the room and stood in front of it.

"Welcome my fellow Elysians. You have waited for twenty-three years and today is finally the day you will give back to the gods for all those years of life they have granted you. In return, you will be blessed with the dynamis that the gods believe represents the deepest parts of your soul."

Chuckles arose from the guards in the back of the room, and Brietta's eyes slitted into a deadly glare. They caught her gaze, and silence fell over the room once more.

"As you know, there are five gods, one each for Terra, Fire, Air and Water, and the goddess of Healing. When they left the realm of Ehora, they left us with five sacred trees. A tree grows in each of the cities, and the final in the middle of our lands."

She placed both hands over her heart. We all lowered down to our knees, one hand placed over our heart, while the other we placed inside the cool sand of the circle.

"These sacred trees are meant to connect us, to bind us not only to the ground beneath us, but the spirit within us. The gods believed in our sacred number of five as well. It stems from the five gods, five trees, and the combined numerals of your age when you receive your dynamis. Today, you will transform into who you are fated to be. This Ascension marks the beginning of your journey."

She placed her other hand beneath the sand now, and we all followed. When we lifted our hands and spread our fingers, the sand trickled through as we repeated our blessing. "May the light always guide you, and the gods surround you."

Once all the sand had slid from our fingers, we stood. Bri guided us to one of the wooden benches that filled the other half of the room. Before Will and I could sit, however, she summoned us.

A knot formed in my throat, and my trembling palms slickened with moisture. Will reached over and threaded his fingers between my own, giving them a squeeze.

"We'll be fine, Lena. Just think, when we walk out of here, we'll also have a brand-new tattoo right here." He raised my hand to his mouth and pressed his lips against the top of my right hand.

That was where a symbol of our dynamis would appear encased in a triangle once we received our gifts. Our true nature would be illuminated, providing us with the clarity necessary to discover our purpose and direction as we transformed into the next versions of ourselves.

Intriguing, yet utterly terrifying.

We made our way towards Bri. She ushered me towards her and Will towards her assistant. I gave Will one last smile before I entered the room.

There were only two rooms for Ascensions inside the small temple. The inside of the room would normally be dark, since there were no windows, just cold stone walls. However, the flickering candlelight drew me in. Candles of various sizes covered the room, as well as several pots full of calming flowers and herbs. Sage-scented smoke tickled my nose, as Bri carried a small satchel of it as she blessed the room for the ceremony.

She motioned towards my feet, and I removed my boots and placed them near the door. Bri set the sage aside in a ceramic bowl and picked up the small tray next to it before she walked back towards me.

"In you go." Her words were like a calming breeze as she motioned towards the small circle of sand in the middle of the room.

Sand squished between my toes as I stepped towards the middle and lowered, gently falling to my knees. Bri bent over and dipped her finger into a smaller bowl. She slid the oil over my forehead and behind my ears, the scent of lavender washing over me.

The tension that had been building inside of me began to ease. Warmth filled my hands as Bri handed me a cup of soothing tea for deeper meditation. Delicious flavors of honey and cinnamon, and a hint of something else that I couldn't distinguish, collided inside my mouth.

I handed back the cup. She placed it down on the tray and grabbed the small knife before placing the tray aside. Nerves swirled once more as I tried to take slow, even breaths, letting the lavender oil soothe me. Extending my trembling hands forward towards Bri, I turned them over, so my palms faced up.

"With this blade, I slice through the barriers that hold you back from reaching your full potential." She nicked both palms, and blood began to spill out. My eyelids began to feel heavy as the effects of the tea were beginning to kick in. "A drop of blood sacrificed, to give back to the realm for the gifts that will be bestowed upon you."

I sat back on my heels and buried my hands beneath the sand as Bri continued the ceremony. "It's time to become connected with the gods, and to discover your fate." She rose and made her way towards the door. "Elena, may the light always guide you and the gods surround you."

The door behind me was still open, and I let the hum of the singing bowls being played outside help me deeper into my meditation.

Every one of my limbs felt numb as I drifted into the deepest meditative state I have ever been in. I barely registered Bri's words as she left. The door closed behind me. I was alone. My eyes remained closed as the world around me faded away.

Darkness enveloped me, pressure building within my chest. Waving my arms in the abyss surrounding me, I stumbled to find my bearings.

The more I stood in nothingness, the more my palms began to sweat. The rapid pants of my breath were the only sound that filled my ears.

Fear prickled over me. My thoughts spiraled inside the silence. Perhaps the gods had deemed me unworthy of dynamis, and I would awaken a failure. If anything was consistent about me, it was the fact that at one point or another I always failed. Why would my Ascension prove to be any different?

Just before my panic fully possessed me, violet swirls of light flooded into my vision. They beckoned me with their glow as they danced about, illuminating a path.

They circled around me and I felt an overwhelming sense of being safe and protected. Surrendering to the pull, I let them guide me forward. The darkness melted away, revealing thousands of sparkling stars all around me.

Gasping in awe, I extended my arms out to the shimmering spheres of light. They wove in and out of my fingertips, gliding over my hands like the ripples of water in a pond.

Something about the night sky had always mesmerized me. Every time I looked up at the stars, it made me feel like each of them was listening to me, watching over me as I made my way in this realm.

As I continued to follow the lights, it started to get much brighter ahead of me. The closer I walked the more I had to shield my eyes from the brightness. After walking for what seemed an eternity, I heard the crunch of something beneath my footsteps. My body froze.

No longer was I in the darkness. Luscious green grass surrounded me as far as my eyes could see. The orbs of light I had followed were much smaller now and danced about like tiny fireflies. The sky was hooded in stars. I took a moment to bask in its beauty.

I took a deep breath. My body suddenly became very aware of a presence approaching me. Warmth, happiness, serenity—these feelings spilled into me, almost like they were being purposefully projected into my body. It was like the feeling of Bri's Empath dynamis when she would use it to calm me.

I came face to face with what I hoped to be the goddess.

It was hard to make out her face, as her body was bathed in golden light. Her ethereal hair whirled around her body like she had her own personal breeze that surrounded her.

My eyes narrowed as a sense of familiarity began to bloom in my mind. How could someone I had never met feel so intensely like an old acquaintance? Also, I know I've heard that voice before, but no matter how hard I tried to remember, I couldn't. Palming my tight chest, I rubbed the throb in my heart as it awakened again.

"Welcome, Elena." She paused, her eyes lingering on me for a moment longer, like she too found familiarity in me. "Take a seat and rest. I have much to show you, and even more to give you."

A log appeared on my right as my eyes widened. The goddess glided towards me until she was right in front of me. As she placed her palm against my chest, the heaviness of every emotion hit me all at once. I swallowed deeply trying to control it all.

"Your fate is calling to me. Let me see who you are."

Every part of me trembled. Terror built, the fear of finding out what I was fated to overwhelming me. The more I fought against it, the more my body ached.

"Have faith, Elena, trust me and stop resisting."

The pressure was intense, and I couldn't fight it any longer. As soon as I released my hold, a swell of light washed over me. The burst of light blinded me for mere moments before it vanished in a blink, leaving the goddess and I right back in the middle of the prairie.

Air flooded back into my lungs as a grin blossomed on the goddess' face. "When I first laid eyes on you, I knew you'd be an Empath."

"I can't be." The words escaped my lips without thought.

Her lips twitched with mirth as she shook her head. "You can, and that's exactly who you are meant to be, Elena."

"M-m-my mother was a Healer, my father a Tempest." The words stumbled out between my ragged breaths. "Empaths are calm, collected...they don't—" Panic was clouding my thoughts, making it much more difficult to deliver my words. "They don't fail, they don't let people d—"

"STOP!" The boom of her voice made the prairie quake around us, and my lips sealed shut. "I know exactly who you are, Elena Morrigan. Rise."

On trembling legs, I struggled to stand. She wrapped her hands around my biceps lifting me upwards. She tapped my forehead with her pointer finger. "You live too much in here." She lowered her finger, tapping where my heart dwelled. "This is where you should reside, this is your path to transformation. My advice is you start listening to it."

"How?" I asked. "How am I an Empath?"

The goddess' face softened. "It's precisely because of reasons like this. You don't even know the depths of your compassion, the care you hold for everyone other than yourself. You feel deeply, and when you feel responsible for the emotions or actions of other you brand yourself a failure. Am I right?"

Nodding my head, I bit my lip.

"You are an Empath because you were meant to enlighten this world. They need your care, they need your strength. They also need you to be something a little more, and as an Empath, only you can handle this task."

The significance of her words filled my body, locking me in place.

"Elena." The golden goddess' voice was smooth as silk. "We have been watching you for a very long time. There is a strength in you that not many people possess. It's unyielding, just like your spirit. No matter what this life has thrown in your path, you take it with grace and compassion. You have given yourself fully to help others, even to those who are not always worthy of it. We know that some small part of you believes that you were meant for more. That you are meant to find a way to help those who struggle and suffer around you."

The ache in my heart stirred once more, evidence that every word she said was true.

"Elena, we know that you feel like you are never enough. My dear, that is the farthest thing from the truth. You have always been enough, and we want you to step into this new chapter in your life allowing these words to resonate as truth within you. Do you feel that in your heart?"

I pressed my palm against my heart and dipped my head in agreement. Tears of shame streamed down my cheeks. I'd always known these truths but had always let my fear and anxiety fill me with doubt. I'd lived my entire life afraid of the unknown, always assuming the worst outcomes.

The goddess lifted her hand and placed her palm over mine, which was still pressed against my chest. "Elena, it's time for you to illuminate your inner strength and shine bright with your glorious light. Whether you believe us or not, you are a very powerful woman. We are confident you will use this extraordinary dynamis with compassion and grace."

Fear curled in circles around my stomach. Though I heard what she said, my mind struggled to grasp why they'd chosen me. Why would they give me a power that was meant to be controlled when I was unable to control my own emotions?

All at once an immense burning feeling seared over my body. When I glanced down, light radiated from my body, pulsing as it rippled underneath my skin. As she continued to pour more dynamis into me, her radiant glow made it difficult to fully see her, but I saw what looked like a faint upturn of her lips. It felt as though the dynamis that was flooding into me was embracing me tightly, wrapping me in the essence of love itself.

When she was finished, she took a few steps back as my vision started to blur and everything around me grew hazy. Panic bristled inside my chest. I still had so many unanswered questions.

"Lena, along with this power, I must also share with you another truth. Your future path will not be easy. Hold on to all you have found here today. Promise me that you will have trust in who you are."

I hesitantly whispered as I felt my body floating further and further away, "I promise."

"Remember, Elena, even when faced with darkness, you can always find your way back to the light. Never stop searching."

As she spoke her final words, her body shimmered away into the abyss. Squeezing my eyes shut, I sent a prayer to the heavens, hoping that I would be able to live up to the fate that I'd just been handed.

"Wake, Elena! Wake!"

A rush of energy flooded my body as I was jolted back into awareness. I opened my eyes, and the air fled out of my lungs in a gasp.

The ground around me had been scorched, the clay pots of flowers shattered to pieces. Stray petals were tossed about the room, the cream candles charred and melted in odd shapes. The only parts of the scene in front of me that didn't leave me filled with terror were little remnants of glowing light that fluttered around the room.

When I tried to move, every muscle in my body cried out in protest. The shuffling of boots and armor made me aware of the presence of others behind me.

"Oh, gods, Elena! Are you alright?"

Turning, I winced at the pain that radiated through me. My gaze landed on Bri's flustered face. Then, it traveled to the gaping mouth of one of her assistants, and the deep scowl of the Royal Guard from earlier.

He gripped the hilt of his sword, taking one step towards me. Instinctually, I flinched backwards. He paused, his lips shifting into a thin line.

Bri looked disheveled, her hair falling out of her pristine braid, almost like she had been tugging and pulling at it for hours. All their eyes were wide, faces stricken with terror. All directed towards me.

"Of course I'm alright, Bri." My raspy voice made me pause. My throat ached.

"Elena, you were screaming!" Bri exclaimed. "You were screaming so loud, it felt like the walls were rattling inside the temple. I've never heard you make a sound like that before. It sounded as if someone was trying to hurt you." Bri fidgeted with her hands as her eyes shifted towards the other guards now gaping at me in the doorway. "The guards saw me running. They followed me in as I opened the door. That's when … that's when—"

"That's when what, Bri?"

She spoke calmly, like she did when she was trying to ease me out of a panic attack. "That's when we saw you were—are—*glowing.*"

My eyes widened and my breathing became erratic. Looking down, I was indeed glowing. Every inch of my body was enveloped in a warm, golden glow.

Alarm bells rang inside my head. I was acutely aware an attack of panic was approaching.

As pressure built inside my chest, a flicker of light on the back of my hand caught my eye. My newly acquired tattoo shimmered with light, as if shouting for my attention. Inside the triangle were millions of stars in all shapes and sizes. A delicate feather floated on top of them.

The space between my brows creased. Etched permanently into my skin was a mark I knew all too well. Only one other had ever borne it, and she had died to give our kingdom a chance for peace.

The Light Phoenix.

Overwhelmed with a combination of shock and fear, my view became hazy. When was the last time I'd taken a breath?

The lack of oxygen finally caught up to me. I caught Bri's distraught eyes one last time. The ground inched closer as my body gave into its pull. She lunged forward to catch me as I collapsed.

CHAPTER 6
DECLAN

"Don't let anyone escape! Go! Now!"

Scorching embers flew all around us as the flames spread through the campsite where we had found the Nightshades. Bushes and trees blazed, but our main goal now was to make sure none of these bastards escaped.

"Down!" Liam roared from behind me, just in time to catch my attention as a Nightshade's Flame dynamis flew over my head. A plume of frozen snow shot out from Liam's fingertips as I hunched my body. It collided with the flames, dousing them on contact. As I rose, the air around sizzled with steam.

The Nightshade was draped in all black, but even the hooded cloak and dark bandana couldn't hide the look of terror that flooded his eyes. The moment his eyes locked with mine, he turned and sprinted into the cover of woods behind him. I rolled my head from side to side, and my lips twitched with delight.

I'd always liked a chase.

Liam gave me a nod, and I transformed into a gust of wind as I zephyred towards the Nightshade. I collided with his body in a matter of seconds and rolled him over to face me. Inky shadows poured through my fingertips, wrapping around his body and squeezing.

I stood, pulling my shadows towards me, as his body followed. Now we were face to face.

Rustling arose from all around me as the rest of my guard of twenty men rushed towards me. Ash and blood covered their faces, clothes and some of their swords. A few bent over, hands on their knees as they tried to steady their breaths. My gaze caught Killian's. He lowered his gaze, shaking his head.

Damn!

It had taken us months to discover their plans for the attack we'd interrupted. Now, this man was the only one we had left, so we better make our questioning count. Rage swirled inside of me, causing my shadows to squeeze the man within an inch of his life.

As I approached, the parts of his face that were exposed were turning a delightful shade of red. I ripped the bandanna from his face and tossed it aside. Then, flicked the hood down.

Amber eyes full of fury met mine as he spit, missing my face by mere inches. Grabbing the rough material of his cloak, I tugged him close.

"Wrong choice," I growled. My fist collided with the left side of his face as he groaned. Grabbing his chin with my hand, I pulled his face back towards mine. "Want to try that again?"

"I'll never tell you anything!" The man snarled.

I forced my shadows to wrap around his neck. "We'll see about that."

Raising my hands, I summoned my shadows to lift him off the ground a few inches. Liam snorted from behind me as the man's legs twitched and gurgles fled his lips. He clawed desperately at the shadows around his neck, his face now a deep shade of burgundy.

"Are you ready to talk now?" He raised his middle finger towards me, and I chuckled darkly under my breath. "I'll take that as no."

My fingers clasped around the hilt of my sword, just as the ground quaked beneath me. The force shook me so violently, I stumbled forward, rising just in time to be hit by a blast of violet-tinted air. The force of the burst sent me flying backwards, and I landed with a crash straight into the solid trunk of the tree behind me.

The back of my head throbbed as I took in the sight around me. What looked like little white embers twinkled in the breeze, remnants of whatever had just assaulted us.

Grunts rumbled from all around me as I realized that everyone had been knocked over by the mysterious blast of energy. Another swift realization was the fact that I no longer felt my dynamis swirling within me, which meant my shadows were no longer wrapped around our captive.

Scrambling to my feet, I zephyred towards the last place I had left the Nightshade. I frantically circled around the empty space, searching for where the man might have been tossed. A twig snapped behind me, and I jolted around to come face to face with a dagger.

"All of you will fall." His words solemn, and his body had a hint of a tremble.

His iron dagger jabbed towards me, causing me to lean back, just narrowly avoiding it. Ever since we'd started hunting them down, they had upped their attacks with iron weapons.

"If you tell us what we need to know, we'll spare your life." I stared into his eyes, hoping that he would make the right decision.

The man broke out in crazed laughter as the rest of my men gathered around us in a circle. I raised an eyebrow at Liam, who shrugged. He was just as confused by the man's reaction as I was. When I looked back, the man's dagger was no longer pointed at my face but angled directly under his chin. His hand trembled, eyes wild.

Raising both hands, I took one step toward him. "You don't have to do this."

"Ah, but I do." Closing his eyes, he dragged the dagger across his throat. He crashed to the ground.

"Well, I certainly didn't see that coming." Killian winced as we discussed last night's events as we saddled our horses.

"I should have." I dragged a palm through my hair, regret clawing at my insides. "That burst of energy was just so unexpected, my mind was a little hazy afterward."

"Yeah, I felt the same after it hit too. That blast was wild. I don't think that I've ever witnessed anything like that," Liam said as shoved his satchel into the saddlebags on the back of his horse.

"I agree. When the blast hit me, I felt like it tangled around my own dynamis before tearing back out of me." I sighed. "There are too many strange and evil things rising in this kingdom. I feel like I'm drowning just trying to keep up."

The two men next to me nodded solemnly in agreement. It had been a long twenty-three years since my mother and brother were murdered. Some days, it felt like we would never get closer to fulfilling our goal, no matter how hard we kept pushing forward.

Liam squeezed my shoulder. "I think it's time Declan. We've been trying for several years, but I think it's time we finally head to Oria."

"I agree," Killian said beside me. "We can continue our efforts from there. You know Clara is so close to discovering a cure."

"You've sacrificed enough, and you've tried valiantly for years, Declan, but we all know the time for your father to change has passed."

Truth ran rampant inside my head. I knew they were right, but I was still dangerous. I couldn't imagine what would happen if I were to leave. "I can't leave yet. I—I just don't trust myself." The words left my mouth on a breath, as I watched both men lower their heads.

"We will follow you, brother, whatever decision you make." Liam patted my back and returned to preparing his horse for the journey back to Vrine.

The City of Shadows. Once my sanctuary, now more like my prison.

I opened my mouth to reply when the flap of wings hovered around us. A raven circled above. Extending my arm, I gave it a place to land.

I unraveled the scroll attached to its leg and handed the raven over to Killian. When I scanned over the contents of the correspondence, anxiousness coiled around my stomach and my jaw clenched.

"What is it, Dec? What's wrong?" asked Killian.

I handed the scroll over to him. His eyes widened as he read. Liam extended his hand towards Killian, taking the note from him after he was done.

We stood in silence until Liam finished. He brushed his palm over his face as I sighed deeply.

"That town...and that last name, Morrigan? That can't be Warren's daughter, can it?" Killian asked behind me as I grabbed a quill and ink from the depths of my satchel. With a huff, I strode over to a boulder and scribed out a response.

The men stood patiently behind me as I finished the response to my father and attached it back onto the raven Killian was holding before I answered his question.

"It's his daughter," I breathed as I watched the raven take flight north, back towards the capital.

"Well, this changes a lot of things," Liam said, handling the parchment back to me, worry lines etched into his forehead.

"Indeed, it does," I said. "Although, I think this might change things for the better for us."

Liam stared long and hard into my eyes before he finally nodded in agreement.

"Alright gentlemen," I shouted, making sure I had the attention of all my guard. "Change of plans. We now have a Light Phoenix to acquire. Saddle up, and let's head out."

CHAPTER 7
ELENA

The warmth of the daylight over my face awoke me from my deadened slumber. Shining light filtered through a sliver of a window at the top of the room, illuminating the cold, stone walls that surrounded me.

As my eyes further adjusted, I realized this wasn't a room. Thick iron bars had replaced the door and one of the walls. It was barren besides the cot that I was lying in, sending shivers down my spine.

An ache throbbed inside my head. Instinctually, I lifted my palm to rub the ache and was confused by the heaviness of my wrist. Shackles circled around my wrists.

Iron, to inhibit the use of magical powers.

"Hells!" The room rattled with the sounds of my frustrated snarl and the clank of the heavy chain binding my wrists.

Memories began to rush back as I flashed back to what had happened before I blacked out—screaming, glowing, then total darkness. Scorch marks adorned the edges of my dress.

No wonder I was tied up. They feared me.

Boots shifted against the floor of the other cell. A body slumped against the bars in the corner, fingers running through familiar honey-blond locks.

I shuffled over to him, falling onto my knees as I grasped the cold bars. "Will," I whispered, but his body didn't budge. I tried again, this time a little louder. "Will!"

A few moments of silence passed as I held on to the bars. Slowly, his head rolled up, his blue eyes meeting mine. The light once within them had dulled. Staring back at me were cloudy, red-rimmed eyes full of sorrow and disdain. The heat of his glare caused me to fall back onto my heels.

"What do you want?" The bluntness of his tone startled me.

"W-what d-do you mean, Will? Why are we in here?" I paused to swallow down the fear that was rising within me. "Will...what happened, and why are you acting this way?"

My words must have snapped the final cord of his restraint because he rose to his feet with a snarl. I scooted a few more inches away.

Will's boots thundered back and forth against the floor as he mumbled erratic words underneath his breath.

"Will—"

"NO!" he seethed, as the words I was about to say fell dead on my lips. "You! This is all because of you, Elena!" His knuckles turned white as he gripped the bars before tilting his head against the iron. He closed his eyes, mumbling more words under his breath. However, this time I could hear them. Every. Single. One. "This is your fault. It always is."

Each word sliced a little deeper, and my trembling hand pressed against the piercing wound that tore wide open inside my heart. "What do you mean by that, Will?" I breathed.

A faint scoff left his mouth, his eyes still closed as he turned his back towards me. Will's body slid down the bars until he hit the floor and slumped over his raised knees. "Your screams woke me out of Ascension just in time to feel the full impact of the blast of energy from your dynamis. Also, just in time to realize what you had done to my own."

The creases between my brows furrowed. My anxiety built, and I wished he would get to the point.

"The entire room, everything around me, was engulfed in flames." The bars of the cell clanged as he thumped his head against it with a heavy sigh. "Everything, including the assistant who had run in to help me."

The iron links clinked together as I covered my mouth. "Oh, Will ..." Tears began to well in my own eyes as I spoke softly. "I'm so sorry that happened."

He turned his body towards me and banged his fist against the bars, startling me as tears streamed ran rampant down my face.

"Sorry? Dammit, Lena that's all you have to say? All I've done since I saved your ass that day after school is take care of you. Picked you up after every mistake, handle the town after every one of your healing blunders. Made excuses for your panic attacks. And you know what? I did it. Everyday, because I was attracted to you. After yesterday..." He paused, his eyes shifting down towards my lips, then back up to meet my eyes. "I thought maybe for once I would have a reprieve from those burdens."

The contents of my stomach churned as I stared back into the cold eyes of the boy I'd once known, his cruel words rotting every kind memory I had with him. Apparently, I didn't know him as well as I'd thought I did.

"Then you went and turned me into...this!" His chains rattled against the iron divider between us.

"I—I didn't mean to! I've never meant to hurt anyone. I'm so s-sorry!"

"Hells, Lena! They're going to take us away from here. Today we're both getting shipped out to the cities. I'll be taken to the City of Ash, and you, *Light Phoenix*, you're being sent to the capital, the City of Shadows. Apparently, the Prince is coming to escort you himself."

"What about your mother and your s—"

"Don't you dare!" He screamed, shaking his head violently, before forcefully blowing out a breath of air. "Don't talk about them. Ever. Again. We go alone, Elena."

My mouth opened to reply, but he shoved away from the bars and fell into the farthest corner of the cell, ending our conversation.

I willed my body forward towards the bars. Wrapping my fingers around them, I whispered, "I'm so sorry, Will."

Rising on shaking legs, I turned to make my way back to the tiny cot. From behind me, Will's voice fluttered through the air.

"'Sorry' can't fix this, Elena."

―――――――

A few hours later, metal keys clanked against the lock of my cell. Will was no longer inside the other cell. After our encounter, I had cried myself to sleep. He must have been taken while I was out. I rose, tossing my legs over the side of the bed. With my heart pounding, I awaited my fate on the other side of the iron door.

It swung open as my back stiffened, hands fidgeting in my lap. Immediately, I knew the man who now stood before me wasn't the prince. Ladies in town discussed the prince's appearance in great detail, and this man didn't fit the description at all.

This man was tall like the prince, but had long black hair pulled back in a messy bun. His skin was tawny, his jawline harsh, highlighted by the scruff of his short beard.

As he folded his muscled arms in front of his breastplate, the definition of his muscles became more pronounced. Glaring at the feather etched in the armor, I rubbed the same mark that was now permanently tattooed onto my skin. Realization hit me like a rock, and my breath hitched from the blow.

I was now the living embodiment of the Stallard line. A living symbol of the only thing that had brought the kingdom of Ehora out of our time of darkness and into a time of peace.

His eyebrows furrowed as he looked upon me with fierce chestnut eyes. Pausing in the middle of the room, he glared down at me as if assessing me the same way I did him.

"Does everyone who walks through this door receive the same appraising gaze, or should I feel special?" His deep voice shook me from my gawking, and I replaced it with a searing glare. He chuckled, before opening his mouth once more.

"Lady Elena Morrigan, by order of King Alaric Stallard, I am here to escort you to the capital of the kingdom of Ehora. We head to Vrine, the City of Shadows."

"Why are you addressing me as a 'Lady?'"

"Because the King has given you the title, and it's my duty to address you as such, whether I believe it or not." He shrugged.

His head tilted towards the door. The Royal Guard did not move an inch to let me by, forcing me to squeeze around his brute of a body just to get through the door. The man even had the audacity to smirk as I slid by. I shoved my way out of the door and my face slammed straight into the armored chest of the other guard standing outside.

"Well, that's going to hurt in a couple of hours." The second guard towered over me as I rubbed my sore cheek and nose.

I was by far the tallest Elysian female in my town, but he was still an inch or two over my head. Elysian men seemed to grow like weeds and were always enormous. These two men were easily over six feet.

His shoulders were not as wide as the others, but you could still tell he was toned from the way the armor bulged over his arms. Messy golden locks tossed about his head as he leaned over and whispered, "Next time, maybe watch where you're going. You wouldn't want to ruin that pretty face of yours," he chuckled.

A scowl grew on my face as I rolled my eyes beneath my lashes. My face was burning hot with anger, which I was sure they assumed was from blushing, as they smirked at each other over my head.

The second guard cleared his throat. "My lady, I am Killian Ashford, second captain of the Royal Guard, and that brute behind you is Liam Hart, first captain. We will be your personal guards as we make our journey." He bowed mockingly with his arm extended showing me the way forward. I stormed by him stomping on his foot as I went.

"Ouch, woman!"

Turning to face him, I caught his glare and tossed him back a smirk of my own. Liam tried his best to cover a smile with his fist, but failed miserably. A flustered Killian grabbed me by the arm forcing me forward towards the main hall of the temple.

I whispered to the captain, making sure it was loud enough for Liam to hear behind us, "Perhaps next time, you should be more careful where you're standing. You wouldn't want me to ruin those pretty feet of yours."

Killian's eyebrows shot straight up. Even his mouth hung open. More stifled chuckles rose from the first captain behind me. Even in all my fury, I couldn't help but laugh as well. Releasing a grunt, Killian tugged me a little tighter as we finally made our way into the hall.

Declan

After I set the boy Will on top of a horse with the group of my father's guards, my gaze caught on Warren pacing back and forth in front of the temple. With a heavy sigh, I made my way over to him.

"Warren," I said, extending my hand out for a handshake.

He grabbed my hand firmly and pulled me into a quick embrace. When he released me, I scanned the area around us to make sure no one had seen our interaction. Thankfully, only a handful of the members of the town were out and the other guards were still preparing their horses for the journey. All of them seemed distracted.

A deep chuckle rumbled beside me. "Don't worry Declan, a hug won't shatter our secret. You know, it wouldn't hurt your façade to actually smile every once in a while."

"Who said it was a façade?" A smirk spread across my lips as Warren's grin spread, but then quickly fell. He turned to face me, worry lines now evident across his forehead.

"How did the raid go last night?"

My head fell as I shook it.

"Damn," he cursed as he ran his palm through his hair. "I'll keep searching. We'll make this our top priority. We're so close now Dec. It will help distract me while she's—"

The stoic man in front of me began to chip, his voice cracking, heavy with burden over what we were about to do with his daughter. I placed my hand on his shoulder and gave it a squeeze of reassurance. "We'll take care of her—"

"Elena," he interrupted.

"We'll take care of Elena. You have my promise, Warren."

"Good, because if anything happens to her, I'll kill you myself." His fierce gaze locked on mine and I knew that was a promise he would indeed keep. Clearing his throat, he dropped his gaze to the dirt below us. "I haven't told her. She doesn't know about anything."

My brows rose at his admission. "Warren—"

"Don't even start." He pointed his index finger into my chest. "She is *my* daughter, and I have my own reasons why I haven't disclosed things to her yet. I plan to keep it that way. Only I will be the one to tell her, so keep your mouth shut."

"Warren, she can't go into all of this blindly." My finger jabbed into his own chest.

"You focus on protecting my daughter from your father and Alastor, and I'll work on protecting her in my own ways."

Closing my eyes, I shook my head. This was not a good idea at all.

"Lena, she's—" He paused, his hand tugging over his mouth as if searching for the right words. "She may appear feisty at first glance"— he chuckled, but sadness hung on each note— "but she is extremely sensitive, Declan. She can't handle this right now. The truth…it would push her over the edge."

His words trailed off, his gaze now locked onto the entrance of the temple. "Let me protect her from this, at least for now. Please."

Warren's pleading eyes roved over mine, and I couldn't help but concede. Nodding in agreement, I heard the faint sounds of voices as a small crowd began to grow near us.

"Oh, and Declan?"

"Hmm?"

"Don't get any ideas with my daughter. She's too good for you." His lips pursed into a thin line as he stared at me, awaiting my answer. "Swear by all five gods you'll keep your hands to yourself."

I bit my lip in an effort not to laugh at the very serious man standing before me. "I swear by all the gods I will not try anything with your daughter, Warren." A small snort slipped free, and his eyebrow rose. Clearing my throat, I tried to convince him again. "You don't have to worry about me pursuing your daughter. That will never be in the fates for me."

"Good," he grumbled, shaking my hand once more and dismissed me to greet Brietta. I stood behind, left to absorb the sting of his words.

CHAPTER 8
ELENA

"Time to go, my lady." Killian tugged me along the narrow gravel path towards the front of the temple. I shuffled along, trying to keep up as we rounded the side of the street and the temple came into view in front of us. Horses chuffed as their riders saddled them for the long journey ahead. Much to my dismay, a small crowd had also gathered.

My eyes roamed over the faces until they locked on my father's, and I dug my feet into the ground causing both Killian and me to come to an abrupt stop.

"What the—" Killian looked down to meet my eyes.

"Please, it's my father. Can you just"—a sob threatened to escape, but I forced it back down— "let me say goodbye? Please, he's all I have left. I don't know when I'll ever see him again."

Killian let out a heavy sigh and lifted his gaze toward Liam who nodded with approval.

Words could never convey the feelings bottled up inside of me. So instead, I just leaned into my father the best I could, my shackled hands hanging between us. Both guards took a step back, turning their heads to allow us privacy. My father enveloped me in his arms, making me never want to leave the safety of them. Tears burst free, despite my hold over them, and I sobbed into his chest.

"Love you," I whispered, my voice hoarse from all the crying.

"I love you too, Lena." He placed a kiss on the top of my head. "I'm not giving up on you. I'll find a way to bring you back, that's a promise."

Just as I stepped away, Bri's voice rang out beside us. "Wait!" she gasped, pushing her way through the small crowd. As she caught her breath, she placed a satchel over my shoulder. "There's another change of clothes, your favorite book, and"—briefly looking over my shoulder, she raised a finger over her lips as she silently mouthed— "this."

My dagger appeared in her palm, and she slipped it inside the satchel as well. Before I could speak, her arms wrapped around me and a sob broke free from her lips.

"Love you," she sniffled. "Stay strong, sweet girl."

More tears began to flow down my cheeks as I leaned into her. "I'll try my best." My father pulled Bri away from me as I walked back towards my two guards.

When we approached the horses, Will was already mounted on top of one, a guard in front of him on the saddle. Noticing the riderless horse next to his, I started towards it. Before I took another step, a muscled arm extended in front of me blocking my path.

"And just where do you think you're going?" Killian folded both arms over his chest.

"To mount this horse, *sir*." My tone was full of disdain. "Is that okay with you?"

"My lady, how do you suppose you'll mount the horse, much less ride it, with those shackles?"

Hells.

How had I forgotten about these wretched things? Hanging my head low, I silently screamed, because he was right, which meant I would have to ride with someone.

"Well, then I'll ride with that guard." I tossed my thumb over my shoulder towards a random guard behind me.

"Nice try, but you'll be riding with me." He scoffed.

"I'd rather walk."

"You're going to walk for five days?"

"Watch me."

Both of us were locked in a glare, silently tempting each other to be the next to add kindling to the fire of our fury. To my surprise, he mounted his horse. Over his shoulder, he looked down at me with a mischievous grin.

"Enjoy your walk, my lady."

A smile tugged at my lips. If they were going to drag me from my home, they had better believe I would be putting up a fight the entire way.

Will's eyes widened as he looked behind me. Before I could even turn around, strong hands grabbed me by the waist and lifted me from the ground.

"Hells!" I shrieked, trying to kick my feet. "Put me down at once!"

Arms swooped underneath my thighs, flinging me onto the horse in front of Killian. The sound of snickering spewed from behind me, and now Liam rode up beside us. I elbowed Killian in the gut, causing him to grunt alongside a few curses under his breath. A stern voice boomed next to me, making me very aware of a firm grip still squeezing my thigh.

"You will sit, and you will stop acting like a babe throwing a tantrum! Believe me, my lady, the last thing you want to do is make me angry." The snarl was so deep, it made goosebumps erupt over my arms. "Sit and stay put. There will be no more outbursts from you. Do you understand?"

My eyes widened and my breath hitched as I took in the *Shadow Lord* standing below me. There was no mistaking that this was the prince, as his appearance and demeanor were everything the ladies in town had described, and so much more.

His olive-toned, sun-kissed body hovered next to me. Defined muscles rippled in his arm as he gripped my thigh, his shoulders broad. Outlining his chiseled jawline was a well-trimmed short beard. Wavy, hazelnut locks flowed over his head. A few strands fell into his face. Hints of black tattooed ink peeked along the side of his neck and over his breastplate. More ink peeked through this rolled up sleeves, exposing swirls that curled around his arms, like waves of smoke.

Prince Declan's striking emerald eyes bore into me, his thick lips pushed together in a line. There was a coldness about him that made goosebumps ripple up my arms. The man was devastatingly handsome, with just enough malevolence in his presence to remind me this was a man I should fear.

He crossed his arms in front of his chest. I realized that keeping this man waiting would not end well for me.

"My apologies, Your Highness." With some reluctance, I bowed my head, biting my bottom lip to force myself to not say more. For a mere moment, his glare softened as it roamed over my face before hovering on my mouth.

Heat blossomed up the sides of my neck and onto my cheeks. My traitorous body was reacting in ways it shouldn't. I shifted in the saddle, unsuccessfully trying to avoid the searing sensation as they continued to hold his gaze on me for longer than felt comfortable.

It felt as though he could see right through me, exposing me all the way down to my soul itself. All the way down to the darkest parts of me, parts that I kept hidden from everyone else in my life.

A sharp ache bloomed inside my chest, and I rubbed my palm against it in soothing circles. Thankfully, the prince averted his eyes before I melted into a puddled mess on top of the horse. He cleared his throat. "That goes for you as well, Captain Ashford." Prince Declan spoke, raising an eyebrow towards Killian.

"Yes, General, my apologies." Killian shifted in his saddle a bit, obviously flustered. Will shook his head and turned back around in his saddle.

"Good. Now that we are all in agreement, let's get on the road. We've wasted enough daylight already. We have a long journey ahead of us."

The prince stalked over to his massive black stallion and in one leap he had gracefully mounted his steed. Straightening my back, I positioned myself as close to the front of the saddle as I could. The more space between me and the guard behind me the better. Breathing deeply, I exhaled as Killian nudged our horse into motion.

Dread coiled inside my stomach as my bottom lip began to tremble. Glancing over my shoulder, I took one last look. An uneasy feeling stirred within me, whispering into my mind the thoughts I feared the most.

This might be the last time I ever laid eyes on my home.

O utside of the town was eerily quiet, with just the clicking of hooves as our horses trotted over the valley floor. I was lost in my thoughts, which was never a good place for me to be. Shaking my head, I desperately searched for something to distract myself.

Everywhere my eyes drifted appeared so peaceful, quite the opposite of the chaos I'd experienced the past two days. The sun spread over the meadow's luscious foliage. Wildflowers blossomed in endless colors, sprinkled as far as the eye could see.

All this beauty that I was no longer free to roam in. My freedom had become as fleeting as the breeze that now tossed strands of my hair about my face.

Will was still ignoring me, just as he had done the entire way thus far. Every time Killian and I closed the gap beside him, Will's guard nudged his horse to gallop ahead. In all the years we'd known each other, I didn't think we had ever been upset with one another. He'd also never been this silent.

Guilt clouded my peaceful view. It was because of me that he was on this journey. I'd turned his entire life upside down, but he must know that mine had been as well. If he'd just speak to me, he would realize that we didn't have to battle this alone.

Leaning forward with a sigh, I massaged my forehead. When I looked back up toward Will, he was gone. Panic slammed against my chest. Frantically, I whipped my head around, leaning around both sides of Killian in search of Will.

That was when my eyes landed on him paused at the back of the group, alongside the prince and a small handful of guards. My heart pounded, my neck straining as the prince nodded and all at once the group set off to the east, towards the City of Ash.

"No wait! Stop!" I cried out, gripping Killian's shoulder so tightly, my knuckles turned white. "Please...Will! Don't you dare leave me without saying a damn word!"

I waited with bated breath for any response from him. Any hint that he might still care. Nothing came. Fury burned through my eyes as I glared at the back of his head until I could no longer make him out in the distance.

Crestfallen, I slumped into the saddle. The leather horn squeaked beneath my twisting hands as I battled between sadness and rage. All the years we'd known each other, everything we'd been through, every moment we'd shared, apparently it all mattered little to him. Perhaps I'd just been a burden to him this entire time.

Could he so easily ignore what had happened between us only yesterday? My fist kneaded against my chest. I tried to tame the storm of emotions that thundered within my heart, from the gaping hole that had been torn into it. Both of us left wanting more than we had been given.

The gods really did have a sense of humor. They'd told me that what was coming next wouldn't be easy, but since I had awakened my life had been nothing short of cataclysmic. I didn't care how strong they claimed I was, I wasn't immune to pain.

Something else was brewing underneath my skin as well, that same fiery feeling I'd felt ripple under my skin the night after I awoke from my Ascension. It felt as though every part of my body was reacting to my emotions as my muscles tensed. This must be my dynamis trying to course its way out of my body.

With every fiber of my being, I clawed for restraint. Crying in front of these men would only prove how weak I truly was. I wouldn't give them that satisfaction.

Clinging to that restraint, I shoved down the emotions that felt as though they were flowing beneath my skin and imagined locking them away into the depths where I'd hid all the darkness in my life. Running a palm over my face, I tried my best to regulate my breaths.

A warm hand gripped my shoulder, jarring me so unexpectedly that I nearly slid off the saddle. Killian tightened his hold, pulling me back to my spot.

"It will be okay, my lady." His words were calm and steady, just like the hand resting on my shoulder.

Placing it back on his own thigh, he continued riding. Silence fell between us. Liam was now trotting alongside us, his eyes also on me. I wanted to bury myself inside a hole. If I thought crying in front of them was unbearable, the feeling of pity was far more unsettling.

Clearing his throat, he asked "If I may be so bold, my lady, who was he to you?"

Numbly, I shifted my eyes forward, taking note that the prince had slowed down to a trot in front of us, likely in earshot of whatever I was about to say. Doubt filled my mind about my ability to even voice an answer. Also, I wasn't sure these men needed to know any personal details about me. However, the heaviness of being alone weighed on my soul. I was probably trotting towards my imminent demise, so I supposed it no longer mattered. With a deep exhale, I turned to face him.

"Honestly Captain, I'm not so sure what he is to me anymore." My shoulders lifted in a shrug. "Will and I grew up together. He was my best friend, and yesterday maybe even something more." I scoffed at the thought. "Fate sure has horrible timing."

Liam nodded, as if he understood entirely too well. Killian chimed in from behind me. "I'm sorry about the way that it all ended. If he was that much to you, he should have at least bidden you farewell."

Agreed.

Fighting back the anger, I opted for a different response than the one that growled inside my head. "He was probably just as over-whelmed as I am." The words slipped through my lips, my heart unsure why my mind felt the need to defend Will.

I could sense that Killian was being genuine, but something in his words cut deep into my heart. There was so much finality to the word *ended*.

Was that what had truly just occurred?

CHAPTER 9

ELENA

We trotted along for what seemed quite some time, until I started to make out the hazy outline of the town in front of us. Brambles and trees now flanked us on each side, leaving only the dirt road we were on as the clearest path straight through Wilde-brooke, and unease prickled over me.

I'd heard stories of this town from my father. All of them were unsavory. Every bone in my body quivered at the thought of this contingent of Royal Guards storming through it. This far outside of Vrine's walls, you didn't find many supporters of King Alaric.

The ground near Killian and I rumbled, and I was shaken out of my thoughts in time to see the prince and his horse galloping over to us. Once near us, he trotted his horse right next to ours.

"Give me your hand," he said so bluntly, it made me roll my eyes.

"I believe you forgot something."

He scoffed, extending his hand to reach for mine.

"Ah, I see you're struggling to remember," I sneered, causing him to pause as his jaw ticked. "The word you're searching for is *please*."

A snort exploded from behind me, and I had to bite my lip to contain my own. The deathly glare the prince gave his guard was priceless.

The words rolled out of him about as fast as sap oozed from trees. *"Please...give me...your hand."*

"Well, why didn't you ask so nicely the first time?" I winked and handed him my right hand as another chuckle rumbled from Liam on the opposite side of us.

With a forceful tug, the prince grabbed my hand. A tiny growl rolled out of him, only fueling my amusement more. He waved his palm over my hand, murmuring something under his breath as he did.

One moment my dynamis tattoo was there, the next it wasn't. My eyes bulged wide at the sight. This time, the chuckle came from the broody man still holding my hand. "What, you've never seen a glamour before?"

I shook my head silently, because he was right, I had never seen it before.

"Simple magic." He shrugged, letting go of my hand. "Once you have dynamis, you can use it to create glamours or wards around things. I had to glamour you for your own protection. It might seem like seeing the symbol of the Light Phoenix would go over well, but there"—he tossed a glance over his shoulder— "it would put a target on your head."

Swallowing down the anxiousness that rose up my throat, I nodded in agreement.

"You'll also be riding with me as we go through."

The prince's arms wrapped around my waist, and before I even had a chance to blink, I was saddled in front of the Lord of Shadows himself. His warm hands applied pressure to my hips as he adjusted himself further back to give me room. Goosebumps rippled over my skin, and I prayed to all five gods that he wouldn't see. Nothing about this man should be alluring, but my body seemed to disagree.

At a nudge of his leg and a click of his tongue, his horse rode ahead in a trot. As I fidgeted, the iron shackles clanked around my wrists. "If we're going through this town, I need to be free of these shackles,"

"No."

"What if something happens? I'll be defenseless."

"You'll have me," he grumbled.

"What if that's not enough?"

His body shifted behind me, as he sighed. "If I take these off, you must make me a deal."

Looking over my shoulder, I caught his verdant gaze. Wrapped inside his hand was the key to my freedom. I nodded. His lips rolled into a distracting smirk, and suddenly I was aware I'd just made a deal I was going to regret.

He grabbed my shackles and unlocked each one. As he placed the iron inside his satchel, my breath caught as my hands pulsed with golden light. The glow was delicate and comforting, almost like the glow of the little lightning bugs I'd see flitter about as soon as the sun sank behind the horizon. Fascinated, I pulled them closer for a better look, but the glow faded back to flesh.

I rubbed my palms over my tender wrists. It was a vivid reminder of how much I should value my freedom from now on.

A deep voice whispered into my ear as a heavy cloak enveloped my shoulders. "From now on Elena, you will follow my orders." His warm breath trickled down to my neck, and I could feel a slight tremble beginning to form in my hands.

"When I say sit, you sit," he continued, his calloused hands brushing over the sensitive skin of my neck as he buttoned the cloak. "What I say goes, got it?" He pulled my chin towards him.

The horse trotted along, and the town of Wildebrooke was in full view ahead. Left with very few options, I grumbled under my breath and nodded in agreement. A devious smirk spread across his lips, instantly warming my cheeks. He let go of my chin and tossed the hood over my head, covering my face almost entirely.

"Good." His voice was low, sending a shiver down my spine, as something else stirred awake inside of me. It burned its way throughout my body, thrashing against my skin like it needed to be set free.

Grappling with the sensation of my new dynamis, I tried to focus as he gave me my first orders. "Now, keep your head down and mouth shut until we are clear of the town."

It was probably wise for me to follow his directions, but I couldn't help trying to sneak a peek at the town. Lifting my head, I watched as the villagers stopped what they were doing to glare at the man behind me.

Their eyes were aflame with rage, jaws clenched as if trying to hold in the hateful words that needed to be released. Others did not heed the same restraint.

"Get out of here! Go take your bloodied hands somewhere else!"

Another man threw his pot of filth onto the road in front of us. Prince Declan's horse snorted, narrowly sidestepping around the mess. More shouts filled the air.

"Murderer!"

"How can you live with yourself?"

"Go burn in the fiery depths of Hells!"

Shock wafted through me, along with something unfamiliar. I placed my palm over my chest, trying to quell the overwhelming feeling of despair and shame. These words were enough to make anyone feel something, but my brain couldn't process why I was feeling shame. None of these words were directed at me so why was I—

Realization struck me as sharply as these emotions that had invaded my body. How could I have forgotten?

These were not my own emotions. These were coming from the man behind me. Only someone with Empath dynamis could pull the emotions from another. I'd been so overwhelmed with the idea of being the Light Phoenix that I had completely forgotten the gods blessed me with the dynamis of an Empath first.

I curled my hand around the hood of my cloak and carefully turned around to view the prince. He gripped the reins and the veins in his neck thickened with blood, no doubt fueled by the vicious words ringing all around us.

Normally, I would agree with them considering all the atrocities his father (and apparently, he) had inflicted upon our kingdom. In all honesty it should probably make me terrified, but when my eyes searched his, all I saw was remorse. The prince's face remained stoic, almost bored. His eyes, however, were glossy with unshed tears, and the small crease between his brows told me a much different story.

We passed the edge of the town and made our way forward. Releasing one hand from the reins, the prince lowered my hood. Smoothing out my hair, I turned to say thank you when a bloodcurdling scream interrupted me.

All eyes turned back toward the town as a woman ran with a child dangling limp within her arms, both covered in blood.

"Black wolf! She's been bitten!" The woman turned down the road into the town as a small crowd began to gather. "Gods! Help, someone help!"

Blood coursed through me, and I pulled forward on the saddle, readying myself to jump down. Strong hands forced me down.

"No!" The prince shouted.

"They need help. I can help!" I snarled, my blazing glare meeting his own.

"It's too dangerous. Hells woman, did you not just hear everything that they said as we passed?"

"I did," I huffed. "And it's all the more reason why you should let me go!"

His shoulders slumped. Shame swelled within me once more, this time from me. "I'm sorry, I—I just want to help...I need to—"

"They have others who can help. Just let it go."

The burn of my new dynamis thrummed through me as his eyebrow rose, reminding me of the promise I'd made. All I could think about was the overwhelming need to get off this damn horse and go to help.

So that was what I did.

I leapt from the horse, taking him by surprise, but his reflexes were fast. He grabbed my cloak in his fist at the same time as I ripped apart the button, freeing me. I fell straight to the ground with a thud. A groan ripped through me as I scrambled to my feet.

My legs carried me off in a sprint towards the town. I didn't dare look back. All my focus remained on willing my feet to go faster.

Declan

Fury wafted off me in waves, tangling alongside my shadows. I couldn't believe Elena disobeyed me after everything she'd just heard about me, after the promise she'd made. None of it seemed to matter. She had tossed it all aside and gone barreling straight into the fire.

Killian's horse snorted next to me as I groaned into my hands. "Want me to zephyr after her?" Killian asked.

"Hells." I rubbed my hand against the stubble on my jaw. "No, let's all go. I believe she truly just wants to help, but I have a feeling we're going to need all of us, just in case things turn sour."

I tugged at the reins, turning my horse around and back into the town behind us.

All eyes peered at us once more, and I tried my best to not let their glares seep into my skin. I was aware of what they thought of me, and I knew what I had done. Some days I wished I could sit them all down and explain the truth. Unfortunately, that was not an option, and I had a Light Phoenix to track down.

Narrowing my eyes, I scanned through the small crowd until I saw the flash of auburn waves ripple around the corner store. I motioned for Liam and Killian to follow behind me.

As we rounded the street corner, I spotted her kneeling in someone's overgrown herb garden. Raising a hand, I motioned to the men behind to stay put.

"Elena," I whispered, making my way towards her, while keeping an eye on a few men beginning to crowd around us.

"You shouldn't be here, Shadow Prince." One of them snarled.

"What?" Her tone was flat, sharpened with annoyance with me for bothering her search. My teeth clenched, but when she rolled those bright aquamarine eyes, the words on my tongue dried out completely.

In that moment, all I wanted to do was take her over my shoulder and spank the stubborn sass right out of her. Or maybe just silence her with my lips? A rush of dynamis swirled, pressing against my skin, as my thoughts wandered over the idea of smothering those pillowy lips of hers into submission.

When her eyes had met mine for the first time, a dull ache had pulled against my chest, straight towards her. Everything about this woman since then had thrown me off completely.

Not only was the journey unexpected, but so was she. I needed to unhook this pull I had towards her before it got me into trouble.

The tiny hairs on my neck stood at attention. The men surrounding us were a lot closer than before. One gripped the hilt of his dagger.

Hells, Declan. Focus.

I followed the man's eyes, which led straight to Elena's hand, the one that was no longer glamoured. Damn.

"We need to leave. *Now*."

Red tinged her cheeks as she stood up meeting me almost eye to eye. She was taller than most women I'd met but I still had a few inches over her. "I am not leaving until I help that child!" She shoved past me and ripped out another herb from the mass of weeds behind me. How she could even find what she was looking for in all this mess baffled me.

As she reached down once more, the man closest to us began his approach. Throwing myself in front of her, I whipped out my shadows, knocking the dagger straight out of his palms.

The sound of steel drew my eyes towards my guards. Liam and Killian both stood at the ready, swords glistening in the midday sun.

"Move! NOW!" I growled as I unsheathed my own sword.

Her eyes widened as she took in the scene around her. Then, in a flash they turned wild and blazing with fury.

"WILL YOU ALL JUST STOP!" she screamed.

As she did, a burst of white fire blazed through her fingertips along with a turbulent gust of wind that sent us all to the ground.

Scrambling back onto my feet, I froze. Elena stood in the middle of the scorched garden, her face paled, mouth gaping wide. Tendrils of white flame still flickered on the ground as she looked at her trembling hands, stunned by the dynamis that had flown out of them.

The others began to stir on the ground, and the woman who owned the house came out screaming at Elena for destroying her garden. In the distance, more disgruntled voices rang out, but they were all a muddle to me. The only thing I was focused on right now was the terrified Light Phoenix in front of me.

I glanced at my guards, giving a silent order which they returned with a nod. In a blink, they hopped onto their horses as I zephyred towards Elena. The gust of wind twirled around us as she clung to me. My stallion, Shadow gave a high-pitched whinny as we landed abruptly on top of him. Without a second thought, I grabbed the reins, and we all galloped out of the town.

Once I felt confident enough that no one had followed us, I raised my hand to alert the guards behind me to slow to a trot. Finally, I had a chance to acknowledge the trembling woman in front of me. I could hear her muttering the same words under her breath, over and over, as she rocked back and forth.

A lump formed in my throat as her hands folded over each other. The repetitious actions sat heavily in my chest, as it was something I knew entirely too well.

I gathered the reins into one hand and placed my palm gently on her biceps. She flinched, but then her body sagged into my touch.

"None of that was your fault. You know that, right?" I rubbed my hand over her smooth skin as I awaited her response. A sniffle fled from her, and when she spoke her words were almost inaudible.

"No...I don't." The misery in her words caused a piece of my cold heart to chip. "I...I burnt everything. Now how will they help that p-poor child?"

I squeezed her arm, causing her to turn and face me. Elena's once-bright eyes were now reddened, her pink cheeks wet with an endless stream of tears. Before I could think, my thumb wiped them free, causing her lashes to flutter closed.

"They will help the child, I promise," I said, pinching her chin and raising it to meet my stare. "Nothing about this is your fault, you tried valiantly. You should be proud of that."

Elena shook her head out of my hand with a breathy scoff. Her gaze fluttered down, and she fidgeted with something around her neck. I had seen her do it on our way here, but hadn't seen what it was until now. Between her fingers was a smooth white stone in the shape of a feather.

"There was nothing valiant about it. I was reckless and stubborn." She paused, dropping the pendant as her hands curled into fists. "The funny thing is, I've always thought there was so much beauty in our dynamis." A breathy laugh tumbled out of her, doused with sadness. "Mine is supposed to bring about light and peace. Yet there's no beauty in my dynamis, only destruction."

With a heavy sigh, she turned back towards me, then her eyes drifted behind me to my satchel. "Put them back on."

"Elena—"

"Please? Her breathless plea hit my chest like a rock.

"Are you sure?"

"Yes." She swallowed deeply, as if the next words she was about to say were painful. "I don't trust myself right now."

I grabbed the iron chains from my satchel and placed them around her wrists. She took a shaky breath, then turned around to face the horizon in front of us.

Leaving me alone to deal with the storm of emotions spiraling within me.

CHAPTER 10
ELENA

Numb. That was the only way to describe the way I felt right now.

Yesterday, I was already drowning beneath my own failures. Now, I was the owner of a rare and powerful dynamis that I couldn't control. All my fears of going through Ascension had been realized.

Dragging my palms over my face, I tried to wipe away the tension underneath. After Declan put the shackles back on, we rode in silence. My mind was overwhelmed not only with what had happened in the town, but also from the way he had acted towards me after. He'd been tender and caring, a jarring transformation from when we'd first met, and in contrast to all the comments about him from the town members. It left me bewildered as I struggled to process it all.

The sound of clomping hooves around both sides of us averted my attention away from my thoughts. Killian gave me a nod, then Liam's lips curved into a grin. Parting my lips to speak to them, I was rudely interrupted by the ravenous beast that was my stomach. It growled so loudly, I was sure everyone in all Ehora felt its quake. I wished I could glamour myself entirely.

Buried within my hands, I mumbled, sheepishly, "Sorry."

I felt a nudge against my arm, and I lowered my hands to find it was Killian. With a grin, he leaned back, grabbed a satchel from the side of his horse and tossed it into my lap. I made quick work of unwrapping it to reach the contents inside.

Before I knew it, I had not only eaten all of what was inside of Killian's satchel but was devouring my way through Liam's as well. Chuckles shook me out of my stupor. With slitted eyes and a piece of jerky hanging from the side of my mouth, I dared them to make fun of me. Both men put their hands up in the air, surrendering to my glare. I tossed the satchel back to Liam, who tossed it right back to me.

"You hold onto it, my lady. We both know better than to get between a woman and her food."

"Yes, I quite prefer to keep both of my hands intact." Killian wiggled his fingers. With a roll of my eyes, I reopened the satchel and continued to munch away.

"Thank you," I mumbled through a mouthful of jerky, "and you can call me Elena. I think we can all agree that I don't really suit the whole title of *Lady*."

A snort peeled out of the brooding Lord of Shadows behind me. I allowed myself to enjoy this moment of levity and joined in the laughter. Given the unknown fate that awaited me in the capital, this might be the last time I got to do so.

Somewhere along the way my eyes had grown heavy and sleep pulled me under. I awoke to two hands lifting me back up from where I had fallen forward onto the horse's nape to rest. I rubbed my drowsy eyes, allowing me to get a better look at my surroundings.

An endless array of stars sparkled in the inky darkness. Mammoth pine trees towered above us as far as the eye could see.

A warm fire cracked in the center of the makeshift camp. A few tents already flapped in the breeze, but some still needed to be erected.

With a sleepy sigh, I began to make my way towards the others to help.

"No."

Pinching my lips together, I turned to the owner of the familiar voice. "You know," I tapped the side of my cheek with my pointer finger. "I'm starting to feel like that's your favorite word."

His tone lowered to a deep rumble as he leaned in close. "Only around you." He folded his arms across his chest.

Pinning him with my own glare, I copied his posture. "They need help setting up, and I won't sit on my ass like a pampered princess watching everyone around me be useful."

His eyes shifted to my shackles. "You can, and you will." Pulling the key from his pocket, he grabbed my forearm, but I wiggled out of it and took a step back.

"I...no...I don't trust myself." I lowered my head, heavy with shame, as he stepped closer.

"Elena, you used a lot of your dynamis earlier, and you're exhausted. You'll be fine for the rest of the night."

When he grabbed my wrist this time, I allowed him. With a turn of the key, my wrists were free once more. As I rubbed my wrists, I glanced up to see a devious smirk plastered across the prince's face.

"You owe me for breaking our deal."

"I do not—"

"Go now." His body crowded my space and he pointed in the direction of the fire. "You *will* go, and you *will* sit on that log until I tell you to move. Are we clear?"

Fuming, I turned and stormed off towards the direction of the fire. The whiplash of this man's moods was infuriating.

Once I made it halfway to the fire, I looked over my shoulder in search of the Lord of Grumpiness. Finding him nowhere in sight, I made my way over to the closest tent that needed to be built and got to work.

P ressing my hands into the ache of my lower back, I admired my handiwork. With the help of Killian, who smirked when he saw me going against Declan's orders, we were able to construct two tents. When he had to leave to organize a perimeter watch, I managed to construct one fully on my own.

However, I was regretting the last one as my body cried out in pain. My thighs burned from the long ride—a ride that I wasn't accustomed to, since this was the farthest I'd ever traveled out of Lostburrow in my twenty-three years.

Pine needles crunched behind me causing me to jump. With a wince, I glanced over to see Liam walking towards me.

"Don't worry. The pain will get easier the longer we ride. By the end of this trip, you'll be a true horsewoman."

"Well, I sure hope so," I said with a huff as a tendril of hair flew off my face. "The last thing we need is for the infamous Light Phoenix to fall off her horse to her untimely death. The king would be enraged he missed out on the opportunity to do it himself, and pure chaos would reign over the realm." I deadpanned.

Liam's eyes widened, then he burst out in a deep, bellowing laugh. "Where does all that sass hide within such a small thing? You keep on surprising me, little lady."

"First of all, there is nothing 'small' or 'little' about me." I motioned my hand over all of me. "I'm almost as tall as you."

He grunted, though I caught a slight upturn of his lips.

"Second, with all this power, I feel I have a great responsibility to keep everyone on their toes. Or, at the very least, entertained." With a devious smile, I bowed my head and spread my arms out wide for emphasis.

He started rummaging through a satchel that hung over his shoulder. Holding a flask up to my mouth he said, "Drink, it'll help with the pain."

Normally, I proceeded with more caution in my life, but I was tired, sore, and cranky. At this point, I'd take anything to help tackle any one of those situations.

Lifting the bottle to my frozen lips, I tilted my head back, letting the warm liquid fall down my throat. Searing pain flooded my throat, causing me to cough uncontrollably. My nose burned and my eyes watered as I tried to regain my composure.

"Already trying to torture our prisoner, Liam?" a deep voice purred from the side of me. On the opposite side of the fire stood the prince, with hands on his hips and smirking at my misfortune.

"Not on purpose, Your Highness. Just introducing Elena to the medicinal properties of whiskey." Liam grinned and sealed the cap back on tossing it back into a satchel, then turned around to head back to whatever he was doing before.

Before he got too far away, I shouted after him, "Next time you plan on torturing me, at least give me a little warning."

"We'll see, little lady, we'll see." He strode away, his shoulders shaking with mirth.

Clearing my throat, I inhaled a deep pull of cool air to try to chill the burn. I could already feel the warmth of the whiskey flowing over my body. Everything felt a little bit lighter and a fuzzy feeling began to thrum inside my head. Maybe when Liam returned, I could persuade him to allow me another swig of it. Just for medicinal purposes, of course.

As I smiled, a chill rippled throughout my body, the awareness of a heavy presence looming. My gaze shifted beneath my lashes, only to find the prince sitting across from me on the other side of the fire.

The flames whipped wildly between us as he glared through them at me with almost the same intensity. Heat rippled across my skin, not from the fire, but from within my traitorous body.

Something about this dark, destructively handsome man made me unable to peel my eyes away from him. No one, not even Will, had ever looked at me in the way the prince was looking at me right now, like I was some puzzle that he was struggling to solve.

As the intensity of his stare deepened, it became difficult for me to tell whether he might rip me to shreds or leap over the fire and rip off my clothes. Surprisingly, option two felt rather intriguing to my body.

What am I thinking?

The man in front of me was the son of the most vicious,

deplorable king. He was the Lord of Shadows, his dynamis commanded darkness, and gods only knew what else lurked inside him. This man was dangerous, period. Nothing about him should be intriguing. Clenching my thighs together, I broke our gaze lowering my head to the ground to try to knock some sense into it. "So, are you always this grumpy?"

"Are you always this insolent?"

"Hmm," I paused, the next words burning on my tongue. "I save it for contemptuous, arrogant bastards like yourself." Catching the darkened eyes of the prince across the fire, I tossed him a sarcastic smile.

Faster than I could blink, Declan was behind me holding my chin with one hand while his shadows wrapped around my exposed neck. I froze with fear. My breaths became shallow and my heart thrummed erratically.

Muscles knotted tightly inside of me as he leaned close to my ear. The scruff of his chin bristled against my temple, eliciting an emotion I should *not* have during this moment. As he spoke, heat from his breath floated down the side of my neck. My dynamis flared from its slumber.

"Don't ever speak to me that way again, my lady. Or I promise you will regret it." Even enraged, his voice poured out like smooth honey. "Be careful, Elena. That mouth of yours is going to get you in trouble one of these days."

"You can't talk to me like that." This time, my boldness only came out as a timid whisper. Even the wild beast within me was terrified of him.

"I am the prince, Elena. I can do whatever the Hells I want."

Before I could react, his hold against me retracted. The wisp of his shadows evaporated from my neck. My head swiveled, only for me to see him storming off into the distance. Still reeling from the events that just occurred, my mind tumbled over itself in confusion.

For reasons I couldn't begin to explain, I felt a pull towards this unstable prince, tugging at the center of me. Whatever this feeling was, I needed to shove it down and keep it at bay.

Especially if I had any hopes of surviving this whole ordeal.

Declan

H*ells.*
     This was going to be one long journey.

Stomping over the forest floor, I stewed over the day. From the first moment we'd met, Elena had questioned, disobeyed, challenged me at every turn. This was only day one. How in the Hells were we going to make it through four more days of this?

Shadow nickered at my approach. I ran my hand over the mane of the black stallion and fed him a carrot.

"Enjoy that." I rubbed his nose as he chewed happily. "I think you're the only one around here who follows orders from me anymore."

A familiar laugh arose from behind me. "Having a hard time with our little Light Phoenix?" Liam made his way around a tree towards me. "Perimeter's all set, by the way. I'll take my next shift after dinner." I nodded, as he patted me on the shoulder. "What's going on now?"

Anger began to rise again as I stepped aside, giving Liam my back as I ran my hands through my hair. "She—she…" A frustrated growl ripped out of me. "She just—"

"She doesn't bend over backwards to do everything you ask of her?" Liam raised an eyebrow.

"Yes!" The words slipped out in rage. I glared at the thick, black mop of hair on his head as it tousled about as he shook it.

"Elena is a lot like someone else I know," he scoffed. I rolled my eyes as I wiped my palm over my face to erase the irritation of his comparison. "Also, have you forgotten who raised her?"

Warren could be one Hells of a broody man. Another one who always challenged me, pushing me to make the right decisions. Yet he loved deeply and every decision was based around making sure that everyone would be safe and secure. The man had endured just as much as I had and continued fighting. My respect for Warren ran deep, and aspects of who I was today were a direct result of him.

"No, I haven't forgotten." I groaned.

"Good. Then hold on to those reins, because this isn't going to be an easy ride. You're going to have to give her a reason to trust you."

"Did you just compare breaking through to Elena to taming a horse?"

"Well, seeing as you're horrible with women and better with horses, I had to adjust my sage advice in a way you would understand."

Patting my back, he made his way back towards the fire for dinner. Thoughts still intruded in my mind, swirling in a way they hadn't for some time. Instead of heading towards the fire, I drifted off in the opposite direction. Before I faced Elena again, I needed to get back into the right state of mind.

CHAPTER II
ELENA

Wind howled around the towering pine trees as I tried to recover from the adrenaline that was still coursed through me. My mind was still trying to wrap together everything that had happened over the past few days. In all my life, I could never have imagined any of this. It was like my nightmares, but this time, I couldn't wake up.

Sighing, I let my aching body sag into the log. All I wanted to do was curl up inside one of the tents, but the ache clawing inside my stomach forced me to stay out here and wait for dinner.

Hares and potatoes bubbled away in a large pot in another fire beside ours. A few of the guards had gone hunting after they had finished setting up tents. Savory smells drifted through the breeze, causing my ravenous stomach to grumble more.

As if on cue, Liam approached with a steaming bowl of something that smelled positively divine. If my legs were working, I would have leapt towards the man and grabbed the bowl away from him. He placed the bowl in my hands, and I thanked the gods the bowl of food was for me.

Bringing the bowl up to my lips, I slurped the savory contents. When I came up for air, I used the back of my sleeve to wipe my mouth and flashed a glare towards Liam. He stepped towards me, and it was hard not to notice the smug smirk twisting the side of his mouth.

"Liam, I'm starving. Don't you dare give me that look."

He opened one of his hands, revealing a small spoon. "It appears you won't be needing this."

Heat gathered on my cheeks, this time due to equal embarrassment and anger. I ripped the spoon out of his hand and tossed it into the bowl. "Happy?"

"Exceedingly, little lady."

I grumbled under my breath at the nickname, and Liam chuckled as he plopped down on the log next to me. Reaching into his other pocket, he retrieved the silver flask and dangled it ever so enticingly in front of me.

I took a deep swig of it before tossing it back. After today, whiskey seemed like an excellent distraction. "I swear, I'm starting to become a little wary of the guards who are supposed to be watching me. Just how much whiskey do you drink during the day?"

"Enough to handle a little lady, even one who bounces around spewing fire and challenging anyone around her to a fight." Liam smiled, then sipped from the flask.

"Agreed! We drink enough to make sure our fire matches your blaze." Killian snorted, as he sat down next to Liam. "Between the two of us, we make one ruthless enough guard for you, Elena."

"I'll drink to that," a deep voice rumbled from the behind us. Killian tossed the flask over the fire to Declan. He raised it to his lips, taking the longest drink out of all of us.

"Who knew I had so much control over the drinking habits of my guards?" I scoffed, extending my hand to grab the flask back from the prince.

"That's all for you," he grumbled, sipping the whiskey before he tossed it back to Liam.

Rage bubbled up to the surface. I was sick and tired of his mood swings. All the anger, frustration and feeling of being overwhelmed were beginning to crack open the lock I had anchored over them.

Killian handed Declan a bowl of stew, and he swaggered over to a spot on the log beside us. Feeling the heat of my glare, he shot me a smug grin and continued to eat his food.

Boiling hot with frustration, I launched my spoon at the prince's forehead, where it met its target dead on.

"Well, that's one way to use a spoon," Liam whispered so faintly I barely even heard it.

The prince's gaze pierced right through me. His lips curled up like a snarling beast's. The smile melted from my face as my eyes widened. A shiver crept over me.

Gods.

Before I could blink, he launched himself toward me.

My world tilted upside down as Declan tossed me over his shoulder. Frantically, I pounded my fists against the stone wall of his back while he bent over to grab a satchel and strode away from the campfire.

"What do you think you're doing?" I seethed. "PUT ME DOWN!"

Deep, raspy laughter tumbled out of the royal highness below me. The grin plastered across his face told me he was enjoying every moment.

"Help me! He's lost his mind!" I yelled at the men behind me. "Tell him to put me down at once!"

Their eyes widened, and I craned my neck to see Declan toss them a glare as he stalked away.

"Nope, I think we'll just play it safe and stay over here. I'm not really in the mood to be pummeled by the prince tonight."

"Excellent decision." Declan shouted as tossed me a bit higher over his shoulder.

"You miserable cowards!" I snarled, still thrashing about, kicking anything that gave my feet purchase.

The other guards snickered as we passed. Gods, we must really be a sight to behold. With each step Declan took, my ribs thumped against his back, and I began to feel the ache of my dynamis slither underneath my skin.

"Hold your breath, my lady." The prince snickered as he launched me into the lake below him.

My scream echoed into the night, arms flailing against the air, before my body came crashing down into the icy water below. After a huge splash, I flung myself back up to the surface, gasping for air. The piercing cold water attacked my skin like a thousand tiny needles, causing me to tremble uncontrollably. For a moment, even the memory of how to swim seemed to evade me.

I wiped the water away from my eyes as my toes searched for purchase on the floor beneath. As I treaded closer towards the shore, my toe snagged against a rock and my feet finally touched the bottom. Anger quelled within me, as my breaths began to steady.

"How dare you," I seethed.

Arms folded across his chest, he leaned against a tree, a perfect display of a smug prince. "You needed to cool down. I figured this was the best option." He shrugged casually. If that wasn't enough for me to begin thinking murderous thoughts, he added in a devious smirk.

I submerged myself underwater and screamed—first, to avoid my stubborn mouth saying something I shouldn't, and second, to cool my emotions before we had a repeat showing of the chaos that was my dynamis. Only once I felt my dynamis seep back to the depths where it resided did I emerge.

"Toss me your clothes, and I'll hand you some soap."

I shook my head in response, and he sighed, tilting his head back against the tree. "If you're going to continue to ride with me, then I need to fix the lingering problems. Snoring I can handle, but the smell? That has got to go."

"I don't snore, and I absolutely do—not—SMELL!" My restraint snapped once more. My toes searched for a loose rock beneath me until they snagged against one. I bent down, grasped the slippery stone and drew my arm back before I chucked it towards him, releasing all my rage along with it. It hit the tree with a crack, barely missing his head by half an inch.

His voice rumbled deep and low, like a purr, no sign of anger or annoyance, just pure delight. "My dearest Elena, are you trying to kill me?"

"If I was trying, I wouldn't have missed. That, dear prince, was a warning."

His eyebrows shot up as he paused momentarily, running his hand over the scruff on his chin. Pushing away from the tree, he stalked towards me, unbuttoning his tunic with each step.

My heart started to race as he tossed his shirt aside and began to kick off his boots. *Just what does he think he's doing?* When he began to unbutton his pants, my eyes bulged, and Declan cleared his throat. "You may want to shield your little eyes, Elena."

I immediately slapped a hand over my eyes and turned around. A splash arose from behind me as the prince dove into the water.

"You're safe. You can turn around now."

His voice seemed to echo from a distance, so I waded around.

I was completely unprepared for the sight before me.

Water rippled over the prince's clearly defined chest, no doubt constructed from the many years of training and battles. My lips parted as he laced his fingers through his wet locks, sending more droplets of water cascading over his chest. When my eyes finally met his, a faint smile danced across his lips.

I snapped my gaping mouth shut, but I couldn't unlock my eyes from him, and neither could he from me. His eyes rolled to my lips, down to the rest of my body where they lingered. It was only then that I realized that I was still wearing my white Ascension dress. A very thin dress that was now soaked and probably almost translucent.

Flinching, I wrapped my arms around my body and sank my shoulders under the water. Averting his eyes, he put his focus to use elsewhere.

The water cut him just above his lower abdomen and was dark enough to hide whatever was below. Unfortunately, I've always had extremely active imagination, and my mind concluded everything concealed below was probably just as beautifully defined as well. A bar of soap in hand, he lathered his body, perhaps a little too thoroughly, before diving under to rinse.

"Catch!" He tossed me the soap, knocking me out of my trance. The slippery soap floundered around like a fish in my hands as I tried to grab hold of it. "Your turn, stinky."

Unconsciously, a growl rippled out of me. "Declan, I can't—I won't, especially with you in here. Also, I don't even have anything else to change into."

"You must really think me daft, don't you?" He waded towards the shore to get out.

Lost in anger, I almost didn't realize I was about to see a very naked prince. My hand flew over my eyes just in time. When I heard the swish of legs sliding into pants, I slowly peeled my hand away.

"I grabbed your satchel earlier. I figured there was a change of clothes inside. So, now you have clothes and no more excuses."

Fighting hard to not roll my eyes, I mumbled some very un-lady like words instead.

To be honest, I really was beginning to smell. Especially after all the events of the past two days. The idea of a bath sounded amazing, even in this frigid lake.

"Fine," I conceded, "I'll toss up my clothes, but you must agree to give me some space. Also, for no reason are you allowed to turn around while I'm in here."

"Now look who's giving demands." He shook his head, and a little smile tugged at his lips. "Here, I'll lay your new clothes on this rock. I'll be just over there if you need me. Don't get any ideas of running away either."

He laid out the clothes and walked back towards the tree line. Leaning up against one of the tree trunks, he faced towards the camp, allowing me time to bathe.

Peeling off a wet dress with corset strings proved to be an unexpectedly frustrating task. Water thrashed all around me until finally I was free. As I tossed the sopping bundle of clothing back onto the shore, chuckles tumbled through the tree line.

"You can swim, right?"

Responding with an angry grunt, I used the soap to lather my hair and body.

As usual, my intrusive thoughts swirled around inside my mind like the ripples of water, expanding one after another, until finally my brain ached. Submerging myself under the water, I massaged my hair thoroughly to get out all the remaining soap. It wasn't doing me any good to think about so many unknowns.

Leaving my thoughts behind with all the other remnants of the past two days, I swam up to the shore. I tried to squeeze all the water from my hair and body as fast as I could before sliding into the pants and tunic Bri had packed. When I picked up my boots to put them on, water sloshed out from inside, and my shoulders sagged.

Turning my boots upside down, I shook them until I was satisfied that every last droplet had been freed from within. Just as I began to shove my foot inside, Declan swatted the boot away from my hands. It tumbled into the dirt with a thud.

"Really?" I protested.

"Elena, you can't put those back on right now. They'll have to dry by the fire. If you put those back on in the state that they're in, you could catch a cold or, worse, your feet could become infected. Prolonging our trip to take care of your feet is the last thing we need," he groused. "I'll have to carry you back."

"Had it all figured out, did you, hmmm? Perhaps you should have thought about my boots before tossing me into the freezing lake," I cooed, glancing at him from over my shoulder. "I think you just enjoy having me in your arms." I froze, regretting the words that had exploded out of my mouth.

He grumbled something inaudible as he grabbed the wet clothes and the boots and shoved them into the satchel. With a tug, he lifted me up into his arms and proceeded to carry me back to the camp.

When we arrived back at the campsite, only Liam and Killian were left sitting around the fire. Declan lowered me down onto the log in between Killian and Liam, then placed my boots near the fire to dry out. Both men dipped their heads in silent greeting. They looked as though they were on the verge of combusting with laughter. Shooting them a glare, I dared them to jest.

Liam shook his head and averted his gaze towards Declan. "All is clear, I just checked in a few moments ago."

Placing his hands inside his pockets, the prince nodded. Liam squeezed my shoulder as he and Killian stood.

"The tent is all set up for you both," Killian muttered. "There are some extra blankets as well, it feels like it's going to be a chilly evening."

Both guards started to turn away, leaving me alone with the Lord of Sass. Panic forced the words out of me as I called after Killian. "So, which one is my tent?"

He tossed a grin over his shoulder, but his gaze didn't land on mine. Following his line of sight, I landed on a set of striking emerald eyes.

"We're sharing a tent, aren't we?" I whispered as I stood, even though I already knew the answer. The intensity of his stare made my knees threaten to buckle. "Y-you don't really think I'm going to let you sleep that close to me, do you?" Wrapping my arms over my chest, I attempted to cover my nerves with a glower.

One corner of his lip turned up as he leisurely closed the gap between us. With each step, my heart rate elevated, as it echoed in my ears like the beat of a drum. Unable to hold the intensity of his gaze, mine fell towards the ground. Black boots drifted into my view, and I slowly tilted my gaze upward.

My breath hitched as he wrapped his calloused palm around my forearm. It felt like the entire forest surrounding us buzzed with energy. Declan leaned forward, causing my skin to pebble as his breath flowed over the shell of my ear.

"Are you scared, Lena?"

Frozen by the velvety tone of his voice, my answer lay rooted on my tongue and made no attempts to venture further. Everything I'd heard and witnessed today had been evidence of all the reasons that I should fear the man before me.

However, there had also been moments where I had caught

glimpses of another man entirely. There was a lightness buried within him that had flickered through the cracks in his carefully constructed mask. That little flicker of light made me curious what more might lie underneath and how I might be able to coax it out of him.

The hand still curled around my arm fell free. Unconsciously, my body chased after the heat of his palm.

"Let me carry you back to the tent so you don't hurt your feet." Both our eyes dropped to my bare feet, already covered with dirt and pine needles from the forest floor.

"Okay." The words brushed over my lips on a breath. I wasn't even sure they had even been audible, but the crush of pine needles in front of me proved me wrong. Declan wrapped his arms around my back and legs, and lifted me up.

The walk was short, but the tension that simmered between us made it feel like an eternity. His silence as he guided us towards the tent made me wonder if it influenced him just as much. The prince shouldered open the flap of the tent as he walked us through and lowered me onto the canvas floor.

The flap fluttered close behind us, sealing me in with the shadows —some created by the night, the others by a broody prince with a powerful dynamis. Blinded by the darkness, I bent down to my knees, searching the space for the bedroll that had been in front of me.

Grumbles spilled into the air next to me. I shook silently with mirth with the knowledge that he was struggling just as much as I was. A few more grumbles arose until I heard a thump against the side of the tent, followed by a content sigh.

Dammit. He'd found the opening before I had, and hadn't even bothered to help me. Cursing him inside my head, I continued to search for the opening of the bedroll. Every inch of my body ached, from the tips of my toes to throb inside my head.

My fingers combed over the smooth warmth of a surface. Shock coursed through me as I realized my palm now lay on top of a very bare chest that was rapidly rising and falling.

Fingers curled around my wrist and gently lifted it away from the scorching heat below. The sensation spurred the dynamis within me, and my palm transformed into a glowing torch between us.

Our eyes widened. No burst of white flame fled from my fingertips. Instead, a soft golden glow radiated from within my palm, just like when Declan had removed my shackles for the very first time. Perhaps there was a sliver of hope that my dynamis wasn't completely unhinged.

"Well, that could have been useful earlier," I snorted.

Amusement flickered within the prince's eyes as he released my palm and I shimmied beneath the bedroll that had been illuminated. The glow dimmed, flying out of my grasp just like my emotions had done for years.

As I pulled the rough fabric over my shoulders, an intrusive thought clawed into my mind and sunk its teeth into it.

If I couldn't even control something as simple as the thoughts and emotions that swirled within my mind, how would I ever learn to control something as strong as my dynamis?

"Elena, for gods' sake, go to sleep." The prince groaned beside me.

For the past hour I'd done nothing but toss and turn. Sleeping on the hard ground wasn't exactly comfortable. Neither was the overwhelming sense of dread that plagued my thoughts.

"I'm sorry, I just—I mean—I feel…" A frustrated huff ripped through me. "I'm just uncomfortable." *In more ways than one.* "Sorry for keeping you awake."

A shuffling sound rose on the other side of me, right as soft fabric slid underneath my head. Declan had lifted and lowered my head back onto his cloak.

Confusion was written all over my face, and I was thankful for the darkness that hid it. The Lord of Shadows had done nothing but give me whiplash since this morning. One moment he was yelling at me, the next he was brushing away my fears with sweet words and gentle touches. Still lying on my side facing away from him, I whispered, "Thank you. That really does feel a lot better."

I felt a small tug at the end of my braid that I had redone somewhere amid my sleep deprivation. The leather strap holding the ends slid into his palm before he tossed it aside.

"What are you—?"

"Shhh." He curled his fingers through the locks of my hair.

"I—"

"For once, just will you be quiet, woman?" A deep sigh fled his lips. "Just let me help you."

A thousand thoughts flooded my brain about what my hair had to do with my sleep, but exhaustion outweighed my fight. Rolling my lips between my teeth, I ceded to his request.

Once he untangled my braid, his skillful hands combed from the top of my scalp all the way down to the tips of the wavy strands. Stroke after stroke cleared my mind as he worked. The soothing movements almost meditative. Occasionally, he tucked a few strands behind my ear as he went by. Each movement was detailed and precise, almost routine, like something that he had done several times before.

I was no stranger to this feeling either. Memories flashed through my mind of a time when my mother would do the same. Closing my eyes, I swore I could almost feel her delicate fingers comb through my hair as she would hum to help lull my worries away. A deep ache pulsed inside my heart as a tear rolled down the side of my cheek. Discreetly, I ran my fingers over my wet cheeks and wiped away the evidence before the prince could notice.

After some time, the tightness that had taken over my muscles loosened. Every part of my body was deliciously relaxed. With each tender brush of his fingers, my eyelids grew heavier.

A small, satisfied moan slipped through my lips, causing the prince's palms to still within my hair. Declan's deep chuckle rumbled over me, and my cheeks heated.

"Oh, gods. So sorry! I just—it just feels really, uh ...*nice*." Every word I muttered was gibberish, only furthering the redness that spread across my face. Silent curses ran rampant inside my mind as I squeezed my eyelids closed, wishing I could fade into the darkness.

I heard a little more rustling behind me. The blanket I had not realized I had tossed aside was now placed back over my shoulders. Declan leaned in and whispered so softly that I could barely hear his words.

"No more apologies. Just close your eyes and get out of your head, Lena."

Even after only one day, this man read me like a book. Everything about that left me unsettled.

"Sleep," he whispered, as he continued combing through my hair.

Exhaustion tugged at my eyelids, and I finally allowed myself to fall into it.

Declan

Wind rustled against the canvas of the tent, and I forced myself to peel my eyes open. The hazy, clementine light of dawn trickled through an open sliver of the tent flaps. It caressed the long legs that were now spread over mine and illuminated the boundless waves of auburn hair that cascaded over me. Elena's body rose and fell peacefully. Her breaths brushed against my bare chest. My fingers itched to reach out and glide through her hair like they had done last night, but I forced the urge down. It had been such a long time since someone else had been this close to me, mostly due to self-imposed reasons.

Cool morning air gusted through the tent, and the delicate body next to me shivered. Careful not to wake her, I slid the blanket back over her shoulders. She nuzzled her head deeper into me with a little hum, and I groaned inwardly in frustration.

Everything about Elena was forbidden, yet I couldn't seem to shake the unexplainable pull that I had towards her. No one could deny that she was stunning. Vibrant locks of auburn hair that made her ocean eyes glisten. Freckles that kissed the tops of her cheeks and nose. Pillowy pastel lips that only seemed to spew words of indignation towards me.

My lips twitched with amusement. To be honest, it was the dichotomy between her tenacity and tenderness that lured me to her. I was frustrated by the way she had challenged me every chance she'd gotten, but I must admit it had made me want to push her even more. Her unwavering will was alluring. However, it was the way she cared so much about everyone but herself that had cracked a small sliver in my heart.

In another time, another place, Elena and I might have been kindred spirits. We shared more in common than she would ever know. She stirred a little bit, and I used the moment to carefully roll her back to her own bedroll.

Quietly as possible, I got dressed and shoved everything else into my satchel. As I stepped out of the tent, I took one look back at the peaceful woman I had left behind. Unfortunately, whatever was brewing inside of me needed to end right here. I would only bring about destruction in her already turbulent life.

My duty would always come first, and this kingdom needed me to be alert and focused on all that was about to befall it.

The flap of the tent fluttered closed behind me as I went in search of Killian. Space away from her was desperately needed if I was going to survive the rest of this journey.

CHAPTER 12
ELENA

Soft melodies of chirping birds awoke me. The sun's rays broke through the canopy of trees in the forest, cascading over my face through the open crack of the tent. Grasping for this peaceful moment, I raised my head up, eyes closed, and let my body melt into its warmth. Soothing, beautiful sunshine. It was like a hug, and my heart twinged at the thought of my father. What I wouldn't give for his guidance right now.

Gods, please send me strength.

A twig snapped beneath boots outside the tent, and I leaned forward to see Killian open the tent wide.

"Well, good morning, sunshine," he said with a smile as he tugged me forward onto my feet.

Trying to erase the wince that slipped, I turned around to gather up my sleep sack to avoid Killian seeing the tears beginning to roll down my face.

He twisted me around. "Elena, are you okay? I know last night was a little ..."

"I'm fine." I sniffled.

His lips pinched into a thin line as his gaze dropped to his shuffling feet.

"I'm sorry." I sighed. "It's just... my father calls me that name."

Not only did I not want to be reminded about last night, but hearing the term of endearment Father used for me was even worse. Drawing in a deep breath, I tried my best to regain my composure.

"Hells. I'm so sorry, Elena. I hadn't realized."

"It's alright, how would have you known?"

We worked together, taking down the tent, before making our way back towards the rest of the group. As we strolled towards the horses, I patted his shoulder, a quiet reassurance that I was okay. Perhaps it was to reassure myself as well.

Once again, I was the last to pack up, so I quickened my pace. I didn't need to give the prince another reason to repeat last night's events. One splash in the frozen lake was enough for me.

He was regally perched on top of his large black stallion. His lips pursed into a line as he clenched the reins. Keeping my head down, I began putting my belongings into his saddlebag.

Killian reached out pressed my arms down, shaking his head. With a tilt of his head, he silently ushered me back towards his horse. Declan's horse chuffed and he snapped the reins and led his horse away.

Not once did he acknowledge my presence, not even a single glance back as he galloped towards the front of the group. This seemed to have become a trend with the men in my life recently.

After helping me onto the horse, Killian attached my bag to his saddlebag as the uncomfortable sting of rejection crept over me. That same unworthy feeling that I'd had three days ago when Will galloped away.

My anger turned inward. I was frustrated with myself for spending even a fraction of time worrying over the opinion of the unhinged prince in front of me. He obviously wanted nothing to do with me, and I was nothing but a nuisance to him. Yet here I was thinking about him in another light, the one that had me at odds with myself.

The version of him where he smiled so bright that dimples formed on his cheeks, where his firm lips turned up into a smirk whenever I challenged him, where he found a way to calm me when my own worries or dynamis threatened to consume me. My heart pounded against my chest, and I combed my fingers through my loose hair as I tried to lull myself out of the tangled cobwebs of my intrusive thoughts, like Declan had done for me all last night.

Killian climbed up behind me and nudged the beautiful ash-colored mare beneath us into a gallop. Once we caught up to the rest of the group, we fell into a trot alongside everyone else. I sat in silence braiding my hair and hoped it would prove to be an effective distraction.

Both of my guards chatted behind me. I faded in and out of their conversation, smiling here and there whenever they would laugh. I didn't know what was wrong with me, but I just couldn't seem to shake off the melancholy mood I was in. The conversation finally faded out behind me, and silence washed over us for what seemed like hours.

Finally breaking the silence, Killian passed me the waterskin and a handful of jerky. "What's going on in that fiery head of yours, Elena?" he said, gently nudging my elbow, patiently waiting my response.

Liam flashed a not-so-subtle look of concern to Killian as he tied back his long black hair into a messy low bun with a leather strap. In truth, I really didn't know how to answer his question, because I couldn't even understand what I was feeling. A shrug of my shoulders was all I had the energy for.

"He really does feel awful about last night."

"Mmhmm."

"That's the reason he didn't want you riding with him today. He felt that you both needed some…space."

"Hmm," I grumbled.

Anger reared its ugly head as I caught the two of them quietly shaking with mirth. Without warning, it crawled out of me to take over the conversation. "You both could have tried to stop what happened last night." My words came out a little more harshly than I'd intended. I tried to speak a little softer. "I mean, it seems like you three have known each other for a long time. Has he always been like this?"

Their gazes flickered between each other. The skin between my brows scrunched with concern. What made this question so difficult to answer? It was as if they were silently deciding what they could or could not tell me. Curious.

"Yes, this is true, we've all known each other for quite a while, little lady. I consider us to be as close as brothers," Liam said with a soft smile.

"Liam joined the guard first," Killian said from behind me. "His parents had been friends of the queen's for a long time, so he and Declan knew each other beforehand. I, on the other hand, was the outsider. Had to prove myself worthy to be accepted into their little man clan."

Liam snorted underneath his breath, silently repeating the words "man clan," before chuckling some more.

"What did you have to do to 'prove' yourself to them? As far as I can tell, the prince has very high standards for everyone, except himself." I mumbled the last part. "You must have done something pretty impressive."

Killian returned a weak smile, and I got the feeling that the story might be one he didn't want to elaborate on. A wave of sadness flowed into me, strong enough for me to know I had pulled the emotion from him. "Nothing big, really."

Liam scoffed. "I think that saving the crown prince's life was a *big deal*, Killian."

The leaked confession made my eyes widen. Another breeze of sadness flooded into me once more. Puzzled, I gently pushed the emotion out, and a gust of wind tousled Killian's floppy blond waves.

"Really, it was no big deal. I was just there to help a friend when he needed it most." Killian cleared his throat, signaling the end of that conversation.

Liam nodded at Killian with a silent affirmation. This time, a warm wind of pride seeped through me. Whatever Killian had done for the prince, he had more than proven himself to the two men he called friends. Even not knowing the whole story, I was beginning to understand just how kind and compassionate Killian really was. So, how was it that men like Liam and Killian attached themselves to the Prince of Darkness?

Perhaps there was far more to Declan than I'd ever understand. The man continued to be an enigma.

"Well, I'm thankful that he has the both of you to balance him out. I fear without you both, he would be eternally grumpy."

As they both chuckled behind me, I felt my frown melt into a smile. After a few silent moments, my courage rose. I wanted to ask about my impending doom, the capital city. Every day we inched closer, and now we were only three days away. "So, what exactly should I expect when we reach the castle?"

They shuffled a bit on their saddles, and it appeared this was another question they weren't too thrilled to discuss.

"Little lady, the king and Lord Alastor are temperamental like the prince." He winced. "However, they are far more ruthless. Their anger knows no bounds, and they will not take kindly to being challenged. They are dangerous men, Elena."

His eyebrow rose as he looked over towards me. I took it as a silent warning for me to rein in outbursts like the ones they'd witnessed yesterday. *Note to self, no more throwing utensils.*

If Declan was the least ruthless out of the three men, it made me wonder what their wrath entailed. A shiver ran over my body at the thought.

"Cold?" Killian asked.

"No, just mildly terrified." I swallowed down the burn of bile rising in my throat. Killian rubbed his palm up and down on my arm.

"Don't worry, little lady, we will be with you making sure you are safe at all times," Liam boasted beside us. "Also, something tells me the prince would kill anyone who tried to lay a hand on you." He chuckled. "Trust me, you'll be well protected, Elena." They both snickered, like they shared some kind of inside joke.

"What's that supposed to mean? What's so funny?" Turning in the saddle, I set a hard gaze on both with my hands on my hips.

"Oh...nothing at all, Elena." Killian laughed. "Just trust us when we say that the prince will have eyes on you. He'll make sure that no harm will happen to you during your stay with us."

"Hmm, unless that harm is from him," I grumbled under my breath.

"You can't stay mad at him for too long, especially when you have a part in this as well. My lady, you are just as temperamental as he is. In fact, it was you who instigated what happened last night."

I whipped around towards Killian. "I most certainly did not—!"

My words caught in my throat as Liam held up something shiny. The light reflected off the object and fluttered over Killian's smirking face. Held up high like a torch was the silver spoon I had tossed at Declan's forehead last night. Mouth agape, I struggled to find a retort, but there were no words, because they were right.

"I'll keep this in my pocket from now on. Not only has it proved to be a dangerous weapon, but it's proved successful in aiding young maidens in distress from ravenous stomachs." Liam's smile grew wider as he tucked the silver spoon into his pocket with a loving tap. "Seems like it has the potential to save my life on more than one occasion."

With a huff, my shoulders sagged in defeat. They both chuckled as we continued our way.

Sweat beaded in droplets across my forehead as the midday sun scorched the tops of our heads.

"Any way those lovely Frost abilities you told me about could cool us down a little bit?"

Liam caught my smirk as he tugged the collar of his tunic to allow for a much-needed breeze from the stifling sun. Wiping his brow, he waggled his eyebrows up and down then released his dynamis towards Killian and me. A chill fluttered towards us as a few speckles of snow dusted the top of my nose.

"I'm unsure if I should be in awe or revolted." I snorted. "All I can think about right now is the fact that I'm covered in frozen flurries of your sweat."

Laughter burst from Killian.

"I think the words you were looking for are 'thank you,'" Liam grinned.

"Umm ... thank you?"

"Anytime, little lady."

My gaze wandered over the guard behind me. "Your turn, Killian. Why don't you just zephyr us to the nearest place with water, or, for that matter, why not just take us to the capital itself?"

Killian scoffed. "As I told you earlier, there are limits to our dynamis."

I rolled my eyes. "I know, I know," I sighed dramatically. "You just said you could only zephyr for about five trips. Any further and you would drain your dynamis. So...why don't you just zephyr us to the closest stopping point then? It can't be that far, right?"

"Though my dynamis may be strong, unfortunately I cannot zephyr all of us and two horses. Tried once, it did not end well." He grimaced.

My mouth hung wide open and it sent Killian and Liam into a fit of giggles. I elbowed Killian in the gut. "Truly though, if I could, I would have done it by now, because it's as hot as Hells out here!" He sighed as he rubbed where I elbowed him. "Alas, that is just one thing we cannot do. As I said—"

"—*everything* has its limits, including dynamis."

A whistle pierced through the group, averting all eyes to the broody leader at the head of the pack. Declan pointed to the left side of the road, and I sighed with relief at the sight of the creek that came into view. After we dismounted our horse, Killian guided her by the reins towards the edge of the rippling water, and I took the opportunity to cool myself down as well.

The knees of my pants became damp from the wet ground beneath them as I splashed the water across my face. It slid down my face as I rubbed my wet palm over the back of my neck. The trickle of the creek murmured against my ear as I took a moment to soak it in.

Tension that had been caged in my shoulders and back began to melt away. Nature had always had a way of bringing me back to life, healing me in a way no elixir or dynamis could. A familiar awareness prickled the hairs of my arms.

Opening my eyes, I turned towards the direction of the pull I felt, and my gaze landed directly on the Lord of Shadows. One hand rested on the mane of the brawny stallion beside him while his mouth hung agape. When our eyes collided, his lips slammed shut as he turned his body and gave me a full view of his back instead.

My curiosity lingered only a moment more before I rose from the edge of the lake. Mud clung to my pants as I worked on brushing it off, just like the thoughts that swirled inside my head about the prince.

Another guard sauntered up with his horse beside me. Before he bent down to refill his waterskin, he tossed me a nod. It reminded me that I should refill my own water before we got back on our journey. Killian had already taken his horse back to the road, so I began to make my way towards them.

After a few short paces, a high-pitched squeal startled me. I turned just in time to see the chaos that unfolded before me.

The guard who had been next to me now rolled on the ground, avoiding the hooves of his horse as she reared. Before I could figure out what had caused her distress, she changed directions and barreled straight towards me. My breath hitched as my legs froze. I begged every part of my body to move, but it was too late, fear had taken over.

With eyes slammed shut, my hands rose in front of my body, my only shield against the scared mare. Panic filled my veins with fire as I felt it pulse against my skin. As I closed my eyes, I braced for an impact that never came.

Shouts echoed all around me, but all were muddled as white light burst from inside me. The horse reared up once more, squealing as she changed direction and galloped away. A heavy hand landed on top of my shoulder, and I almost jumped out of my own skin.

"Elena, it's okay," Killian soothed. "You alright?"

I stared down at the scorched ground underneath me.

Am I alright?

"Elena?"

"I...uh..." The words were stuck in my throat. I swallowed, wetting my dry lips before trying again. "I—think so."

He eyed me cautiously, probably noticing my wild eyes and trembling hands. "Good, because we need your help."

It took my brain a moment to catch up on his words. "Oh, no, the horse—d-did I hurt it?" Tightness coiled around my throat as it threatened to close at the thought. My bottom lip stung under my teeth as I balled my hands into fists, as if the action would stop the dynamis from being spewed from them once more.

"No, Elena. The horse is fine, I promise. A guard was bitten by a snake, and he's not doing so well." Killian's brow furrowed.

Clearing my throat, I forced every hint of my own panic down deep inside and replaced it with a mask of tranquility. "Then let's go help him."

———

There wasn't a Healer among the small group of guards, but they did have a small satchel of cloth wraps and a few elixirs for different purposes, none of which were useful for poison. I had known it was poison from the moment I saw the guard's bloodshot eyes. When I lifted his pant leg, dark lines had already spread like vines underneath his skin from the bite wound. My greatest fear confirmed. This man didn't have much time, and I had to work fast.

There was one plant that I knew would work, at least until we reached the nearest town, but I had spotted it a while back alongside the road.

"I need you to take me to a specific plant I saw on our way here." I said hastily, as I swiped away a bead of sweat as it slipped over my brow.

"I'll take you." Declan's deep voice stirred from behind me. Another guard took the reins of the spooked horse from his hands.

Declan must have gone to fetch her when she galloped away. His lips formed into a thin line as he took in his guard lying in agony on the grass behind me.

He extended his hand towards me. When I hesitated to grab it, his eyes thinned into slits. "Elena," his tone so low it made me shiver. "Take. My. Hand."

I jumped at his forceful command and took his hand. He tugged me into him, then a gust of wind enveloped us.

When we finally landed, my hand flew to my lips and I tried desperately not to retch.

"Sorry, I should have warned you." He smirked. I returned it with a glare, removing my hand now that the nausea had dissipated. "Longer bursts of zephyring will have those affects."

"Noted," I said tersely.

We'd landed precisely in the area where I had observed the overgrown field of sidra root. To the untrained eye, this would just look like a field of weeds, which indeed it was. However, these weeds had one of the strongest medicinal benefits for removing anything unwanted that poisoned the body. In certain times of the year, they blossomed like white flowers in the shape of a star. Thus, how it had received its name.

Suddenly, I realized I had never mentioned any of that to Declan or where exactly to take me.

"How did you know that this was what I needed?" I rapidly plucked as many green leaves as I could and shoved them into my pockets.

Running a hand behind his neck, he chewed on the inside of his cheek.

"Well?" I raised an eyebrow. My pockets overflowed with enough sidra root to help the guard and keep him comfortable until we could get him a more powerful elixir, or a Healer.

"My cousin is a Healer and my mother..." he breathed, his voice faltering. "She had a fascination with anything flora."

Adoration for his mother flowed through in each word, and the familiar ache tugged inside my chest. That same feeling that had curled itself around me whenever he was around.

Clearing his throat, the prince wrapped an arm around my waist, shoving me into his chest. In two blinks, a gust of wind and shadows consumed us, and then we were back with everyone else.

Lying on the ground, paler than when we'd left, was the guard. I wobbled over, remnants of nausea from being zephyred still wafting through me. Pulling out all the items, I got to work, determined not to add another name to the list of those I'd lost.

CHAPTER 13
ELENA

As the sun began its descent behind the horizon, the Royal Guards began to pack up once more. Griff, the injured guard, had been making great progress. Before taking a moment to rest against this boulder, I'd told Declan I was positive Griff would be able to make the journey to the next town. It was a few days away, but I had collected enough sidra root to make more poultices to help in the meantime.

Shortly after our conversation, he'd growled at me when my eyelids drooped and ordered me to rest. I'd grumbled right back, but hadn't argued.

With my back against a boulder, I tried my best to rest my eyes, but as usual, unwanted thoughts invaded my mind, keeping me restless. Lost deep in thought, I hadn't even noticed the body that had slid down next to me.

Not until a warm palm slid over my upper thigh, sending a million volts of electric tingles running through me. Noticing my shock, he slid his thumb back and forth in calming circles. It did quite the opposite—it sent even more shivers down my spine and a flush of heat to my center.

I winced as my cheeks burned. Every emotion seemed much more sensitive, almost heightened, since my Ascension. Declan pulled his hand back, his hand clenched against his thigh.

"I—I apologize," he choked out. "I was just trying—I can imagine these two days were...well, a lot to take in." He cleared his throat. "Your dynamis seems to react when you're faced with extreme emotions. Controlling them is something we're going to have to work on."

"Ha!" I snorted. "That's an understatement for sure. Gods only know the reason they would bless someone as unstable as me with an equally unstable dynamis."

"Perhaps they're getting bored in their old age? Maybe they needed a little excitement? A good laugh?"

My mouth gaped wide. A flicker of a smile twitched against Declan's lips before it faded.

"Dearest Shadow Lord, did you by chance just try to make a joke *and* smile?"

"Perhaps. In my ripe old age, maybe I needed a little excitement myself."

"How old?"

"A man never tells."

Another snort escaped. "I think you have that saying a little backwards, but I'll excuse it. You can't help it if your memory is starting to falter now that you're ancient."

Leaning into him, I gave his shoulder a nudge and laughter passed between us for a moment. Then, silence. My hands fidgeted relentlessly on my lap.

"Thank you for helping today." His eyes bore into mine, and there was a sincerity there that made me hold my focus. "This group of guards..." Declan cleared his throat and shifted his body so that his arms were resting on the tops of his knees. "They've become like family to me. They've done a lot for me." He paused. "If anything ever happened to them or if I couldn't protect them from harm, I would never be able to forgive myself."

I nodded, his words striking a familiar chord in my own core values. I knew all too well the burden of never being able to find forgiveness for yourself.

A rush of emotions crashed like a tidal wave into me again. My body jarred against what felt like sadness and guilt. The emotions took on a life of their own; it was almost like they were trying to pull me under.

I used all my might to shove them out of me. As I did, a gust of wind flowed through my hair.

Stunned, my lips parted. Had that happened the last time?

"You felt something, didn't you?"

"Huh?"

My body stilled under his intense scrutiny. Green eyes blazed at me, his jaw clenched. Then, he slammed them closed, exhaled, and then opened them slowly.

Declan was suddenly the portrait of calm. What was going on with this man? Perhaps I wasn't the only unstable Elysian in the kingdom?

"Try again," he commanded harshly, making me flinch.

"You really need to learn how to spea—"

"Again!" he growled, and my eyes widened. "Try. Again."

Flustered by his impatient tone, I huffed, turning my body to face Declan. "I don't understand what you would like me to do...y-y-you... *ass*!" Trembling with rage, I realized the filter over my mouth had slipped, and to none other than His Royal Highness. *Kill me now.*

He leaned impossibly closer. His leg brushed against mine and I could feel his breaths against my temple. "Try to feel it."

"Excuse me?" I scoffed. "Yeah, there's no way that I'll be doing tha—"

His hand slapped over my mouth before I could continue. Declan's nostrils flared as he ran his other hand through his thick wavy hair. He took another deep breath. When he spoke this time, he was a little more careful with his words. "I want you to try to read my emotions. I'm curious if you can feel them."

"Oh," I mumbled against his hand. "You could have just said that the first time."

He dropped his hand. "Try again, Elena. Please."

Inhaling deeply, I prepared myself for whatever was about to happen. "Fine, I'll try."

Instantly, my body jolted, overwhelmed with a searing sensation. This must be what rage, anger, or maybe even frustration felt like. Its flames scorched their way through my body. I could feel it burn *everywhere*. My skin sizzled uncomfortably, my legs squirming. The pressure was unbearable. There was no way could I hold onto this any longer. I needed to release it, *now*.

A bead of sweat slid down my neck as my teeth pierced my lips. Grasping an imaginary hold of the feelings burning through me, I shoved them out of my body. A rush of wind tousled our hair.

"Whoa," I whispered.

"What did you feel?"

"Anger...I think? A whole lot of it." I shivered, remembering the feeling. "It felt like I was burning alive."

"Hmmm..."

"What are you thinking?"

"Something tells me that you may have several more layers inside of your newfound dynamis we'll need to uncover."

I swallowed deeply. If only he knew that there was so much truth in that prediction, in the form of a whole other dynamis I hadn't told another soul about.

"Try again."

"I—I don't know if I can handle that again."

"Just—" He pinched the bridge of his nose, and his tone grew impatient. "Trust me, Elena."

With a heavy sigh, I debated whether to share the truth of my dynamis or not. Uncertainty hovered over this entire journey, and I wasn't sure if admitting I had two unique dynamis to the king's son was such a brilliant idea.

"Try again," he pleaded.

Against my better judgment, I met his gaze. They lacked any anger at all. Only genuine curiosity stirred inside them as they stared patiently into mine.

"I'm also an Empath." I paused as his brows rose nearly to his hairline. However, he didn't utter a single word. My nerves clawed their way up my throat, and I swallowed them back down. "The gods blessed me with Empath dynamis before they made me the Light Phoenix."

Silence passed between us for longer than felt comfortable. He ran his fingers through his hair as he processed my words. Finally, he shifted his body back towards mine, and there was no escaping the full attention he was giving me. "Right, well...let's try one more thing then."

I sat stunned, surprised that that was all he had to say. "*Okay.*"

"Good. This time, I want you to use your dynamis to search inside for my emotions. Without me sending them out to you."

Hesitation prickled for a second before I relaxed my body and cleared my mind. Eyes closed, I waited for the worst. It was an unnatural feeling to be searching for someone's emotions, but I tried my best to will my mind and dynamis to continue its quest.

When I was ready to surrender, I felt something dark and turbulent ahead. The skin between my eyebrows scrunched together as my mind felt its way around this seemingly inflexible emotion. Impatiently, I launched my mind forward, trying to capture it.

Instead, a flurry of clouds, thick and gray, swallowed me up and shoved me. The feeling of falling felt so real that it wasn't until my body twitched that I realized I was sitting firmly on the ground.

"What in the Hells was that?" My fingers wrapped around my nauseous stomach. "I don't think I ever want to feel that again."

A smile spread across his lips as he opened his own eyes. Smug bastard, he really did like watching me in pain, didn't he?

"That was my ward."

"You ready, Elena?" Killian shouted as Declan and I approached the rest of the group.

"As I'll ever be." I sighed dramatically, causing Killian to laugh.

He was already mounted on top of his horse, so he adjusted

himself to the back of the saddle to provide room for me to join. Killian lowered his hand and I reached up to grab it when we were interrupted by His Royal Highness.

"No, you'll be riding with me, Elena." He bellowed the command from on top of his saddle. The man was fast. How the Hells had he got up there so quickly? He sat staring at me with furrowed brows and lips pursed in their infamous thin line.

"Seriously?" I began to argue.

"Now. Hurry up."

Gone was the soft-spoken man who had combed through my hair last night, helping to lull me to sleep. All that was left now was the Lord of Grumpiness.

Rolling my eyes, I lifted my hand and placed it into his. Before I could lift my foot, he yanked me and I flew into the saddle in front of him. Several obscenities tore out of me under my breath, until a sharp pain poked my side.

"Ow! What the Hells was that for?" I rubbed my tender side where he had pinched me.

Anger fueled my fist as I tried to punch him in the gut. He grabbed my wrist and swung me back around, trapping me with his arm cinched uncomfortably tight around my stomach. With a harsh tug of the reins, we were off in a gallop. A chorus of snickers arose from behind us as the guards followed.

Once there was a sizable gap between us and the rest of the group, Declan slowed the horse down to a trot. I tried to tug my arm away from him, but his grip tightened as he pulled me in closer. Still trapped between his arm and his chest, I shivered as I felt his heavy breaths rolling over the side of my neck.

"That was for arguing with me, Elena, and the pinch was for rolling your eyes at me yet again," he growled next to my ear.

I forcefully blew out a breath, still wiggling to try to escape his hold on me. "Gods, are you always this surly?"

His broad chest crashed against my back as his mouth hovered next to my ear once more. "No, I just save that for contemptuous, arrogant bastards like yourself."

He'd used my own words against me. *Touché, Prince, touché.*

I curled my neck around just in time to see the delighted smirk stretched across his face. Whipping my head back around, I murmured several fouler obscenities under my breath.

"What was that, Elena? You're mumbling again and I can't hear you."

Extending my elbow with maximum force, I launched it back into his stomach.

A deep grunt bellowed out of him as he shoved me away. "Was that necessary?" He growled.

"Absolutely, Your Highness." A devious smile spread across my face.

CHAPTER 14

ELENA

For a long part of our journey, it was eerily quiet, as I strained my back to keep away from the hard wall of a chest behind me. My shoulders were already starting to throb almost as much as the pain in my head. I released a groan, slouching as I applied pressure to forehead. The events of the past two days were starting to catch up with my body.

Declan leaned back on the horse as I heard shuffling from within his saddlebags. "Here." His words were softer than earlier. "You'll need to drink more water today. Also, eat this. It'll help."

He handed me his waterskin, then placed a strange, orange-tinted shard of what looked like glass in my hands. I raised an eyebrow, holding up the glass rock, silently questioning how I was supposed to ingest it. He laughed, rubbing his large hand over his face before he spoke.

"I'm not trying to poison you, Elena. I'm trying to help. It's ginger candy one of the cooks makes for me when I'm out on the road. The ginger in it is supposed to help with upset stomachs, hangovers..." He tapped his index finger on my forehead. "Headaches as well. She likes to make me things." He shrugged casually. "Apparently, I'm her favorite."

"Favorite, huh? Mmhmm." I waggled my eyebrows up and down, but all I was met with was a blank stare. "Is she pretty?"

Silence.

"Since you're neglecting to answer, I'll assume that she's gorgeous. Also, she must be one fierce woman to put up with your particular aura of ... *surliness*." I snickered.

"I can already hear the gossip now. 'No shadows can hide the prince and cook, as they were caught red-handed with a bun in the oven.'"

Snorting quietly to myself, my shoulders shook widely with mirth. I was either delirious or hilarious, but the glare burning the back of my head confirmed it was the latter.

I popped the candy into my mouth. The feel of his chest against my back made me jump. He was close enough to whisper into my ear. "Well, considering Alana, our cook, is old enough to be my grand-mother, that would be quite the royal scandal indeed, Elena."

My mouth gaped wide open as he waggled his brows up and down with a sinister grin.

A burst of laughter launched the ginger candy out of my mouth somewhere into the depths behind us. Declan's head flew back from the sight, laughing so hard tears leaked around his eyes.

For a moment, I paused and took all of him in. Dimples formed across both cheeks, quite the opposite to the stoic face and harsh atti-tude that he paraded around daily. It made me wonder if this man—the one who was kind, combed my hair to help me fall asleep, and had a beautiful roar of a laugh—was the real Prince Declan.

After he wiped his eyes, he caught my lingering gaze. I turned back around, taking a long swig from the waterskin. I could hear him rustling again, and not too shortly after, he handed me another ginger candy.

"I noticed you lost yours somewhere back there."

"Thank you, Declan. I really hope it helps, because my head is killing me." At his wide eyes and smirk, I winced, realizing I'd just called a royal by their first name.

Gods.

"I'm sorry, Your Highness."

"No apologies necessary."

The tension in my shoulders eased.

"*Actually*—" He drawled, in a deep velvety tone. "I enjoyed the way my name sounded rolling over your lips," Declan whispered against the sensitive shell of my ear.

Once more, a twinge pulled at my chest, and my body became tense all over. The control I had over my dynamis snapped, kindling to my internal flame. Every inch of my body ignited in a warm, bright glow.

My dynamis pulsed greedily throughout my body. No spot was left untouched. Even the space between my now clenched thighs throbbed from the power inside me begging to be released.

Another jolt of dynamis sent my hair flying in the air all around me. Power hummed through my entire body, thrashing against my skin, trying to force me to release it into the world.

Oh, gods.

I'm in trouble.

E very muscle in my body constricted, leaving me feeling as though I was about to rip at the seams. My eyes felt like hot coals as my dynamis swirled behind them. I could almost hear the sizzle of my tears as they evaporated instantly on my cheeks from the heat. This was too much, too powerful, too emotional.

Every feeling that coursed through me created a storm inside of me—a turbulent pulse of fear, worry, anxiousness and something that felt an awful lot like desire. At first, I assumed these emotions were entirely mine. It was as if they were calling me to action, whispering silent commands to me. However, some of the emotions had a signature feel to them, unique to only one other's I'd felt before.

My dynamis instinctively targeted the foreign emotions threatening my body. The small hairs on the back of my rose. Another tug of my chest and I was suddenly hit with the answer.

Declan.

I was pulling emotions from the prince as well as struggling to maintain my own.

Great gods above.

Ears flicking back and hooves clomping, Declan's horse whinnied. The stallion reared back on his hind legs, and the two of us crashed onto the dirt road beneath us.

Pain radiated through my body, but I couldn't even force myself to stand up. Instead, I lay helpless in the dirt, and relived an unwanted memory of my past that I wished could be wiped free from my mind.

Before panic completely consumed me, blackness flooded every inch and crevasse around me. Around *us.*

In my moment of insanity, I had forgotten that the Lord of Shadows had also fallen off the horse.

"Control your dynamis Elena! Find your calm."

I tried to respond, but a high pitch cry tore out of me instead.

Darkness enveloped both of us. Swirling shadows secured themselves around my waist, but not in a menacing way. Instead, it felt more like a protective caress. Up and down. They cascaded over my arms, intertwining with my hair, which whipped wildly above my head. They continued their efforts to calm me as I continued to fight against my dynamis.

That was when I heard it.

Smooth and rich with emotion, a deep voice rang out from behind me. Another tug of my chest, this time more painful than the others, as my body arched. It felt like my dynamis was trying to tear me away from the luscious, melodic sounds dancing around behind me. Clawing my hands into the dirt, I tried to force my dynamis back to where it resided.

The gods had granted me this dynamis because they believed in my strength. Strength that I needed to use right now to rein in the chaos that I had created.

Steady breaths became my main objective. I leaned into the rhythm of the song, letting it lull me back to control. The shadows continued to caress me, and I let my mind clear, shoving the turbulent storm aside to let the warmth of the light shine in.

Remembering my lessons with Bri, I chanted my mantra in my head, the one that had carried me through each of my downfalls, each moment of panic, and each tear of my heart.

"I am the light. No darkness can bind me. I have it within me to hold and to guide me."

Over and over, I chanted those words, softly at first, then with increased forcefulness as I worked to rein in my dynamis.

Cool breeze rolled over my body, and I relished the fact that I could feel it over my skin. The shadows that surrounded my body swept back to their owner. The melody that had once played inside my ears now faded into the distance until the only sound that was left was the whisper of the breeze passing through the leaves of the trees surrounding us.

The warmth of the day tapped against my sealed eyelids. With some effort, I managed to peel them open. My lungs finally allowed me to pull one long, deep breath. I raised my head towards the sky and thanked all five gods for allowing me to breathe in the fresh air of the beautiful day once more.

Controlling this power, *my power*, wasn't going to be easy as I had hoped. How was I going to do this alone?

The words must have left my lips, because a strained voice from behind me replied, "You won't. That's what I'm here for, Lena, to train you."

He was on his knees a few inches behind me and watched me cautiously as I wiped away the beads of sweat that had taken residence on my forehead.

"Why, Declan?" The words felt rough against my throat. "Why would anyone take this on?" I paused momentarily as the enormity of what just happened struck me. "Why didn't the king just... kill me?"

Tears burned behind my eyes. If I let them out now, it would open the gates to uncontrollable sobs, a breakdown that I would not allow to happen. Not today, and not in front of him.

A sigh wafted through the air between us. I took in his pale face and rumpled hair. He was as fatigued as I was. Wiping away beads of sweat with his palm, he then rubbed his fingers between his furrowed brows.

"That's a story for another time and another place." He tucked strands of loose hair behind my ear. "Right now, we need to focus on being calm. I don't think either of us could handle another surge of your dynamis in the state we're both in."

The prince stood, lifting me onto two legs as well. Silence fell between us and he gently picked me up like the night before.

Liam stood a few feet away, the reins of a much calmer black stallion wrapped around his hand. Declan helped me onto the saddle, then crawled on behind me. With a few gentle clicks of his mouth, the stallion underneath us cantered on.

Exhaustion flooded my body as my shoulders began to sag. Declan's arm carefully weaved through mine and wrapped around my stomach as he slid my aching body back against the warmth of his chest. This time I didn't fight it because something about it felt comfortable and safe. I let my body relax into his.

This time, it felt right.

CHAPTER 15
ELENA

The high-pitched whinny awoke me from my slumber. Drowsiness still hung on my eyelids, but I forced them open with a sweep of my fingertips.

The clang of chains and the heaviness of my wrists made my breath hitch. My gaze fell to the iron shackles wrapped around my wrists, and a mix of emotions I invaded my mind.

Shame over the way I'd lost control of my dynamis. Guilt that I could really hurt others during the chaos. Terror that these chains might never leave my wrists again.

"Lena…" Declan whispered as he turned my chin to face his. His face crinkled with concern as my lips rolled in on themselves. Even caged within my teeth, they still trembled. "Let me see your wrists."

Extending my hands towards his, I closed my eyes to keep the sadness held within. I heard the click of the lock and felt the heaviness being lifted away from my wrists.

"Thank you," I breathed, opening my eyes just as he shoved the iron shackles into his satchel. A tear slipped free, and my hand shot up to capture it. Declan's steady hand covered my own and lowered it into my lap. With his other hand, his thumb swiped away the tears that had escaped against my will.

Heat warmed my cheeks as his knuckle brushed against the edge of my jaw before he rested his hand back on his thigh. He cleared his throat. "You drained a lot of your dynamis. Anymore would have been dangerous, so I put these on."

"I understand, it's okay." I turned around to face forward. He stopped me with his palm as I gathered the courage to meet his eyes again.

"I'm sorry. I should have taught you how to ward after you used your dynamis the first time." His gaze fell from me as he ran a palm through his already mussed hair. "You passed out, and I wanted to make sure you were protected in case you woke up in a panic."

"Passed out?"

"You've been asleep since you fainted, then the entirety of the next day, Lena."

"An entire day?" I exclaimed, as the beats of my heart raced alongside my breaths.

Declan nodded solemnly. "Fortunately, we're very close now to Pinepeak." He nodded to the horizon behind me, and I followed his line of sight. Sure enough, the town was only a few paces away.

I awaited his orders for me to pull up my hood, awaited him to reach out and glamour my dynamis tattoo. None of that came.

As we entered the gates of the city, my eyes widened at the sight. Smooth gray stone paved the walkways, and buildings appeared to also be made with sturdy stone and other materials that didn't look inches away from blowing away with the wind. However, it only took one glance into the eyes of the Elysians as we passed to see the king's toll still weighed heavily here.

Beggars held out bowls for food or slept in alleyways. Clothes were tattered, and carts of food for sale were only half full.

Our horses paraded down the main street and allowed me to observe just how different the looks we received here were. Some eyes narrowed or fell to the ground as we passed, while other people gave smiles or nods like they were almost happy to see the Royal Guards. The entire interaction left me even more puzzled than I was before.

Laughter and lively music spilled out of the well-lit building ahead of us. The closer we inched toward it, the more intrigued by it I was. Declan let out a whistle, and his stallion pulled to a halt just outside the door.

"Wait here," he said, so low I could barely hear him over the music.

He walked towards a gentleman lingering around the front door. They leaned their heads together, as if trying to make sure that no one else heard their conversation. The man nodded with a smile, then held out his arm towards Declan.

He embraced the man's arm and then turned it over while staring at his wrist. Both smiled, then shook each other's arms once more before Declan made his way back towards me. That was the most peculiar handshake I'd ever witnessed, or there was something more to it.

Confusion must have been written all over my face, because Declan's eyebrow rose as he assessed me. "Everything alright? You look in pain." He snorted as he reached up towards me, but I swatted him away and slid off the horse myself.

"More like suffering from a royal pain in my ass." I murmured under my breath. A laugh slipped from my lips, as I leaned my forehead against the soft fur of his horse in an attempt to hide it.

When palms rested on each side of my forehead and the heat of his body warmed my back, I knew he'd heard me. Caged between his arms, I felt his beard tickle against the side of my neck as he spoke.

"Keep talking like that, Lena, and that can be arranged," he threatened in a deep voice, rich with promise that I had no doubt he would fulfill.

The heat of his body fled as quickly as it had come, leaving the chilly air to consume the empty space. "Let's get you inside and get you something to eat. Perhaps something to distract that mouth of yours before it gets you into trouble." Boots clattered against the stone road as he swaggered away towards the guards who awaited his orders.

Dragging my palms down my face, I sent a prayer to all five gods that I had wiped the blush off along with it. With a deep sigh, I shuffled over to the saddlebags to distract myself by unhooking my satchel.

By the time I had finished, Declan had come up beside me with Liam and Killian in tow.

"How are you feeling, little lady?" Liam's grin widened as he guided us into the tavern.

"Fantastic," I drawled sarcastically.

Liam shoulders shook with silent laughter. Declan and Liam approached the bar to speak with what I assumed to be the owner. Killian threw his arm over my shoulder and guided me away from the door. "Glad to see that sass has made a reappearance." He smiled, and my elbow found purchase in his side. Killian groaned and dropped his arm from around my shoulder. "That, however, I didn't miss."

Patrons at the table beside us gave us scowls, which only spurred our laughter more.

"What's so funny?" a deep voice asked, and both of our gazes shifted towards Declan's.

"Oh, none of your concern, Your Royal Grumpiness." I patted his cheek with my palm. "I mean your Highness."

Liam's eyes bulged as his fist covered his mouth. Killian just shook his head and folded his arms across his chest as if he knew what would happen next.

Declan leaned in and hovered just in front of my nose. Nerves spread like wildfire inside of me as my teeth clenched down on my bottom lip. His gaze dropped before it reverted towards my eyes. "Lena..."

"Yes, Your Highness?" I said with a little more sarcasm than I had intended.

"Why does something tell me that you'd like for me to carry out my promise from earlier?" He hummed, raising an eyebrow as he awaited my response.

My mouth flapped open and closed like a fish's, but I found no words. Declan stood back to his full height, arms crossed over his chest, chuckling darkly. "Mmhmm, that's what I thought."

Liam interrupted. "They only have a few rooms available, so we'll have to double up and sleep in rotations. We'll stable the horses and tell the rest of the men. Killian and I will take the first watch, if you need us at all. You two enjoy your meal." With a nod, he and Killian strolled out the door, both with grins pasted on their faces.

The man before me, nodded to the tables behind me. Once I was seated, he went and grabbed us two plates of food and a bottle of wine to share.

It was silent between us still, and I watched intently as Declan filled my glass almost to the brim. Both of us ate, taking glances at each other every few moments, until I had drained my glass completely.

A smile warmed the prince's cheeks as he filled my glass once more. Pushing his plate aside, he leaned back in the chair and adjusted his legs to a more comfortable position. As he did, his legs brushed against mine and I inhaled my drink from the spark it created within me. Declan's eyes widened as he began patting my back.

"I'm fine," I managed to squeak out, as I took another gulp to calm the tickle that still lingered inside my throat.

"So, tell me a little about yourself."

I gave him a blank stare. He sighed, then both elbows landed on the table as he leaned forward. "We've been riding for three days and I know nothing about you besides the fact that you're feisty, don't take orders well, and care more about helping others than you do yourself."

"Sounds like an accurate description." I said as I raised my glass toward him before taking another sip.

"I'll make you another deal."

Now he had caught my attention. "Continue," I ordered, watching his lip twitch with satisfaction.

"For everything you share with me, I'll share a little bit about me as well."

"Seriously?"

"Seriously."

"Okay, ask away, Your Highness." I raised my glass to his as we clinked them together.

Perhaps it wouldn't be such a terrible idea to get to know the Shadow Lord a little more.

"So, horses?" I asked.

Hours had passed, and most of the patrons of the tavern had left. Declan and I still sat chatting about our past. We'd already moved to another bottle of wine, which might or might not have influenced my loosened lips.

"Yes, horses. Whenever I have a free moment away from my duties, the first thing I do is go for a ride on Shadow."

"Of course the Lord of Shadows would have an all-black horse named Shadow. Very creative." I smirked into my cup. "I'll make sure to warn your future wife to avoid letting you name your children."

"I'm sure she would appreciate the advice."

I'm not sure why, but a little wave of jealousy drifted through me at the thought of seeing someone being Declan's wife.

His lips quirked as gaze fell to his glass. All mirth faded as he swirled the wine within it. "Truth is, it was a pastime that my older brother and I used to share. We loved riding along the shore in the mornings and over the hillsides in the spring when the wildflowers would cover them in a blanket of colors." He paused, but I could tell there was more he wanted to share. "When I was younger, sometimes even my father..." He winced and drained the glass. "He used to go with us, before ..."

His father was not known for his kindness, so for Declan to reveal this fact about him was surprising.

"So, books?" He smiled weakly as he attempted to change the conversation.

"I didn't get to leave Lostburrow much, or at all really." I shrugged nonchalantly. "Books became my chance to explore, my friends...my escape when I needed it most."

My shoulders dipped low as Declan leaned his elbows on the table once more. "What were you trying to escape?" he asked, genuine concern intertwined with his tone.

A sigh fled my lips as I brought my finger up to my forehead and tapped it against my head. "I'm always trying to escape the darkness that taunts me inside here."

"It's hard to imagine you with any dark clouds swirling inside of you. Especially when all I've seen is sunshine."

Declan's brows shot up to his forehead, almost as if he hadn't meant for those words to slip. I covered my smile with my glass.

"Oh, it's there." I made sure not to mention his comment, and Declan's shoulders visibly relaxed. "It's always there." I said quietly into my glass before draining it. "So, any love interests?" I piped, not wanting to linger anymore on the past conversation. "Well, besides the one I already know…your cook."

Declan's lips quirked, but he only responded with his own question. "What about you? What about…Will?"

Hearing his name sent a jolt to my spine I hadn't expected, and my body deflated into the chair.

"I'm sorry, I shouldn't have—"

"No, it's alright," I interrupted. "If I were you, I would have been curious too, especially after the way we parted."

An ache blossomed in my head, and the walls of the tavern began to wobble a bit. Either that, or the wine was starting to affect me.

"We were friends. He was my only friend, to be honest. I always wanted more between us, but he never looked at me that way, until…" I sighed as the memory of that day assaulted me. "The day of our Ascension, he kissed me and told me he'd been interested in me for a long time."

Declan's jaw clenched and his fist curled into a ball on the table.

"It's okay though, because he'll never look at me again that way again," I scoffed, and Declan's brows furrowed.

"Why?"

"Because h-he…" My lip began to quiver, and my eyes glossed over with unshed tears. Declan released his fist and rubbed his open palm against my arm. "He blames me for everything that happened, and apparently I've been a burden to him since the day we met."

Declan stopped rubbing my arm and instead gripped it, forcing my eyes to meet his. "You don't believe that, right?" He snarled.

"I'm not really sure what I believe anymore," I whispered, averting my gaze. His palm left my arm but found my fingers and laced them between his.

"Elena, you need to listen to me. You did absolutely nothing wrong that day. None of those events were anyone's fault, especially yours. Do you understand?"

A shrug was all I could offer in response.

"I need you to say it." His eyes locked on mine in a silent demand.

"Say what?" I whispered as a tear rolled down my cheek.

"'It's not my fault.'" He brushed away the tear with his finger. I shook my head, but he gripped my chin. "Say it, and then we can finally go to bed."

"I c-can't."

"You can."

We stared at each other for a few moments. His gaze never faltered from mine until I caved under the intensity of his stare.

"It's not my fault," I whispered.

"Good, now let's go to our room."

"*Our* room?"

Declan stood, pushed in his chair, painstakingly slow, then rounded the table and extended his hand towards me. He wiggled his fingertips until I placed my palm inside of his and he pulled me up.

We were just a few inches apart when I mustered the courage to grab his chin and pull it down to meet my glare. "It better have two beds, Declan."

His face transformed into a mischievous smirk.

Hells.

CHAPTER 16

DECLAN

E lena swayed back and forth all the way up the stairs. I chuckled inwardly every time she slipped and a curse flew from her lips.

"Dammit!" Her shoulder hit the edge of the wall, and her face flushed crimson. When we finally reached the top floor, she got on her knees and kissed the wooden floor beneath them. "Bless the gods. I've finally ascended!"

As I tried my best not to smile, I slipped my arm through hers and lifted her upright. We had gone through two bottles of wine at dinner, and I was pretty sure she'd drunk the majority of it. On top of that, she'd barely eaten anything. I made a note to make sure she drank water tonight.

"Don't think I didn't hear you back there laughing at me, oh great Lord of Shadows." She turned and shoved her dainty little finger into my chest. "Oww!" Her freckled nose crinkled as she glared at me. "What's underneath there, armor?"

"Muscles," I deadpanned.

She slapped her palm against her forehead with so much vigor that it echoed inside the tiny hallway. Another little chip of my heart chipped away at the sight of her hunched over in a fit of contagious giggles. The sound alone spread like rays of sunshine all over my body. I peeled her hand away from her face and used it to guide her towards our room.

Making it to the door, I fumbled with the stubborn old lock. No matter how many times I twisted it, the lock wouldn't budge. Elena wobbled over and slumped against the door just as the lock clicked.

It swung wide open, and both of us toppled onto the floor. A meek groan rang out from underneath me, where Elena now resided.

"Your muscles are squishing me," she wheezed, and I couldn't help but chuckle as I rolled off her and stood up.

Laughter had been a foreign concept for me lately. It had been a while since my cheeks had hurt from smiling so much. This wide-eyed inferno who was staring at me from the floor was melting the frozen façade I'd been building for years.

Grabbing her hands, I lifted her up and helped her over to the bed. Next to the side table there was a ceramic pitcher and two cups. Lifting the pitcher, I filled a full glass of water and held it in front of her. "Drink."

She raised her hand to her head in a salute. "Yes, sir," she mimicked as she drained her cup.

The heat from her lingering stare burned into my side as I refilled the cup and handed it back to her. Her eyes stayed locked on me the entire time, and I got lost in them. When she finally came up for air, my bottom lip slid between my teeth as bead of water fell down the slope of her neck to the depths below.

She wiped her mouth with the back of her hand. Mesmerized, I tracked her fingers as they smoothed over her soft lips and wiped the remaining dampness from her neck. Heat pulsed up and down my body. *Gods.*

Elena was a temptress, and she didn't even know. I tried to erase the forbidden thoughts that swirled inside my head.

"Declan, there's only one bed." Her whisper was full of anxiousness.

Closing the distance between me and her where she sat on the bed, I leaned into her, watching her eyes go wild as she fell back against the headboard. My arm slid over her, and delight sparked my dynamis at the sound of her breath hitching as I did.

"Dec—I..." she whispered, he breath brushing against the side of my cheek.

My fingers curled around the pillow next to her and I pulled it with me as I stepped backwards, distancing myself from the bed and her. "I know, Elena, that's why I'll be sleeping on the floor."

The rosy flush that was beginning to be one of my favorite sights warmed her cheeks, making her freckles stand out even more. As she nodded, I grabbed a spare wool blanket from the foot of the bed and began to build a makeshift bed on the floor.

Just as I kicked off my boots and crawled under the sheets, the bed frame creaked beside me. Two aqua eyes peered down from me from the edge of the bed, and unbraided auburn waves dangled around her face.

"You've been riding all day, and that floor looks miserably hard." She scowled at the floorboards. "Please, let me switch with you."

"Absolutely not." I rolled over and tucked the scratchy woolen blanket around me.

She must be crazy if she thought I would let her spend even a second on this hard floor when she didn't need to. A huff fluttered over me, followed by a heavy sigh and even more rustling.

"What are you doing up there? Go to slee—"

Another balled-up blanket crashed into my face before I could finish my sentence.

"Stop being so grouchy and take the extra blankets at least." Elena smiled sweetly before she crawled underneath the covers. Inwardly, I smiled at the kind gesture that was rolled up inside of an insult. One of the many reasons this woman intrigued me.

Exhaustion ached everywhere, including my mind. With a heavy sigh, I allowed myself to fall asleep. Any worries I had were just going to have to wait a few more hours.

Elena

Sleep evaded me as I lay restless staring at the beams of the ceiling. Just like every night, my thoughts had spiraled into a tangled web in my mind and I was struggling to find my way out.

With each thought, my chest became heavy and the familiar fear prickled all over my body. It was an uncomfortable itch that no matter how hard I tried, I could never scratch. Trapped, I lay there and tried to fight against it.

I replayed the past few days in my mind, and the fear spiked even more. Even with my eyes closed, my mind replayed the events in vivid detail.

All the times I'd failed and let others down. The moments when I had been reckless and stubborn in the name of healing, only to cause destruction instead. What good was I supposed to do for this realm if my dynamis only led to ruin?

Inwardly I screamed, angry at how helpless I felt inside my own body. Tears rolled down my cheeks as I came to the inevitable conclusion—there was no way I could go to the capital or back home. The only place I needed to be was away from anyone else. A place where my failures would never hurt someone ever again.

I knew at that moment I had to leave.

The remnants of the bottle of wine still hazed inside my head, and it continued to throb as I rose from the bed. Peering around the edge of the bed, I could see Declan's eyes were still closed. His chest rose and fell in steady breaths.

He looked so peaceful as he slept, no furrowed brows, no scowl etched across his beautiful lips.

I froze. *Beautiful lips?*

Gods.

My eyes scrunched closed as I groaned inside my head. Thoughts like those were another reason I needed to leave this place. In no way should I have any kind of attraction for the son of the king. A king who had a complete disregard for anything that was different or unique in this realm. Like the humans, or like me...the Light Phoenix.

Fear soured my stomach, and I tiptoed over to the water pitcher and poured myself a cup full. After I gulped it down, I sat on the edge of my bed to put on my boots, then slung my satchel over my shoulder and made my way to the small window facing the back alley.

There was no way I could exit through the front door. There were probably guards on duty all around the tavern. The window looked big enough for me to slip through, and as I peered through the foggy glass, there seemed to be no one else around.

Thankfully, the window was already open. I only needed to raise it a few more inches to squeeze my body through. I wrapped my fingers around the sash and eased it up. The hinges groaned.

Panic stilled my limbs as I sent a prayer to the gods that I hadn't woken Declan. Timidly, I looked over my shoulder and held my breath.

The moonlight cast enough light in the room that I was able to see his eyes were still shut and he was still in the same position as before. Relief washed over me as I slung my legs one by one over the side of the windowsill.

There were only two stories of the inn, but the alcohol that still ran through my veins made it seem a lot steeper of a jump. Fate must have been on my side, because below there was a wagon full of hay. As I gathered my courage, my eyes wandered one more time to the man behind me.

Tonight at dinner had actually felt normal. Like we had just been two normal Elysians sitting inside a tavern, with all the time in the world to get to know one another. The reality, however, was there was nothing normal about us at all. There never would be. With a heavy sigh, I turned back and jumped to my fate below.

Landing in the hay bale went exactly how I imagined it would, loud and painful. My legs absorbed most of the shock before I fell forward on my knees and hands, all of which now ached incessantly.

Voices rang out from the stable across from me. Shoving my pain aside, I buried myself deep into the hay. Heavy boots walked by, and I waited until the sound ceased before I crawled out of the wagon and shuffled into the stable.

A man's voice yelled out from the street, startling me so much that I barged into the first open stall I saw. The beautiful tawny mare inside snorted.

"Shhh...sorry, girl, didn't mean to startle you," I soothed as I brushed my hand over her soft fur. "Want to help me get out of here?"

This time she whinnied, and I took that as a sign. The saddle was still on her, which meant someone had just left or someone was about to come soon. Either way, I better hurry.

Extending my leg toward the stirrup, I gripped the seat of the saddle and willed my body to leap onto her. Immediately, my foot connected with air, and I realized I'd missed the stirrup entirely. Instead of mounting the horse, I cascaded down to the ground.

"*Hellllls*," I groaned, knowing tomorrow my entire body was going to hate me. Shuffling and the click of boots echoed throughout the stable and into my stall.

"Your owner's coming, girl, we've got to move fast." I rolled onto my feet once more.

The horn of the saddle felt slick with the sweat of my palm as I gripped it. Just as I lifted my leg into the stirrup, a heavy hand grabbed my shoulder and pulled my body backwards up against the wall of the stall.

Thick shadows swirled around the body of my captor. As they cleared, I came face to face with a pair of lethal verdant eyes.

"Just where do you think you're going, *Wildfire?*"

CHAPTER 17

DECLAN

E lena's eyes were blown wide, her body frozen between fear and shock. The longer the silence passed, the more energy seemed to fill the air around us.

"Are you going to answer me?" I growled, taking another step towards her, caging her body with my own.

I already held her wrist above her head, but her other palm had found its way to my chest when I stepped closer. Shoving my knee between her thighs, I had her completely immobilized.

"I—I..." she stuttered, trying to shove me back. Her head dipped in defeat as I grabbed her free wrist and made it join the other.

Clutching both her wrists in one palm, I let my free hand fall to her forehead where her hair concealed her face. Using my index finger, I traced over her temple, eliciting a faint whimper from her lips.

"Wildfire, I warned you what would happen if you angered me." My voice scratched against my throat, making it sound deeper than usual. "You broke your deal, *again*," I hummed as I tucked the hair around the shell of her ear.

Leaning back, I trailed my fingertips along the side of her jaw, tilting it upwards to meet my eyes. Our chests were so close together that the rapid pulse of her heart thundered into mine. My bottom lip hovered dangerously close over hers.

"Whatever shall I do with you now?" I breathed.

Her eyelids fell shut as she captured her bottom lip between her teeth. If only I could trap it between my own.

A low rumble of laughter filled the space beside us, and it felt like we had been doused in cold water. The electricity evaporated from the air instantly. Our heads tilted in the direction of the sound as I separated our bodies.

"Well, hello, you two." Liam's smile was about as large as his ego. As he waggled his eyebrows up and down, I groaned into my palm.

"I was just about to escort Elena back to her room." My voice taut as I scowled back at him.

"Mmhmm, I bet you were." Liam crossed his arms across his chest. Elena tried to cover her crimson cheeks with her hands.

"Move," I barked at Liam and grabbed Lena's wrist while pulling her behind me. "Don't you have a watch to be on?" I snarled behind me.

Only a faint laugh answered as I stormed away with Elena in tow. Shoving the front door of the tavern open, I barreled through the dining room and stomped up the stairs.

It wasn't until I stopped in front of the door and fiddled once more with the most insufferable lock in the entire realm that I heard her sniffling beside me.

Lena slumped against the wall, her back towards me as her body shook. In my haste to leave the stables, I hadn't stopped once to look back at her.

She flinched as I wrapped my palm around her shoulder. "I'm fine," she whispered, angerly wiping away the tears that had fallen.

"No, you're not, Lena," I turned her towards me and gathered her into my arms.

Sobs unleashed in waves as I nuzzled my head on top of hers. She twisted her hands around the back of my tunic as if she was holding on for dear life. Each tear felt like a rock as it crashed inside of me, vibrating all through-out my dynamis. In that moment, I wished for nothing more than to absorb all her pain so she would never have to feel an ounce of it ever again.

"Come on, let's get you back to sleep," I hummed against her lavender-scented locks. When I felt her head nod against my chest and her fingers unclench from my tunic, I tried the lock once more. Bless the gods, it opened on the first try.

Once inside, I herded her towards the bed and helped her sit down on the edge. With every movement she winced, no doubt from the ungraceful leap she took from the window earlier. As she stared off into the distance, lost in her thoughts, I bent down and unlaced her boots.

Her tunic was covered with dirt and hay, not something I wanted her to be sleeping in, especially in the state that she was in. In the chair behind us were our satchels. I rummaged through hers but only found another pair of pants. Without a second thought, I grabbed one of my tunics instead and handed it to her. "I'll turn around, but you need to change out of that." I nodded towards her tunic.

Lena avoided my gaze and her hands fidgeted inside her lap. "I…I may need some help," she whispered. "Everything is so sore. I don't think I can lift my arms above my head without help."

Her red-rimmed eyes rolled up towards mine, and a shiver ran down my spine. I had to fight every muscle in my face to not react. All I mustered was a grunt and nod as I made my way over to her.

Smooth, real smooth, Dec.

Lena's arms quivered underneath my touch while I struggled to raise them without causing her pain. She winced as I tugged the fabric over her arms. With one more pull, her limbs were freed, and I lifted the rest over her head before I tossed it to the chair behind me.

Even though her breasts were covered by a thin band of fabric, she shielded them from me with her arms. As she did, I noticed a long pink scar that ran along the inside of her right arm. The sight stirred my dynamis as my lips pursed.

Elysians didn't scar. Either this had happened before she'd received her dynamis, or someone had used an iron blade on her. The only Elysians who utilized those were the Nightshades, and sometimes my father. The thought made a growl tumble out of me as I clenched my tunic in my hands.

Elena shivered under my stare as I slid the new tunic over her and lifted the covers back for her to climb inside. Kicking off my boots, I lifted my own tunic off and stuffed it inside my satchel, where I grabbed something else I needed.

Her gaze followed me as I grabbed my pillow and blanket from the floor and rounded the bed to the other side. When I climbed under the covers, her breath hitched, which she smothered with a cough.

"Give me your wrist, Wildfire."

Wide eyes turned thin as she glared at the iron shackles within my hands.

"Please..." Her lips trembled as she pleaded with me. "Please just let me leave, Dec."

The way her eyes clouded once more ripped me wide open. It made me want to tell her everything I had sworn to her father I wouldn't.

"I just don't want to hurt anyone any m-more." She sniffled into the rough blanket clutched between her fingertips. "I'm tired of feeling like I can't control anything in my life."

Her confession shook my soul. If only she knew how much we shared that in common. Elena swallowed deeply, closing her eyes. "My weakness, one way or another, always finds a way to bring everything around me to ruin."

Just as another tear fell from her lids, my thumb brushed against her cheeks and swept it away. "Lena." Her cloudy eyes opened and met mine. "It's in our fears and our weaknesses that we reveal our strengths." Her brows furrowed as I spoke. "Let me put it this way, if we were never knocked down, how would we ever learn the strength we have inside us to get back up and try again?"

She chewed on her lip as she pondered my words. "But every time I get back up, those fears and weaknesses just knock me right back down. Declan, I'm exhausted from fighting a battle I'm never going to win."

She grabbed the shackles and locked one around her wrist before I could stop her. Before she latched the other, I swiped it from her hands and latched it around my own. "I'll help you fight the battle. You don't have to do this alone, Elena."

"Why—"

When I silenced her with my palm, her eyes grew wide. I lifted our wrists, causing the heavy links of the chains to clink together. A grin spread across my lips. "This is just so you don't try to run away from me again, Wildfire."

Releasing my hand from her lips, I pulled the sheets over her shoulders and began to comb my fingers through her hair. "Like I said, we're in this together now. Rest, and I promise you in the morning we'll begin to figure out your dynamis." This time, I was the one who pleaded. "Please, let me help you."

With a heavy sigh, she nodded against her pillow as she closed her eyes. I stroked her hair for a few more moments until her breath became slow and even. Only then did I allow myself to sleep as well.

M orning rays cascaded over the wavy locks of the woman lying peacefully beside me, making them look alive with fire. I'd been staring at the ceiling for hours. The mess I'd thrown myself into weighed heavily on my mind. The beats of my heart tripled in pace, just like the intrusive thoughts that flooded my mind.

All the while I felt a steady throb inside my chest, an unmistakable pull towards the woman tucked snugly underneath the sheets. Everything about my building attraction towards Elena was forbidden.

The more I learned about Elena, the greater the need had grown for me to keep her away from my father and his advisor. Unfortunately, if I didn't deliver the Light Phoenix to the capital, there was no doubt in my mind that both men would use every resource they had to hunt her down.

Warren had persuaded me that Elena would be the perfect distraction inside the castle while we continued to get closer to finding the mole. He was positive my father would gather all the dignitaries together to show off the dynamis of the Light Phoenix. It would give us a chance to reassess their roles in this kingdom and uncover any leads that might help us. There was also the possibility that the strength of her dynamis would be enough of a lure to entice someone to slip their cover.

Another reason why Warren trusted me to take Elena. He believed I was the most capable of teaching her how to embrace her dynamis, and the most capable of keeping her safe.

The pressure of these tasks threatened to cave in my chest. Every muscle tightened, creating a cage over the upper half of my body. The more I thought about it, the tighter it constricted. My mind flashed back to when I had told her I would protect her in the first town, and she had replied, *"What if that's not enough?"*

Those words had ruptured through the secure hold I'd had on my intrusive thoughts. Now, they roamed freely inside my mind, and that was never a good thing.

Anger lashed its way through me. That last thing we all needed was for me to doubt myself, but here I was worrying about not being able to protect the Light Phoenix.

My head began to feel hazy, the breaths flowing faster than they should have. Closing my eyes, I began to count the stars the way my mother had taught me during the first time panic invaded my body as a child.

"One... two...three," I whispered between shallow breaths. "Four... five...six..."

While I focused on the counting, the claws that dug into my chest began to lift. Licking my lips, I steadied myself to keep counting when I felt the unfamiliar warmth of fingers interlocking within my own.

Elena hovered over me. Concern creased her brow as she placed her other palm over my chest and rubbed soothing circles with her thumb. Lena's aqua eyes glistened in the morning sun, as they rippled over me like a tranquil river. Her delicate lips moved, and I realized she had begun counting where I had left off.

"Seven...eight...nine...ten." She paused, raising one eyebrow. "Keep up Shadow Lord."

My lips curled up as she gave me a playful tap across my chest, and I counted alongside of her. When Elena had interlocked her fingers within mine, it had jolted me out of my spiral. However, pure selfishness took over and I continued to count along with her until we reached twenty. I savored a few more moments of her peaceful gaze before it vanished.

Once my breaths had steadied, her thumb stopped its circles as she asked, "How long?"

"I've been like this for as long as I can remember."

Her head dipped. "Me too."

There had been several signs I'd picked up through our journey that had made me wonder if she was afflicted with the same burden. Now I had my answer. It appeared that Lena and I had a lot more in common than either of us thought.

Reaching over to the table beside me, I grabbed the heavy keys and unlocked the shackles chaining both of us together. Releasing the heavy iron weight from around my wrist should have felt freeing, but instead it felt more like a loss. Like a severing of the connection between us. The way Elena longingly smoothed her hand over the empty space around her wrist made me believe she felt similarly.

The pull within me took over, all other fears tossed aside, as I cupped her chin. Lena's eyes went wild as I pulled her towards me, leaving her lips hovering inches from mine. Her mouth barely opened to accommodate more air for her increasing breaths. I dragged my thumb over her bottom lip and watched the skin pebble across her arms.

We lingered in silence, our chests rising and falling against the tension that sizzled between us. I ran my thumb over her lips, inwardly groaning as a meek whimper fled from her.

"*Wildfire*," I rasped as I continued to trace her pouty lips. "Do you know how much I think about these?" I pressed my thumb harder against her bottom lip. "How much I crave to find out what they would feel like against mine? How they would taste?"

Desire clouded my gaze as her body shivered in reaction to my words. It only fueled me further. My hand left her lips and leisurely trailed down the sensitive skin of her neck.

There was nothing I wanted more than to cross the line, to rip it apart and tear it to damn shreds, but reality started to claw its way back into my mind. As I pulled away, the lusty haze in Elena's eyes fell, replaced with one laden with disappointment.

"Time to go, Lena."

The silence in the room was stifling. We shifted tentatively around one another as we got dressed. With my satchel thrown over my shoulder, I opened the door and motioned Elena towards it.

As she walked past me, the air filled with the scent of her. The sweet scent of lavender overwhelmed my already sensitive senses. I'd watched her place the lavender oil behind her ears for the past few days, and the scent had become uniquely her.

I closed the door behind me, and her shoulders slumped as she walked down the stairs. As I tilted my head towards the ceiling, I prayed to all five gods to give me strength.

It was going to take divine intervention to keep me away from that woman.

CHAPTER 18

ELENA

There were no words. None.

Nothing could describe the way that I felt as I walked down the creaky stairs of the tavern. Overwhelmed, I tried to make sense of everything that had happened last night, and this morning. Particularly this morning.

I was baffled by the man stomping down the stairs behind me. When he wasn't brooding over his Lord of Shadows ego, he was capable of being tender, kind, and even humorous at times.

When I was at my lowest last night, he hadn't punished me for trying to escape. Instead, he'd offered to help me, and the anxious part of my brain wondered why.

Once outside, I leaned against the outside wall of the tavern while the guards prepared the horses for the rest of the journey. None of them were anything like the guards I'd met at home. Every single one of these men smiled as they packed up their horses. A few politely nodded their heads towards me.

For a moment, I wondered if this was some kind of elaborate ruse to get me to like them, so when I got to the kingdom I would bend the knee willingly. However, their actions were far too genuine to be feigned. Even those who appeared to have a carefully constructed mask, like the Lord of Shadows, whose gaze had found its way to mine. As he motioned for me to come to him, butterflies quailed inside of my stomach. No one could act with that level of sincerity.

Right?

"Ready, Wildfire?"

His voice was low as he said the nickname. The one he had given me last night in the stables. With a nod, I grabbed the horn of the saddle and made extra sure I placed my foot in the stirrup before I lifted my leg over. As I did, warm palms connected with my thighs, supporting me into the saddle.

"Thank you," I squeaked out as I adjusted myself forward to make room for him behind me.

"Anytime." He leaped up in the saddle behind me. As he adjusted into the saddle, I swore every part of his body collided with mine. His thick thighs brushed against mine, his arms swept against the pebbled skin of my arms, and the heat of his chest scorched my back. My dynamis swelled inside my overly sensitive body, and I suddenly wished those chains were still wrapped around my wrists.

Hells.

I might not survive this journey…or this man.

I t was an excruciatingly quiet ride until Declan finally spoke. As he did, the tension in my shoulders released, along with the swirl of my dynamis.

"Time to learn how to ward," he said while placing both reins into one hand.

"On the horse?" I asked. My voice was a little higher pitched than I expected. "The last time horse and dynamis mixed, it did not end well. Or did you forget the part where I ended up in the land of dreams for an entire day?"

"Your sarcasm knows no bounds."

"It knows it's welcome and it cannot be tamed."

A snort erupted behind me, followed by the loudest sigh I'd ever heard. The wind even ruffled a few of my hairs.

"Alright, that's enough procrastinating."

"Yes, sir." I mimicked his deep voice and turned around to salute him. His eyes had darkened, and a dangerous smirk danced across his face as he leaned forward.

"You're going to regret that sass, Wildfire."

"**G**ods, Declan! That hurts, you insufferable ass!" His eyes blazed as he wrapped his fingers around my knees, squeezing hard. "Good. Now, focus."

I growled inwardly, but tried again to rebuild the wall in my mind in the way that he had taught me. Before we had taken a break in the afternoon to feed the horses, he had described the process of building a ward to me.

To build the wall, Declan had told me to reach down to the deepest parts of my soul. My soul had figured out a way to keep those shut away from the rest of the world. Now, it was up to me to use that same strength to construct a mental blockade to shut out those who might choose to hurt me.

Since then, we had been at it for hours and my brain felt like it had been hit with a thousand punches. Each time I thought I had finally got it, he would send his emotions towards me and my ward would shatter to pieces.

A bead of sweat rolled down the side of my face as I gripped the sides of the saddle horn. I slammed my eyes shut and focused once more on building my ward.

Inside my mind, my wall manifested into a tidal wave, different from the swell of shadows inside of Declan's mind. Each time we practiced, I began to memorize the feel and shape of the wave, as I made it tower over my mind. The towering wave gave me a sense of strength I'd never felt before. It crept into my bones, and I opened my eyes.

"Give it a try," I whispered.

"I already have." He smiled, peeling his fingers off my knees. A playful smirk danced about his face as he folded his arms across his chest.

"Why that look?"

"You still keep surprising me."

"The feeling is mutual, sir." I winked before turning back around.

The sun had finally set beyond the horizon, but there was still enough light from the moon to see some of the landscape around us. Grass and fronds towered over the marsh pools spread about. Some trees curved and bent in awkward angles, while others were darkened by decay. Mist rolled low over the ground, which added unease to the already eerie landscape.

Declan pulled at the reins, and we began to slow.

"We're going to sleep here?" I whispered.

"Wildfire, we will be fine."

I mumbled under my breath. "Sure, we will."

Declan dismounted the horse and lifted his arms towards mine. Placing my hands over his shoulders, I swung my leg over and his hands gripped my hips as he helped lower me to the ground. They fled from my body the moment my toes touched the surface.

Clearing his throat, he reached behind me, grabbed my satchel and thrust it into my hands. He nodded towards the other guards already beginning to make camp. Then he turned without a word and stormed off. I took that as a silent order for me to make my way back to the camp alone.

Thick mud caked my boots, squishing beneath me with every step that I took. A glacial chill ran down my spine at the thought of the few hours I had left before we entered the City of Shadows. Before my freedom would no longer be mine and my fate would lie in the hands of the king.

I found a spot up against a tree while the others made camp for the night. Guilt and shame left a dull, pulsating sting throughout my body. My mind wandered back to my small town, my father, and my life before. Since I'd been gone, they had been without anyone with knowledge about making elixirs that could aid healing. Although my skills were novice at best, I'd still left them stranded, without care.

I massaged the pressure building in my forehead. Ophelia's husband flashed in my mind, reminding me of the elixirs he would no longer have in my absence. Why had I never taken an apprentice to help me with healing these past two years? Now, they had no one.

The forest spun around me as regret tugged at my stomach, leaving me uneasy. The rest of the town would suffer because of my selfish mistake. I clung to the hope that my father would find a replacement. One more weight that I would add to his shoulders, as if the burdens he carried weren't already heavy enough.

Thankfully, I was distracted from my spiraling thoughts by the crackle of a fire. I pulled myself aways from the tree and forced my body towards the warmth. It was too late to hunt, but thankfully some of the other guards had thought ahead and caught some extra hares for tonight. They were tossed into a pot for another stew.

It was no surprise when my stomach grumbled as the delicious smells began wafting out of the pot. The guard stirring the pot of stew lifted his gaze towards me with a grin, then continued stirring. A few moments later, he quietly handed me a bowl and a spoon before continuing to pass out the rest.

There was laughter and merriment all around the camp tonight. Everyone was eager to get back home and continue where they had left almost two weeks ago. Even Killian and Liam seemed excited to return. They chuckled about a tab they'd forgotten to pay at the local tavern and how someone named Lucille would be after them the moment they reached the city gates.

I struggled to smile at their conversations as my mind wandered a thousand different places. The impending doom that awaited me and the guilt of leaving my town without a healer consumed my thoughts. Killian must have observed my blank stare, because the log creaked beside me as he took a seat.

"Not hungry tonight, Elena?"

Half a bowl of stew still swirled within the bowl. So much that I even surprised myself. "I suppose not." My voice faded as I shrugged off the question.

"Something is weighing heavy on your thoughts, Elena. I've learned it's always better to let it out than ruminate on it."

Firelight danced about his golden locks. I didn't have to pull emotions to know there was genuine kindness behind his smile. Desperately alone, I yearned for someone to trust. Seeing as how my time might end shortly, what harm could come from opening up now?

"Everything is just—" I paused, noticing my trembling hands. "It's beginning to feel overwhelming." I dug my fingers into my knees, clinging on so I didn't get emotional in front of Killian. With a knowing nod, he didn't speak, just patiently waited for me to continue.

"As you saw a few days ago, I have some knowledge with healing. My mother was the only Healer in our town, and she taught me several healing techniques growing up—ones that didn't need magic, just someone who cared enough to pay attention to the ingredients with healing properties. I loved learning and experimenting alongside my mother. Together we were able to create powerful healing elixirs and salves. Together, we were able to help a lot of people."

Tears pressed behind my eyes, and I rubbed my fingers over them to try to alleviate the ache. After a deep breath, the words continued to spill from me.

"I—I did the best I could after my mother passed away, but I don't have the dynamis that she did. No matter how devoted I was, there were some I couldn't save. Now, my town is left without anyone to help them. I've left them to suffer." I cringed at my own words. "It's been two years, Killian, I've had two years to have someone learn alongside of me, but I didn't. Gods, why was I so selfish...so irresponsible? I've let everyone down, just as I do everyone in my life, it seems.

"The gods are torturing me with this power, this strength inside of me." A frustrated huff tumbled out of me. "It's almost hilarious, you know? You've only known me for four days, but even you can see through the mask I wear daily. How am I supposed to pretend to be strong, powerful, brave when the real Elena is weak, insecure and unstable?" Tears began to flood down my cheeks. "I fear I will not survive whatever fate awaits me at the capital."

Killian pulled out a small cloth from his pocket and offered it to me. "Elena, I've only been around you for a few days, but I can see that you seriously underestimate yourself."

As I wiped the cloth over my cheeks, my face froze in bewilderment.

"Lena, since the very first day you have always put others first. You've worried about your father, that boy Will, the child in Wildebrooke, and now the people of your town. You've never backed down from your fears this entire trip. We didn't make it easy for you in the beginning, yet you still fought with us, challenged us at every step. Hells, you even saved one of our own guards from poison, Elena. You showed compassion to the very people who took you from the safety of your home.

"Best of all, you've constantly challenged Declan, which I must say, my lady, very few do and live to tell stories about it." He chuckled under his breath. "What I'm trying to say, Elena, is that you are a fighter. As a captain of the Royal Guard, it's my job to discover a person's character and strength when they are presented before me."

Embarrassment flooded my cheeks, and I averted my gaze towards the fire. How could someone I'd only known for days see those things within me when I couldn't even see them in myself?

"I'm not a fighter, Killian. My weaknesses have been on display this entire trip." I held his gaze, challenging him to tell me I was wrong.

"Resilience is by far the most powerful strength one can have. Anyone who can survive being beaten down and yet still rise with the sun each day is someone I would stand next to in battle any day. As a good friend once told me, it's in our fears and weaknesses that we discover our strength."

The words resonated in my soul, just as they had the night before when he had said them.

Declan.

The thought of him made me wonder where he had gone off to. Narrowing my eyes through the shadows around the camp, I finally spotted him at the farthest end of the clearing, his shoulder perched against a tree, his gaze fixed towards the horizon. Towards the capital.

My eyes shifted towards Killian, asking for permission to leave. He followed my line of sight, then gave my shoulder a squeeze before joining the others.

I rose as well, trying to make my exit without too much distraction. I made my way through the muck and tried my best not to slip.

A branch snapped underneath my boots. My body stiffened as I shut my eyes and winced, preparing myself for the worst. When I realized that there was no yelling, I peeked open my eyes to see that the prince hadn't even flinched. He was lost in thought, his eyes glued to the castle on the horizon.

I narrowed my eyes to get a better glimpse of it myself. The castle was built with white stone that looked faintly blue under the moonlight sky. Foliage crept along the sides of the walls, and vines climbed over four large towers. Torches lit the castle, and the warm light reflected a colorful hue from what looked to be several stained-glass windows. On top of each of the towers navy blue flags waved in the sea breeze. Each adorned with the familiar kingdom crest. I had expected a dark and gloomy castle, but the sight before me was nothing like that.

I inhaled to gather the courage to tap the man before me on the shoulder. With my arm extended, ready to make contact, Declan peered over his shoulder. His eyes met mine as I shoved my arm down, trying my best not to look ridiculous. A smile formed on his lips as he pushed away from the tree he was leaning against. He took a step towards me until he invaded my space.

The night air was chilly tonight. I could almost smell the salt from the ocean in the air, as the City of Shadows resided alongside it. The wind tangled between us, causing my arms to become pebbled with goosebumps. A shiver followed as I rubbed my arms to try to create some warmth.

Observing my chill, Declan slid off his cloak. I raised my hand to stop him, to which he scoffed and pushed my hand away. Once the cloak was over my shoulders, he tugged the button through the loop, which sat snugly over my collar bone. The warmth of his touch on my skin sent shivers all over my body; however, this time it wasn't from the cold.

Neither of us had spoken a word since my arrival, and the silence continued as Declan finished buttoning the cloak. Suddenly, the air around us felt warm, almost electric, as his fingers traced my neckline all the way up to my chin. He lifted it slowly to make me meet his gaze.

"Come to check on me, Wildfire?" As his hand fell, my body leaned forward, chasing after the heat of his touch. Clearing my throat, I took a step back to give us some distance.

"I..." I swallowed, trying to regain my composure. "I suppose I came here to apologize for all of my sass from earlier." A smile blossomed on my lips. I knew damn well I wasn't sorry at all.

He crossed his arms over his chest as he peered at me with a smirk. "Yes, I can see just how much it has tormented you."

I couldn't help but smile and roll my eyes, as I let out a small laugh. Honestly, the way this man's moods shifted so quickly, he deserved all my sarcasm and more.

In a flash, Declan grabbed me and shoved my back up against the tree. His knee was wedged between my thighs, his body was flush against mine, locking me into place against the tree. He anchored himself above me with one hand while the other gripped my shoulder.

Wide-eyed, I watched breathless as he leaned towards my face. Heat rushed through my body, and there was an overwhelming worry that his lips might press against mine. Guilt began to creep in, because I knew deep down inside, I wouldn't stop him this time if he tried. Surrendering, I shut my eyes.

Instead of feeling our lips collide, I felt his drag across my cheek towards my ear. My toes curled inside my boots. Calloused fingers brushed against the side of my neck as they tucked a few strands of fallen hair behind my ear. They trailed down my braid and played with the loose hair at the end as he spoke. The deep, rumble of his voice roused what felt like tiny ripples of lightning to course throughout my body. Everywhere he touched my skin, my dynamis ignited, almost as if it yearned to follow his touch as much as I did.

"Elena...what can I do to ensure you never roll those beautiful eyes at me ever again?"

All that came out of me was a soft hum.

"Tell me, Wildfire," he purred.

Dear gods.

As my mind went blank, my body took over. I could no longer formulate words. Declan's fingers traced a slow, delicate path down my arm, finally settling on the top of my waist. I squirmed against the tree, my thighs squeezing against the sides of his knee. His grip around my waist tightened as I tried to shift my body out of his grasp. All that did was provide enough pressure to relieve some of the throbbing erupting between my inner thighs.

"Maybe this will teach you a lesson." His words faded, replaced by teeth grazing the side of my neck. I gasped, holding my breath as he continued. My body quivered underneath him.

"Or perhaps *this*..." His warm lips trailed down my neck towards the opening of the cloak. With a swift maneuver of his hands, the cloak puddled around my feet. His lips caressed the spot where the cloak once was, and I felt as though my body was melting into the tree. My breathing quickened, heart racing into oblivion. That same pull in my chest that seemed to only happen around him tugged voraciously.

That was it. I'd officially lost my mind.

There was no way I should want this. Hells, we'd been fighting since we'd met. As usual, my traitorous body had other plans. Everything inside me called out to tell me that this was right. It was almost as if my soul knew him more deeply than I did. Like they were old flames, reunited once more.

Once again, Declan grabbed my chin, tilting it back to meet his gaze. He gazed upon my lips, his chest rising and falling at the same rate as mine.

"Actually, I think there's only one way to smother all the sass." He tapped his index finger against my lips. "And it has to do with these."

Just as his soft lips brushed mine, a bloodcurdling yell followed by a thundering growl came from behind us.

Declan's body tensed. More shouts arose from the guards on duty, and the clang of metal swords clamored against the wind. He quickly turned around, arms out to shield me from whatever had made that growl in the distance. However, nothing could shield me from seeing the mammoth beast that drew closer to us.

The beast before us was twice the size of any wolf I had ever laid eyes on. Its paws were enormous, probably the size of my head. Each claw looked like it could rip us to shreds with one swipe. Blood coated its snout. A guard's body lay lifeless beneath it. Black sludge also oozed from its fur. If that wasn't enough to make me go pale with terror, I was staring into two dark voids where eyes should have been.

The beast roared ferociously this time, causing me to jump. As it arched its neck back, its mouth hung wide open, displaying its sharp, yellowing teeth. The smell of death and decay clouded around us, and it took everything I had in me to not lose my dinner in the bushes. I swallowed deeply, cautiously bending down to grab my dagger from my boot.

As soon as I rose to my feet, the beast began its sprint towards us.

"RUN!" Declan growled, unleashing his shadows and all the darkness along with it.

"No!" I pushed around him and threw my dagger straight towards the beast's head.

The dagger found its target, but the beast didn't flinch or stop its charge towards us. All my muscles tightened with fear. My heart was racing uncontrollably, and my feet felt frozen to the ground. This feeling was all too familiar. I'd felt it once before—the night fear froze me in the doorway of our home as I watched my mother being murdered before me.

The beast snarled as some of the guards began to use their dynamis. As it turned its sights on them, Declan grabbed a hold of my arm and tugged me behind him.

More screams pealed from behind us before the chill of silence replaced them. Our feet slid over the mud, but Declan dug in his heels and continued to run for the thick cover of trees ahead of us.

Behind me, I could hear muffled shouts and the sound of padded feet as they rumbled against the ground. When I risked a look over my shoulder, my foot rolled over a rock, sending me barreling into the mud. Waves of anger, panic, and desperation crashed into me as they slipped out from under Declan's ward. My hands kept slipping against his arms as he tried to lift me up. Forgoing my arms altogether, he threaded his hands under my armpits and lifted me up. In another burst, he tossed me behind him and launched his dynamis.

He threw everything he had at the beast. His shadows struck, ripped and tore. Bits of flesh and sludge flung through the air. Shadows wrapped around the beast's body, weaving tightly to slowing it in its tracks. This was no ordinary animal. This was something darker. It felt like something made of pure evil.

"Go now, Elena!" he rasped through gritted teeth. "Listen to me for once, *please!*"

Declan's muscles visibly shook, and I knew he couldn't hold on for much longer. As death stared me in the face, I couldn't just stand by and watch again.

No longer would I stay frozen.

I was never going to lose anyone because of my fears again.

I let a deep pull of air wash through me. My eyelids slammed closed, shutting out the world. As I did, I imagined myself extending my hands towards Declan, needing to pull more emotions. My dynamis was already bubbling under the surface. Maybe the more emotions I pulled, the more of a blast of air I could create when I pushed them out of me.

Desperate, I grasped for whatever I could. It seemed to work, as I felt emotions crashing into me like rocks. Combining them with my own fear and rage, I funneled it down to the dynamis that was collecting deep in the center of my body. Now, I just had to figure out how to use it.

Taking a chance, I opened one eye to see Declan staggering bac, creating more space between him and the beast. Time was up. I just had to make a run for it.

I bolted forward. The power inside of me thrummed. Warmth spread through me, and I began to see its familiar glow bathe my body. I could hear the prince yelling my name and the sounds of others approaching to help. Arrows, shards of ice and blasts of fire whisked through the air, dancing all around me as I ran faster. Some hit the beast, causing it to sway. However, nothing seemed to stop it.

The beast swung its head, its void eyes locked on my own as it roared, heading straight towards me. All sounds muffled around me, but I could feel Declan zephyr over to me.

My power had other plans and unleashed on its own. A powerful gust of wind tossed him into the air, sending him flying back somewhere behind me. I was just inches away from the beast, and my skin burned from the dynamis I withheld beneath it.

Leaping into the air, I flew over the beast as it charged. I gripped the dagger still embedded into the beast, and together we crashed to the ground. The force of the fall dislodged the dagger from its head and I pulled it with me.

Just as I rolled onto my back, the beast leapt onto me, its teeth chomping into my shoulder and its claw slicing through my side. Screaming out in agony, I slammed my dagger into its thick neck over and over again. Each time my dagger hit flesh, black sludge spilled into my mouth. It reeked of decay, and I gagged as I tried to spit it out.

Thick claws sliced again, this time over my chest. Tears streamed down my face mixing with the blood that pooled around me. Fueled by pure rage to save those around me, I rolled on top of the animal and slammed my dagger straight through its neck. The beast let out a guttural howl, and I screamed so loud my body shook.

In that moment, I erupted.

Blinding white light exploded from me, creating a circle around me. The burn of white-hot flame followed. It streamed through my fingertips, right into the beast that continued to shriek in pain as flames engulfed its body. The smell of burning flesh overwhelmed me.

My entire body writhed in pain, but I continued to unleash my dynamis.

When nothing was left but a pool of sludge and bones beneath me, I let my body fall back and hit the ground. I cradled my body, trying to stop the warm blood from escaping. My eyelids began to grow heavy, and the thoughts in my brain began to grow hazy.

They were safe. Alive. There wouldn't be another lost soul haunting my nightmares tonight.

Muffled shouts burst around me, along with the sound of boots rapidly approaching. Arms scooped me up and cradled me close.

"Damn it! Why, Elena?" Declan roared over me, but I didn't have anything left in me to open my eyes or respond.

"Dec, she's losing blood too fast! There's no way she'll be able to heal herself fast enough. You need to get her to Clara, now!" shouted Killian.

"We've got things here, Dec. GO!" bellowed Liam.

"Hang on, Lena. Please, just hang on a little longer," Declan whispered, pulling me closer as the winds gusted around us and I collapsed into darkness.

CHAPTER 19

DECLAN

"Elena seems to be healing well. You're lucky you got her here just in time. She lost a lot of blood." Clara rubbed my shoulder as we stood outside on the balcony of Lena's room. "Relax, Declan. She'll wake up soon. I can feel the tension all over you."

The warmth of her dynamis flooded my body. It healed my tense muscles, as it washed over them. Exhaling deeply, I was finally able to relax my shoulders.

"Thank you for that," I breathed.

A smile spread across her face. "Of course. I did it for purely selfish reasons though."

"Oh, really?" A hint of a smile tugged at my lips.

"Absolutely. I only healed you because when you're in pain you become an insufferable brooding ass."

Laughter poured out of her, just like the ocean waves crashing back and forth below us. I shook my head as her laughter dulled into a lighthearted sigh.

"So, what will happen now?" Clara tilted her head toward the open balcony door, toward the direction of the sleeping Light Phoenix.

"You know my father and Alastor are going to want to parade her around. However, we're going to teach her to understand and strengthen her dynamis...teach her how powerful she really can be. After that, no one should be able to stand in her way."

Something mischievous flickered in her eyes for a moment before she rested her elbows on the smooth, white stone of the ledge. "Sounds like a good plan." Silence passed between us. "I'm close, Declan. By the end of the month, I really think... I—I think I'll have a cure."

Emotion swelled inside my chest as I imagined what it would feel like to be free of this leash that Alastor had put on me years ago. Clara had been working herself into the ground day and night trying to find a cure ever since. She and I were no strangers to the feeling of being caged inside this castle.

Wind whipped around the thin white curtain of the open balcony door, diverting my attention through it to the woman I feared I'd begun to have feelings for. Clara leaned over, her eyes followed my line of sight, and a small grin danced about her face again.

"Who knows"—she cleared her throat—"maybe the Light Phoenix might be a little part of the cure as well."

A scoff tumbled out of me as I crossed my arms in front of me.

"I've never seen you look at someone like that before."

"What do you mean?" My lips pursed together. I hated the fact that she could see right through me. There was no fooling her.

"Like she's something precious, something you've been longing for," she whispered, and my eyes fell to my boots. Fear festered inside of me, because she was right.

"Speaking of something precious..." Clara pulled something out of her pocket and placed in my palm the smooth, white stone feather pendant that had been around Lena's neck. The entire necklace had been drowned in blood and mud, so I'd had Clara clean it up the best she could for her. It must have some importance, because I had caught Elena running her fingers through it several times during the journey.

"I couldn't clean the twine that originally held it, so I replaced it with an old chain I had."

"It's perfect, thank you." I placed the pendant in my pocket and pulled Clara into my side, watching the waves as they rolled back and forth in the midday sun.

Elena

The ground crunched beneath me as I ran through the trees, barefoot and only in my nightdress. Branches clawed at me as I sprinted, tearing away pieces of my hair and ripping into my sensitive flesh. Tears streamed down my cheeks as a scream tore out of me. "Help me!"

My head whipped back so I could see how far the beast was, only for me to trip and slam hard into the dirt below. The beast pounced on top of me, howling as it turned me over with its paw, claws slicing into me.

The act ripped a gargled scream from me as it lowered its foul snout to hover above my face. Its void eyes glared upon me as a branch cracked beside us.

Stepping from the shadows behind him, cloaked in darkness and death, came the same hooded figure that had haunted my dreams for far too long. Its voice was low, raspy and ominous. It sent a wave of nauseousness throughout my body.

"Join me," it growled. "Give in, Elena. Release your dynamis, and together we will make this world feel our pain."

"Never."

The being chuckled, sounding more like spurts of growls. "One day, Elena, one day soon, you will give in to me. Consider it a promise."

My only response was spitting in its face. The beast roared as its teeth plunged into my neck.

"Wake, Elena! Wake!"

I woke up breathless, with my hands wrapped around my neck. *Thank the gods.* A dream. Only a dream.

Using both of my hands, I rubbed my face, trying to regain a sense of my surroundings. Warm golden light illuminated the massive room, and the breeze from the balcony made the sheer white curtains dance. My eyes roamed over the luxuries that filled the space: soft blue velvet chairs, paintings of ocean waves and sunsets hanging in elegant gold frames. On the side table next to the bed was a vase of white peonies. Each petal looked as smooth as velvet.

The massive oak bed that had swallowed me whole was filled with cream sheets and cloud-like pillows. My body sank into the softness of the mattress. It appeared I had made it to the capital, Vrine, the City of Shadows. The castle that was meant to be my home for the unforeseeable future.

The realization made my stomach fill with unease. Staring at the ceiling, I felt surprised, yet entirely thankful that I was alive. When I'd last closed my eyes, I'd assumed that was the last time they would open.

My hands lay over my stomach, reminding me of the attack. I lifted the silk nightdress that I was now wearing to peek at the damage, only to find nothing but smooth, pink skin. The signs of healing.

The king must have an incredibly strong Healer, because from what I could remember, my body had been torn to shreds before I passed out. I massaged my temples to release the memory of the blood that had spilled over my hands.

Hums of conversation spilled into the room from what I assumed to be others on the balcony. Carefully, I slid my legs over the side of the bed. Without the warmth from the covers, my entire body shivered from the coastal air. The sheer slip I was wearing did nothing to cut the chill. Draped over a chair was a silk robe in the same navy shade as my nightdress. Grabbing it, I threw it on before my teeth chattered their way right out of my mouth. I tightened its sash around my waist and wobbled my way towards the balcony doors.

As I approached the doors, I could distinctly make out Declan's voice, but it was the voice of a female that halted me in my tracks.

Stepping onto the balcony, I gazed upon two bodies entangled in each other as they overlooked the ocean from the railing. Anger and jealousy coursed through my body as Declan rubbed the shoulder of the tall, slender brunette next to him.

She was stunningly beautiful. Her skin was smooth and sun-kissed, almost the same shade as Declan's. Her long, dark chestnut hair swirled in the wind as they spoke softly. They appeared to be laughing about something as she turned to give him a sweet smile and he bent down to kiss the top of her hair. My heart sank and my shoulders sagged.

Something inside me deflated at the sight. It was a ludicrous feeling to have, especially since I knew the man before me was forbidden in every way. However, I wasn't blind to the fact that something inside of me yearned for the affections of the dark and mysterious man who had been my travel companion these past few days.

Perhaps this was divine intervention, the gods telling me this wasn't the path for me. I should have known that a man as handsome as the prince would be in a relationship. It was silly that I'd even entertained the thought that he might have feelings for me.

Suddenly, my gaze heated on the back of his head. How dare he try to kiss me when he had someone else waiting for him at home!

An audible snarl rumbled through me, and my breath hitched from my mistake. Pivoting out of the doorway, I made it about halfway towards the bed before a strong hand grabbed my wrist, whirling me around to face him. Once our eyes met, Declan dropped his grip, slipping his hand back inside his pocket.

"Elena, it's good to see you awake." He spoke softly as his eyes dropped down towards his shoes.

A polite cough arose from behind Declan, breaking the tension between us. Gracefully, like she floated on air, the slender brunette strolled around the side of Declan. She paused next to him and folded her delicate hands in front of her, giving me a warm smile. It took everything in me to return a smile as I bent into a small bow.

"My apologies, Your Highness, my lady." I spoke sullenly. "I didn't mean to intrude on your conversation. I'll just return to the bed. Sorry again for disturbing you both."

Nope. Not sorry at all.

Declan was shielding the smile on his face with one hand. Crossing my arms in front of my chest, I wished my glare could kill or at least induce some sort of bodily harm.

"Elena, it is such a pleasure to meet you." The sweet voice approached me from the right, dislodging the lock I had on Declan's face. "I'm so glad you're up and awake. When Dec brought you to me you were in such a terrible state. It took practically all the dynamis in me to heal you. I had to sleep for a whole day! I haven't had to do that since I first received my dynamis years ago." She giggled, reached out for my hands and held them between her own. My mouth gaped wide. "Oh, I'm not complaining at all though, it was my pleasure, truly! Declan was just telling me all about you."

"Oh, really?" I mused, wondering if he had indeed told her *everything*.

Clearing his throat, Declan spoke with amusement in his voice. "Lady Elena, this is Lady Clara Estridge, my cousin."

He smiled down at me as I pinched my lips together and redness bloomed across my cheeks. Shoving aside my embarrassment, I returned my gaze to the sweet woman in front of me. The hints of resemblance now became blazingly apparent. Dark chestnut hair, golden tan skin, similar slope of their noses. The only difference was her hazel-colored eyes.

Gods, how did I miss that the first time?

Slipping my hands out of Clara's, I desperately tried to cover the shame written all over my face.

"Goodness, Elena! Are you okay? Your cheeks are so red. Come over to the bed, let me feel your forehead." Clara herded me like cattle towards the bed. "Let's make sure you aren't coming down with a fever."

She forced me under the covers with a tsk, and I had to bite my lip to stifle a giggle at her sudden bossy demeanor. Clara ran the back of her hand over my forehead, then picked up my wrist, closing her eyes while counting. Once I was deemed in good health, she poured me a glass of water and placed it on the table next to the bed. Glancing over at Declan then back at me, she politely excused herself from my beside.

"Declan, make sure she drinks all that water. If she doesn't, you're helping me apply wart salves to Lord Alastor's feet for a week!" She winked, throwing a mischievous smile toward her cousin. It was a pleasure to meet you, Elena." Clara headed out the door, closing it behind her.

"Gross." Declan winced, shoving the glass of water in front of my face. "Drink."

Taking a sip, I tried to stifle my laugh. "I like her," I said, as the cool water calmed my parched mouth.

"Yeah, I'm pretty sure you two will get along a little too well for my liking." His lip tugged up.

As I continued to sip my water, Declan shifted back and forth on his heels. It was as if he was trying to decide whether to leave or stay. Moving my body over in the extremely large bed, I patted the spot I'd made vacant as I spoke softly. "You can sit with me, if you'd like."

He glanced at the empty space, then back towards me. Slipping his hands back into his pockets, he shook his head. I focused on the rim of the water glass. Silence passed between us for a few moments before the prince spoke.

"How are you feeling?"

"Surprisingly well, considering I was almost cut in half only a short while ago. Clara is truly a gifted Healer. I've never seen such a clean wound." I rubbed my hand over my stomach.

A deep scowl covered his face as his eyes traced my movements. Palming through his hair, he paced to the nearest wall and leaned against it. "Elena...you were badly injured. By the time I got you to Clara, your lips were blue." His fists clenched by his side as he continued to speak, "Your skin, it was so pale."

The events of the forest replayed in my mind, and my heart swelled with guilt. It had been incredibly stupid to go after the beast like that. I could have died. I set the empty cup on the side table, then twirled my fingers idly within the sheets.

"I'm sorry," I whispered.

It was all I could muster, but I knew his Elysian ears could hear me. We all had an unusually strong sense of hearing, and some had sight as well.

A pained expression etched across his face, he shifted his glance outside. "Don't ever do that again, Lena."

I opened my mouth once, twice, then closed it once more. Unfortunately, I couldn't make that promise. No longer would I be frozen. I couldn't lose another person, another innocent life, because of my fear.

"How is everyone else? How are you? I think my dynamis tossed you aside at one point." I tried my best to divert the conversation off me.

"The others are well. Killian and I spent the night transporting the rest of the men back to the castle. A few stayed behind to bring back the horses. Liam is okay as well, a little fatigued after using so much dynamis to throw shards of ice at the monstrous beast. He and Killian have been taking turns guarding your room the past few nights." Declan shoved his hands back into his pockets and walked back towards the edge of the bed.

"And you?" I asked tentatively. "Are you well?"

"No, but seeing you awake definitely makes me feel …lighter." He held my gaze before releasing it to rub the back of his neck. "My father and Lord Alastor will want you to attend dinner tonight. They're very curious to meet the Light Phoenix, who has also now become known as the Slayer of Beasts." He shuffled his body back and forth. "The king and Lord Alastor, they are—"

"Temperamental?" I interrupted, a smirk dancing across my face.

"Hmm, yes, that's one way to put it." His tone was more serious now. "They will not tolerate outbursts, objections, disobedience—"

"So, you're telling me I need to be quiet and watch my mouth? Is that what I'm hearing?" I chuckled.

"I'm serious, Elena, it's for your own safety. We are not good men."

I raised an eyebrow at the term "we" in that sentence—if he wasn't a good man, he wouldn't have saved me—but he just stared at me, waiting for an answer.

"I make no promise," I said. "I will try my best, Your Highness."

"See that you do."

I nodded, and it was silent again until he explained that he would send up my lady-in-waiting, along with a selection of dresses for me to choose from for the evening. A flutter of excitement rushed over me at the mention of dresses. He told me that dinners in the castle were always formal, meaning elegant attire only.

"Before I leave, there's a few things I want to show you." He extended his hand to mine.

Sliding back over the edge of the bed, I let my feet fall to the floor and allowed Declan to help me up. Though I was almost fully healed, I had to admit that I still felt exhausted.

His gaze was no longer on my eyes. Following his gaze down to my chest, I realized why. My robe had fallen open, exposing the slip of a nightdress that barely covered me. I gasped, withdrawing my hand from his, and tugged the ends of my robe closed. The prince's mouth hung ajar, and I couldn't resist tilting his chin up to close it. He cleared his throat, following me as I walked towards the center of the room, away from the bed.

"What did you want to show me, Declan?"

"First, let me show you the bathroom."

"Hmm, that wasn't what I expected." I tried to stifle my laughter as I began to roll my eyes before I caught his gaze.

"Watch it, Wildfire," he said in a low growl as he led me into the extremely oversized bathroom.

Now, my mouth fell open. The floor was covered in a beautiful white stone with strands of gray and black that ran through it. Large windows let the light in, but also let you see the ocean below.

Declan spun my body around to face a copper bath to the side of me. Stone tree-like roots supported the bottom, lifting it off the ground, and it had a faucet like the one I used every day to pump water from our town's well.

"I thought you might like this better than me tossing you in the lake...or the ocean." He smirked, gazing out the window at the view of the waves below. I shook my head, ignoring his jest, as he pulled on the faucet and water began pouring out.

"You have running water?"

"We've always had aqueducts beneath the cities, and a few centuries ago we figured out how to pump the fresh water through faucets into homes. We also figured out how to heat it as well." He waggled his eyebrows up and down.

"I'll be doing this immediately."

Declan cleared his throat.

"Without your company this time, of course." The towel he had picked up slipped between his hand as I sucked in my lips to contain my laugh.

"Of course." He tossed the towel into the basket he'd taken it from, then motioned with his head for me to follow him back into the bedroom.

"Well?" I asked impatiently.

He reached within his deep navy jacket, trimmed in gold, retrieved my dagger and handed it to me. The sight stirred a squeal of delight from me as I embraced the prince in a hug. His entire body stiffened, so I released him.

"Thank you for finding this for me. I thought ... I imagined that I would never see it again. This dagger is really all I have left of them." I almost choked on the words.

That was when he surprised me once more and pulled out my mother's feather pendant. It was on a new chain, one that he was now draping over my neck as I stood there at a loss for words.

"All you have left of who?" Declan whispered, his thumb brushing against the side of my neck.

"My parents," I said, so quietly that I didn't even know if I had made any sound.

"I'm sorry we took you from your home."

"Don't be, it wasn't your fault. Your father is the one I blame." I let out a laugh, looking up at the prince to try to lighten the mood. Instead, I was met with a solemn expression.

"We are not good men, Elena," he said, repeating his earlier statement.

"You saved my life, Declan." I lifted my hand to place it gently over his heart. "That makes you good to me."

His throat bobbed, still not making eye contact. The prince's hand rose to cover my own. We stood there for a few moments before he lifted my hand off his chest and I let it fall to my side.

"I'll see you for dinner tonight, and please don't be late," he said, walking towards the door. He opened it wide, then began to close it before he peeked around once more. "Wildfire," he said.

"Mmhmm?"

"Thank you for stepping in front of that beast … and for saving *my* life."

The door closed with a soft click, leaving me alone and speechless.

CHAPTER 20

DECLAN

E verything about Elena fascinated me and terrified me at the same time. My body seemed to be pulled toward her by some invisible force every time she was near. Closing the door to my room with a flick of my shadows, I stormed over to my closet to get dressed for tonight's dinner.

What a complete fool I had been on the journey back to the castle. I'd tried so hard to bury myself within my frigid heart, pushing her away with the only things I knew how to do, fear and gruffness. Unfortunately, that only unleashed her fiery spirit, making me burn for her tenaciousness even more.

I'd even let my ward slip on more than one occasion. The black fabric of my pants slid against my legs as I sighed deeply, thinking about the mess I'd created. I needed to do better, needed to be smarter. There was too much to risk and too many important factors at stake for me to lose all my senses by falling for a woman I knew that I couldn't have.

She deserved someone far better than me, someone not filled with so much darkness. In just a short time, being around me had led to her almost death, all because she was trying to save me. A shiver trickled down my spine at the memory of the blue tint of her lips and the feeling of her lifeless body hanging over my arms. Elena deserved a lifetime of happiness, especially after everything that she had been through. Sadly, happiness was not something that I had within me to offer.

Impatiently fumbling with the buttons on my black dress tunic, I heard a knock on my door.

"Come in."

"Good evening, Your Highness." Eloise gave me a polite bow and a smile as she walked into the room. Once my mother's lady-in-waiting, now she served me.

"Eloise, you know by now that a bow is not necessary," I said with a shake of my head.

"Of course, just as you know that I find manners to be everything in life," she hummed, then strode over to hand me my dress jacket for the evening—a deep navy blue, trimmed with a fine golden embroidery around the collar and down the opening. Formal dinners were the only time I wore the kingdom's royal colors of navy and gold. Normally, my wardrobe consisted only of the color of my heart, black.

"Manners are everything, huh? I'll remember that the next time I hear you swearing foul words that would make even Liam and Killian shudder," I said, a small smirk tipping up the corner of my lip.

She slapped my arm while letting out a huff of air. "One time! Gods, I impaled my finger with a sewing pin! What would you do if that was you?"

"You're right, if that happened to me, far fouler words would be spewed. The sewing pin would have also been launched into the depths of the Hells," I said, launching out a slip of shadow like a whip.

She threw her head back in laughter, and I couldn't help but laugh along with her. Laughing wasn't something I did very often, in fact I could probably count the number of times I laughed within a week on my hands. Just the thought of that brought me back down to reality, and once again my lips pressed together in a thin line.

"You're worried about tonight, aren't you?" Eloise said, placing a hand on my shoulder.

"Elena is not prepared for the wrath my father and Alastor can unleash." I should have stayed in her room longer, walked her through what to expect. However, I'd run like a coward. The longer I lingered around her, the more my control slipped.

"I'll look after her, Your Highness. As I get her ready for this evening, we'll have a little chat, woman to woman. You can trust me to make sure she's well prepared."

I gave her a nod, slipping the jacket over my shoulders. Even though I trusted Eloise, my stomach twisted in a knot. I was about to send Elena into a den of vipers.

"You know you need to tell her, no matter what Warren says." She tugged a loose gold thread on my jacket. "Secrets fester like wounds when we keep them from the people we care about."

"If only I could, Eloise, but I fear he may be right. It should come from him, and only him. I'm not sure how I would handle hearing I'd been lied to for years, and I can only imagine that with everything Elena has just been thrown into, it would completely overwhelm her."

Eloise folded her arms across her chest. The scowl that formed on her lips told me that I was in for a reprimanding.

"Sometimes you men can be so...exasperating. The way she leapt in front of that beast last night tells me she's capable of a lot more than you both are giving her credit for."

One look into her knowing glare and my shoulders sagged. My stomach churned as I weighed the truth within her words.

"If you won't tell her about that, then you should probably tell her about the other thing."

"What other thing?"

The fabric of her dress slid against her fidgeting fingers. Her eyes shifted around the room, avoiding contact with mine at all costs.

"Eloise." My voice deepened as I tried to coax the words out of her.

"Last night, I felt something between you two when you brought her in. It was faint, but it was unmistakable." Her throat bobbed, and her eyes clouded with tears. "I felt the bond, Declan."

Hearing the words said out loud sent my mind reeling. During our travels, I'd had my suspicions, but fated mates had dwindled after the original Light Phoenix had passed. Since then, it was a rare occurrence.

"How could you feel it?"

"Because there is something that I have been keeping from you for a very long time." She lifted her trembling hand and waved it over the one that had her Flame dynamis marked into it. "Something that allows me to feel the presence of those who bear a similar mark."

As it passed over the back of her hand, what was revealed below caused my knees to weaken. Wrapped around her wrist shone a golden vine. "Eloise," I breathed. "Is that—"

"Yes." Her voice was meek, and she wrapped her arms around herself. "It's the mark of a fated bond between me and my mate."

"Who?" I whispered.

A tear slid down her cheek, as her eyes rolled up to meet mine. She didn't have to tell me anymore because I already knew. "It was Keir, wasn't it?"

I tucked her into my arms. The month before his death, I had noticed something different about my brother. In a way, he had seemed lighter, happier, pushing us even harder towards getting things settled in Oria. Like there was a deeper purpose fueling his devotion to getting us out of the castle. Now I knew exactly what that purpose had been, and it was wrapped inside my arms sobbing into my chest.

"Why didn't you tell anyone? Or tell me afterwards, Eloise?"

She pulled herself away from me and grabbed a handkerchief from inside my wardrobe to dry her eyes. "You know as well as I do that our relationship would have been forbidden because of our social status. Your father would have never allowed his son to be bound to a lowly lady-in-waiting. Even if we were fated mates."

The truth in her words hit me like a blow to the gut, only further fueling the anger that I harbored against my father and Alastor.

"I have a feeling your mother knew." She sniffled again, wiping the cloth across her reddened nose. "We were going to tell you both, and then...I—I should have told you, but you were already burdened with so many other things. I didn't want to add one more thing to your shoulders. Keir told me to leave if anything happened." Eloise lifted her head, and her brown curls fell across her tear-stricken face. "But I couldn't leave. Declan, you are the only family I have left."

"Eloise"—my voice thickened with emotion— "please don't ever feel like you must keep things from me any longer. I've always thought of you as being a part of this family, even before you told me about Keir. I'm so sorry you had to shoulder this secret for so long by yourself."

With a deep sigh, she smoothed her hand over her face. "It's okay, Declan, just make me a promise."

"Anything."

"Just tell her before it's too late."

A rock formed in my throat, and I struggled to swallow it down. Eloise patted my shoulder and started to walk towards the door.

I wanted to answer her, tell her I would honor that promise. However, I couldn't make a promise I knew that I would eventually break.

"You be careful tonight," she whispered as she looked over her shoulder, hand curled around the open door. "I'll see to it that Elena is prepared for whatever your father and Alastor launch at her."

With a nod, she stepped out the door.

I walked over and slumped into my armchair and threw my head into my hands. Alone in my room, I allowed myself a moment to release all the sadness, anger and frustration. Just one moment. Then, I'll begin to sort through where to go from here.

CHAPTER 21

ELENA

As soon as Declan left, the tub beckoned me. Warm water filled the tub as my fingertips roamed over the little glass bottles filled with different bath oils and salts. They paused over one that looked like it had violet petals inside of it. Lavender. I poured the salts into the bath, along with another bottle with a milky liquid inside it. The aroma of the sweet flora wafted about the room, awaking my senses. Taking a deep inhale of the calming scent, I turned off the water and placed my clothes aside.

My muscles cried out in elation as I sank down into the warmth. Laying my head against the edge, my eyes closed, I hummed with contentment. This was truly divine. I wondered if they would notice if I spent my entire time at the castle in here.

Time seemed to melt away. One moment the water was warm, the next I was staring at the shriveled state of my fingers. Begrudgingly, I pulled the plug of the enormous tub. The water swirled into the depths below, taking with it all the stress, emotions and pain from my journey here.

Droplets of water from my hair dripped onto the marble floor as I wrung out the excess water and wrapped a fresh towel around it to dry. After tying my robe's sash securely this time, I stepped out of the bathroom just in time to hear the light tap on my door.

When I opened the door, a woman filled the doorway. She brushed a few soft curls that had fallen into her face behind her ear.

"Lady Morrigan, my name is Eloise. I'll be your lady-in-waiting during your stay in the castle," she said, bowing her head.

Opening the door wider, I motioned for her to come inside. A group of servants also came in. I watched in awe as they carried in elaborate dresses, handfuls of tunics, leggings, and even several pairs of shoes and boots. Every dress that filled the closet seemed elaborate and over the top. I couldn't imagine where anyone would wear some of these gaudy pieces. One was even made from thousands of feathers, no doubt a play on the Light Phoenix name.

Servants diligently folded and placed everything into the dresser and armoire. Eloise must have noticed me gaping, because she grabbed my hand and gave it a small squeeze as they filled my room with more clothes than I had ever had in my entire life.

"It will seem a little overwhelming at first, my lady, but the prince wanted to make sure you feel comfortable during your stay here with us."

Eloise walked back out of the room and rolled in a cart filled with small sandwiches, fruit and what looked like a pot containing some kind of warm liquid. She nodded towards the closest velvet armchair and poured a cup of the steaming liquid.

"This should help with the nerves." Eloise handed me the beautifully painted teacup. Inside was a dark brown liquid, and it smelled divine.

"Is this a different kind of coffee?" I sank in my chair, embarrassed that I even had to ask.

"Oh, no, my lady. This is better. It's hot chocolate, and it's positively sinful. I've found that there is nothing that a pot of hot chocolate cannot cure." Eloise gestured for me to take a sip. Warm, rich, flavorful liquid hit my tongue, and my eyes widened in delight. It took a few more long sips of the heavenly liquid before I was able to speak again.

"Wow," I whispered breathlessly. "You're right, this is sinful."

She piled a variety of fruits and sandwiches onto a plate and slid it in front of me. "Eat, my lady. You're going to need your strength for your dinner tonight."

I winced at the reminder of dinner with the king. My appetite immediately diminished. A warm hand patted my shoulder as Eloise stood up.

"Don't fret, my lady. His Highness will be there with you, he will keep you safe." She spoke softly as she began to pick out a dress.

"So, this is where I'll be staying the entire time?" A look of bewilderment washed over Eloise. "I...I just assumed, since I was a prisoner, I would be located somewhere less comfortable."

"Oh, heavens, no. You will absolutely not be staying in a dungeon, my lady! You are our prestigious guest and will be treated as such."

Her fingers threaded through the endless variety of garish dresses before she pulled out a simple, but elegant black dress. It had thin straps of black lace and a heart-shaped neckline. The silk dress was long, with a slit cut into both sides that made me wonder how I was going to walk without showing off too much of my legs.

Eloise hung the delicate silk dress on the outside of the oak armoire. She ushered me towards the small desk with an oval mirror attached to the top. The glass was enveloped in beautifully carved wood. Leaves and vines intertwined between petals, all delicately carved into the frame.

Our dynamis derived from the elements because the gods believed in the transformative strength and beauty of nature and all living things, so naturally artisans were inspired by the beauty of nature as well. The craftsmanship was exquisite, and it made my heart ache.

I would always love my life in Lostburrow, the simplicity of it. My town had made me the person I was today. However, somewhere deep down in my soul, I also longed to experience life outside of my small town—to experience culture, art, and libraries with shelves filled with endless amounts of knowledge.

Here I was surrounded by all those things, but instead of feeling excited, I felt full of remorse over the fact that I didn't have anyone to share my experience with. I realized, even if I saw all the wonders in this world, it would never feel complete without the ones I loved alongside me. My chin quivered at the thought, and I slumped into the back of the chair.

Eloise paused combing through my hair, and I could feel her peering at me through the mirror. I didn't have the courage to meet her gaze for fear my eyes might flood with tears, so I kept my eyes lowered. She continued working with my hair. She must have been a Flame, because I felt her warming my hair as she brushed. With every pass of her fingers, my hair became dryer.

"My lady, just how much do you know about King Alaric? I just want to make sure you're prepared for dinner tonight."

The tightness in my shoulders relaxed. Something about Eloise made me feel comfortable enough to trust her. Trust was something that I knew I would have to keep well-guarded, especially inside this castle.

"I know that he despises all Elysians who live outside of the capital and lords' cities, almost as much as he despises the humans and half-Elysians. Ever since the humans began to develop dynamis, King Alaric targeted all his anger towards them. Even though their dynamis was mediocre. When Elysians and humans began to marry and reproduce, all Hells broke loose. The king felt Elysian power was strongest when it was pure, untainted by humans. Hatred grew, and tempers flared on both sides, which became the start of the Rebellion."

Eloise nodded as she continued to work on my hair.

"I'm also not naive to the fact that he must have brought me here for a reason, and that reason is likely not one that I will enjoy. I'm not expecting a very warm reception tonight."

Eloise winced. She finished curling and braiding my hair in a beautiful arrangement. Half of my hair was braided and pinned in the back, while the rest of my hair draped over my shoulders.

"You're right, my lady." She sighed. "King Alaric and Lord Alastor aren't exactly known for their pleasant personalities. They don't shield anyone from their opinions, including the prince. You would do best to stay as quiet as possible and try not to react. They *will* try to push you to your limits, but you must promise me that you will hold your own and stay strong."

I closed my eyes at the thought of yet another person encouraging me to stay strong when I felt like a limp puddle of emotions. Sighing heavily, I opened my eyes to meet Eloise's.

"Well, I'm your girl. You don't have to worry about me holding my own; however, I'm going to have to practice some serious restraint when it comes to keeping quiet."

"Yes, I would definitely try to control any outbursts tonight." Leaning in a little closer to my ear, she whispered, "I find that screaming inside my head while squeezing my hands together into a fist seems to help."

My lips twitched into a smile when I saw her amused face in the mirror as she started to apply my makeup. "Eloise, why are you telling me all of this?"

"I've been here for a long time, my lady. I pride myself on being able to sense those who need help, or perhaps maybe even a friend." She smiled as she ran her hands through my curls to loosen them.

"A friend would be greatly appreciated," I said, as she grabbed my chin to hold it in place while she applied blush to my cheeks.

"Friends we shall be then," she hummed. "Now close your eyes and let me charcoal them. I'm going to make you look so stunning that all those broody men will be so distracted by your beauty that they leave you alone." She chuckled.

Instantly, embarrassment flooded my emotions as I bit my lip. "Eloise?"

"Mmhmm?"

"You said you've been here for a long time," I said softly, trying not to be rude. "How long exactly?"

"I was the queen's lady-in-waiting, before—" Her words stopped as she took a deep breath. "Now, I look after prince Declan and have the pleasure of assisting you." She spoke with a bit more happiness in her tone.

"I'm so sorry about the queen, and the prince's brother. As I grew up, my father would sometimes share stories with me about his life in the capital. I remember him telling me they were both wonderful. Completely selfless and kind. It was a shame that they met the gods so soon. Did they ever catch who was responsible?"

Eloise placed the brushes down on the small desk and was silent for a moment. Almost long enough to make me fear I should have never asked that question. Her mouth formed a tight line as it quivered. Guilt weighed inside me as I fidgeted with my hands.

"They were absolutely wonderful people," she said as she placed a warm hand on my shoulder. "I think that you and the queen would have gotten along splendidly. You remind me of her a little." Then she spun me around to look at myself in the mirror.

"Eloise ..." I gawked at my reflection in the mirror. "I don't even recognize myself."

My eyelids were painted a light shade of violet that made the color of my eyes brighter. The charcoal that lined my eyes made them look wider, and my lashes looked fuller than I had ever seen them. A rosy blush dusted each of my cheeks, and my lips were painted a light shade of mauve.

Her face sparkled with delight as she helped me into the sleek dress. The straps of the corset were so tight, I wasn't sure how long I'd be able to breathe with it on. Even bound tightly, I couldn't stop the shiver that ran down my spine, forcing me to clench my hands into fists. Eloise helped me into a pair of flat slippers, but I caught her gaze lingering over my clenched palms.

"Hold your head up high, my dear. Remember that strength that's inside of you." Eloise squeezed my hand. She left my side to begin cleaning off the desk we had used.

"Eloise?"

"Hmm?" She placed a brush inside the dresser.

"Elena. It's my name. Friends call each other by their names."

She gave me a bow. "Of course, Elena."

Head held high and shoulders back, I strode out of my room ready to take on anything in my path.

That path ended quicker than I expected when I slammed right into a giant chest of armor.

"You know, we really have to quit meeting like this." The slow drawl of Killian's voice slid towards me. I massaged my aching forehead and nose. "For someone who seems to have a keen grasp of her senses, sight seems to be not one of them."

"Hilarious," I said flatly. One side of his lip curled up as he wrapped his arms around me. "It's good to see you too." My words were muffled by his armor.

"We're so glad to see you safe. You gave us a good scare, Freckles."

I choked on a laugh. "Freckles?"

"Everyone's got a nickname for you. I was feeling a bit left out."

"Keep trying," I deadpanned, which earned me a laugh.

Killian extended his arm for me to hold. We began to walk down the corridor in silence. The pounding of my rapid heartbeat echoed in my head. The surge of dynamis within me tingled at the surface, taunting me. Before I entered that dining hall, I needed to gain control.

Inhaling deeply, I did the best I could to pull a mask of calm over my body. I let it wrap around me like a blanket. It was nothing more than a flimsy shield, but I hoped it would be enough to get me through the entire dinner.

As we approached the white doors trimmed in gold, my knees buckled. Killian placed a palm over mine on his arm, forcing me to meet his gaze. "It's just dinner, Elena, you can do this."

"Ha!" I grumbled. "*Just* dinner?"

"Declan will be with you the entire time."

"I still haven't decided if that's a good thing or a bad thing." A small shaky laugh escaped my lips.

"I believe you'll find out for yourself sooner or later that it's indeed a good thing, Freckles. Boy, do I wish I could see his face when he sees you in this dress."

Suddenly, I was very aware of my rosy cheeks. Oh, gods, was I wearing the wrong dress?

As if Killian could hear my thoughts, he replied, "Oh, you definitely chose the right one, Elena."

Some of the tension released from my shoulders. I'd only just met these two men, but knowing that they would be the ones looking after me made me feel a whole lot safer.

"Deep breath," Killian said as he knocked on the doors and they both opened wide on command.

Rolling my shoulders back and tilting my head up high, I glided into the room. *Here we go, Elena.*

CHAPTER 22

DECLAN

"I can't believe you put the girl in the room next to you, Declan. What message do you think that will send? By tomorrow morning the entire city with will think we've begun to go soft on the lesser Elysians." My father seethed.

The piercing ache in my head reminded me why I avoided these dinners as much as possible.

Rubbing circles over my temples, I tried to erase the fury that burrowed inside. Nothing would make your appetite evaporate faster than sitting across from the man who had killed your mother and brother, and beside your father, who still refused to believe it.

Since I'd arrived, my father and Alastor had begun a torturous interrogation about the past few days with the Light Phoenix. Still heartbroken and fuming over what Eloise had told me earlier, I couldn't contain the glare that was currently locked on their faces.

My shadows rippled like steam along my arms and I took long draws from my whiskey glass. That seemed to quiet them for a while, and they got lost in conversation about plans for the ball that they would be holding to show off the Light Phoenix's dynamis.

My insides coiled in knots as I waited for Elena, feigning boredom while I homed in on their conversation. I'd been sent to retrieve the

Light Phoenix for one reason. They planned to make her a pawn in their vicious game, holding the rebels under their thumb, invoking fear in anyone who dared to challenge the kingdom.

My father's reputation was slowly ripping by threads, and he was grasping at everything he could to make sure it didn't rip wide open. In his mind, he believed Elena will mend the tears and bring him back into the kingdoms favor. Little did he know I had other plans for her. I took another long draw from my whiskey glass, but my plotting was interrupted by the sound of the dining room doors creaking open.

Time stood as still as my heart. My Wildfire glided into the room like a damn warrior ready for battle, shoulders back, head held high, and a look of pure confidence on her face that was enough to make any man go weak at the knees. Thankfully, I was already sitting down.

A small smirk began to rise on my face as she walked towards me with more grace than any courtier in this kingdom. Pride thrummed through me as we all rose to meet her.

"Father, Lord Alastor, let me introduce you to Lady Elena Alexandria Morrigan, otherwise known as the Light Phoenix."

Elena's eyebrows twitched at the mention of her middle name, and I could feel the heat of her questioning eyes as she fell into a bow.

Yes, Wildfire, I know your middle name.

Doing my best to keep my face controlled, I let my attention fall back towards my father and Alastor.

"Lady Morrigan, let me introduce you to King Alaric Benjamin Stallard and his advisor Lord Alastor Grimshaw."

After they bowed their heads towards Elena, I pulled out her chair for her. She was to the left of me, my father was on my right at the head of the table, and Alastor was directly across from me. Seating arrangements in the castle were always made by rank. The higher the rank, the closer to the king we sat. For once I could thank the gods for my father's attention to that detail, for that meant that Elena would be seated the furthest away.

Servants entered from the kitchen, placing platters of meats, seafood, vegetables and an assortment of breads on the middle of the table. As they lifted the silver lids, I struggled not to break composure as her lips parted. She was trying so hard to maintain a stoic persona, but I had to shove down another smile when a breathy gasp escaped her when they revealed the platter of chocolate desserts.

My eyes roamed over her as I filled her plate with different foods and desserts. She was breathtaking. The simple black dress she wore highlighted every one of her assets.

Every. Single. One.

An overwhelming urge grew within me to throw her over my shoulder, carry her away to my chambers, and never look back.

Mesmerized, I watched as she twirled her auburn hair between her fingers. It seemed to be a nervous habit of hers, one of the many that I had come to notice during our journey. The others included biting her bottom lip when she was overwhelmed or rolling her eyes when she was frustrated. All of which seemed to have a direct line to my...

I cleared my throat, setting the plate in front of her. Lena's eyes found mine, silently asking for permission to eat. When I nodded, a grin spread across my face as she went straight for the chocolate dessert.

Alastor's loud chewing was the only sound that echoed inside the massive room. Dinner seemed almost peaceful for once in my life, that was until my father decided to speak.

"So, Elena," my father bellowed from the end of the table. "Let's discuss why we summoned you here."

Alastor wiped his smug mouth with his napkin as his eyes lingered on Elena for longer than I appreciated. I slammed the glass in my hand against the oak table, shaking Alastor's glare off her and back onto me.

"Since you have been blessed with this extraordinary gift from the gods, it will be your duty to share it with your kingdom."

Elena cleared her throat and took a long sip of wine, no doubt in reaction to the fact that she had just been told her dynamis was theirs to utilize.

"Alastor, my advisor, has arranged a ball for you and that other boy—"

"Will," she interrupted. My father's eyes narrowed. I awaited my father's anger to be unleashed, but it didn't come. Curiosity twinged against my chest as to why.

"Yes, Will." He took a sip of wine, while Alastor's stare affixed on Elena once more. "You both will train for a month while entertaining the dignitaries of our kingdom for brunches, dinners, or whatever else we need you for. You will be expected to be the face of our Stallard line, supporting all the same ideals as we do."

Elena fidgeted uncomfortably in her seat beside me.

"At the end of the month, we will display the strength of your dynamis. If you do well, child, you may keep the title of Lady, as well as all the gifts that are currently on their way to your town."

Elena's eyes met my father's, as the wheels spun inside my head. All my guards were here in Vrine, so that must mean he had sent his own. Something told me that their journey was about more than bearing gifts. A piercing pain stabbed inside the pit of my stomach. I made a note to send a raven to Warren immediately.

"Yes, child, I've sent several wagons of coin, livestock, even some of our finest elixirs."

Her breath hitched, and I knew she was thinking about how much all of that would mean to her town.

"A few of my guards will also remain there to provide extra protection for your town as well."

Silence passed as my father swirled the wine inside his goblet, glaring at his pawn, waiting for her to choose her fate.

"Does this sound like something you would be capable of doing, *Lady* Elena?" Alastor rumbled across the table.

"Y-yes." Her voice trembled.

"Good," he purred. "Then we will continue to provide aid to your town, as long as you continue to speak highly of our king and abide by our deal."

Both men smiled toward each other and their glasses crashed together in a cheer. Elena, on the other hand, sank into her chair, burdened by the role that she was now expected to carry. All to ensure her town stayed safe.

"Elena," my father grumbled, drumming his fingers against the marble table. "I'm curious, just how did you manage to defeat this dark beast?" As he spoke his fingertips around the edge of his wine goblet. "My son's dynamis is the most powerful in the kingdom. There has never been anyone more powerful."

I caught the slight flicker of disgust in his tone at that admission. Elena simultaneously winced then glowered towards my father. Discreetly dropping my hand to her thigh next to me, I squeezed. Her face shifted back to the bored, stoic mask she'd worn when she walked in this evening.

Good girl. Don't let them get to you, Wildfire. Withdrawing my hand from her thigh, I lifted my whiskey glass to my lips. Father and Alastor wore a scowl at the lack of reaction from me. Sometimes I can't control my anger, but I was trying my best to reign it in for Elena's sake tonight. "Declan told me you have some sort of white flame dynamis. Please, enlighten me on how your flame managed to accomplish such a feat where he could not."

Blood boiled within me, my dynamis slamming against my skin. The taste of metal hit my tongue as I clenched my teeth. My lips parted as I prepared to snarl a response, but someone unexpectedly beat me to it.

"Well, Your Majesty, someone should probably reassess who's the most powerful dynamis then." Face bored, she continued to pick at her plate of food.

Gods, this woman never ceased to astonish me. A laugh threatened to rise from within me, so I shoved a piece of beef in my mouth to stifle it. A purplish-red hue painted their faces. My father's mouth hung agape.

Obstinate behavior was not something that they were accustomed to, unless it came from me. Alastor was the first to lash out, and I leaned back into my seat, preparing for his inevitable tantrum.

"Why, you insolent little—"

"Careful." My voice boomed across the table as my fingers clawed at the chair's armrest.

"How dare you speak to your king in such a manner. You must have had lousy excuses for parents if you come to us at your age lacking manners befitting the title we have given you." Alastor paused, a devious grin tugging at his lip. "We may have dressed you in our finest clothes, let you stay in our finest accommodations, but you are still nothing more than an insignificant child parading around with stolen dynamis inside her blood."

There it was. It was only a matter of time before their true prejudices spilled out. I wasn't surprised that it was Alastor who'd cracked first. Alastor glanced towards my father, who raised his glass of wine in salute. Outside my face portrayed my well-practiced glacial demeanor, on the inside I was seething hot.

It shouldn't have surprised me that they'd attacked Elena's spirit so fast. My nails pierced the ends of the armrests as a blast of emotions slammed into me. Prickling and burning pain shot across my body, all signs of anger, rage and shame.

Delicate fingers wrapped tightly around her golden fork, her knuckles white from the pressure. A flush of red stained her cheeks, and her beautiful eyes were overrun by the black of her pupils. Panic flooded within me. I needed to push some calming emotions her way before this dinner turned into an execution.

Maintaining my bored face the best I could, I reached down to my well of dynamis and thought of the most uplifting and cheerful emotions I could think of, like the memory of watching my mother tend to the flowers in her garden each morning or hearing my brother's roaring laughter as we raced down the mountainside on our horses, or the way that Elena's smile seemed to be the only one able to thaw my cold heart. Every happy moment I'd ever had hummed beneath my skin. In one quick blow, I used my dynamis to shove them towards her.

She let out an almost silent gasp. The fork tumbled onto the napkin below. Slowly, the redness faded away from her cheeks, her shoulders fell, and her body sagged back into the chair. Relief washed through me and I peeled my hands off the chair, swiping away the sweat that had taken residence on my forehead.

I was just about to take another drink of my whiskey when my

Wildfire cleared her throat beside me. My dynamis sprang to life once more.

"Yes, it is true, Your Majesty, my lord." Beautiful blue-green eyes full of daggers locked gazes with my father and Alastor. "I do come from outside your 'Blessed' bubble of powerful Elysians. However, the gods have chosen me to carry the monumental power of the Light Phoenix. Not one of your 'Blessed' Elysians, or even your own sons, was given a dynamis like mine."

An audible growl rumbled inside my father's chest.

"The gods chose me, an *insignificant, meaningless child*, from a town far away from here. The same insignificant child who managed to save the life of your most Blessed Elysian, the prince. The same insignificant child who was taken from her town and dragged across the land because His Majesty requested *her* presence." She paused to take a deep breath before she continued, "So, you see, gentlemen, I believe that I am not quite as insignificant as you may want to believe. On the contrary, I believe that it is you who will be needing me to ensure your claim on this land and your title remain a little more...*significant*."

Elena leaned back in her chair with the slightest smug smile spread across her beautiful face. "Oh, and Lord Alastor?" His blue eyes darkened. The glare bore into her face so viciously, I wanted to rip his eyes out with my shadows. "I am not a child, but in fact, as you said, a lady. You would do well to remember that in the future."

In one breath, my Wildfire had managed to do something that I hadn't been able to in my entire life. I watched with glee as my father and Alastor squirmed in their seats, stunned into silence. Proud was an understatement for the feelings that spread like fire in my tainted, cold heart over what Elena had just done. This woman continued to surprise me at every turn, and it was making it damn near impossible to restrain myself from her. She was unlike anyone I had ever met. An enigma that I couldn't wait to figure out.

Alastor's face turned several shades of red, where my father's face suddenly seemed eerily calm and collected. It took me a moment to decipher that he was already beginning to scheme and calculate exactly what to do with my Wildfire. His face rose into a smug smile as he raised his hand to silence Alastor, who had begun stuttering a rebuttal.

"My dear, it seems that I have greatly underestimated you. I'll be wise to ensure I don't repeat my mistakes from now on." His words were laced with more threat than sincerity. Shifting his gaze towards mine, he took a heavy draw of wine. "You have a month to train the Light Phoenix. I want her strong enough to give a demonstration of her exquisite dynamis in front of the entire court. See to it that you also teach her some proper manners as well."

He lifted his glass to Elena before draining his drink. "If you want to be a lady, then you'll be trained to act like one. First and only rule, *Lady* Morrigan—no one challenges the king. You'll do well to remember *that* in the future." I caught her slight flinch out of the corner of my eye, and my protective instincts roared within me.

"You start tomorrow," Alastor seethed. With a snap of his fingers, the servant standing against the wall behind us jumped to his side. "Remove their plates, they are both dismissed."

A small huff of frustration fled through Elena's lips. Rising from my chair, I extended my arm for her to hold. Mirroring me, she rose and gave a silent bow to my father and Alastor.

"Oh, and Elena?"

We both halted and our heads turned to face my father.

"You do not leave this castle. No letters. No communication to the outside. You will do nothing unless I say so." His lips curled up into a smug grin, as Alastor chuckled into his goblet.

The hair on my neck stood straight up, and I could feel the muscles in my neck pulse as I began to charge towards them both. A delicate hand wrapped around my wrist, and as I whipped around to meet her eyes, all the fury died like a sail with no wind. Elena nodded her head solemnly, and tears clouded her lovely blue eyes.

With a deep breath, I placed her hand over my arm and guided her around the long table and out the dining room doors as fast as I could.

CHAPTER 23

DECLAN

Only our footsteps echoed against the wooden floors as I ushered her back through the castle hallways. It wasn't until we turned the corner towards our rooms that I felt her entire demeanor change. Face slick with sweat, her complexion blanched. The tension around my arm loosened as she released her grip and raced down the hallway, swung her door wide open and disappeared within. Without hesitation, I stormed after her.

Barreling through the open door, I was surprised to find the room vacant. Until the sounds of retching thundered from the bathroom.

Strolling into the bathroom, I paused to grab a small white cloth and ran cool water over it. Elena hunched over the toilet, holding on for dear life.

"Ugh, go away… *please*. You don't need to see me like this," she gurgled, taking a breath only to retch again.

Little did she know I'd seen my fair share of unmentionable things, and this was exceedingly low on that list. I swept the hair back away from her face, holding it for her as she disposed of the last remnants of her dinner. An ache in my heart blossomed at the sight, as well as the desire to sweep her into my arms and rock her back and forth until she felt better. Instead, I watched as she pulled away from the toilet, sitting back on her heels.

She went to wipe her mouth with the back of her hand, and I lowered her hand while placing the cool, wet towel over her forehead and over her lips.

"I'm so embarrassed," Elena groaned, her freckled nose wrinkled with disgust.

"Nothing to be embarrassed about, Lena." I extended my hands to help her up. "Let's get you out of here."

When she placed her hands in mine, I lifted her to her feet. The hem of her long silk dress tangled underneath her, sending her crashing into me. One of my hands now held the back of her head, while the other arm ended up wrapped firmly around her waist.

Even through the thin fabric I could feel the zing of energy from our connection. Elena twitched underneath me, her body's reaction similar to mine, fueling my confidence. My fingers slid against the cool, black satin and stopped at the small of her back. Her lips trembled as I rubbed calming circles as I swept away the hair that had fallen into her face with my other hand.

Elena tilted her head up to meet my gaze, her eyes glistening, face flushed in the most beautiful shade of pink I have ever seen. She placed both of her hands over my chest, pushing herself back onto her feet. Taking a few steps away, she caught my glance again through her lashes and whispered, "Thank you…Declan."

"Anytime." I nudged her with my shoulder, coaxing her to follow me back into the bedroom.

Once she made it to the bedroom, she slumped into one of the velvet armchairs near the fireplace. The fire crackled in the silence, and my heart stumbled at the sight of the light illuminating every inch of her body. She glowed like a goddess herself. Every couple of moments, her eyelids dipped. Exhaustion threatened to pull her under. If I wanted to speak with her, now was the time. Training started tomorrow, after all.

"Elena?"

"Mmhmm?" Drowsiness clung to her mumble.

This woman stirred emotions I hadn't felt within me in so long, much like the nerves that swelled within my stomach right now. "What you did tonight, how you stood up to my father and Alastor...I have never seen a more astonishing feat."

No words left her lips. Those deep aqua eyes pierced into mine, questioning my statement. Elena was intuitive to so many things around her, *except* when it came to her own self-worth. I genuinely thought she had no idea the strength and beauty she possessed. I was learning that she was a very powerful woman.

Taking long strides towards her, I lowered to my knees in front of her. Her eyes became more alert as I grabbed her hands on her lap. She squirmed a little further back in the chair, her chest rising and falling with her breaths.

"Not many have been graced with the pleasure of me kneeling before them, my lady. Look at me, Elena."

The words were a gentle order, just like the caress of my fingers as I held her chin. Glossy eyes watched me from beneath heavy lashes. A tremble rippled over her skin beneath my touch.

"Wildfire, you have done something tonight that I have never been able to do in my entire life. You managed to stand up against my father and Lord Alastor, and your will was unfaltering. My dear, your spirit continues to amaze me. You blaze through every barrier placed before you like it never even existed. I work with several brave and strong guards daily, but you, sweet Lena, you are one of the strongest people I have ever met."

There was no mistaking the hitch of her breath, even when she broke my gaze to stare into the fire instead. With one last brush of her cheek with the back of my hand, I pulled back and rose to my feet.

"Try and get a good night's rest tonight and make sure to eat a big breakfast tomorrow. You'll need it. We'll start training with your dynamis first thing in the morning."

She dipped her head, and I began to make my way back to the door. Full of adrenaline, I knew that sleep would not come swiftly tonight. My night was about to consist of a few glasses of whiskey and a *very* cold shower.

"Declan?" Her sweet voice flooded my senses, pulling me to turn around once more. "You...um...you don't suppose there's someone still awake who could bring me some of those chocolate desserts from dinner, do you?" A sheepish grin tickled her lips.

"Of course."

I bid her good night, then alerted the guard at the end of the hall to send up some desserts for her. As I walked back towards my bedroom, the grin that tugged at my cheeks was so large it hurt. I'd kept my heart guarded for so long that the swell of happiness that was crashing within me felt foreign.

Clara might have been right. Maybe Elena truly would be a part of the cure for the darkness that lurked inside of me.

CHAPTER 24
ELENA

The morning came entirely too fast for my liking. I groaned as I heard tapping against my door. There was only a flicker of light in the sky; it had to be barely dawn. I forced myself out of the bed and wrapped my robe around me as I scurried over to the door.

Somehow, in one short evening I'd managed to offend two cruel and powerful men, not once, but twice. A hysterical laugh fled my lips. I placed my head into my hands. *Who is this woman I'm becoming?*

That wasn't the only eventful activity of last evening, however. A shiver ran down my body as the memory of Declan's palm brushing across my skin invaded my mind. All at once, heat rushed back to my cheeks.

When I'd walked into the dining hall earlier, I could instantly feel the fire of his gaze upon me. Declan's emerald eyes had roamed over my entire body. I could have sworn a shimmer of desire flashed across his face as he tried his best to distract himself by filling my plate with food. When he grabbed my thigh under the table, I almost lost myself completely.

Somehow, I managed to hold it together until after dinner when the events of the night came flooding in, leaving me hanging over the toilet. I cringed at the memory of the prince seeing me in such an embarrassing state. This man had already seen me at my worst more times than I could count, and yet he had taken care of me in each moment.

I recalled the intensity of his stare as he kneeled before me. His gaze had sent my body aflame, and I had melted under his touch when he gripped my chin. The attraction that was building between was something that neither of us had expected. However, that was where it must end. There was no point in starting something that was doomed from the start.

There were more important things to focus on, like getting through this training to ensure my own survival and protect my town. My father was waiting for me at home, and if I had to pretend to believe in the king's ideals for a month to help the people of my town, that was a burden I was willing to carry.

It was time to stop pretending to be something I was not. Declan Stallard was a prince, the next in line to be king. Elena Morrigan was an *insignificant Elysian, from an insignificant town* outside of these walls. Our story must end here. Time to face reality and leave the fantasy to my books.

Another tap at the door shook me away from my thoughts. I opened it. Grinning, Eloise stepped through the door, holding a tray of food.

"Sorry, Eloise, I guess I was exhausted after last night's dinner. I hope you weren't out here waiting for too long." I gave her an apologetic look as she strolled into the room and placed the tray down on the wooden side table near the navy armchair.

An assortment of breakfast items were piled high on top, and suddenly I felt like I had died and met all five gods. The heavenly smell of fresh bread and salty bacon wafted through my senses. My mouth watered as my gaze roamed over the fluffy eggs and pastries as well as the pot I hoped would be filled with steaming hot coffee. On cue, my stomach grumbled as I shut the door behind her.

"Oh, hush! I wouldn't have bothered you until much later in the morning, but the prince insisted that you begin your training bright and early this morning. Gods only know why it had to be *this* early."

She herded me towards the small table near the fireplace. "Now, sit and eat a big breakfast and enjoy a cup or two of coffee. I'll lay out your training leathers, gambeson and boots on the bed. Would you like me to braid your hair, my lady?"

"Remember, it's Elena." I smiled before I shoved a piece of bacon in my mouth. "I can manage that myself, but thank you for asking, Eloise. Thank you for the amazing breakfast as well."

"You're welcome, Elena." She passed by the wooden desk and noticed the letters I'd scrawled out to my father last night. The king might have ordered me to not send them, but nothing could stop me from writing them. "Would you like me to mail these?"

"Normally I would say yes, but I was forbidden to leave the castle or to communicate with anyone outside of these walls."

Eloise's lips pursed, her fist clenched. "That's just ridiculous. Let me work on that. You just keep writing them."

The act was so simple but meant everything. I didn't have many friends, much less those who would risk something like this for me. Eloise barely knew me, yet she was willing to figure out a way for me to send letters to my father.

"The prince left instructions to join him by the cliffs behind the castle when you're done." She turned once more to leave.

"Thank you again, Eloise."

Once she left, I continued to work my way through the tray of food. The prince had told me to make sure to eat a lot this morning, so that was exactly what I intended to do.

CHAPTER 25
ELENA

After making a sizable dent in my breakfast, I tugged on my training leathers and boots and made my way out of the castle. Tossing my hair into a quick braid as I sauntered through the halls, I couldn't help but feel gazes on me. A few guards watched me with stern expressions, clutching the hilt of their swords. Servants paused their work to bow, bursting into whispers after I passed. By the time I approached the back doors of the castle, I let out a small sigh of relief. Tying a leather band around the end of my braid, I shoved the doors open, stepping into the morning light.

The sun was finally rising, setting the sky ablaze with color. Shades of yellows, vibrant oranges and crimsons were painted across the sky. It appeared the gods had decided to spend their morning using it as their canvas. A cool breeze whipped across my face, tickling my nose with the salty smell of the sea. Waves hummed back and forth beneath the cliff. Everything about this moment felt peaceful, a welcomed change from the stressful events I'd endured recently.

Surprisingly, there was no sign of Declan yet. I made my way over to the cliff and lowered myself down to dangle my feet off the edge. Time seemed to fade away as I lost myself in the serene view around me.

A few moments later, a deep voice cleared its throat behind me. I glanced over my shoulder and took in the exquisite man who towered above me.

"Why am I not surprised to find you here, dangling inches away from your death?" Declan huffed, notably quite a few paces behind me.

"Well, if you're so worried about me falling to my doom, perhaps you should come sit beside me?" I patted the smooth edge of the ground beside me.

The lines creased between his eyebrows as he shook his head. "I'm perfectly fine enjoying the view from here," he said sternly.

Could I have just discovered something that the Lord of Shadows is afraid of?

"You're afraid of heights, aren't you?" I turned my head back towards the horizon to hide my smirk.

All I heard was a grumble from behind me, leaving me to chuckle inwardly at his refusal to answer.

"Come on, we have much to do today."

I scoffed and gave one more longing look at the picturesque view in front of me before shuffling to my feet. As I stood, some of the rock gave way. Panicking, I released a shriek as my arms waved through the air. In seconds, something caught me and whipped me back towards the grass, tossing me several feet away from the edge of the cliff.

It happened so fast that I hadn't even realized that Declan's shadows had pulled me away from the edge. As the shadows slithered their way back towards their prince, I stood up with a laugh, dusting myself off. "Well, thank you for—"

"Dammit, Elena!" He stalked towards me.

"I—I'm sorry, I—" My voice cracked as Declan grabbed me by the shoulders.

His harsh tone radiated through me. "Why do you keep putting yourself into these positions? Stop being so naive and start using your brain. What if I hadn't been here to save you?"

The words hit me like a slap in the face. Back once more was the frustrating, hot-headed Shadow Lord.

"Get off of me!" I shoved my way out of his grip.

The beats of my heart became erratic, as though it was about to leap straight out of my chest. We both stood glaring at each other, no sounds but the crashing waves from below. *Damn him for calling me naive.*

If my memory served me well, I seemed to remember that not too long ago that same *naive* woman had saved his life. He had struck a nerve far deeper than he would ever know. No matter how much I fought to be strong and independent, somehow, I always ended up needing saving—an ever-present reminder that I was a failure. Anger surged within me, calling forth my prickling dynamis.

"You're mad at me? Good. Maybe now you'll take your training seriously." He stormed off towards what looked like stairs that led down to the beach.

Fuming, I paced back and forth until I felt the prickle of my dynamis crawl back to its depths. Begrudgingly, I forced my legs to follow him. He might be the worst person alive right now, but I needed to learn how to tame the unstable swell of this power within me. Swallowing my pride, I made my way down the stairs and traversed the sand to the now seated prince.

"Sit," he said a little more calmly, but there was no denying it was still an order.

Tiptoeing around him, I sat cross-legged in the warm sand across from him. My eyes roamed over him. Eyes closed, legs crossed in front of him, palms resting on each thigh. Meditating.

Wonderful. How was I supposed to fall into a state of calm in the presence of this man? Letting out a grumble, I rolled my neck, releasing the pressure forming beneath. I closed my eyes, gathering all my teachings from Bri, and began to chant my mantra inside my head.

I am the light. No darkness can bind me. I have it within me to hold and to guide me.

Repeating it over and over, I tried to force my body to fall into a peaceful state. However, my mind began to wander, a usual occurrence whenever I tried to meditate. Brietta had tried for years to use meditation to help me with my anxiousness and I'd mimed the part of calm well. I never had the courage to tell her the truth—that during all our times of meditation, I never actually reached a state of peace. Instead, I thought of new recipes for healing elixirs, plants that needed tending in the garden, what I was going to make for dinner, or the last chapters I had just read in my book.

Half of the time my anxiousness faded away not from the meditation, but from me being bored to death from sitting with my own thoughts for hours. The memory roused a smile, just as something slapped me across my right cheek. My eyes flashed open as I searched for the culprit behind the attack.

Nothing sat before me but the Shadow Lord. A smug smile had formed on his face. I looked behind me, only to find no one near us at all. Frustrated, I rubbed my cheek, closed my eyes and attempted to meditate once more.

Just as I began my mantra again, something tugged on my braid, forcing my eyes wide open.

"What the—"

"Is something wrong?" Declan interrupted before I could finish my string of curses. I glared at him, hoping he could still feel it while his eyes remained shut. His body was still, except for his raised eyebrow.

"Why do I feel like you have a hand in whatever is going on here?" I replied bluntly.

His eyes rolled open. "What are you trying to insinuate, Wildfire?"

A frustrated snarl passed through my clenched teeth. "You're telling me you know nothing about whatever slapped me across my face, then pulled on my braid?"

"I have absolutely no idea what you're talking about. I thought you've had extensive training in meditation, Elena. Perhaps I should have started with something a little easier for you." He gave a devious smile before he shut his eyes again, ending the conversation.

My body trembled with rage. *Just who does he think he is?* Growling as I bit my lip, I tried to coax away the anger that was stirring the dynamis beneath my skin. Every part of me wanted to prove Declan wrong. Show him that I wasn't that naive little woman who needed protecting.

Shoving down my rage, I blew out a breath and forced my eyes shut. Rubbing my forehead, I resumed my mantra. Eventually, everything faded back to normal, causing me to question whether I had made up those events in my mind this whole time or not.

Until I was hit with a barrage of attacks from all sides. I opened my eyes, but not fast enough, as I was shoved face first into the smooth sand in front of me.

Sand filled my mouth as I snarled into it. Digging my fingers into it, I shoved my body up, spitting the sand out as I went. Sitting back on my knees, I wiped away the rest of the sand so I could look upon my opponent. Whoever had just done this was about to come face to face with my wrath.

My head swung from side to side until I realized there was nothing but an empty shore in front of me. Where had he gone? My heart was racing as I spun around.

A little too late, again. Freezing water splashed my face, drenching me. A roar of laughter spewed from a few paces in front of me. The dynamis within me sizzled back to the surface and I swore steam emanated from my skin where the residual water resided.

Suddenly, my entire body became swollen with power. It felt as if I might spontaneously combust if I didn't release it soon. The taste of metal hit my tongue as I bit my lip to distract from the increasing pain of my dynamis.

"HOW DARE YOU, DECLAN STALLARD!" My hands curled so tightly in fists that my nails were biting the skin of my palms.

"That's it, Wildfire. Glad to see you finally joined the fun." He shot out a blast of his shadows, aiming straight for my legs.

The shadows swept underneath the back of my legs, launching me onto my ass. My dynamis pulsed in tune with the rapid beats of my heart, begging me to release it into the world. It was time for Declan Stallard to learn a lesson or two.

We circled each other. Our eyes blazed with so much intensity it was predatory, both of us intrigued to see who would be the first one to strike.

"Meditation is one way to find the dynamis within you, Elena. However, you won't be able to stop and meditate to call it forth when you need it," he said as we continued to circle each other. Whips of shadows taunted me as I dove around them while still trying to hold my stance. "You need to learn how to pull from your dynamis, no matter what's happening around you. Whether you're in the middle of a sword fight or struggling against the hold of an assailant, you need to be on the ready."

Another stream of shadows leapt towards me. I narrowly dodged them.

"Remember in the forest? You managed to pull the strongest of your power while simultaneously attacking a massive, unearthly beast. Elena, if you can do that, then you can surely call forth your dynamis right now to halt a few of my shadows..." He taunted me again with a mischievous smirk. "Maybe."

Pulling on the well of my dynamis I felt burning inside of me, I decided to try to force it out, just like I had done before with the unwanted emotions. Perhaps I could create a blast of wind swift enough to knock him on his ass.

I began to call forth my dynamis, until unease crept into my mind. What if I accidentally released the light power that had burned through my hands on the night I'd melted the beast?

Don't get me wrong, I was furious with the man in front of me, but I didn't want to incinerate him...*yet*. A dangerous smile pulled at my lips at the thought, and Declan lifted his brows.

Shoving out my emotions alongside a wisp of dynamis, I launched it forward with everything I had. The blast of air was so strong it ripped the leather off the end of my braid, releasing it into the wild wind I had created. The rapid rise and fall of my breaths gradually simmered to a calm, just like the dust and wind from the gust I had created.

My breath hitched when I saw the powerful gust of wind had flung the prince all the way down to the shore. He lay still and unmoving as the tide rolled against his body. Damn! *Too far, I went too far.*

I scrambled over him, fell to my hands and knees and pressed my head against his chest. *Breathing, thank gods.* As the waves crashed against my thighs, I pushed my fingers against his wrist and counted the beats of his pulse. My grip on his wrist stirred a groan from him, and I sighed in relief.

Leaning over his listless body, I placed my palm across his cheek. It was amazing how peaceful he looked while unconscious. *Maybe I just need to knock him out more often?*

I chuckled to myself, placing my palm against his chest to push myself up. I'd need some help getting him back up to the castle. There was no way that I was carrying him up those steps. I was halfway up when strong arms shoved me to the side and I tumbled over him, falling flat onto my back.

In the blink of an eye, Declan was on top of me, caging me in with his arms and legs. A devilish smile danced across his face. I rolled my eyes, my head sinking into the wet sand beneath it. This man was truly infuriating. How either of us was going to survive training together over the next month was beyond me. The idea of him becoming a pile of ash had become more appealing.

"Never underestimate your opponent, Wildfire," he said, as a cocky grin spread across his face. His gaze rolled lazily over my body beneath him as I huffed and rolled my eyes. Declan leaned closer, halting my attempts to get out of his cage of arms. "How brave of you, Lena. You know, we've talked about you rolling your eyes." A low growl rumbled deep within his chest.

It sent warmth to more places in my body than I'd care to admit. *Damn this man!* How could he make me so furious in one moment, and in another have me trembling with feelings quite the contrary?

"Do you suppose we could continue this conversation somewhere else?" I scoffed as the tide swept against the side of my face. "I don't know, maybe somewhere with less sand...and water?"

A smile replaced the devious twitch of his lips. He was on his feet instantly, extending his hand for me to take.

"I'm not sure I trust you after everything that just happened," I jested, pretending to withdraw my hand.

"Just take my hand, woman." he said, shaking his head as he chuckled quietly.

"Fine."

Before the word finished leaving my lips, he had pulled me back onto my feet. As I dusted off the wet sand from my leathers, he gathered my hair and twisted, wringing out the salty water. It felt far more intimate than it should have, and my body reacted uncontrollably. Heat flushed my cheeks, and my skin pebbled with goosebumps. Thankfully, what I was wearing had my skin mostly covered, and he wouldn't be able to see. Hopefully.

We walked across the shore and back up the stairs, no sound but the scrunch of wet leather as we continued towards the back door of the castle. Its stark white stone was breathtaking against the bright blue of the morning sky. I paused for a moment to take in the rest of the city.

We were high enough to see the city below. Each shop and home were vibrant with color—warm sunshine yellows, pale peaches, blues and magentas. It was curious to me how the City of Shadows could be alive with so many brilliant colors. I had always imagined it to be cold, dark, and distant, just like its ruler. Observing the city below, I realized how wrong I had been.

"Enchanting, isn't she?"

As he whispered into my ear, shivers spread through me. I tilted my head, coming nose to nose with the prince. "Who?"

"The city." He breathed, swallowing deeply as he took a few steps to the side.

"Mmhmm," I whispered. "Yes, she is."

In the back of my mind, I had a feeling he wasn't talking about the city at all, because his gaze had never once left mine.

"Let's get you inside and out of those wet clothes before you catch a cold."

Nodding, I turned around, following him back inside.

"Change into another pair of leathers. We still have some more training to do this afternoon," he said with a sly wink.

Of course we do.

"Oh, and Elena?" He paused, noticing my eyebrow quirk up. "Don't forget your dagger."

A grin grew on my lips as he strutted towards the kitchen.

Continuing towards my room, I was startled by a squeal of excitement from my right. Arms squeezed around me and waves of chestnut hair flooded my vision.

"Elena! I'm so happy I ran into you!" Clara beamed as she released me. It was so infectious that I couldn't help but join her. "Oh, gods, you're soaking wet." She wrinkled her nose in disgust as she looked down, realizing she was now soaked as well.

I burst out laughing. The feeling of lightness spread through my body like the rays of the sun. There was something relieving about laughter. It was almost like a dynamis itself, with the power to erase every worry, stress, and fear. If I could, I would do it every hour of every day.

Once we both calmed down, she told me she wanted to check the state of my healing and followed me back to my room.

After entering, I excused myself and took a quick rinse in the shower Eloise had introduced me to last night. It was even more amazing than the bathtub. It was like being inside of a waterfall—truly magical. Wrapping a fluffy cloth around my hair when I was done, I threw on another set of leathers and tunic. Leaving the tunic untucked so Clara could look at my healing injuries, I waltzed back into the room.

She seemed pleased with the progress, but she placed another palm on top of the pink flesh. "I just want to make sure everything heals internally as well. This will speed it up even more."

Her palm felt warm, and the heat seemed to spread within me across my entire scar. When she was done, she had a smile on her face, waiting for me to look. I gasped at what I saw. Where the pinkish flesh once resided, now all that was left was normal skin, as if nothing had ever happened.

"Clara, that is absolutely amazing," I said, still frozen in awe. "You truly have one incredible gift. So much good you can do with your dynamis, so many you can help."

A forced smile spread across her face before it wilted. "Unfortunately, I only get to help those within these walls. Even then, there are limitations. My dynamis can only be used when the king allows me to." Her voice faded into a whisper.

My eyes widened at her confession. "I'm so sorry, Clara, I can only imagine how difficult that must be for you."

"There have been so many people I could have helped if I'd been allowed...even my own mother."

"No!" I gasped. "Clara, he didn't."

She swallowed back a sob. "Even his own sister was deemed unworthy of my gift. She was extremely unwell, and my father sent word to have me return home. When I went to ask His Majesty's permission, I was denied. His excuse was that my dynamis was far too sacred, and I needed to remain inside the castle walls in order to protect the kingdom, *him*, at all times. He felt that two days away from the castle was too much of a risk, then proceeded to blame my mother's illness on her own decision to leave Vrine. Two days later, she passed away," Clara said, tears silently falling and splashing onto the wood floor beneath us. "I didn't even get to say goodbye."

"I knew the king was cruel, but what he did to you and your family is unforgivable, Clara." I pulled her into an embrace and gave her a tight squeeze.

How could someone deny their own flesh and blood something so precious as the gift of healing, of saving their life? Gods, he was more despicable than I had ever imagined.

"So...you've never been outside the city walls?"

She shook her head. "Once the king found out about the strength of my dynamis, I was sent here to live indefinitely."

"How long?"

"Since the day after my Ascension. Over fifty years ago."

My mouth gaped open, and not at her age—as an Elysian, she had been locked into ageless beauty the day she went through Ascension. Instead, I was appalled by her admission that she had been stuck inside this city for so long. Clara was being kept like a bird in a cage.

Something spurred inside me, and my dynamis flared. I made a vow in that moment that I would figure out a way to get Clara out of here. One day, I'd find a way to help her spread her wings and fly.

Unraveling the cloth wrapped around my hair, I wiped her tears away with it, guiding her to sit in the velvety armchair. I plopped my body down in the one beside her.

Eloise had snuck up some chocolate when she brought me breakfast this morning, telling me I'd probably need it after training today. Gods, if only she knew how right she was. Tossing Clara the box of chocolates, I reached for two glasses and poured wine into both. Mouth half stuffed with chocolates, she smiled.

"I knew from the moment I talked to you I was going to like you." She picked up the wine glass and raised it towards me.

Giggling, I lifted my glass towards hers until they clinked together. She handed me back the box, at which I shoved two delicious chocolates in my mouth.

"Just wondering." She paused to take a sip of wine. "How exactly did you get so wet during your training with Declan this morning? I could have sworn Declan said he was going to teach you some meditation techniques to help harness your dynamis."

"Your cousin does have some interesting training tactics, that's for sure," I scoffed.

"Is that all you find *interesting* about my cousin?" she hummed playfully.

"Clara, I have no idea what you're talking about."

Lie.

"Well, my cousin sure seems to find himself quite distracted as of late. I wonder what must be on his mind. Curious, isn't it?" Her smile wrapped around the lip of her glass and she took another sip as I tried to become invisible inside the chair.

Standing up, she took the last swig of her wine and leaned down to give me a hug. "I think we are going to be great friends, Elena."

"Me too. Clara, thanks again for healing me...for saving me."

A warm smile spread across her face. "I'm glad I was able to do some good. This kingdom needs more of it, and I think you might be the one to help us achieve that." She left the room before I had a chance to respond.

The sound of swords clanging against one another flooded through my open window. Sighing, I pulled my boots over my feet and laced them. After tucking my tunic back inside my leathers, I strapped my leather sheath onto my thigh and slid my dagger inside.

Time for round two of training, here we go.

CHAPTER 26
ELENA

I made my way through the castle and out to the training ring, but only after getting lost a few times along the way. The endless hall-ways had me twisted around, and I somehow ended up in the kitchen. Twice.

Fortunately, I met the infamous Alana, head cook and the sweetest soul I had ever met. On my second return to the kitchen, I had to admit I was terribly lost. Her charming laugh bellowed throughout the kitchen and warmed my heart. A few minutes later, she was shoving berry muffins into my hands and giving me directions to the training ring, which was only a few doors down from the kitchen.

Pushing open the wooden door leading outside to the ring, I became immediately aware of the sweltering heat. I slung off my gambeson, leaving behind only my thin white tunic. The gambeson was meant to protect my chest and stomach during practice, but if I was going to be training in this heat, I might as well be comfortable doing it.

I was so distracted by the delicious blueberry muffin in my hand, it took me a moment to notice the striking woman standing at the side of the ring. She was a few inches taller than me and had legs for days. Her deep umber skin glistened in the sunlight and her long, onyx-colored hair bounced in the breeze. She must have noticed me gawking at her with a muffin in my mouth, because the smile she gave me could have touched her ears.

"Lady Elena, I'm guessing?"

Swallowing the chunk of muffin, I finally spoke. "Just Elena, no 'lady' here."

"Liam told me you had a fiery spirit. It's going to be a pleasure training with you, Elena. My name is Nayla Bahl. I'm a captain of the Royal Guard. Someone has got to keep those three in line."

Nayla tilted her head in the direction of the practice ring. When I saw the image in front of me, my mouth went dry instantly. I was so shocked by the view, I fumbled the muffin in my hand and it rolled onto the dirt beneath me. "Oops," I breathed.

"It's quite a sight to behold, isn't it?" Nayla smirked.

"Indeed," I whispered as I gawked at the men.

Three incredibly handsome men sparred in the middle of the ring, flaunting their perfectly sculpted bodies in front of us. As they sparred, sweat glistened on their beautifully sculpted abs. Swallowing, I watched as Declan wielded two swords against Liam and Killian. They were so in sync with each other's movements, a dangerously choreographed dance.

"You're drooling, you know."

I closed my gaping mouth as my cheeks flushed with embarrassment.

"It's okay." She let out a breathy laugh. "I had the same reaction when I saw them all training for the first time as well. It's natural to not be able to peel your eyes away."

We both observed them for a while before I mustered the courage to ask Nayla the questions burning within me. "How are you able to be captain?"

Her brow shot up, and I quickly recovered. "Personally, I think it's amazing. I used to have to train with my father in the early hours of the morning just so the other members in my town wouldn't treat me like an outcast. It's ridiculous that society can't handle women learning how to protect themselves."

With a smile, she began to tell me about her path to the castle.

Nayla was a Terran, someone who could use their dynamis to wield the earth. We had those in our town as well, but mostly all they could do was break up the soil so we could cultivate crops. Nayla's dynamis, however, was incredibly strong. She could move boulders, even stones. She could bring whole buildings down with just a flick of her dynamis. Declan had observed her dynamis in action during a Rebellion attack and had recruited her.

"My father wasn't too thrilled about it. When I decided to take the position as captain, he disowned me."

"What? He disowned you for wanting to be a captain in the Royal Guard?"

"Their loss," she shrugged. "I've never been one to follow along with their expectations. I was never going to enjoy living the life of a courtier, wasting my life in fancy dresses and being married off in a loveless marriage at the first chance my father got. I believe I was meant for more in my life. I was meant to make a difference, you know?"

"Yes, I understand completely," I said.

"Want to practice a bit until these boys are ready to have you join in with sparring? I see you brought your dagger."

A smile spread across my face as I answered, "Absolutely."

We made our way over to an area full of targets for archery, as well as training dummies stuffed with hay to practice sword fighting. I drifted towards the targets, noticing a selection of daggers sitting on a wooden table next to them. We both grabbed a few and aligned ourselves several feet away from the targets.

Nayla launched her dagger. It flew fiercely, landing in the closest ring next to the bullseye. She nodded toward me to take my turn. Finding my stance, I inhaled a deep breath and let my dagger fly. It landed smack dab in the middle of the bullseye as pride thrummed through me. I would never have been able to do that without the help of my father.

"Bullseye on the first try. Impressive...or just good luck," she hummed, tossing me another dagger. "Let's see if you can do it again."

She motioned for me to go again, so I did. Bullseye. Her eyes widened as she retrieved the dagger and had me repeat it five more times. Each time, the dagger hit its mark.

After my last attempt, clapping arose from behind us. Liam, Killian, and Declan were all perched on top of the training ring fence, mouths open in awe.

"I should have guessed you would be a natural at throwing daggers. Especially after witnessing you throw spoons with the same precision." Liam pulled out the silver spoon from his pocket, and I couldn't help but combust with laughter. "Come here, little lady."

He swept me up into his burly arms, then set me back down on the ground. Killian smiled big, jumping off the fence for an embrace as well.

"I feel like we haven't seen you in forever, Freckles."

"You saw me last night," I scoffed. "Still sticking with Freckles, I see?" He tossed his shoulders up in a shrug.

"It appears you've met our beautifully talented counterpart," Liam said as the biggest grin I'd ever seen him have spread across his face.

For a moment, I swore Nayla's cheeks flushed, but my line of sight was interrupted by something flying through the air. The rock that crashed against Liam's chest sent him barreling backwards off the fence. A plume of dirt exploded around him, and we all combusted in a roar of laughter. Liam scrambled back up to his feet, trying to wipe off the dirt now caked onto his sweaty chest and back. He glared at Nayla as she strolled over, patting him on the chest.

"Always have to be on your guard, *Captain*," she hummed playfully before returning to throwing daggers.

Liam growled under his breath as he stalked towards her. Killian shook his head as he followed them. Once again, I was alone with the prince.

"Are you ready for some more training?" he said, his voice gravelly.

Emboldened by my time throwing daggers, I strolled over to where he still sat on the fence. I gripped the bottom of his chin. "I think the real question is, Declan, are *you?*"

His throat bobbed as he rolled his lips between his teeth. Delighted, I sashayed into the training ring.

I could feel the heat rolling off him as he stalked behind me, like he was preparing for the hunt and I was his prey. A shiver ran down my back at the thought, and I turned around to face him, preparing my stance.

"Not bad, Wildfire," he cooed. "Raise your left arm up a little higher though, closer to your face."

Pursing my lips together, I adjusted my arm.

"Good girl," Declan whispered. Inhaling sharply, I tried to hide my visceral reaction to his words.

"There will be times where we might not be able to use our dynamis," he instructed as we circled each other once more. "Like when you've exhausted your well of dynamis, leaving you without your gift. There may also be times when we find ourselves without a weapon. This is when hand-to-hand combat and physical strength become important. Let's see what all that training with your father has taught you."

In the next moment, he leapt towards me, aiming for a blow to the shoulder. I spun out of his path, in turn leaving his side vulnerable. Right where my fist found purchase. I jumped back before he could launch another attack on me. Smiling, he nodded in approval as we began to circle again.

We each made a few more attempts but continued to evade one another. Sweat dampened our bodies, our chests heaving for air.

At last I saw an opening, so I rushed to take it. However, I was too slow. Declan grabbed my wrist and whipped me around until my back hit his chest with a thud. With me caged between his muscled arms, he leaned down and whispered, "It was a good effort, Wildfire, but it will take a few more sessions before you can take down the Lord of Shadows." The scruff of his beard bristled against my cheek, making me shiver.

As I thrashed against his hold, I searched my mind for a strategy from the multiple times I'd sparred with my father and Will. Frequently as they won, there had been an occasion or two when I had been able to take them both down.

With all my strength, I threw my head back into his, at the same time lifting both legs and kicking them back, right between his legs. Immediately, I was released from his clutches. His snarl was gargled as he hunched over in pain. I scrambled away, but I couldn't contain the laughter that fled out of me. That only caused Declan to growl even louder as his eyes blazed with fire when they met mine.

An involuntary shriek left my body as he zephyred towards me so quickly I didn't even have time to blink. The force of our collision was so abrupt that the thunderous sound radiated over the training ring as we cascaded into the ground.

Declan's heavy body weighed me down, knocking all the air out of my chest. Gasping for the little bit I had left, I gazed upon the prince's vicious smirk. He rolled off me with a huff, wincing as he rose to his feet. Sweat glistened down his body, and he extended his hand to help lift me up.

"Almost, Wildfire."

He towered over me, smirking, thinking that he had bested me once more. Little did he know I had one more trick up my sleeve.

I swung out my leg and swept it underneath his feet. The look of pure shock and terror would forever be embedded in my brain. I watched with glee as Declan fell back into the dirt with a crash so hard you could have probably heard it echo against the walls inside the castle.

Shouts and whistles rang out from behind us. Killian and Liam were shouting praise, and Nayla had a huge smile on her face as she jumped up and down alongside of them.

Pain radiated throughout my entire body, but I managed to pull myself up onto my feet. I strolled over to where Declan lay in the dirt. He groaned a little, palming his face. When his eyes met mine, I couldn't help but smile down at him. The muscles in my legs cried as I squatted next to him. Leaning down close to his ear, I whispered wickedly into it.

"Never underestimate your opponent, dear prince."

The corners of his eyes crinkled, and a smile tugged at the corners of his lips.

"**B**y the gods, who knew our little lady had it in her. She knocked the great Shadow Lord straight on his ass!" Liam slapped his knee.

"That deserves a few rounds of drinks." Nayla tossed her arm over my shoulder. "What do you think, Elena? For once, we all have a day off at the same time. Let's introduce you to the City of Shadows tonight."

"That is if the prince can walk that far." Killian smirked over at Declan.

Everyone burst out in infectious laughter again, as Declan's scowl only grew deeper as he grumbled behind us.

"A night of drinking sounds fantastic." I bounced giddily as we walked. "Can I invite Clara? Also, will there be whiskey?"

Liam pat my back. "You can always count on whiskey with us, little lady."

Nayla pulled me into her side and whispered, "You should definitely invite Clara. I know someone who would be *very* happy."

Glancing between the three men with curiosity, I noticed one in particular with rosy cheeks. Killian shot me a shy smile.

Oh, tonight is going to be fun indeed.

CHAPTER 27

ELENA

As soon as we parted inside the castle, I ran up the stairs and down our hall towards Clara's room. She accepted the invitation, on one condition—I had to let her help me get ready. There was no argument from me. Even the gods knew I needed help in that department.

After taking an extremely long, steamy shower, I made my way over to the armoire to find something to wear tonight. Pulling out a pair of black leather leggings and some high-lacing boots, I thumbed through the different tunic options I had. I settled on a black one with flowy arms and lace around the plunging neckline. It needed a little cinching around the waist, so I found a black corset. Clara would have to help me put it on when she arrived.

Just as I was finishing lacing up my boots, I heard pounding at my door. I shook my head as I made my way over to the door. Before I could open it all the way, Clara shoved her way in.

"Let's get you ready for tonight! Full disclosure, I brought wine." Her face dropped. "Oh, and Alaric wanted me to bring this to you as well."

In her hands was a small envelope sealed shut with a wax stamp bearing the king's crest. With trembling hands, I opened it and read the contents.

Clara pushed me over to the small blue velvet chair next to the desk where Eloise had helped me get ready the night before. "Well, what did His Majesty have to say?"

Tossing the envelope onto the desk, I sighed.

"Tomorrow begins my first parade of the dignitaries. An early brunch, and I must wear one of those hideous dresses."

Her eyes darted to the open wardrobe and cringed at the sight of some of the feathery gowns. "Does he want you to literally embrace the Phoenix?" We chuckled in unison.

"That is a lot of extravagant feathers."

She shook her head while she helped me lace up the corset. "Declan is going to have a *very* hard time concentrating tonight with you wearing *that*." She began working on braiding parts of my loose hair.

"Your cousin doesn't look at me in that way." I smiled weakly, knowing that was a half lie. "Even if he was, it would be forbidden. Also..." I sighed heavily as Will rushed through my mind. "I'm not sure I'm ready to open my heart again."

The brush stilled against my hair and she held my gaze in the mirror. "Elena, you'd have to live under a rock to not see the way he looks at you. In fact, I haven't seen him look at someone the way he looks at you in...well, I don't think I've ever seen it. Until now," she mused, until she noticed me gnawing on my lip. "The Flame, the one who lived in your town. Is he the reason you don't want to open your heart again?"

"Yes." My stomach churned just thinking of it all again. "We were friends. Well, until one day when it became...more." The memory flashed before me. "Everything seemed great, until he—until he blamed me for ruining his life and being the reason he has his dynamis."

"That's horrible, Lena. You don't believe that though, right?" she hummed from behind me. "Right?"

"No." The lie was barely audible as it fled my lips.

Clara must have felt my mood turn sullen, because she didn't say another word. As she finished arranging my hair into a beautiful half-up, half-down style, I observed my transformation from peasant to courtier. She spun me around and told me to close my eyes as she began to work on my face.

"Speaking of people being distracted tonight..." I stole a glimpse of her biting her lip. "What do you think Killian is going to think about what *you* are wearing?"

Her chestnut locks were braided into a similar style as mine. The rest hung loose and curled down around her waist. She wore a long satin dress that was a deep shade of plum, setting her bright eyes alight. "Changing the subject, I see?"

"Can you blame me?" I shrugged. Clara chuckled to herself, as she applied a vibrant peach shade to my lips. "You know, he was blushing when I asked if I could invite you to go with us tonight."

"Really?" she whispered.

"Really."

The cutest pink tint flushed her cheeks. "We've been dancing around each other for years. Every time I thought he was going to take a chance, he would talk about his duty to the kingdom. He has always been extremely focused on making sure nothing gets in the way of their mission...they all have."

I sat for a moment as I considered her words. Assuming "they" was the group of captains and a brooding lord, I was curious what mission they were all so intent on fulfilling at all costs. It had to be something important enough to overlook finding happiness with someone they loved.

Instead of falling into the spiral of what ifs, I chose to cling onto hope. Hope that Killian and Clara would have their chance one day. I couldn't think of two people more perfect for each other. Just the idea of it made my heart sing.

"All done, Lady Elena."

She turned me around so that I could look at myself in the mirror. Gold flecks sparkled over my eyelids, and the way she used the charcoal to line my eyes made them appear more open and wider than ever before. Just like Eloise, she had managed to me feel beautiful, something I didn't feel often.

"Thank you."

"Anytime, Lena." She tilted her glass of wine to her lips, finishing it in one gulp. Clara noticed my raised eyebrows and let out a snort.

"Being trapped inside this castle for so long, you learn how to grow a tolerance for a hefty amount of wine."

I followed suit and drained my glass in one gulp. "I might as well join you then."

"You're a quick learner, Lena." We assessed our appearance once more in the mirror, and she squeezed my hand. "Let's get going before Liam drinks all the whiskey."

Clara practically dragged me down the stairs. I thought my arm might detach from my body. By the time we set foot in the open-air Killian, Liam and Nayla were all waiting outside.

Clara ran ahead and jumped into Nayla's arms, knocking her over, and they tumbled onto the ground. The men chased after them, trying to bring both back to their feet. Nayla and Clara just pulled them straight down to the ground alongside them.

An ache blossomed in my heart as I watched the four of them laughing on the ground. The only friend I'd ever had was Will, and now I was questioning if that friendship had been as real as I'd thought it had been.

I'd known this group of people for an incredibly short time, yet somehow, they'd filled a void in my soul that I hadn't known I needed filling. They replaced the emptiness that I'd had since the day we rode out of my town.

They'd been a flicker of light in the dark. Despite the fact they lived in proximity to such evil—the king and Alastor—here they were thriving, living proof that light could still grow in the darkness. I might not always understand the decisions of the gods or fate, but a glimmer of hope settled in my heart that these people had been brought into my life for a reason.

As I started towards them, a thick arm wrapped around my middle, pulling me back.

"You look absolutely enchanting tonight, Lena."

"Dec—?" I breathed. He spun me around before I could finish speaking.

With one hand still wrapped around my middle, he smoothed away a rogue hair that had fallen into my face. Just the slightest caress of his calloused fingers, and I melted like a puddle.

"Are you ready to see the city?"

"Yes."

One word. That was all I was able to squeak out. Declan spun me around and gave me a gentle shove to the small of my back towards the direction of our friends. Adrenaline rushed through me, and I couldn't help but feel giddy. The night air felt electric, and my soul felt alive with pulsing energy.

"Let's go have some fun—that is if you wild animals can find your feet again," Declan quipped.

In unison, they all shouted back.

"To the tavern!"

CHAPTER 28

DECLAN

Though my smile was fixed, underneath I was boiling over with nerves. I hadn't been lying when I'd told Elena that this city was beautiful. It held so many memories for me of a time before evil crept its way into it.

There was still beauty within it, but its light had been forever dimmed by my father's actions. Just like Pinepeak, there were some who knew the truth of my purpose here in the city, but the rest? They only knew me as the malicious Lord of Shadows.

As we crossed the bridge connecting the castle to the rest of the city, Elena's eyes sparkled with wonder. The closer to the castle, the more affluence was evident. Flowers blossomed on top of pristinely painted windowsills, larger homes with extravagant gardens and balconies. Those outside nodded their heads toward us as we walked, but as soon as we came closer to the main courtyard of the city, the looks began to shift.

There was still a vibrance of life here, but its luster had begun to wane. Children ran laughing through the street around us, some wearing shoes so worn that their toes peeked out. Merchants stood outside with carts only half full of products to sell due to the tariffs

Alastor issued. While we lived comfortably in our lavish castle, the rest of the city was struggling to put dinner on the table.

It was one thing to observe my city with my own eyes, but no one could have prepared me for the feelings I would get watching it through Elena's. Her eyes gleamed as she took in the city, pausing every so often in front of a merchant, dazzling them with her charm.

They adored her, placing pastries, bracelets, and even a pair of earrings into her palms. Of course, my compassionate Wildfire tried her best to turn them down, telling them she couldn't possibly take their hard-earned pieces for free. The merchants hushed her, telling her how honored they would be for the Light Phoenix to have something of theirs. A smile tugged at my lips every time she thanked them profusely, often to the point where I had to pull her away to keep us walking towards the pub.

Even when the looks turned disgruntled towards my captains and I, she surprised me, inching closer towards me or pulling me into her as they spoke, forcing them to interact with me in a more positive manner.

The gesture ignited a flame inside of me that I hadn't felt in a very long time. Every time I glanced at her beautiful face, she continued to melt my cold heart. She was like no one I have ever met before. This woman challenged me at every turn and had so much compassion and strength inside of her, strength that she didn't even believe that she had. There was a deep-seated need within me to help her realize it for herself.

It had become increasingly hard to resist the pull that I felt in my chest, the one that tugged me towards her whenever she was around. My entire world shifted when she entered the room, and I was desperately struggling to maintain my balance. Elena had no idea the power that she held over me.

Reality cut me deep as a man shoved against my shoulder and shouted, "Go wash the blood off your hands!"

Rage snarled through my lips, and my shadows rippled from my arms as my fist wrapped around his throat.

He spit onto my tunic while yelling towards Elena, "Stay away from him, all he brings is destruction."

My grip tightened around his throat until he made a choking sound.

A meek voice reached my ears. "Dec...don't." Lena's eyes were wide, but not full of fear. They were full of concern. For me.

I lowered the man to his feet and shoved him away. As he scurried away, I wiped the spit off my tunic with a cloth from my pocket. The concern on her face grew.

How could I give this woman all of me when I was nothing but a shell of my former self? Too much darkness resided in my soul. It would shatter all that was good about her. I didn't even love the person I was, so how could I give her the all-encompassing love that she rightfully deserved?

A sting formed behind my eyes, but I reined it in, tugging it back down into the depths and locking it away. No one needed to see those dark parts of me. Tonight, I'd put that away and embrace the little bit of light for however long she would grace me with her presence.

Elena

A piece of my heart chipped when the man tore Declan's grin from his face. Especially when the man told him that all he brought about was destruction, words that I had spoken about my own self only a few days ago. One more thing that Declan and I seemed to have in common.

It had taken all my energy to remain calm when others had given him scowls or whispered disparaging words as we stopped at the merchants' booths. I was well aware that the man wiping the spit off his tunic before me must have a troubled past, but the more I got to know him, the less I could wrap my mind around why there was so much animosity towards him. Especially when he had more compassion in his pinkie than either his father or Alastor. Things just didn't add up.

Even though it was evident there was a clear line between the affluent and underprivileged within this city, it somehow still felt full of such vibrance and light, it astounded me. Some of the merchants had genuine, vivacious personalities. They lured me in with bright smiles and thoughtful words. Their carts being sparse with products, and clothes showing signs of wear, made this place feel a little like home. There were people still struggling inside the capital walls as well.

Declan shoved the cloth into his pockets. When he caught my gaze, it was as if the frustration in his body shifted elsewhere. His shoulders relaxed and his feet found their way towards me. As I spread the widest smile I could across my face, his own lips lifted. He took my shoulder and guided me towards the rest of our group. Together, we made our way inside the Electric Eel tavern.

For a quaint little tavern on the outside, the inside was bursting with vitality. Musicians played a lively tune, while others danced in front of the large hearth. As we entered, some patrons vacated their seats. Liam shook his head as they passed, none of them acknowledging us. It was almost like they were scared to do so.

Nayla and Clara tugged me to join the dance while the men found us a table large enough to contain us all.

They twirled and swung their hips back and forth to the music as I stood to the side smiling and clapping to the beat. As fun as it looked, I'd never really danced before and I wasn't about to embarrass myself by flailing around on the dance floor. Nayla frowned as soon as she observed me being a wallflower. Linking her arm around mine, she pulled me in and started to help me sway back and forth in time with the music. Eventually, my body took over, and we each took turns twisting and turning each other as we bounced up and down to the lively tune.

We were exhausted by the time the song ended, so we made our way back to the table. Each of them slid into a seat, leaving only one spot left for me. *Thanks, ladies.*

I slid into my wooden chair with a little more vigor than intended, causing me to bump shoulders with Declan. The contact sent a bolt of lightning sizzling through my body. To cover my gasp, I took a hefty swig of the pint of ale in front of me. Liam concealed his grin within his glass.

A woman with long, striking blonde hair approached the table, leaning over to talk with Nayla and Clara. As I sipped my ale, I pretended to be focused on the men's conversation rather than the one that was going on next to me.

"I'll make them some more potent elixirs tomorrow and bring them to you." Clara spoke softly.

"It's started to spread. We're up to four now." The blonde's eyes fell to the table. "I'm afraid that we won't be able to save them if we can't figure out what is making them ill."

Nayla placed a hand on the woman's shoulder. "I wish there was a way to get Clara out there." The woman nodded in agreement, and Clara's lashes fluttered closed.

Wherever this place was must have been outside of the capital, or her body would not be drooping with remorse. Nayla lifted her glass to change the subject.

"We should play a drinking game," Nayla suggested, as Clara knocked her glass of ale to hers in agreement.

"I don't think I've ever played a drinking game," I mumbled, hoping no one would notice.

"What?" Liam slammed his glass down on the table, splashing ale over the side. "We must fix this travesty immediately!" Liam shouted over the crowd of people who filled the small tavern. "Lucille, dear? Come over here, please."

The woman who had been talking to Clara and Nayla made her way toward Liam. "You better not ask me for favors, especially since you still owe me for the last tab you left behind." She raised an eyebrow, then placed her hands on her hips.

Killian and Liam both dove into their pockets, each tossing a handful of coins into her awaiting palm. My mouth hung open. "Just how large was your last tab, gentlemen?"

Everyone at the table burst into laughter, even Lucille. I slunk down in my seat, but I couldn't help the smile that stirred within my lips.

"This coin is for our past tabs, and tonight's, Freckles," Killian said, tossing a wink my way.

"Well, if that's the case, here you go, Lucille." Declan tossed her a purse of his own. She leaned over and whispered something into Declan's ear. "This should cover all the supplies they need," he whispered back, giving me a small clue to the puzzle I was trying to figure out.

"Now that's all settled, what can I get you fine ladies and gentlemen?" Lucille slipped the small purse into her apron.

"Another round of ale for us all, and two bottles of your finest whiskey with some glasses, please."

"Of course, Your Highness."

"Oh, and Lucille?"

She paused, whipping her hair around.

"You wouldn't happen to have a set of dice, would you?"

She nodded, and Declan settled into a satisfied smile as she left our table to retrieve our order.

"Ale *and* two bottles of whiskey? I fear my liver may not survive the night," I winced, partly joking, but also remembering what happened the last time that I'd had my fair share of whiskey.

Everyone laughed, then they got swept away in conversation. Declan leaned down close and whispered into my ear. "Wildfire, just relax and be yourself tonight." His tender gaze assessed my doubtful one as he tucked my hair over my ear. "I'll take care of you."

Be myself. Sadly, I didn't even know how. Twenty-three years of life and I was still trying desperately to figure that out.

Lucille dropped off our ales, whiskey, glasses and dice. The men poured whiskey into glasses and slid them in front of us all. Killian rolled the dice between his fingers. "I should probably explain the rules to Elena, eh?"

"Of course, you brute," Clara said, slapping Killian in the shoulder.

Nayla caught my expression at the same time, both of us sharing an amused smile.

"Yes, please explain, you brute," I said, causing both Killian and Clara to blush.

"Okay, Freckles. The object of the game is to roll even numbers. You roll anything else, and you'll have to take a sip of your whiskey. If you run out of whiskey, well, you can start sipping your ale. Got it?"

Dear gods, I really might not walk out here alive.

"Got it," I declared with all the false bravado in the kingdom.

Declan, Killian and Liam all exchanged a mischievous glance.

"I propose that we put a wager on the game," Declan proclaimed. Both Killian and Liam raised their glasses in approval.

"Why am I not surprised?" An annoyed sigh followed Nayla's words. "Alright, what is your wager, gentlemen?"

Liam and Killian both looked towards Declan, waiting for him to make the decision for them. "Ladies versus men. The best of five rounds wins."

"Seems too easy." She folded her arms as she lifted her brow. "What does the winner receive?"

Declan leaned back, stretching both hands behind his head, taking his time to ponder the request. All our gazes were locked on him, and I lifted my glass of ale to take a long sip. His malicious gaze shifted to mine, causing me to inhale my drink. Mirth spread over his face as I cleared my throat a few times to recover.

"If you ladies win, the three of us must get up in front of the entire tavern and do a little song and dance for everyone. If we win, you all dance with us for the rest of the evening."

Killian's face went pale. Either he wasn't the best singer or he'd realized he might have to dance with Clara.

"Deal." Nayla said.

"Ladies first," Declan placed the dice in my hand.

The dice shook between my anxious hands for far too long. Tension formed on everyone's faces. I finally let go and watched the dice as they rolled to a painfully slow stop.

"A six?" Liam grumbled. "Damn beginner's luck." Raising their glasses to their lips, they begrudgingly took the first sip.

Killian was up next, rolling a three. Clara rolled a five, Declan a ten, and finally Nayla rolled a two. By the time we made it through our first round, the burn of the whiskey had awakened my body. We also all had to refill our glasses.

It was a thrill, as I hung on the edge of my seat with each roll of the dice. The night lingered on, and we eventually made it to our second bottle of whiskey. The stakes were high; we were tied four to four. Anticipation tingled all around me, and we all went still as Declan prepared to take his turn.

As he shook the dice, my heart began to beat faster. It would be fine if the ladies won, but what if we lost? I could think of only one person I would be forced to dance with.

The breath froze in my lungs as the dice tumbled across the thick wooden table. One stopped as the other continued to spin, then fell to a halt. Twelve. The men had won.

Their glasses clinked together as they took a celebratory sip of whiskey alongside us. As if on cue, the group of musicians in the corner started to play another lively tune, and people flooded to the tiny dance floor.

Declan's hand slid across my thigh under the table and my heart pounded with anticipation while I waited for him to ask me to dance.

Our intense gaze was broken as Killian pulled my arm and yanked me onto the dance floor. Declan seethed at the back of Killian's head as everyone else's mouths dropped wide open.

Killian swung me around the dance floor with ease. I was shocked by my ability to keep up. Alcohol appeared to do wonders for my dancing skills. Liam and Clara joined us on the floor, and a few minutes later Declan and Nayla. As we kept dancing, curiosity and my need to meddle overtook me.

"You can't avoid her forever," I whispered to Killian.

He looked longingly towards Clara, her chestnut waves swaying back and forth as Liam twirled her around in circles. "I could say the same about you."

I scoffed. "My situation is entirely different."

"Is it?"

"It is," I said firmly, trying not to show the faltering in my emotions. Our movements slowed to a sway as everyone else danced around us, still lively.

"You're right, Elena." Killian sighed. "I can't avoid love forever. I've spent too long listening to my head instead of my heart. Every moment in our lives is precious, and it's about time I learned to find life in each of them. Instead of waiting for those moments to stumble upon me, I must find the courage to seek them myself."

His words hit me so deeply, my feet froze to the floor. Killian playfully tugged on a strand of my hair to get my attention. The music changed from the upbeat tune to a slow melancholy ballad. Before Killian left to chase after Clara, he leaned close to my ear and whispered, "Go live in your moment, Elena."

He kissed my palm, leaving me standing in a daze, as he tugged Clara away from Liam and into his arms. Clara's eyes sparkled up at him as he pulled her closer to his chest, both hands cinched around her waist. Liam grinned so wide that the warmth of happiness cracked through his ward, sweeping across to me as my dynamis pulled it in. He grabbed Nayla by the arm and pulled her into a dance. I could feel the intensity of their gaze from here as they stared into each other's eyes.

The whiskey and ale had begun to have its effect. The room swayed while my feet remained planted to the floor. Darkness flooded my vision as I took in the sinfully gorgeous man before me. Dressed in black from head to toe, he wore his sleeves rolled up to his elbows, the top two buttons unbuttoned, showing slivers of the tattoos of his shadows inked across his body.

"Dare to dance with me, Wildfire?" The timbre of Declan's deep voice rumbled through me.

At a loss for words, I simply dipped my head. His hand slid around to the small of my back as the other slid down my arm until it found my hand and intertwined it with his own. He pulled me closer into him, and I let my throbbing head rest against his chest as he rocked me back and forth to the music. His heart thundered against my ear, and I tried my best not to smile. Declan was nervous too.

Leaning back, I searched for his gaze. I was met with a lazy grin as Declan's thumb brushed back and forth against my back. He dropped his other hand, which had been squeezing mine as we danced. The absence of it made my already weakened knees wobble. Declan's knuckles skimmed alongside my cheek, and the air hummed with electricity around us.

Time seemed to stand still for us, our eyes and bodies locked by an invisible tether. In the background, the music switched to another upbeat tune. With chaos swirling around us, we swayed slowly back and forth.

"You want to get out of here?" he said softly, lifting my chin to make sure I answered.

My mouth went dry. Nothing good could come from the two of us being alone together, but I couldn't help the anticipation that was building from the thought. The pull towards this man was growing stronger each day, and I was finding it difficult to keep fighting against it.

I took a deep breath and surprised myself with the words that fled my lips. "Let's get out of here."

CHAPTER 29

ELENA

Placing his hand in mine, Declan intertwined our fingers, tugging me through the bodies surrounding us. He leaned into Killian's ear and told him we were leaving. From behind Declan, I sheepishly waved at Clara as we made our way to the exit. Nayla and Liam had returned to our table, laughing and clinking their glasses of ale together as we approached.

Liam grabbed Declan's cloak from his chair and tossed it over to him. The three of them exchanged a knowing smile. My gaze fell to my feet, the heat warming my cheeks as usual. With a tug, Declan nudged me in front of him. Hands gripped my hips as he guided me through the mass of Elysians inside the tavern until we finally made it out the door.

Night air cooled my heated cheeks as we strolled through the cobblestone street. I trembled under the proximity of Declan's presence. His hand brushed against mine, catching me off guard as I stumbled over a cobblestone. He grabbed my arm swiftly, righting me before I could blink.

When I looked up at him, a sinfully handsome grin made my legs wobble once more. Golden light from the shops shone across his tan skin as his forest green eyes glistened. For once, he seemed calm, perhaps even at peace. He swept his fingers through his hair. My teeth pinched the flesh of my lower lip as I watched. His darkened eyes caught me and rolled down to my lips, where they lingered.

"We're going to have to work on those little habits of yours, Lena. Before they completely undo me."

The sound of his voice rumbled all the way down my body, warming me. He placed my arm inside his own and we continued to walk back to the castle.

"The people seem to struggle here, like we do outside the city walls. Yet, beneath it all, I can still see the vibrance of the city that once was. The one you still find beautiful." I spoke tentatively, trying to distract the tension between us with conversation. "I suppose I don't understand how opinions about you differ so much from one Elysian to the next."

Declan flinched before wiping his face clear of emotion. "They do the best they can to thrive, even when my father and Alastor do nothing but blockade their happiness." He paused his steps, considering how much more he wanted to share.

"The city lives in a constant state of fear, always afraid of what might happen. If something rubs my father or Alastor the slightest way, disastrous things happen. My father will deprive them of food, block their access to our aqueducts. Sometimes"—his gaze dropped from mine— "he'll even enforce raids, taking men and boys right out of their homes, conscripting them into the Royal Guard."

My lips parted in disbelief. Guilt flashed across his face, and his eyelashes lowered to the cobblestones.

"I told you, Elena, I am not a good man." The words hung in the air between us. An argument formed on my lips, but he placed his thumb over them, pinning them closed. "I'm the general of the Royal Guard, Elena. Who do you think enforces all their commands? Who do you think has to watch the faces of my people fill with agony or terror as we approach? I have done terrible things in the name of my father. Actions that will haunt me for the rest of my life."

"I'm aware of your broodiness and your occasional moments of rage," I jested, trying to lighten the mood, but the joke fell flat. I cleared my throat and tried again. "However, the more I get to know you, the more I see how compassionate you are. It's so genuine that I don't understand how others cannot see it as I do. You're clearly nothing like your father."

Declan's entire body tensed as he absorbed my words. "I wish that was true, but I fear I'm more like him than you think."

"Explain it, then."

He smoothed a hand over his mouth. "Not tonight, Lena."

Observing the tension rolling off him in waves, I concluded this part of our conversation was over. "I'm still trying to figure out why everyone was so cordial to me tonight. I'll be honest, I'm not used to this much social interaction, much less ones that are positive."

"Having the Light Phoenix alongside us seemed to lighten their spirits a bit. It gave them something to focus their attention on. It filled them with something we all haven't had in a while." Declan played with the ends of my hair that had fallen across my chest. Shivers ran down my back as the heat of his fingers brushed against me.

"What could my presence possibly fill these people with?" I questioned, still trying to find distraction from this tension between us.

Though I might be the Light Phoenix in their eyes, I was just Elena Morrigan. They didn't know the real me, the one consumed by fear and weakness lurking underneath her mask. What could I possibly offer these people?

"Hope." His words silenced my thoughts. "You've given them hope, Elena. You are a living symbol of a chance for all of us in this kingdom to find peace once more." He stepped closer as my breathing picked up pace.

"You've given *me* hope. Just being around you makes me want to be a better version of myself. Wildfire, you radiate so much light and goodness with everything that you do. Hope is the most powerful magic within us. It's unwavering faith that no matter what shadows the darkness tries to cast over us, we will always be able to find our way through. Hope is our light in this darkness."

"Dec, I'm not all light and goodness. I know what it feels like to be judged, looked down upon for your failures...your differences." The tears began to well, but I blinked them back. "I've lost patients because of my failures. I wasn't enough to find a cure, or create an elixir, or even save..." My throat swelled up, and I couldn't bring myself to mention my mother. "I have no right to inspire hope in these people. They deserve better," I breathed.

"Elena," He wrapped his palms around my arms and held me straight. "You've been underestimating yourself from the moment I met you."

He tucked my arm underneath his and started to walk towards the castle. I wasn't sure if it was from the whiskey or our conversation, but I was still feeling a little unstable.

"There's something I'd like to show you."

We walked in silence up the hill and over the bridge towards the castle. Instead of heading through the door we'd come out of earlier, we took a turn, walking through the courtyard in front of the castle. The fragrant smell of herbs and flowers could only be described as heavenly. Violet wisteria swayed in the breeze above us as we walked under the arches that lined the gravel path. Approaching a stone wall covered with layers of ivy, I noticed a smaller wooden door.

"I'd like to show you one of my mother's favorite spaces in this castle. One that has become special to me as well." As he pushed the creaking wooden door open, my breath stilled. Declan gently nudged me inside.

This garden was the most magical place I had ever laid eyes on. Little orbs of light, no doubt summoned by simple magic, hovered in lanterns hanging from the trees around the garden. There were flowers in every color, shape and size, all in glorious bloom. The light from the lanterns made everything shimmer in a golden haze.

My eyes landed on the twisted trunk adorned with vibrant citrine leaves that looked aflame under the moonlight. It lured me towards it with its ethereal wonder. Declan followed behind me and paused when I stopped underneath the canopy of branches.

"I've always wanted to see a gods' tree in person. It's absolutely breathtaking."

Declan rounded the side of me, and we both stared in awe. "It is. We used to hold ceremonies here, even bring in members of the city... until..." Declan's throat bobbed. My hand found his and it tightened around my own.

The trunk was darker than I had imagined, but not entirely. In fact, it almost seemed like it had darkened from the roots up. I reached out in curiosity to touch the bark of the tree.

The moment my fingers touched the bark, my dynamis flared, jolting my body. A loud hum vibrated inside my head, like the buzz of thousands of beehives.

I jerked my hand back and the connection was broken. My gaze fell to my hand. A dim glow pulsed where the dynamis still swirled beneath.

"You alright?"

"The bark just scratched me a bit," I fibbed, and tucked my hand out of sight. With a nod, he turned and walked towards a bench surrounded by pastel-toned peonies.

Confusion swirled through me almost as quickly as my dynamis. I decided whatever had just happened must have been a result of the whiskey still muddling around in my brain. As I walked towards the bench where Declan was sitting, I beheld the most alluring sight in this entire garden.

As if he could feel the heat of my gaze, his eyes rose to meet mine. Declan stared at me the same way I had viewed this garden, in awe.

I sat down on the cold stone, and he placed a hand on my thigh. Goosebumps prickled over my arms.

"May I?" His grin widened at my shocked expression, then he dropped his gaze to the dagger strapped to my thigh. I palmed my red face and nodded.

He removed the dagger, then stepped behind me towards the peony bush. With a quick slice, Declan cut off a bloom from the bush, twirling it around in his fingers as he walked back towards me. Then, he bent down on one knee and placed my dagger inside its sheath. With his other hand, he lifted the flower towards my face. "For you."

My heart pounded against my ribcage as he rose to his feet and sat beside me. "Thank you," I breathed as I inhaled the sweet, floral scent of the petals. "This garden is truly ethereal, Declan. Peonies must have been your mother's favorite. There's a bush in every color imaginable."

"They were." He spoke softly as his eyes roved over the bushes. "She once told me that they were the greatest symbol of the transformation of our spirit—the way that they take their time to bloom, unfurl their petals a little at a time, until finally they're full of life, ready to show the world their vibrance. When I look at them now, I must agree. There's no better representation of enduring life in all its stages."

"That's beautiful, Declan," I whispered. "It's no wonder why this garden is so special to you."

"I truly thought nothing could ever outshine its beauty." He paused, the silence unnerving, as he rubbed his palms over the top of his pants. "However, seeing you bathed in golden light, surrounded by all the things I hold dear..." He swallowed deeply. "Nothing will ever compare."

Declan's eyes fluttered closed, as if he was painting a mental picture of this very moment inside his mind. My heart swelled, feeling the tug in my chest from that invisible string that always seemed to pull whenever we were near each other.

The night sky beckoned my gaze. I inhaled a deep, calming breath as my eyes roved over the shadowed sky illuminated by thousands of twinkling stars. This was my favorite place, underneath the stars.

"What are you thinking about, Wildfire?" His deep voice rumbled beside me.

My mouth became void of moisture, and my tongue rolled over my bottom lip. Declan's pupils widened underneath his thick lashes. As I bit my lip, he clenched his jaw. The air around us thickened with tension.

"I was thinking about what we were talking about earlier."

"Mmhmm," he hummed.

I glanced back up at the sky and his gaze trailed mine.

"Something about the night sky has always entranced me. Nobody knows this, but I've always feared the dark, even to this day." I shrugged my shoulders as I divulged my secret, catching Declan's grin out of the corner of my eye. "However, every night I gathered the courage to climb on the roof of our house and look up at the stars. The stillness of night has always felt peaceful." I sighed, twirling the ends of my hair. "Alone, just me and the stars, I'd tell them about my day. Pouring out every secret, every fear, every happy or sad moment became a nightly ritual. As silly as it sounds, it always gave me a sense of peace, maybe even hope that the gods were up there listening to me, that I was still on the right path in my life. I'm reminded of that hope every time I look up at the sky. It's really the perfect balance of light and dark." I paused to steady my rapid heartbeat. "Maybe you and I are like the night sky, a perfect balance of both..."

When I glanced back towards Declan, I met his hopeful eyes, glistening with wonder, as if he already knew what I was about to say next.

"You can't have the light without the darkness, Declan. Without the darkness of the night, we would never notice the brilliance of the stars. Someone wise once told me that it's through our fears and weaknesses that we discover our strengths. I agree, because it's in the darkness that our light shines the brightest."

At the sound of his breath hitching, something inside of me broke. Every shield I'd built within myself for years came tumbling down.

Twisting my trembling hand in his tunic, I pulled him towards me. With a heart beating outside of my chest, I slid my hand around the back of his neck as I hovered my lips above his. It was now or never. Was I to be smart and think with my head, or was I going to give into the pull of my heart?

"Oh, Hells...fuck it."

As our mouths collided, I could feel his smile spread across my lips.

Our kiss was slow and tender as he explored every curve of my lips. He treated my mouth like an uncharted land that he was desperate to discover. A low rumble rose from his chest as he wrapped his hand around the back of my neck, pulling me tighter. I gasped at his touch, and he pulled me on top of his lap.

Every kiss became more needy, passion blooming within every caress. Grabbing the back of my head and tilting it up, he deepened our kiss. His tongue invaded my mouth, swirling with the same intensity as his lips as they crashed against mine. The earthy scent of forest and spice invaded my nose, and he tasted like sweet whiskey, a seductive combination that overloaded my senses. There was nothing I wanted more than to devour a whole bottle of him, to be intoxicated by his entire being.

If I was honest, I'd wanted this from the moment he'd slammed me against that tree in the forest. Everything about this moment was all-consuming. I craved to feel this good *everywhere*.

As if reading my mind, fingers tightened around my hips, and my entire body felt aflame. Declan's hand slid its way up my back, tracing along the ridges of my spine. He tugged at my hair, exposing my neck to him. Lips wrapped around my earlobe, followed by the sting of his teeth as they scraped over the smooth surface of my skin.

There was no stopping my thighs as they clenched around him, and his hands dug deeper into my body in response. Each delicate kiss he pressed into my neck sent my emotions spiraling even further. Sharp pain pierced my body as the thrum of dynamis shivered against my skin.

It was all too much, yet not enough. I never wanted the moment to stop, but I knew it needed to. No matter how much I wanted Declan, deep down I knew it could never be, and the emotions created by those fears were crushing me.

"Dec," I panted, placing my hands on his chest, struggling to push away from him.

My swollen lips quivered, tears building behind my eyes. This was the most incredible moment of my life, and here I was ruining it. Declan made me feel like no one else had ever made me feel. Whether

I liked it or not, he always told me the truth. He'd seen me at my worst, most vulnerable moments, and still pursued me at every turn. A strange sense of familiarity arose every time he was near. Sometimes when he was around me, I even caught myself feeling like we'd been here before.

However, the overwhelming guilt of what I had just done was dragging me under. The king and Lord Alastor would never allow anything to happen between us. Gods, if they ever found out what happened tonight, I could only imagine what terrible things they might do to Declan or the people in the city he cared so much for.

Guilt tugged at my stomach as my mind wandered to the first boy to have tempted my heart, Will. The tear he'd sliced in my heart still felt raw and unresolved. Yet here I was, on the lap of another man. Lately, I was starting to not recognize the person I was turning into.

Each sting throbbing inside me was a reminder to stop being so selfish and remember what I was truly here for. Silly romantic feelings weren't important, and I should never have let them get in the way. If the king followed through with his deal, I'd be free to go back to my town. All I needed to do was follow his orders, and I'd be able to go back to protect the ones I loved. As delusional as that idea might be, it was a hope that I clung to.

"What's wrong, beautiful?" Declan tilted my chin with the tip of his finger.

"I—I'm so sorry..." My voice trembled as I spoke. "I want to, but I —I just can't," I whispered, choking down a sob, a tear running down my cheek.

Swiping it away tenderly with his thumb, he looked at me with such a sincere and heartfelt grin that I almost abandoned all common sense and kissed him all over again.

"There's nothing to apologize for. Wildfire, you have completely entranced me. I fear you have sassed your way into my cold, brooding heart and I can no longer evade my feelings."

My lips twitched at his attempt at humor.

His forehead pressed against my temple as he continued to whisper. "Patience is not something I'm well known for, but for you, I would do anything. Especially when it's something I've grown to value more than all the wonders of this realm." A mischievous smirk tugged against his lips.

"So, Elena. I'll wait. For you, and *only* you. No matter how long it may take. In this life or the next, I'll be waiting." He placed his hand over my thundering heart. "When you are ready to open this to me"— he tapped my chest, then placed my palm over his—"I'll be there with open arms ready to protect it with all of mine."

If those words weren't enough to shatter me completely, he leaned forward and placed a tender kiss upon my forehead. The same warmth that had enveloped me at dinner with the king cascaded over me. All at once, the pain that penetrated my body from my emotions ceased. Hushed were the endless rambling thoughts of my mind.

"Let's get you back to your room. You've got to sleep off all that alcohol before we train tomorrow." He waggled his eyebrows and I couldn't bury the laugh that welled out of me.

Shoulder to shoulder, we walked all the way back to my room. Each brush of his body against mine ignited shivers through my already sensitive skin. When we came to my door, he lifted my hand and pressed a kiss into my palm. "Sweet dreams, Elena."

With a nod goodbye, he strolled down to his room, opening and closing the door behind him as I watched, frozen in the moment. Every instinct in my body shouted at me to run after him and jump straight into his arms.

Instead, I forced my legs to carry me into my room. Once inside, I leapt into my bed, clothes and all, and curled into a ball.

Tears tore out of me until I faded to sleep from exhaustion.

CHAPTER 30
ELENA

I wrapped my arms tightly around myself, trying to stop the shivers. Our town was quiet, perhaps a little quieter than normal, even at this time of night. Father and I had been out hunting to feed ourselves and those in town who were unable. Both of us were exhausted as we walked in silence towards our cabin. The only sound was the crunch of soil underneath our boots.

That was until the screaming began.

All at once, shouting tore from homes around us. My father's eyes locked on mine as he reached out to grab my arm and pull me closer. Just as he did, the cabin next to us exploded in a burst of flames, and the people within let out agonized cries.

The streets were filled with Elysians running out of their homes in hordes. They scrambled around as men dressed head to toe in black, heavily armed, chased after them. My body grew numb as air faded from my lungs.

Two strong hands wrapped around my arms and shook. My father was shouting at me, but for the life of me I couldn't make out what he was saying. He continued to shake me until I slammed back into my body and back into consciousness.

"Elena, go! Find your mother—I need to find the other guards." He gasped. "You need to run, Lena!"

"I—Father!" Everything was happening so fast that I couldn't seem to form words.

"GO, ELENA!"

My father shoved me hard in front of him, and I sprinted towards my house. After a few seconds, I mustered the courage to turn around, but he was already lost in the sea of bodies.

I dodged and leapt around the chaos that filled the streets. Finally arriving at our cabin, I made my way around the side when I noticed our door was wide open. The light from inside spilled onto the ground.

Slowing to a stop, I crept towards the door. When I went to reach for my bow, I let out a hushed curse. It must have fallen off my shoulder in my sprint over here, and my new dagger from my birthday was still sitting on top of the dresser inside the cabin.

Shards of rock lay askew around my boots. I wrapped one tightly in my clutches as my heart thumped rapidly against my chest. Inches away from the front door, a muffled cry emerged, followed by a vengeful laugh.

My lungs collapsed, cut off from air entirely. I pushed forward. My grip tightened around the rock, nails scraping against its jagged edges. When I set foot in the doorway, my legs went weak.

Nausea hit me like a tidal wave as I saw my mother standing in the middle of our cabin, hands held behind her back, a sword held against her neck.

"*Elena*," she mouthed silently. "*Run!*" Desperation pleading through her eyes.

So many emotions were flooding into me, and I began to feel the onset of panic. *Gods, not now.* I needed to be strong. I needed to protect my mother.

But every muscle in my body tightened, freezing me in place as my mind spiraled uncontrollably. As fear took over, I lost control over my limbs, and the rock I was gripping crashed to the floor with a resounding thud.

The hooded man whispering threats into my mother's ear was alerted to my presence. A gasp escaped my lips as his ferocious, amber eyes locked on mine.

His mask was pulled down, allowing me to see the malevolent smile that rose on his lips. "How the gods bless me today…two stunning ladies under my blade instead of one."

A growl was all I could muster from beneath my clenched teeth as tears flooded down my cheeks, my body still frozen stiff in the doorway. Grinning at my discomfort, the man ran his nose through my mother's gorgeous locks. My mother winced, but kept her gaze pinned to mine, trying her best to shield me from what was occurring.

"You smell like heaven, angel. Such a shame I have to end your life today." A wicked smirk flooded his mouth. He ran his foul lips against my mother's ear, as he spoke loud enough for us to both hear. "You don't mind if I have my way with that one do you?" His hungry eyes rolled towards mine as bile crept up my throat. "I'll be kind and let you watch. Maybe I'll even let you join in."

My mother flinched, and whispered the last words that I would ever hear grace her lips.

"I love you."

She threw her head back, crashing it into the man's nose. Frozen in fear, I watched helplessly as he cursed out loud, grabbing her before she could reach me. His blade sliced through her neck and he threw her to the ground. The thud of her delicate body smashing into the wooden floor reverberated all the way down to my soul.

Everything felt too heavy. The shock sent my body crashing to the floor. Sobs rushed out of me and every muscle in my body convulsed as I lay helpless on the floor in our entryway.

Heavy boots echoed against the wooden floor and the smell of leather wafted in front of my face before I could open my eyes. I felt the sting of his blade as it sliced down the inside of my arm. Again, all the air fled my body as his boot crashed into my stomach. I groaned in agony between endless sobs. The man spit on the ground next to me before stepping over me on the way out the door.

"Pathetic. You're not even worth my blade." He hissed and stormed off to find another innocent victim.

I dragged myself over to my mom and slumped down next to her. With the little strength I had left in me, I pulled her limp body onto my lap, rocking her back and forth as I combed through her hair with my hand.

Why, gods ... why?

Eyes almost swollen shut, I prayed to the gods that this was a horrible nightmare that I would wake up from soon.

My subconscious knew that indeed it was. Unfortunately, everything that occurred in this nightmare had happened for real and it played repeatedly in my mind as a reminder each night. Biting down hard on my tongue, I tried desperately to wake myself back up. I couldn't take the pain anymore.

Guilt began to consume me, and the light inside of the cabin dimmed. An eerie wind blew in from the open door as a deep, otherworldly voice chuckled. Another hooded figure stormed through the door, this one familiar as well, but I'd never been able to see its face. Only darkness resided in the depths of its hood. It was followed by a dark beast.

They stood beside me as the beast's void eyes sliced deep into my soul. Raising its beastly head, dripping with a foul, black sludge, it howled a guttural howl. I tried to cover my ears, but a barrage of voices flooded my head. They were the voices that haunted me— everyone I had lost, everyone I had let down.

"You never do enough."

"You're worthless, Elena."

"You couldn't even save them."

"Selfish."

"Pathetic."

"Weak."

Their voices swirled around me in a chorus as my entire world spun. My father's voice rang out from where he crouched in front of me, his eyes blazing with fury as tears cascaded down his cheeks. He didn't even look up at me, but he didn't have to. I could feel the disgust in his words.

"Elena, what happened?" He sobbed, cradling my mother's lifeless body in his arms.

I let you down. I'm so sorry, Father. I'll never forgive myself.

Declan

Sleep evaded me. Tonight's events left me tossing and turning in my bed. The memory of her body against my own lingered within my mind, the taste of her lips still sweet on my mouth.

When she'd pulled away, I let my ward down and was bombarded by several waves of her emotions. Elena's body trembled with fear, guilt and shame, so much so that it had cracked her own ward.

Everything about that moment frightened me, the same emotions threatening to overwhelm my own dynamis. I'd meant every word I said when I told her that I would wait for her. It was a promise I intended to keep. Whether it be in this life or the next, she would be mine.

I was shaken from my thoughts as a bloodcurdling scream echoed off the walls.

Elena.

Fear launched me from my bed. Using my dynamis, I zephyred into her room. Shadows spooled around me as I waved away a stunned Killian and another guard who had barreled through the door at the same time.

My breath hitched as I gazed upon my Wildfire engulfed in white flames.

"Close the door behind you," I growled. Killian's wide eyes met mine, and I gave him a nod, reassuring him I could handle the situation. He closed the door behind him and my attention returned to Elena.

Soft, auburn locks of hair floated turbulently above Elena's head, as if she was swirling in her own personal storm. Lena's body was glowing gold and white, and her face was full of terror as she continued to scream. I had witnessed her dynamis try to take over her body while we were traveling, but this was nothing like that day.

When I bounded over to her, there wasn't one thought that crossed my mind about what her dynamis might do to me. All that fueled my actions was the overwhelming need to protect her.

Sliding my body behind hers, I caged her lower body between my legs and pulled her close to my chest. Icy skin stung against my own, the opposite of the heat I had expected from the golden glow surrounding her body. The chill frosted over my cheek as I leaned into her. Elena needed to wake up before she hurt herself.

"Elena, wake!" I continued to shout while rocking her body, doing anything to shake her out of the deep trance she was in.

"FORGIVE ME!" she screamed as her eyes flung open.

All at once, her entire body tightened and she gasped for breath. Pieces of my heart tore apart every time that she went to pull in air and nothing but shallow breaths entered her lungs. She gripped my thighs with desperation. Eyes wide, face struck with fear, she was trying with all of her might to force herself to breathe.

I'd seen this before. Hells, I knew firsthand what she was experiencing all too well. Shivers ran through my body at the memory of the time my father nearly whipped me to death for succumbing to a panic attack in front of the staff. No matter how much dynamis I had thrumming through my veins, from that day forward, he would always consider me weak because of it.

Pulling her as close as I could, I kept one arm wrapped around her waist and the other I used to grab her hand and place it over her chest. Placing my palm over hers, I began to guide my Wildfire down from her ledge.

"Lena, it's me." I squeezed her body tighter, so she'd know it was me. "I'm here with you."

Her eyebrows scrunched, as she continued to gasp for air.

"Breathe, Lena." A short puff of air pulled in, but nothing came back out. "You can do it. Focus on my breaths, Lena, try to breathe with me." I emphasized every breath so she could feel the rise and fall of my chest. Desperation began to build within me, and my own chest tightened at the sight of her wild eyes. "Count the stars with me, love. One ..."

Gasp.

"Two..."

Another rattled intake of breath.

"Three..." I pressed my palm harder against her chest.

Air flooded into her lungs, but none came out.

"Four." Panic flooded through my dynamis. "Fight, love, fight the darkness."

I felt a tiny puff of air finally flow through her lips, and then another. Until I heard the slightest breath whisper between us. "Five..."

Relief washed over me. "There you go, sweetheart. Come back to me, back to the light."

We rocked back and forth, my arms secured around her the entire time. Right now, her thoughts held her hostage, and my job was to tear them away. Little by little, the muscles in her body loosened, finally allowing her to take in deeper pulls of air.

Her head fell back onto my shoulder, and I clenched my jaw as I gazed over her face—eyes red and swollen, her lip bloody from biting it. Removing my hand from her waist, I swept her wild hair away from her face. It was drenched in sweat like the rest of her as I tucked it behind her ears. Finally, her entire body surrendered and she melted into me.

Elena's head lay heavy against my shoulder. My hand was still intertwined with hers over her chest. Silence passed between us for a few moments as I ran my fingers through the lengths of her hair. My lips grazed the top of her head in a tender kiss, and her lips began to quiver. Tears streamed down her cheeks, and everything inside me shattered. Seeing her cry, seeing her break into a million pieces, left me undone. As carefully as I could, I folded her body into mine so she faced me and brushed my lips across her wet cheeks.

"You're safe now, love," I whispered. The sting of tears pressed behind my own eyes. "I will always guide you out of the dark and back to me."

Lena's breath hitched, and her arms tightened around me. "I'm so sorry." She erupted into sobs.

"Shhh." I pressed a kiss into her hair. "You never have to apologize for feeling. Good or bad, our emotions are the most authentic parts within us. Never be afraid of allowing yourself to feel them."

She nodded against my chest as I wiped away more tears from her rosy cheeks.

"Would you...like to talk about it?" I asked hesitantly.

"Not yet—no...I—I'm sorry." She sniffled, small tremors of panic still rippling down her body.

"No more apologizing. Let's get you back to sleep."

After fixing the rumpled sheets, I tucked her body inside. The sound of muffled weeping filtered through the pillow as she curled into herself.

"Could you stay with m-me? Just for a little while?" The plea in her voice wrapped around my icy heart and tugged. There was nowhere else I'd rather be than right beside her.

"Of course. Just give me a moment. I'll be right back."

I crossed the floor in three strides and leaned my head out the door to tell Killian that everything was fine. After closing the door behind me, I slid into the bed behind her. I slipped my arm underneath Elena's head and wrapped the other around her middle, pulling her into me. Everything about this moment felt right.

Every time I was around Elena, I felt compelled to be as close to her as possible. She drew me in with every sweet smile, every flush of her cheeks, every compassionate part of her soul, and every damn elbow to my gut. No matter how hard we both fought this connection between us, I feared the invisible force pulling us together was far stronger.

"Good night, Lena," I whispered, hoping to not wake her.

"Good night, Declan."

Breathing in the sweet smell of lavender from her hair, I nuzzled my head further into it. As I melted into her warmth, my arms curled tighter around her. Eventually, lulled by her soft, steady breaths, I fell asleep.

CHAPTER 31

ELENA

G roaning, I tried to open my swollen eyes. Every muscle in my body felt sore as I tried to sit up in bed. Pain radiated throughout my body, and my head fell back onto the headboard with a grunt. Today was my first brunch with the king's dignitaries, and afterwards another grueling training session.

Declan.

The spot next to me was vacant, but the sheets still felt warm to the touch. He must have stayed the entire night. I threaded my fingers through the ends of my hair, twisting around and around as I lost myself in my thoughts.

Declan's words from last night felt ingrained in my soul. My heart ached from the heaviness of them. For someone who had recently inherited monumental amounts of dynamis, at this moment I felt completely powerless.

There was a battle going on within me. If I didn't find my strength soon, I was going to go down like a sinking ship, never to be seen again.

Exhaustion rang warning bells inside my body, telling me to stop and go back to sleep. However, the tiniest whisper of my consciousness reminded me that I was not a quitter. I needed to pull myself together and keep moving forward. That was what I'd always done and today would be no different.

I'd been blessed with another day of life, and I shouldn't waste it wallowing in past events I couldn't change. Just one step. That was all I needed, and the rest would follow.

Wincing, I pulled my feet over the edge of the bed and placed them on the floor. *Just one step, Elena.* With every bit of strength left, I pulled myself up off the bed and took a step, then another.

I was about as wobbly as a newborn doe, but I eventually made it over to the table. Sliding down into the chair, I looked over the tray of breakfast foods and tea that Eloise must have left for me this morning. As I reached for a fluffy blueberry muffin, my arm brushed over a folded piece of parchment. Written on the front was a name I knew all too well. *Wildfire.* My fingers began to tremble as I slumped back into the chair and unfolded the parchment to read his note.

I hope that you were able to get some much-needed rest. After your brunch with my father, take a rest and then find me afterwards. I'll be in the library, collecting some books for you to read about dynamis and the Light Phoenix. We will do a less physical form of training today. See you soon.

P.S. There is ginger candy for the hangover, and some chocolates...because chocolate solves all problems, right?

—Declan

I folded the parchment and set it aside, a smile caressing over my cracked lips. Somehow this man awakened all that was good inside of me. I wasn't entirely sure that I would be able to restrain myself much longer. Last night was a perfect example of how easily I let my walls crumble.

However, I knew I'd made the right choice. My dream last night was a visceral reminder of what happened to the people close to me. Declan and I simply couldn't be, no matter how much we might both want it.

The door of my room creaked open as Eloise's tiny body slid through. Hazel eyes roved over me as they assessed the damage from last night. "I'm so sorry, Elena. I should have knocked first, but I need to get you ready for brunch with the king."

I nodded as a yawn slipped loose. She made her way to my wardrobe. "You aren't going to like this one." She chuckled, pulling out one of the monstrosities of the dresses the king had ordered to be brought in for me while I was training yesterday.

Golden feathers covered every part of the fluffy gown, from the capped sleeves all the way down to the hem. Bits of golden tulle peeked out between the wide skirts, and lace covered the bodice and the high-necked collar.

I ate as she readied my hair and my face. Then she helped me into the hideous gown, all while feathers poked us both.

"I'm going to look like a giant yellow bird," I huffed, trying to smooth down the puff of the skirt with my hands.

A snort came from behind me. "Wait...there's more."

"Fantastic." I grimaced.

In her hands was a navy velvet sash. Embroidered in gold thread was the kingdom's crest, and to attach it to my dress was a golden feather pin. Eloise placed the sash around my body, and I faced the mirror and scowled at my reflection.

"Be careful today." Eloise's voice shook me from my glare. "One of the king's maids stormed into the kitchen today and warned us of his foul mood. Nothing good ever comes from those."

I patted her shoulder. "I'll try my best."

"Good luck, Lena."

The moment I entered the dining room, the heaviness of all the stares halted my steps. Whispers spread throughout the guests as fast as kindling on a fire. Pulling down deep, I found my courage and straightened my spine as I locked eyes on the host of today's event.

The guests parted as I passed. Some smiled and dipped their heads while others scowled at the sight of me. With a heavy sigh, I tucked the emotions beneath my ward and tried to calm the dynamis that had begun to awaken.

Alaric turned around from his group of dignitaries and strode over to me. "It's a pleasure to see you, Lady Elena." His voice boomed as he interlocked our arms. "Let's take a stroll around the room, shall we?"

Before I could even nod, he tugged me along and began parading me around the room.

"I would like to apologize for my behavior the other night."

The king's apology sent my eyebrows to my forehead, and I struggled to rein them in. His lips twitched into a smirk.

"Elena, a king apologizing is a rare occurrence. You would do well to accept it, before I decide to not ever do it again."

Dull green eyes assessed mine, his lips pursed into a line as he awaited my answer. They lacked the life that warmed Declan's. Alaric's were cold and reddened around the edges.

"Apology accepted, Your Majesty," I said, trying to calm the swell of nerves.

"Have you made a decision about my offer?" he asked, taking two golden wine goblets off the passing server's tray and handing one to me.

Wrapping my fingers around the stem, I dipped my head. "Yes, I'll take your offer. As long as my town stays safe, I'll do as you ask."

"Good." He guided me towards Alastor and another man. Both stared at me with such intensity that it made my skin prickle. "Elena has decided to take my offer," he said, and the other men's lips tugged into cruel grins.

Their looks of satisfaction made my stomach ache, and doubt blossomed within it. Even though I knew this was going to save my town, I couldn't help feeling like I had just joined hands with the enemy.

Hells, I hope I'm making the right decision.

"This is Lord Edan Drake. He runs Vragos, the City of Ash."

Edan dipped his head, his pointy nose crinkling at the king's introduction. "Yes, I *rule* over the City of Ash." His sharp jaw clenched, dark brown eyes shifting to the king. "It's nice to meet you, Lady..." His thin lips pursed together as he tried to recall my name.

"Elena," Alastor interjected, taking a deep draw of whiskey as his icy blue eyes studied me.

"Oh, yes, that's right." Lord Drake cleared his throat, waving Alastor off. "So hard to remember all these courtiers these days."

"Seeing as how she possesses the dynamis of the Light Phoenix, the savior of our realm, I suggest hers is one name that you should commit to memory," Alastor drawled, and the king nodded with approval.

Edan's shoulders cowered before he shook it off and apologized. "Forgive me for my error, Lady Elena."

"You're forgiven," Alaric grunted, and pulled my arm into his once more. "We have mingling to do and promises of your protection to make. Time to circle the room, my lady."

This entire interaction had left me stunned and confused. Only two nights ago both men had belittled me over my plate of salmon. Now, they were being eerily respectful. Something didn't sit right, and the dynamis that had roused within me once more agreed.

As we walked away, Alastor stared at me from his glass of whiskey. The intensity of it burned through me as it tracked me around the room, through every interaction the king and I had, and even during conversations with the other guests about my dynamis. I could look up and always find Alastor's eyes.

Even after the king excused me from my duties, a shiver ran down my spine as I exited through the gold-trimmed doors. There was no need to look over my shoulder to know that his gaze still lingered upon me.

As I walked down the long hallway and up the stairs towards the library, there was only one question that crossed my mind about Alastor's stare.

Why?

CHAPTER 32

ELENA

S unlight spilled over the dark oak floors of the hallway as I approached the library doors. One was ajar enough for me to hear the stern voices within, and my legs stiffened. Rocking back and forth on my heels I contemplated turning around until Declan's voice barraged through the open space.

"Damn!"

I leaned against the smooth wood of the door. The fury within his tone should have stopped me from eavesdropping. Instead, it stirred an unavoidable need to stay.

"I warned him, Killian! Numerous times we've told my father and Alastor that these beasts were roaming the outer walls of the city." The slam of a fist reverberated against a hard surface inside. "Those miserable bastards. Hells! One almost killed Elena, and now three families must mourn the loss of their children—children, Killian… Gods," he breathed. "Please forgive us."

A heavy sigh shuddered, followed by an uncomfortably long silence.

"The guards on duty were ours." Killian's voice sounded strained, and my curiosity ran rampant with what he meant when he said "ours." Weren't all the guards theirs?

"Damn the Hells!" Declan seethed as another crash came from within.

"They said one moment they were awake, and the next they woke up lying on the ground, the sounds of screams in the distance. You know it had to be him."

Who?

"After one attacked Elena, I should have foreseen this." A groan slipped from Declan, and though I couldn't see it, I imagined he was probably running his palms through his hair in frustration.

"Dec, you know this is not your fault, right?"

Inching closer to the opening, I strained my neck to hear Killian's hushed voice more clearly.

"Dec—?"

"It's entirely my fault!" He interrupted with a snarl. "Don't deny it, Killian. If my mother and brother were still here, things would be different. They wouldn't have let this get so out of control."

"Declan, no one knows where our paths will take us. Their lives could have easily gone down the same one as yours."

"I know I've made a mess of my life, but I refuse to ruin the lives of everyone else in this kingdom more than I already have. These people deserve a better life…we all do."

Slow steps treaded across the floor, pausing for a moment before Killian's voice strained through the silence. "We'll add more guards to the city wall, as well as more patrol shifts. We do this together, brother. You don't have to walk this path alone."

The endearment tugged against my chest. Killian and Liam might not be blood, but it was easy to see that they had formed their own bond of brotherhood, just as strong, with Declan. It warmed my heart to know that this trio of men were looking after each other.

Footsteps padded once more, but this time it was headed towards me. Panic bristled through me as I tried to shuffle away from the open door and not get caught.

"Freckles, whatever are we going to do with you?" Killian stepped through the open door and leaned against the wall beside me.

"I—umm—I just—" The words jumbled out of my mouth, none making any sense at all.

Killian towered over me, his arms folded in front of his chest. Slowly a smirk danced across his face, his honey eyes filled with the faint glimmer of amusement. "Take care of him today, will you? That man is going to need every bit of your light today." He patted my shoulder has he passed, then left me behind without another word.

As I faced the open door, my nerves bundled themselves into knots. This would be my first time seeing Declan after last night's events. Last night's version of Shadow Lord had been tender, caring. When I stepped into this room, however, I might encounter the quite the opposite. Gathering my courage, I stepped inside.

Nothing could have prepared me for the sight I beheld before me. Resplendent light illuminated the room, filtering through the floor-to-ceiling glass wall. Rows of bookshelves lined the remaining walls, filled with thousands of books in every shape and size. Smaller shelves sprinkled throughout the room, also overflowing with books. Inhaling the heavenly smell of parchment and leather, I sighed, letting the calming scent wash through me.

Declan hadn't noticed that I had entered the room. Lost in his thoughts, he stood staring at the ceiling, as if silently praying to the gods to give him the strength to keep going.

Cautiously, I crept over to him. His shoulder was slumped against the side of a bookcase, his broad back facing me. When only mere inches separated us, he shoved himself from the bookcase, both hands combing through his thick, chestnut waves. Then he let out a roar so loud, the entire space rattled. Grabbing the closest chair, he launched it over the floor. It splintered into a thousand pieces.

I flinched, my arms wrapping around my body.

As if he sensed me behind him, he abruptly turned, hands clenched in fists.

Wild eyes locked onto mine, and the fury that raged within in them began to melt. His breathing evened, while his fingers began to unlock from fists. Then a look that I had never seen on Declan before flashed across his face.

He slid his palm over his glossy eyes as his head tilted towards the floor where it remained. Shame was written all over his body, but it was also floating through me. My heart pinched at the sight of him. Eyes swollen from exhaustion. Defeated. Broken.

One way or another, I would find a way to get my revenge on the king and Alastor.

"Elena—I didn't mean for you to see—" He paused, his throat bobbing up and down.

"Dec..." I said softly. "I believe it was you who told me last night, 'Never apologize for feeling.'" Closing the gap between us, I grabbed one of his hands and rubbed my thumb soothingly over the top. "What happened wasn't your fault. Deep down, Declan, you and I both know who is truly responsible for what happened to those children."

His forehead scrunched.

"I, umm, overheard it all," I said sheepishly, biting my lip. One corner of his lips tilted up and the smile spread across his face, which I considered a victory. "Don't carry this weight on your own."

He opened his mouth to interject, but I raised a hand to silence him. "How about tonight we go to those families? We can say our condolences. Together, we can tell them that we will avenge their children."

There was no way I would let him bear the weight of this terrible situation on his own. The baggage that this man carried on his shoulders already seemed heavy enough. Though I didn't have to know all that he carried, it reflected in everything that he did. It was a feeling I knew all too well.

Perhaps we'd been brought into each other's lives to help each other understand the burdens we carried on our shoulders were too much for one person to hold onto. Just maybe, we were fated to teach a lesson to each other on the importance of letting others in to help and letting the past go.

He sighed, taking in my words. From this point forward, like Killian had said, we would do this together.

A smile grew on his lips as he stared at me longingly. "You just keep surprising me." He spoke so softly the words floated in a haze surrounding us.

I shrugged my shoulders. Lightening the mood felt needed at this moment. "I could say the same of you, Your Highness." I winked.

"Ah, I'm back to being Your Highness again? I believe I already told you, Wildfire, I like the sound of my name on your lips." He stepped closer, his eyes darkening with every move.

"If you're lucky, maybe I'll surprise you again."

"Let's hope the gods bless me with such luck soon." His eyes roamed over my ensemble. "That's a lot of feathers." He covered his mouth with his fist, trying to conceal the laugh that was bubbling through.

I rolled my eyes dramatically as I did a little spin. "In place of real wings, your father thought it best they be plastered all over my body." I snorted.

Declan extended his arm towards the table with books on top of it. "I figured after last night, we could do some less strenuous activities today. Today's training involves strengthening the mind. There's also something I'd like to share with you."

We both sat down at the table, and he slid the books he had selected over to me. Giddily, I started pulling them from the stack, reading the titles as I went. There were so many, but a few caught my eye, like *The Histories of Ehora,* and *A Complete Guide to Elemental Magic.* Excitement hummed through me as I thought about diving into each one of these books by the fire in my room tonight.

Declan laughed quietly, and I peered over the open book I was holding long enough to see his eyes sparkling down at me.

"What?"

"Nothing."

"What's so funny, Declan?"

"Something about watching your entire body light up when you are looking at books makes me unable to draw my eyes away from you. If I'd known it would cause this enchanting reaction, I would have brought you into this library on the first day."

Warmth spread over my cheeks. "This library is incredible, Declan. I think the only thing I love more than books is…food."

"You sure that's the only thing you love more?" His eyes darkened as his gaze roamed slowly over me.

"I'm sure." My voice faltered. It came out more like a question than a statement.

He tilted his head away from me. However, I could still see a smile forming on his lips.

"Alright, Shadow Lord, say what you need to say so I can lose myself in these books for the rest of the day."

He pulled his chair closer to mine. When his knee brushed mine, it sent shivers across my skin and my heartbeat accelerated.

"Business outside of the kingdom will require me to be gone in a few days, and I'll be away for a week. I want to make sure that you have a strong enough ward before I go. Nobody knows you're an Empath yet, so this ward will help you keep your emotions in check and stop you from pulling them from others unconsciously."

Panic rose up my throat at the thought of him being gone for an entire week. My emotions must have been written across my face, because Declan laid a hand across my knee.

"I promise no harm will come to you when I'm gone, Lena. I've spoken with Nayla, Liam and Killian. Each of them will take turns watching over you, as well as continuing your training." He removed his warm hand from my knee, and I already missed its heat. "Close your eyes, Elena."

Sighing, I closed my eyes, preparing for what was to come.

"Let's see if you can read the emotions I send to you."

Instantly, I was hit by a blast of wind, carrying the warmest feeling I'd ever felt. Its silky caress floated over my skin like sunlight. It reminded me of the night that I had dinner with the king and Alastor. I remembered anger had surged within me when they had repeatedly called me insignificant. Before I could unleash my fury upon them, this warm feeling had spread across me, calming me enough to refocus and say what I needed to say in a more eloquent manner.

Stillness captured my body as the answer struck me. My eyes flashed open to find Declan's intense eyes already set on me.

"You are an Empath too, aren't you?" I whispered.

He smiled and held a finger up over his lips.

I lowered my voice to a whisper. "So, the entire journey, dinner with your father, last night...you could read everything I was feeling?" The words floated through my lips as I adjusted to the shock.

He nodded.

Dear gods.

Declan cleared his throat. "Now you understand the importance of learning how to build your ward." He chuckled.

"Absolutely," I squeaked, palming my face with my hand. "Why didn't you just tell me that day when you found out that I was also an Empath?" Curiosity was beginning to arise within me, so many questions flooding to the surface.

"I still wasn't entirely sure you were an Empath. I know only a little about the dynamis of the Light Phoenix. Being an Empath is wonderful; however, it is also extremely dangerous in this kingdom, as I've learned."

Running a hand through his hair, he sighed and leaned deeper into his chair. "Before I explain it all, it is important that this stays between you and I."

I nodded silently.

"The only others who know of my Empath abilities are those closest to me. It's a small circle that includes my three captains, Clara, and Eloise."

"You can trust me."

"I know. It all started when I was young. Being an Empath herself, my mother noticed my unique awareness of the people around me. In a room full of people, I could always read everyone. I knew when to be compassionate, when to be bold, and when to show restraint. Most children with these abilities show signs of anxiety, even before they are blessed by the gods with the dynamis.

We're hypersensitive because we feel the heaviness of the world around us."

My hand fell over my chest, rubbing it to soothe the ache that had crawled its way in.

"When I was young, she learned to shield me from my father and Alastor, but as soon as I came of age and received my dynamis, she began to instruct me on the true meaning of our magic."

Why would his mother shield his dynamis? It was true, the Empath power was a rarity, but it was considered a lesser dynamis in our kingdom. I scrunched my nose as my eyebrows furrowed.

"Elena, you've been taught all your life that our dynamis is derived from the elements of this kingdom. My mother, brother and I had been researching dynamis for years. Mother was always curious about how Empaths' and Healers' dynamis fit into the elemental magic. She was always bewildered by the fact that there were so few of us inside the realm. Together, we discovered that our dynamis does not derive from the elements at all. Instead, it originates from something far deeper."

I curled my fingers around the sides of my chair, anticipation pulling me to the edge of my seat.

"Emotions."

My mouth gaped wide open as I hung onto the chair for dear life. "What does that mean, Declan? I don't understand what that has to do with being an Empath."

"Emotions control the power within us. When we ascend, our dynamis is gifted into our entire being, bonding to the blood that flows within us. We can use our emotions to bend our dynamis at will, shaping it to fit our needs. Our emotions can transform our dynamis into any element we desire."

I gasped.

"For example, those who are Flames, their strongest emotions could be anger, sadness, ambition, fear, and sometimes extreme passion. Those with dynamis that involve the element of water, like Liam, who's a Frost, are often full of compassion and optimism. They are cool-tempered and solve problems easily. Our Healers, like Clara, have similar emotions. Those with earth or air elemental powers, like your father, Nayla and Killian, and the men in my family, are often the most grounded individuals. They demonstrate confidence, strength, and trust. Also, they love fiercely and deeply."

"And Empaths?"

"Empaths feel it all, Elena."

The enormity of his words caused me to pause while my mind processed the meaning. Declan waited patiently. My head rested on my hands in deep thought as I tried desperately to figure out what Declan was telling me.

Emotions. If our dynamis was attached to our emotions, what would that mean for an Empath? Wheels in my brain began to turn rapidly. As Empaths, we could sense all emotions. We felt everything deeper, allowing us to have a stronger connection to the world around us. Someone who knew emotions inside and out could potentially control multiple forms of dynamis. Was this why Declan and I both exhibited multiple dynamis?

"I think I'm finally beginning to see why being an Empath could be dangerous in this kingdom." I chewed on my lip. Knots began to form inside my stomach. If I was right, that meant that I had access to all the dynamis, and not only me—everyone could potentially access other powers as well once they fully understood all their emotions as well as us Empaths did.

The thought of what that knowledge could do to an already broken kingdom sent a shiver down my spine. I prayed to the gods that if we all truly had access to all that dynamis we would choose to use it for good, not evil. However, where great power grew, so did great evil. Access to unlimited dynamis could be disastrous in the hands of those whose souls were full of darkness. My body trembled, fingers fidgeting in my lap.

"You're fearful if your father and Alastor knew the truth, they would use that knowledge to enhance their dynamis and create more harm throughout the Kingdom, aren't you?"

"Yes."

A chill ran across my body. The skin on my arms pebbled. Declan placed his hands over mine. "Now that you know the truth, let's work on learning how to use your emotions to access and protect yourself. Are you ready?"

"Absolutely."

Declan smiled and brought my hands to his lips, brushing them with a featherlight kiss.

"There's my Wildfire."

CHAPTER 33

DECLAN

Lena's face lit up with her lust for knowledge. It quelled the nerves that had risen when I'd decided to share this secret with her. Perhaps, if she could handle this secret, she would be able to handle one more when I finally gained the courage to share it with her.

"Are you ready?"

The question floated between us as I placed her trembling palm in mine. Her head bobbed timidly.

"Close your eyes."

She raised one eyebrow. Our gazes formed a standoff.

"Gods, Lena," I groaned. "You're incapable of taking orders, aren't you?"

The little hellion shrugged as her lips twitched mischievously. A heady mix of mirth and frustration curled my lips.

Leaning forward until I felt her nose brush against mine, I whispered, "One day, Wildfire, you'll enjoy when I order you around." I smirked.

Delighted at the way her pupils blew wide, I leaned back and began to brush circles with my finger on her palm. "Do you feel this?"

"Y-yes." Her voice quivered.

"Good. Now, concentrate on following that feeling and holding onto it."

Her brows pinched together, alerting me that she felt the dynamis tingling underneath her skin and had latched onto it.

"Still feel it?"

"Declan…" Her tone was laced with frustration.

"Lena…" I countered, releasing her hand and zephyring to the nearest bookshelf. A breeze created from my zephyring loosened a few tendrils of hair into her face, causing her eyelids to flutter.

"Keep those eyes closed, Wildfire," I demanded. The little groan she made had me chuckle inside. "Can you still feel me making circles?"

"Yes, Declan, I can still feel it," she sighed, no doubt rolling her eyes underneath those scrunched eyelids.

"Good. Now, open your eyes."

With an indignant scoff, she opened them, glaring into a blank space in front of her. Her mouth hung wide as her eyes searched the room for me. I folded my arms across my chest and a wicked smirk danced across my lips when her gaze landed on mine.

"How can I—how is this possible? How can I still feel your touch when you're way over there."

"Are you willing to listen to your wise elder now?"

"Old, yes. Wise? That's still debatable."

"Watch it," I growled. Shadows rippled over my arms. Lena giggled.

I unfolded my arms and stalked back towards my little spitfire. Her mirth faded into something a little more dangerous. Her cheeks flushed when I grabbed her and gently lifted her up to stand next to me.

"Emotions are the energy that flows within us, Elena. With every beat of our heart and breath from our lungs, we keep that energy in a constant state of flow throughout our bodies. Our dynamis is embedded deep with our blood, intertwined around the very essence of our souls. Our emotions are just another way to help us navigate the world, much like our senses."

As I lowered my hand from her chin, my knuckles brushed down her neck. Lena shivered, but her attention remained fixed on mine.

"Tell me, when you are sad, do you not feel it physically? Is there not a dull ache that twists within your body?"

Her tongue moistened her bottom lip, teeth grazing the pouty flesh. She closed her eyes and nodded solemnly. The ward she built in her mind was still standing strong, but her scrunched forehead and glossy eyes told me everything I needed to know about the depths of sadness Lena had buried within her.

"When you are angry, does your body feel like it is burning with an unquenchable inner flame? Like at any moment, you may combust? Does your face not become flushed and heated?"

Her gaze shifted from mine, finding the ceiling above. Delicate fingers clenched into fists.

"And when you love..." I paused, my voice cracking under the rush of unexpected emotion. Lena's cheeks pinkened as I tried to cover my slip with a cough. "When you love, does your entire being not feel like it's no longer yours to control? Does everything feel overly sensitive to touch?" My fingertips brushed against her arms as the tension sparked in the air between us. "Do you feel your heart become so enlarged that it aches against the cage of your ribs? Is there warmth that radiates throughout your entire body, so strong, so intense, like an insatiable hunger that begs to be fed?"

There was no hiding the flush of deep red that burned her face. The sight of goosebumps trailing up her arm made a wicked grin spread wide across my face.

"Our emotions are not only feelings, but they also manifest physically within our bodies. Each of those reactions are signs of our dynamis building beneath our skin. To become in tune with your power, you must allow yourself to feel the physical presence of emotion within you. Once you feel it, you must hold onto it with every fiber of your being. Only then will you be able to master the fury of power within you, Lena.

"Give it a try," I coaxed as I wrapped my fingers around her wrist and flipped open her palm. "Reach deep and find the emotion that will make this glow once more."

"I'm scared I won't be able to control it," she breathed.

"You are more powerful than you allow yourself credit for, Elena. Trust in yourself." I took a few steps back, distancing myself from the pull towards her—that familiar pull of the bond that threatened to tug me under if I wasn't more careful. The air in this library had become heavy with the intoxicating tension between us.

Elena steadied herself and took a deep pull of air before her focus shifted towards her palm. Concentration furrowed her brows, and the glow within her palm began to flicker.

It faded in and out as a huff of frustration fled her lips. Instead of jumping in to help, I let her stumble and recover. I wanted her to feel empowered by her own resilience, the inner strength that she had shielded away from herself.

One more deep breath passed over her lips as she tried again. Brighter and brighter her palm began to glow. Gathering my shadows, I darkened the space around us, allowing the golden glow to illuminate her entire body. I'd been alive for several centuries and the glow that happens when her dynamis flared still astounded me.

A single tear slipped down her cheek as I brushed my thumb over it to capture it.

"It's b-beautiful," she breathed.

"It's mesmerizing," I whispered, glancing not at her dynamis, but at the most enthralling thing inside this room.

Elena.

CHAPTER 34
ELENA

S till reeling from the earlier events inside the library, I made my way down the stairs to meet everyone for tonight.

After making myself glow in training, I'd dashed up to my room to ease my turbulent emotions and change out of my hideous dress. Nothing could have prepared me for the secret of our dynamis that Declan had revealed today, or the way I'd felt when he'd helped me control my dynamis for the first time.

Control had evaded me my entire life. It slipped like grains of sand through my fingertips, no matter how hard I tried to grasp it. Today had empowered me in a way I never thought possible, and I owed Declan for guiding me through it.

The crisp night air nipped at my bare skin as I trudged down the hill towards the four somber figures awaiting below. Each of them wilted under the weight of the task we were about to embark on. The mood was as heavy as the baskets of food that hung from each of their arms. They dipped their heads in silent welcome. We turned and began our journey over the stone bridge to the far edge of the city.

"It's good to see you again, Elena." Nayla joined her arm with mine as we walked down the hillside and over the stone bridge into town. "I hear we're to be training next week while Declan is away?"

"Yes, I believe so."

"I'm looking forward to spending more time getting to know you, oh great Light Phoenix." Her ruby lips twitched up ever so slightly, a welcome attempt at levity given the anxiousness that churned within me.

We were walking further into the city than I had gone last evening. Each street was vacant of the warmth and liveliness of the prior night. Doors were closed tightly, no merchants were out on the streets, and even the lights seemed to have lost a little of their luster.

Liam must have noticed my observations, because he scooted over to the other side of me and hooked his arm in mine. A low grumble arose from Declan behind us, which Liam shrugged off. "We ordered a temporary curfew until we get these attacks under control."

That made sense. A curfew would ensure no one else would get hurt by these beasts that had somehow managed to breach the city's walls.

As we walked towards the farthest edge of the city, only the sounds of our heavy footsteps over the cobblestone streets rattled in my ears. Declan and Killian had taken up walking in front of us, until they came to a stop in front of a door painted a vibrant shade of blue. Declan knocked on the door. The window curtains next to the door parted a smidge before we heard rustling behind the door.

"Go away!" A snarl rang from inside.

"Please, I understand your feelings, but we wish to offer our condolences."

"You've never apologized for any of your atrocities before. Why start now?" the voice grumbled from within.

Declan's stoic mask melted as he pushed away from the door and paced in the street behind.

Liam walked over towards him, placed a hand behind his neck and brought their temples together. Whatever he whispered seemed to release the stress from Declan's body.

I made my way towards the door. "It takes a great amount of courage to try to change and admit your mistakes. Sometimes it can be expressed within words, and other times it's shown through action, like we're doing tonight. The question is, do you all have the courage to forgive?"

Silence loomed over the space, and when it appeared the door would remain shut, Declan told us all to leave the baskets by the door so we could return to the castle.

As we turned to leave, a frail woman appeared in the doorway. Redness lined her swollen eyes. I let my newly constructed ward down and was rushed with the despair in her soul. She opened the door a little wider, extending her arm, ushering all of us inside.

Once inside, I observed other families huddled in the middle of the living room. There was not one dry eye in the room. Faces were pale and sadness hovered above the room like heavy rain clouds. Nayla grabbed the basket out of my hand and joined Declan and Killian as they handed them to the parents of each of the lost children.

I felt outside of my body as I watched them hug and console the families. Declan's glossy eyes met my own, and he extended his hand for me to join him.

I hugged, cried, and consoled each person inside the house. Tears saturated my cheeks as we sat and listened to stories and memories the families had of their children. I had known letting my ward down when I entered would be overwhelming, but I *wanted* to feel. It made me experience everything right along with them. It helped me to find the right words to say and know when to be silent.

Everyone shared stories well into the evening until the others started to yawn and eyelids began to droop. We gave them all one last embrace before leaving, and as the door closed behind us, I could feel that some of the weight of their sorrow had lifted.

Our hearts were heavy, yet full, as we walked down the cobblestone street back to the castle. Tonight was a reminder of the strength that was still left in this kingdom. Even after such a tragedy, these people's resilience was truly admirable. Even with all the darkness surrounding them, they had chosen to let the light in.

Declan slowed his pace, falling into step beside me. Fingertips brushed against my own as if silently asking for permission. I folded my hand into his and he gave it a squeeze.

Pausing, I took in the group of people around me. Even in the silence of the night, you could see the strong bond that they all shared with each other. I wanted to be a part of that bond. I was beginning to let myself believe that this was truly all in the gods' plans. My fate had set me on this path to a dynamis that could help so many, meeting this amazing group of people, and finding this inner strength in myself that I'd never believed I could obtain.

Declan turned my chin up to face him, eyes wide with concern. I met his gaze.

"Thank you for taking me with you all tonight. Being around those families...comforting them in their times of need"—I swallowed back my emotions— "it made me feel like I had a purpose again. Helping others has always made me feel whole."

Declan brushed the back of his fingers along the side of my chin. His touch always elicited delicious shivers throughout my body, but something felt more alive tonight. As his touch cascaded down my arm, my dynamis thrummed against my skin, trailing a fiery path where his flesh touched my own.

His hand whipped back, like my skin had bitten him. I'd only felt my dynamis react to him a few times before, but he had never once reacted to it until tonight. My dynamis seemed to have been calling out to him, and he had finally answered.

"Did you feel that?" I whispered.

He nodded. "Every time I've touched you tonight, it's as though your dynamis is trying to reach out to touch mine. I can feel my shadows rippling against my skin as well."

He lifted my hand so that my palm was now flat against his. He nodded towards my left hand to do the same. We stood close together in the dimly lit street as goosebumps rippled over my skin. The other three had strolled a few yards away, giving the two of us some space.

"Can we try something?" His voice was low and soothing.

"Dec—"

"I know you're worried about your dynamis, but something inside me is telling me that we won't hurt each other."

I dug my heels in to maintain my newfound courage. "I trust you."

Declan intertwined our fingers. Already, I could feel my dynamis rippling up and down my arms and crashing like waves into my palms. A shiver ran down my back.

"Breathe, Wildfire," he whispered.

I nodded, exhaling the breath I'd been holding.

"I'm going to count to three, and then we slowly push out our power, alright?"

My nerves twisted like thorny vines inside my stomach.

"Reach down deep, Elena, find the light within you, and call to it. Remember, our dynamis bends to our will. If you don't want it to hurt someone it'll listen." He squeezed my hands. "You are in control. You are its captain, it just awaits your command."

Biting my lip, I stared into his eyes. They glistened with hope and wonderment.

"On three, we do this together."

I nodded.

"One ..."

I dug down deep, reaching for the warmth hidden within.

"Two ..."

When I called to it, the dynamis dancing underneath my skin became even more alive. It flooded my entire system, and my hands became heavy as stone. Power waited to be unleashed; all I needed to do was to open the gates.

Please, don't harm him.

"Three ..."

Closing my eyes tight, I released it.

The feeling was unlike anything I had ever felt. Warmth enveloped me. My body felt entirely at peace, as if nothing in the world could ever harm me. Strength flowed through every muscle as my soul hummed.

Wild and all-consuming. It made me feel... invincible.

"Open your eyes," he breathed. We were standing so close together now that I could feel his warm breath tickle my forehead.

Violet tendrils of light shimmered between us, wrapping around our palms and rippling along our arms.

"Wh-what is this?"

"This is us."

His grin ripped down every wall I had been trying to build. Everything else melted away. Every fear. Every worry. Time stood still, and in that moment nothing else mattered.

Our eyes collided, his vibrant green eyes aflame with an intensity that stole my breath. Declan raised our right hands up towards the night sky, then released my palm while motioning for me to the same.

"Push your dynamis, Elena. Let it flow and release it into the night."

I did as he said and let the warmth cascade through my fingertips. A beacon of violet light flashed into the sky, launching all the way to the stars. Laughter tumbled out of me, my grin so large it was hurting my cheeks.

Our display had caught the attention of the three captains. All of them made their way back to us, eyes wide and mouths hanging open.

"By the gods..." Nayla whispered.

"How is this possible, Declan?" I asked.

"I don't know, but maybe you were right."

"Right about what?"

"Maybe we really are the perfect balance of light and dark," he said. "You are my guiding light in my realm of darkness, Elena."

My heart stumbled, colliding right into the man right in front of me. I let down my ward to let the feeling in and pushed mine out towards him. It felt warm, like the rays of the sun that danced across my face on a sunny day. Or like the cool lick of water as it rippled over your skin. It was like the sting of the thorn of a rose; though it hurt, you couldn't help but be entranced by the beauty it had created.

Everything about this man was so familiar. I felt as if I needed him just to breathe, as if our souls were so connected that our hearts even shared a beat. I feared that I was falling in love with Declan Stallard.

Collecting myself, I mustered the courage to say the words on my lips. "Together, we shine the brightest," I breathed as he reverently stroked his fingers though my hair and cupped the back of my neck.

"Indeed, we do, love."

Before I could respond, the air around us became numbing cold. The eerie feeling made every hair on my neck stand at attention. Something wasn't right.

A guttural growl came from behind us.

Declan's faced blanched. My teeth sank straight into my bottom lip. Only one thing could make a sound that horrifying.

"Hells...a beast!" Liam shouted.

CHAPTER 35

ELENA

"We do this together!" Declan commanded.

The mammoth beast stood about twelve feet away from us, snarling as it crouched down, preparing to attack. The captains rushed forward, flanking Declan and I on both sides in the narrow street.

Our hands still intertwined, he spun my body in the direction of the beast. All of us prepared for the battle in front of us as the beast raised its snout into the air and howled. It was low, deep, and rattled against my bones. As a group we extended our hands forward, waiting for Declan to give us the signal.

Growls echoed between the buildings, drawing our attention away from the beast in front of us. Two more foul beasts appeared from the side streets behind the first beast. Goosebumps rippled over my skin, and I began to tremble. Declan and I had barely survived one of these beasts last time.

How the Hells will we take down three?

Declan's thumb stroked over the back of my hand. In that small second of calm, his commanding presence filled me with hope that we might be able to survive this.

Anchoring my feet firmly into the ground, I set my sights on the dark beasts in front of us. Once more, I dug down deep to my well of dynamis, summoning it forth. In the corner of my eye, I could see that both Declan and I were glowing a faint violet shade. His hair whipped around wildly, as did mine.

"NOW!" he shouted.

Dynamis of all manner leapt forward towards the beasts. Screeching howls pierced through my ears, but our efforts didn't halt their attack. We watched in horror as they clawed their way towards us.

Just like before, scraps of their dark, matted fur flew into the air as our violet light peeled away meaty layers of flesh. Sludgy, dark blood spilled over the cobblestones. Together, our power was doing far more damage than either of us on our own.

Nayla and Liam impaled the beasts with shards of stone and ice. Killian launched several daggers attached to him, conserving his power, just in case we might need to be zephyred out of here.

Declan took a step forward, as I did. More dynamis thrummed through our fingertips, striking the beasts. This time, their momentum did not slow. The sounds of our battle had summoned several people outside of their homes. Concern filled Declan's face.

"We need time," he panted between heavy breaths. "We need to get them away from the people."

Roaring orders back to the captains, Declan pulled me down the next street toward the main square of the city. Two of the beasts clawed their way towards us. The captains fled down another alley, the third beast growling behind them.

As we ran, we took turns launching our dynamis towards the beasts. Each blow carved chunks out of the beasts' flesh, but still they charged for us. Declan tugged my shoulder, pulling me down each alley and street that would lead us out of the city.

Elysians began to open their doors and flood the streets. "Get back inside! Now!" Declan yelled shoving others back into their open doors as we ran by. As we rounded another street, we heard the screams of

Elysians behind us, and I prayed to the gods that they got inside before the beasts reached them.

At the end of the street a little girl with bouncy blonde curls sobbed. Without hesitation, Declan bent down and wrapped her into his arms, ran to the nearest door and pounded. "Open now, I have a child!"

The door swung open, and he shoved the crying babe into a woman's arms. The beasts' howls were getting closer. My heart pounded against my chest.

"Close this door and hide!"

The woman slammed the door shut, while Declan grabbed my wrist and launched us back into a sprint. Claws scratched against the cobblestone, and I glanced over my shoulder to see that a beast was trailing behind us. Turn after turn, Declan helped us wind through the streets of the city that he knew by heart.

My breath rasped against my lungs. Every muscle in my legs burned. "I...I don't know if I can keep up, Dec," I panted, turning to blast another bit of dynamis towards the beast closest to me.

It lunged into the air and its teeth nipped my calf just as Declan shoved us around yet another corner. Warm, red liquid began to trickle into my boot. The pain throbbed with each step.

"Hold on!" We swung around another street. "Elena, just"—Declan gripped my hand tighter as we ran— "hold on, love."

We rushed straight towards the opening of the alley, both turning to launch another assault of dynamis. My fingertips burned from the white light that tore through them. When we reached the opening, my eyes widened at the sight of the captains backed against the large fountain in the middle of the town square. We raced towards them, joining their side.

"This is it," Declan shouted. "Use everything you have left!"

I bottled up every emotion, everything I had left buried deep down inside. He extended his hand, and I placed it inside mine. Dynamis rushed forward at my summons, pressing painfully against my skin, urging to be released. Locking sights on the beast, I let it fly.

A powerful golden wind blasted them all back. Two hit the sides of buildings. The crack of breaking bones rang in the air, and they both lay lifeless on the ground. The final beast whined as it struggled to get back onto all fours.

The captains continued to bombard it with their dynamis. Out of daggers, Killian held his sword at the ready.

The final beast slumped to the ground, but it still tried to use its claws to pull its body towards us. Declan and I approached the beast before it could rise again.

Hollowness filled the depths of where my dynamis resided, and I finally felt what it was like to drain my well. Releasing my grip on Declan's hand, I palmed my dagger tightly. As I kneeled over the beast, I slid the blade through its heart. Black blood oozed out of the wound just as Declan shoved his sword into the beast's neck, severing its head from its body.

Exhausted, I rolled off the beast, falling toward the cobblestones. Before I hit, strong arms slid underneath mine. Declan lifted me back onto my feet. Sweat beaded his brow, his breaths still coming out in short pants. I brushed my hand tenderly over his temple, wiping the sweat away before it stung his eyes.

"We did it," he whispered into my hair as he pulled me closer.

"Of course we did." My words rumbled into his chest as it vibrated with laughter. "Remember, I'm a *very powerful woman*. I suppose you weren't too bad yourself."

We were an exhausted mess. Hysteria had started to set in. He shook his head, and for the first time ever he rolled his eyes. I pinched his side, and he let out a low growl. "Is that a challenge, Wildfire?"

"Perhaps."

A mischievous light danced across his eyes. However, it faded when whispers echoed all around us.

Declan and I took in the people who now surrounded us. Some stood in awe, others continued to whisper to each other.

"Did you see what they did?"

"Their dynamis shines brighter than all the stars in the sky."

"They all saved us. Gods bless the Light Phoenix."

We turned to face the people who had trickled out of their homes. All at once, whispers stilled and silence spread across the street. Heads bowed, and people lifted their fingertips to their lips, then placed them over their hearts. Like a ripple, the same motion was repeated by everyone surrounding us, including Liam, Killian and Nayla.

"Declan." I paused, my voice quivering. "Wh-what are they doing?"

"It's a sign of respect."

"B-but we just did what anyone else would have done—"

"No, Elena, not everyone would have done this. You've given them more reason to love you, to respect you. Reminded them to maintain hope, my love."

I swallowed, shoving down the thick emotion threatening to burst free. Not only had his words shaken me, but also the tenderness that flew through his lips when he called me "love."

"We all did this together, remember?" I whispered, giving a bow of my head to the three captains behind us and finally to the prince in front of me. I raised my fingertips to my lips.

"Elena. W-what are you doing?" He swallowed, trying to grip me around my back as I gently pushed his hands free.

I placed my palm flat over my heart, bending down on one knee in front of my prince. His eyes widened, and a smile grew like a flame upon my face. The crowd that surrounded us all rippled down to one knee.

This time it wasn't for the Light Phoenix.

This time it was for their prince.

Declan's eyes began to gloss over. He blinked rapidly, as he brushed a palm over his face. A tiny crack in his ward slivered away, enough for me to be able to feel the warm breeze of love and compassion wash over me.

"Rise," he said. At his command, we all rose, awaiting the words of our prince. "Tonight, we have learned something invaluable." He reached forward to intertwine his hand in mine. "We learned that we are never alone in this world. We are stronger together, and together we have the prowess to take down our enemies. No longer do you need to live in fear, as we will unite as one to take down the evil that surrounds our city and this kingdom. Together, we will end this."

Cheers erupted from all around us on the crowded street. Each person smiled with teary eyes full of hope. Some rushed to shake the hands of the captains or pat their backs.

The little girl from earlier, probably no older than the age of four, stumbled over to Declan. Her sunshine curls swayed in the night breeze as she squeezed the thickness of his calf in a tight embrace. I chuckled at his shocked face as he peered down to see what was wrapped around his leg. My heart throbbed as he picked her up and swung her around. She squealed with laughter, and Declan's laugh was so loud it could have rattled the windows.

Liam and Killian approached each side of me, and we watched Declan play with the little girl on the street. Liam leaned in, whispering into my ear. "It's been ages since I've seen him like this, Elena. You've mended pieces of him that have been broken for far too long."

I looked up to his smiling face just as I felt a bump against my other shoulder.

"Looks like you've gone and lived your moment," Killian whispered.

Cheeks flushed, I fought back the tears that built behind my eyes. When I raised my gaze again, I was met with a pair of smoldering emerald eyes.

They burned with desire. I felt a shove on my back, followed by chuckles from the men behind me as I shuffled forward towards the prince.

My body tensed as one of his warm hands wrapped around my waist, pulling me in closer. His knuckles slid over my cheek, sending shivers across my skin as my dynamis chased after his touch.

"So, how does one make an exit from here?" My words were breathless.

He leaned in so closely that his lips brushed the edge of my earlobe. "You fear the dark, but how do you feel about shadows?"

His breath tickled my neck. I bobbed my head in approval. Declan gave a nod to his captains, then pulled me into his chest. "Hold tight, love."

A whirl of black surrounded us, and in a blink, we were back in my room in the castle. Taking a deep breath, I filled my lungs, massaging my temples to erase the dizziness left behind. "I don't think I'll ever get used to tha—"

Before I could finish, Declan's lips collided with mine.

CHAPTER 36

DECLAN

Elena's back slammed against the door as I shoved her against it. The gasp that escaped her luscious lips sent a bolt of electricity down my body, straight to my already aching cock. Invigorated by the sultry sound, I devoured every inch of her lips like a starved man.

I'd meant for our kiss to be delicate, tender, a gentle caress of the way she made me feel every day. However, after what she'd done in the city, the temptation had become insatiable. Elena had no idea what that simple gesture meant to me. Shame had always loomed over me like the very shadows I summoned. Darkness might fuel my dynamis, but it had its claws wrapped tightly over my mind as well.

Tonight, when the people of my city kneeled in respect, some of that darkness dissipated from my soul. It had been a long time since I'd felt a smidge of the happiness that seemed to exude from Elena.

There were no words to explain the emotions that had flooded my body when the people of our city smiled, even laughed together with...*me*. Forgiveness was something I knew I didn't deserve, but even in the cold depths of my frozen heart, it was my deepest desire.

Slowly, the weight of my world was being lifted by this gorgeous woman in front of me. Elena's power didn't just reside in her dynamis. Her entire being radiated with kindness, passion, and immeasurable strength. It hummed with hope.

Perhaps hope was one of the strongest emotions of them all? Maybe it was hope that we needed to light our way through the darkness of this kingdom.

I needed this woman.

All of her. Mind, body and soul.

My restraint had shattered into a million pieces, as well as all the reasons that had kept me away from her. Tonight, I was going to show my Wildfire just how much I'd fallen in love with her.

When I'd first laid eyes on Elena, there was no doubt that she would be my undoing.

Tonight, I would be hers.

I sucked on her bottom lip, eliciting a whimper from her. Delight filled my chest at her silent plea for more. My hands fell beneath her thighs, pulling her legs around my waist. Heat radiated off her in waves as she squeezed her legs around my back, pulling me flush against her chest. Our heartbeats danced together as one.

"Declan..." she gasped.

"Yes, love?" I panted in between needy kisses, my hands exploring every gods-given inch of her body. I slipped my hands under her tunic, palming the underside of her breast while my thumb brushed over the thin fabric covering one of her pebbled peaks.

"I—I... oh...gods—"

A chuckle rumbled deep within my throat. "Love, the only name that will leave your lips in the heat of passion will be mine. Do you understand?"

"Is that an order?"

I nodded. Then, the little vixen stared me straight in the eye and smirked. "Yes, sir."

Hells. This woman was going to destroy me.

I twined my fingers in the waves of her hair, palming the back of her head. When I tugged on her locks, she tilted her head back to expose her neck. Lena's vibrant eyes glossed over before they snapped shut when my lips caressed their way down to the sensitive spot between her shoulder and neck. I grazed my teeth over the smooth flesh. Another breathy moan fled from her beautiful mouth.

Pushing away from the wall, I carried my Wildfire towards her bed. Her arms were draped around my neck, fingers gliding through my hair. Our lips began a delicate, featherlight exploration. Each brush became more reverent than the next, filled with the passion our words couldn't express.

Elena's body trembled beneath me as I laid her back onto the bed. I used my legs to spread hers further apart, inching my way closer to her body.

A wince spread across her face, and I looked down to see her pant leg reddened with blood.

"Damn it! Elena, you're bleeding." I reared back.

After tearing off her boots, I saw the bite wasn't as bad as my fears had thought. I wrapped my hands around the wound and summoned the dynamis I had left in my well. She glanced down at me with wide eyes, and I couldn't help but smile at the beautiful sight. As I grabbed a wet cloth to clean both of us, she sat stunned in silence on the bed.

"Clara's been teaching me a few things." I grinned, trying my best to chuckle at her gaping mouth. "Healing dynamis has been a slower process for me to learn, so I'm not the best. It would probably be wise to see her tomorrow to make sure you're completely healed."

Without another word, I enveloped one of her hands in mine. Turning it over, I pressed my lips against her palm. She rolled her lip between her teeth before she spoke.

"I...I've not done *this*," she whispered, "yet."

A rosy flush filled her cheeks, stirring a sly smile across my face. She shielded her head into the covers and her gaze avoided mine at all costs. I held her chin between my fingers as her anxious eyes met mine through her thick lashes.

"Wildfire, while I am honored to know you'll allow me to be your first, I'm more enthralled to know that I will be your last," I whispered into her ear, smiling against her cheek as her breath hitched. "Because after tonight, there will be no other man who lies beside you but me. You will be mine, Lena, and I'm never letting you go."

Guiding my hand leisurely up her thigh and along her body, I paused only to tease the exposed skin at the edge of her tunic. Pieces of her long locks fell into her face, and she gave me a nod, permission to keep going.

I tangled my fingers in the laces of her white tunic until it was loosened. As my calloused palms brushed against her supple skin, her body hitched towards me. Lena's fingers curled around the edges of my tunic as she helped me strip it over my head and toss it to the floor.

Air escaped my lungs at the sight of her. I feared I might have forgotten how to breathe. Delicate, smooth skin sang to me like a siren, my hands unable to stop roaming over the curves of her. Freckles sprinkled over her entire body like constellations in the night sky. Long, luxurious auburn hair spread across the sheets in waves. Gods, her eyes were like crystal pools of water urging me to dive in and never surface.

Elena was breathtaking, and unlike my panic attacks, I'd allow her to steal my breath any day, any time.

Cheeks still dusted in a rosy shade, her arms went to shield her chest, protected only by a thin wrap of material. I gathered her hands in one of mine and lifted them above her head. "No more hiding from me, love."

My lips caressed her forehead, then feathered the tip of her nose with my own. Our eyes locked as I captured her lips once more, pouring into it all the passion that had been pent up inside of me. Her aqua eyes were clouded in a lusty haze, but there was a fire within them that emboldened me.

There's my Wildfire.

"There's nothing that you could tell me or show me that would keep me away from you. I want all of you. No more hiding."

One of her hands wiggled between mine, breaking free. Without tearing away our gaze, she glided her hand across my chest. Fingertips light as feathers trailed a path down my arm towards my free palm.

She trapped my hand beneath hers, and they began an excruciatingly slow path towards her breasts. Together, we began to pull down the material wrapped around them.

Until we were interrupted by a knock at her door.

My head sagged beside hers on the bed. I groaned into the sheets. Her chest shook underneath me, not from trembling but from the laughter she was trying desperately to contain.

"Are you laughing at me, Wildfire?"

Lena's eyes went wide as she shook her head. Her hand slid over her mouth to contain the snort that flew from her nose. Giving a little pinch to her side, I couldn't hide the smile that peeked out at her squeal.

Another rap at the door sent my blood boiling once more. My roar bellowed out to the unfortunate person standing behind it.

"This interruption better be urgent. Especially if you like your head to remain attached to your body. I am not to be bothered the rest of the night otherwise!"

A deep chuckle I knew all too well floated into the room from the other side of the door. Slowly I rose, taking a few steps towards the door. Liam's voice rumbled through it.

"My apologies, Your Highness, but the king has requested your presence...urgently."

Both hands curled against my side as another rumble of frustration rattled inside my chest. A shy smile lifted Lena's flushed face. Entranced, I couldn't take my eyes off her even as she hid her beautiful body with her tunic. Long legs fell to the floor as she rose from the bed and closed the gap between us, intertwining her delicate fingers between mine.

"I'll be waiting." She brushed her smooth cheek against mine as she whispered against my ear, "Come find me when you're done, *sir*."

Lifting my other hand to her face, I rubbed my thumb over her swollen lips. "I will return shortly...I promise."

She pressed her lips against my thumb as she tilted her head towards the door. I willed my legs to leave the room before I could change my mind.

My boots felt full of iron as I stomped alongside Liam. A ripple of nerves flooded through me and wrapped around my spine. This feeling wasn't coming from me. Liam cleared his throat as my gaze drifted towards him.

"S-sorry, my ward slipped a little," Liam stuttered. The man's ward has always been as solid as a rock. He'd never slipped before, much less stuttered.

"Liam," I barked, "just tell me. What the Hells has you so shaken?"

He cleared his throat. "The king and Alastor—as you may have guessed, are not very happy about our little display in the city."

"Yeah, I figured as much," I huffed.

Silence fell as whips of shadows rippled over my arms.

"Hells, just spit it out, Liam."

"Your father—" His throat bobbed. "He asked me to bring him the whip, Dec."

A familiar metallic taste saturated my mouth as more continued to drip against the stone floor. I would not be returning to Lena any time soon. Already, I was breaking my promises to her, just like I ended up doing to everyone in my life.

Somewhere in the night, time had evaded me. Daylight shone from a sliver of a window near the ceiling of the stone wall beside me. This room was all too familiar, though it had been a while since I'd seen the inside of it.

The musty smell invaded my nostrils, evoking memories of all my past visits. Of being hauled in here to remind me of my place and my allegiance to this kingdom. Of the lies that dripped from my father and Alastor about how these "lessons" would teach me to be a strong royal. There were no lessons at all. Rather, my father had attempted to bleed the weakness out of me.

A whoosh came from behind me. The tails of the whip shredded deeper into my skin, and I could no longer hold in my shudder.

Self-healing was a natural ability once Elysians had gone through

Ascension. With the strength of my dynamis, I healed faster than most Elysians. However, when I was brought down here, it was never fast enough. Healers were often brought in to heal me so that my father or Alastor could continue with their "lessons" without me passing out. Over the years, my tolerance to pain had grown abnormally high, but everyone had a breaking point, even me.

Judging by the pain that radiated throughout me, I was getting close to needing another healing. Boots paced behind me, the sounds of more than just a pair. My father must be here with Alastor. Sometimes, they took turns dealing out my punishment.

There had been countless opportunities for me to leave this place, to be free of them. Each time, I'd turned them down, remembering my true purpose. I'd stayed to help those who couldn't help themselves. There was no way I could leave them unprotected.

A small part of me, a very small part, also held on to the hope that my father would wake up one day with a change of heart. My mother had had faith that he would one day find the path back to the light, which was why she'd written to me the night she died. She'd begged me to fight for him, to help him see the error of his ways.

Another promise I wouldn't be able to fulfill.

As if possessed by the Hells themselves, a deep roar bellowed out of me and the whip slashed deeper this time. I felt a chuckle vibrate against the back of my skull.

Fucking Alastor Grimshaw.

I should have known that it would be him handling the whip in place of my father. He had hated me ever since my Ascension, especially once my dynamis became stronger than my father's.

Everything in this kingdom had begun to fester and wither the moment he became my father's advisor. It was Alastor I blamed for the evil that had taken root inside my father. There was no question that I held a hatred for my father, but Alastor? My disdain for him knew no bounds. One day he would meet his end in the same manner that he'd murdered my family, at the end of a blade.

A chill ran down my spine as he gripped my hair, raising my face to his.

"I thought now that you were older, you'd be a little wiser. Then we wouldn't have to visit this room as often, little prince."

Hells, how I despised when he called me that. "You know me, I can't resist a good time."

Alastor growled, his fist colliding with the flesh of my cheek. He leaned down close. Close enough for me to get a deep draw of his foul breath.

He flicked his fingers against the jagged red scar on the back of my neck. "Don't forget who holds the real power here, boy."

When I didn't respond, he merely chuckled and exited the room with a crash of the door.

Before I could regain my breath, the door swung wide once more and the screech of the wooden chair against the stone floor stung my ears. Father slid the chair to where I kneeled, hands bound to iron rings on the floor. Iron to make sure I wouldn't use my dynamis.

He squeezed my shoulder, making me hiss in pain. A smug look of satisfaction grew on his face. Rage continued to build within me as I spit out the blood pooling in my mouth.

Disgust replaced his smirk. He pulled out a handkerchief to wipe away the blood from his pristine black boots. "Is there anything you would like to share about your display in my city?"

Grinding my teeth together, I tried to remain calm. "No, not really."

My father's face turned red, earning me another strike across my already bruised cheek. It took everything inside of me to keep my face in a state of boredom.

"Behave," my father growled, "and this all stops."

Rage shattered my bored expression. "Dammit, Father! I told you about those beasts! They were killing the people inside of our town, outside in the forests...children died! Children! Do you not care about the people in your city any longer?"

"They are weak. I have no room for weakness in my city," he scoffed.

"I don't even know who you are anymore." My voice was ragged.

"I'm your king, and you'll do well to remember that *son*." He tossed the handkerchief at me and rose from his chair.

"I know exactly who you are. The question is, do you? Or has Alastor washed every good part of you away to the point that all that's left is his minion to do his dirty deeds?" I seethed, earning me another slap.

I took a steadying breath. "Once, you were brave, stoic...even compassionate. You helped those in need in your kingdom. You were a loving husband who brought fresh flowers to your wife every morning, and a father who rode horses with your sons every afternoon."

The blood drained from his face. We didn't talk about my mother or brother, ever.

"Can't you see, Father?" My throat became thick with emotion as my father's eyes glossed over. "Don't you see what you're doing is destroying this realm? It destroyed *them*...and every day it's tearing me apart."

We glared at each other in silence. I prayed to all five gods that this would be the day I finally broke through to him.

"This is the only way," he breathed.

"It's not."

Rage filled his eyes once more, burning away any sign of remorse. "Will Elena be ready for her display at the end of the month?"

"She will."

"Good. Maybe you'll be able to redeem yourself. I'm tired of the embarrassment you bring to our family."

My teeth dug into my lips, filling my mouth again with the taste of copper.

"You leave today. I've spoken with Edan. He'll be expecting you. Examine that boy's powers and send me a post of his progress."

"Fine."

He gripped my chin, forcing me to make eye contact. "His daughter, Adara, you remember her, right? She's overseen the boy's training. She'll report to you directly."

Nausea rippled within me at the thought of having to spend even a moment around her.

"Please do try to not make a fool of yourself in front of your potential wife."

I pulled my body as close to my father as the iron would allow me. "As I've told you several times before, I will not marry her," I growled.

"The king decides what is best for this kingdom, not the prince. You will do whatever I say you will, boy." He shoved my chin out of his hand and stood up so fast the chair fell with a crash behind him.

"Also," he growled, "you will be the one to punish the guards who were on duty when the beasts entered the city. The two who were near the gate where the beasts slipped in will be sentenced to execution, by you."

Even when my eyes fell shut, they felt the blaze of my father's glare. "Clean yourself up. I expect you out in the front courtyard in an hour."

With his last words, he stormed out of the door.

A few moments later, the door creaked open and Clara rushed in and fell to her knees beside me. Over the years, she had been the only one who had ever seen the full extent of these "lessons." Now she sucked in a gasp. My back must be one gruesome sight to see.

"Gods, Declan...what reason did they give you this time, cousin?" Her voice broke off at the end.

"Have they ever needed a reason?" I sighed deeply.

A similar sigh echoed beside me as she unlocked the chains around my wrists. "Declan, I'm going to have to clean the wounds before I heal them. Some of these are deep, and I don't want you to get any infections. I think Alastor used iron-barbed tails this time. They're going to scar, and it's going to be a little more painful than usual to heal."

"It's alright, Clara. Do your worst."

She passed over a flask of whiskey. As she pressed the cloth to my wounds, I hissed at the sting.

"When you leave, tell Killian and Liam to meet me in the courtyard immediately. My father is making me take charge of the punishment of the guards on duty."

"Hells," Clara whispered.

"I will also be in charge of the execution of two of them. Two of *our* guards."

"Oh, Dec, I'm so sorry."

"I—" I shook my head to refocus before I fell apart. "I have a feeling Alastor may do something as well."

"You mean summon the curse?" Her breath hitched.

"Yes." Lifting the flask to my lips, I let the spicy liquid burn away the copper tang in my mouth.

CHAPTER 37

ELENA

After Declan left, I did nothing but toss and turn all night. In the morning the bags under my eyes were purple and puffy. The fact that Declan hadn't returned made my stomach churn. All the things that could have happened while he spoke with the king and Lord Alastor ran through my mind in an endless loop.

Breakfast lay on my side table, but the nerves that twisted my insides erased any twinge of hunger. I threw clothes on and rushed out of the room.

The halls were quiet. Too quiet.

No guards standing on patrol, no servants roaming about with trays in their hands. The eerie feeling made the hair on my arms stiffen as I picked up my pace towards the training ring.

Just as I made it to the doors, Clara rushed in. Eyes reddened, cheeks dampened, she pulled me into her arms. It nearly knocked the wind out of me.

"Come," she sniffled, tugging my arm towards the opposite end of the castle. "W-we have to get out to the courtyard before it begins."

"Before what begins, Clara?"

"Alaric is going to punish the guards on duty during the attacks by the beasts. He put Declan in charge of the executions."

The world around me went numb. Executions? Hadn't there been enough deaths already?

Clara tugged me along as I tried to shake away my shock. Pushing open the main castle doors, we stepped out into the crowd around us.

All the Royal Guard were present, flanking the sides of the massive courtyard. Residents of the city overflowed the bridge into the castle, spilling onto the gravel path that lined the grass. Six guards lined the middle of the open courtyard, shirtless and kneeling in the grass. Two more kneeled in front of them. All with their hands bound by iron shackles behind their backs.

My breaths became uneven as my eyes frantically roved over the crowd for Declan. I laid my sights on him, draped in black from head to toe. I pulled out of Clara's grasp and rushed over towards him.

"Declan," I gasped.

A moment of relief washed over me as I wrapped my arm around his back. When my palm smoothed over his tunic, his face wrinkled in discomfort. Declan wiped his expression away, moving my hand away from his back. I slapped it away, ripping his shirt up so that I could see what was going on underneath. Horror struck my face at the scars lashed across his back. Scars that could only be caused by one thing for Elysians—iron.

"WHO DID THIS TO YOU?"

Strong arms wrapped around my trembling arms, holding me still. "Lena, I'm okay—"

Before he could finish his sentence, Alaric bellowed his name. His distressed eyes scanned over mine.

"You should go back inside." Sucking in his breath, Declan pushed past me and made his way towards the row of men in the courtyard.

I took a step after him, to tell him he didn't have to go through with this, but Liam wrapped his hand around my wrist, halting me in my tracks.

Normally calm and collected, Liam silently pleaded with his eyes for me to return to his side. My shoulders sank in defeat as I took my place between him and Killian. Clara and Nayla flanked both captains.

All eyes were locked on the Lord of Shadows pacing back and forth behind the guards.

"These men have forsaken our great city. Their job is to protect and shield those in danger." The king's voice boomed over the courtyard, hushing the nearby crowd.

"However, they let in the darkness. They allowed our walls to be penetrated by those foul beasts. Their failure resulted in the loss of several precious lives, some of which will never get the chance to see this realm through adult eyes."

Cries of sorrow spilled from the crowd, piercing straight through my chest to my heart. Without breaking my stare from Declan, I reached down and grabbed Liam's hand. Instead of letting go after a squeeze, he held it tightly, both of us trying to find balance in the terror that was about to unfold before us.

"These men will receive five lashes each. A lash for every life that was lost, whipped with iron tails. Their scars will be a permanent reminder of their disgrace."

A mixture of cheers and disgruntled cries rang out from the crowd, the division of their opinions clearly evident. Even Alaric's face faltered for a fraction of a second before regaining composure.

"The remaining two guards will pay the ultimate price. For falling asleep during their duty, letting the beasts slip right through our front gates, and allowing the loss of innocent children, they are sentenced to death. May the gods have mercy on your souls."

Enthusiasm and cries of distress roared once more, and the two guards trembled with fear. Alastor handed the whip to Declan and stormed off to join Alaric. Declan ran his hand through his hair as the faintest wisps of shadows skimmed over his body. A crack in his ward, a seam torn through his control.

Killian held onto Clara's hand. Tears streamed down her face as her entire body trembled. Killian's eyes glistened in the sunlight. A tear rolled down the side of Liam's cheek. Nayla gently wiped it away. My eyes fluttered closed, and for once in my life I desperately wished that this was all just a dream.

"We can't allow this to h-happen." My lip trembled. "We have to s-stop this."

"Lena, if we interfere now, it will only become more devastating for everyone involved. Including Declan." Liam scrubbed a palm over his mouth like the words had physically pained his lips.

Numb, we all watched as Declan began the lashings.

The sound of the whip's tails cracking against flesh slick with blood would haunt me for the rest of my life. After each round, Declan paused, as if trying to regain courage and composure simultaneously. By the time he made it to the last guard, the crowd's voices fell eerily silent and I teetered on the verge of passing out.

Limping towards the edge of the courtyard, the final guard took up ranks with the others. The wind swept in from the sea, sending a chill throughout my body.

From behind the flanks of men, Alastor emerged and stopped directly in front of Declan. Both men glared at each other.

Declan shook his head, lips moving in a silent conversation. Alastor grabbed him around his neck and leaned in close. As he whispered, Declan's body became taut, and my heart sank to my stomach when the whip slid out of his hand and crashed to the ground.

Clara's sob beside me was muffled, and I could barely feel Liam's palm as it tightened around my own. All I could focus on was the stranger who now was staring straight into the depths of my soul.

Once-bright emerald eyes were shadowed and dulled. All that was left was an endless void of black. Life faded from his face, leaving pale flesh behind. Shadows unraveled from Declan's body at an alarming speed, twisting around him in a turbulent storm of destruction.

Darkened eyes still lingered on mine as the pull I always felt around him tugged against my chest. I leaned forward into the pull. A wave of remorse and shame slammed into me. It drowned me so heavily with emotion, my legs threatened to give until Killian pulled me back up.

Declan's eyes widened, almost in concern, yet his face remained cold. A burst of air fled out of me as I pushed out the emotions, and I took two steps towards him.

As I did, Declan shook his head, halting me in my path. His lips pursed, like he was fighting whatever had taken over him, as a single tear rolled down his cheek.

Then he turned and charged toward the men.

My mouth opened to shout when Killian slid a heavy palm over it and slammed me backwards into his chest. "Hush now, Lena. It's too dangerous to go after him right now. No one will get through to him in this state."

I was grateful he left his palm over my mouth, because a scream fled my lips a second later.

Declan's shadows surrounded the two men, tightening around them like rope. He launched them into the air, then slammed them into the ground with a deafening quake. Moans tore from the men as he raised them up once more, feet just barely hovering above the ground.

The Lord of Shadows stepped between them, unsheathing his sword and raising it high. When he spoke, all air fled my lungs at the otherworldly sound that crept out of him

If death had a voice, this would be it.

"Every slash and scrape those who died endured, I will make you feel. You will suffer the way they suffered. You'll die the way they died, terrified and alone."

The men's pleas rained over the courtyard, but were silenced the moment Declan's blade met flesh. Each slice of the sword was more devastating than the last, and my head thrashed against Killian's chest.

However, nothing could peel my eyes away from the man hacking the life out of those before me. It was as if I hoped that he'd feel my searing gaze and stop.

No matter how much I hoped, it didn't end until the ground and Declan were soaked in scarlet. The final blow sent a rain of blood over the crowd, misting my entire body.

Lifeless bodies fell to the floor, and Declan turned to face us. Alastor grinned, his lips moving silently. The delight in his eyes made my stomach upend.

Declan's chest rose and fell in heaves, his gaze now pinning the six remaining guards off to the side. With a flick of his wrist, his shadows grabbed one of them by the ankle and dragged his body towards them.

"NO!" I screamed, ripped away Killian's hand and ran towards Declan.

The shadows fell from around the guard and leapt towards me, pushing me down to my knees in the gravel. Shouts rained all around us. His father, Killian and Liam unsheathed swords left and right.

All of it fell away.

The only thing that held my attention was the man stalking towards me, shadows blazing off him like ruinous flames. He towered before me as he wrapped his hand around my throat and dragged me to my feet. Chest heaving, he pulled me in closer until we were only inches apart.

Placing my trembling hand over his heart, I pleaded to the man trapped behind the darkness.

"Come back to me."

His face contorted and his body tensed as if something inside was battling for control. Fingers tightened around my throat with a bruising grip. Just when I began to feel air slipping from my lungs, all at once everything ceased.

He released me, stumbling backwards, his emerald eyes wild. His knees caved underneath him. Tremors broke out over his body, his breath coming out in short spurts as he stretched his arm towards me.

"Elena," he gasped.

Our fingertips brushed just as massive arms grabbed me around my middle and lifted me backwards.

Guards.

"Release me!" I thrashed, kicking and swatting my arms at anything I could.

"Elena!" Declan snarled, trying to claw his way to his feet, but only stumbled into Liam's and Killian's arms.

My elbow collided with the guard on my right, and my body dropped for a second before someone else took his place.

The last thing I saw was Declan's outstretched hand grasping towards me as he screamed my name from behind his brothers in arms.

A fist slammed against my head and my world faded to black.

CHAPTER 38

DECLAN

Unhinged fury burned through me, every part of me ignited and ready to combust when those bastards carried her away. When Elena's flailing body went limp, the roar that tore out of me could have broken the glass windows of the castle.

"Declan!" Liam yelled, struggling to keep hold of my thrashing body. "She'll be okay, we'll—" My elbow crashed against his gut, and he fell forward with a grunt. "Calm the fuck down, brother, so we can take care of her ... together!"

Struck out of my frenzied rage by the distress in Liam's voice, I stilled for a moment. My brothers' terrified faces were drenched with blood.

Blood of two guards who were supposed to be under my care and my protection. Two men I'd failed. I stared back at my brothers, the guards' blood still dripping down my face, as a tremor worked its way down my body. I was overwhelmed by the fear that one day the blood on my hands could be theirs, and I would have no control over stopping it.

The world around me spun as I shoved out of their grips and zephyred down to the ocean. I knelt in the frigid waves, scrubbing my stained skin with trembling hands.

Death and destruction.

That was all that I would ever be in this world.

The water began to turn scarlet, but no matter how hard I scrubbed blood still stained my skin. Just like the shame that lay heavy inside my soul, I feared there was nothing I could do to erase that feeling.

A gust of wind ruffled the back of my hair, and the sound of boots splashing through the waves came closer.

"Brother..." Killian knelt in the water beside me, placing a steadying palm across my back. A similar weight pressed across the other side as Liam joined the two of us.

"I'm so tired..." The words clogged inside my throat as my haggard voice strained to push them through. "I—can't do this anymore."

Killian sucked in a breath, and Liam's hands clawed into my tunic.

"I can't be responsible for any more loss of lives, innocent lives. Lives that I've promised to protect."

The dam of emotions I'd constructed my entire life burst wide, tears rolling over my cheeks in endless waves.

"The worst part is, while under his control I can see everything." I paused to strain a breath, my chest becoming tighter every second. "All my senses are activated. I see every abomination I commit, and all I can do is scream helplessly watching the nightmare unfold in front of me. I can't let anyone else meet their end at my hands. Please." I drew a dagger from my belt and clasped it tightly. "Just let me finish this like I should have that day twenty-three years ago."

Killian swiped the dagger out of my hands and tossed it into the depths of the ocean. His chest rose and fell, his face reddened with frustration.

"Just like I stopped you that night on the cliff, I will stop you now," he growled. He grabbed my arm and fell back into the salty water to face me. "Listen to me. We need you. This realm needs you. The gods did not bless you with the most powerful dynamis on a whim, Dec. Every single soul in this realm has purpose. We may not always know or understand what that purpose is, but maybe that is the point. To learn our purpose through trial and error."

Liam's head dipped in solidarity, as he squeezed my shoulder.

"All I know, brother, is that we are meant to *live*. To find the joy in every moment, to fight for the people we care about, and sometimes even fight for ourselves when the darkness threatens to conceal the light that shines within us." Killian rubbed a palm over his face, removing the tears from his swollen eyes.

Liam's deep, caring voice drew my gaze, his face mirroring the same redness as Killian's. "You are never alone, Declan. I can only imagine the pain that you've carried over the years, but you don't have to be on this journey by yourself. We'll be here to remind you of all the good you've done, all the light you've given back to this kingdom."

I scoffed, shaking my head. "What good?"

"Declan, you single-handedly organized the completion of Oria and made it a thriving and livable community for humans and Elysians seeking refuge from the tyranny of your father. You've built and fostered alliances for the Rebellion, planned several strategic attacks against the Nightshades, all while working hard to discover the mole in our ranks."

"That's just—"

"What, not good enough for you?" Liam snorted, crossing his arms across his chest. "Okay, how about this. You created a family for us all, bringing us together when we needed someone the most. You taught us to find the strength buried within us all when all we saw was weakness."

"Liam…" My voice cracked.

"No, let him finish. You need to hear this and get it through that thick broody skull of yours."

I glared at Killian to which he returned a sly smile.

"One more thing. You've begun to heal a little bird who's lived her life trapped in a cage of her own mind. Declan, you've begun to show her that it's possible to spread her wings, take a leap and fly. Most importantly, you've shown her that it's okay to open her heart."

Tears flooded down my cheeks once more. My head hung low, heart breaking wide open at the mention of my beautiful Light Phoenix.

"I—I'm her mate."

"We know," my brothers hummed in unison.

"H-how?"

They both looked at me with smiles as Killian patted my back. "You'd have to be blind not to see that both of you are hopelessly head over heels for each other. Well, that and Clara told me."

"And who told her?" I growled.

"Eloise." They chuckled.

"Hells. Is there anyone left who doesn't know?" I huffed, wiping my swollen eyes as I stood.

"Elena, apparently."

They rose to stand beside me. My mind whirled as I struggled to figure out my next step.

"I love her." I sighed. "But, gods, I don't know how I'm supposed to keep her safe from me. From all of this. Bringing her into my life could shatter every remaining bit of light inside of her, and I would never be able to forgive myself."

"You deserve to be happy, to feel loved for the person you are." Killian embraced me, releasing me just in time for Liam to do the same.

"She'll never look at me the same way after today." Emotion swelled in my throat once more as I tried to shove it down.

"You need to give our little lady a smidge more credit. She fought like a wild terror just to get to you, even after we warned her against it. Elena was still willing to walk through fire to get to you."

The bond tugged against my ribcage as Liam spoke, nudging me to acknowledge the truth in his words.

"Take care of her while I'm gone?" My voice was strained by the reminder that I must leave.

"Of course, brother. We do this together, always."

CHAPTER 39

ELENA

The throb inside my head beat in time with the drips of water leaking through the crack within the ceiling of the cell. Cool stone stung the side of my cheek.

Moss and dirt crumpled under my fingertips as I wrangled my body into a sitting position. Cobwebs hung in the corners of my stone-lined room, and the air was musty. The faint smell of something metallic elicited a shiver down my spine. I forced the fear building inside me back down.

At the end of the hall, a door swung open with a thud, followed by two sets of footsteps. When Clara wrapped her fingers around the bars of the cell, I almost fainted with relief.

"You can leave us now, Ryder."

The guard, whose nose was now bandaged, grumbled beside her and didn't budge. I had to lower my head to shield the smirk.

"Would you like to tell the king why you wouldn't leave the Royal Healer alone to heal the Light Phoenix?" Clara crossed her arms over her chest, tapping her toe against the damp stone floor.

He leaned in close, trying to intimidate her into submission, but the Healer remained as solid as a rock. With a huff, he blazed past her, grazing her shoulder. The door slammed behind him, and the guard was gone as quickly as he'd come.

The clang of iron reverberated against the cell door as Clara unlocked it and swooped down to embrace me. "I'm so glad you're okay," she said breathlessly, tossing the keys aside.

"What was all that about?"

She gave me a perplexed stare, so I nudged my head toward the door.

"Oooh, that," she chuckled lightly through her nose. "Scorned lover. Easy on the eyes, but the emotional range of a turnip. I love my men like I love my onions—sweet, spicy and full of layers." She gave me a tiny wink. Only Clara could bring a smidge of humor into this disastrous situation. "How are you feeling?" she asked, rubbing her fingers over the tender spot where Ryder had struck me.

I winced. She scooted closer, placing both hands on my shoulders. Warmth spread through my limbs and over my cheek, healing me from the inside out. If only her dynamis could erase the pain, fear, and worry that still dwelled inside me from today's events.

"And now?"

"Better." My voice cracked, the worry crawling its way out, clouding my eyes with tears.

"Oh, honey…" She wrapped her arms around me and pulled me in. "He's okay. What we saw was"—she paused to clear the sorrow from her throat— "horrifying…"

A shudder rippled over my body as unwanted images of this morning flashed before my eyes. "What happened to him?"

Clara's eyes shifted downwards, twisting the gold ring around her thumb. "Can I tell you a story?"

Nodding, I crossed my legs. Clara's teeth tugged at her bottom lip as she matched my position.

"This is really not my story to share, but I feel like it's necessary for you to hear it." She massaged her forehead as she gathered courage.

"I've been surrounded by powerful people my entire life, Lena. Some who choose to use it for good, and others…well, others who don't. I've learned you can be the most powerful person in the world and still feel entirely helpless. Still feel broken inside, no matter how hard you try to piece yourself together for everyone else."

Her eyebrow rose as her gaze locked on mine. I nodded. It was hard not to take note of the insinuation in her words.

"Do you know what happened to Queen Lenora and Prince Keir?"

My lashes lowered, and my reply was filled with sadness. "Yes, they were supposedly killed by rebels who infiltrated the castle."

"Rebels, ha." Her laugh was void of mirth. "Well, I think you and I both know it wasn't the Rebellion, but someone unfortunately did murder them both. All of us will forever regret not being able to be there for them. One person carries that burden, that guilt more than any of us."

"… Declan?"

Sucking in a deep breath, she nodded. "We were all sent away. Each of us had a different task we had to do that day. Sometimes—" Clara's lip quivered. "Sometimes, I almost feel like Lenora and Keir knew. Like they pushed us all away on purpose."

My chest began to tighten as Clara's eyes became glossy and red.

"When everyone returned to the castle that night, we were informed of their deaths. It felt like life was sucked right out of me, out of all of us." She sniffled. "Lenora had become like a mother to me, especially after Alaric kept me away from my own. That night, I lost my mom all over again."

Extending my palms towards hers, I cocooned them into my own. She grasped my hands, steadying herself.

"Though it was painful for all of us, it completely shattered Declan. Rage consumed him, and he wrecked his room. Before we could stop him, he stormed into the throne room, grabbed his father and unleashed his dynamis on him."

A gasp left my lips at the image of Declan and his father brawling. There was no way that they hadn't punished him for that. *Hells, what did they do?*

On bated breath, I waited.

"Declan is strong, but at the time, so was Alaric. In the end, Alaric overtook Declan, knocking him unconscious. The king and his advisor punished him with their usual tactics, but when I was finally allowed to heal him...something was different. I felt something festering within him, and no matter how hard I tried to heal him, I couldn't reach that darkness."

I lowered my ward and was bombarded with a wave of her emotions. Shame, guilt, sadness all seeped into my skin. The heaviness was unbearable, like my body was being smashed underneath the stone walls of this castle. Concentrating on the emotions, I reached down deep for my dynamis and pushed them out of me. A gush of air flew around us, sending our hair twirling.

"We all tried to move on, to find our new normal. It was a struggle for all of us, and Declan...he was lost, cold, distant. Nothing we could do could pull him away from the well of sorrow."

Heat itched against my skin as I imagined Declan's sorrow.

"About two weeks after the murders, the king ordered Declan and the Royal Guard into the city. Alastor claimed to have discovered the queen's and prince's attackers. Later that night, I was summoned below to this very room. As you can see, there are several cells down here. Each was filled with five or more men and women. Every. Single. One."

My hand shot up to cover my shock. There had to be at least twenty cells down here. The ache in my heart grew stronger as her hands fidgeted within her lap.

"My job was...to heal them after they"—she cleared her throat— "interrogated them. Before they began, Declan was pulled behind closed doors by Alastor and Alaric. I heard their shouts as he refused their orders. He yelled about their innocence and how this entire interrogation was a fraud. Declan knew they didn't have anything to do with the deaths of his mother and brother."

My mouth went dry. I had a feeling I wasn't going to like the next part of the story.

"They shouted until all at once everything went still. Alastor stormed out of the room with a smirk, followed by Alaric, who looked like he'd seen a spirit. Declan was the last to leave the room that night. His face was somber, eyes dark. He pushed past me like he didn't even recognize me and began to unlock a cell door. One by one, he began to drag them into that dark room. One by one, I was sent in to heal them. That is, the ones who had life left in them to heal."

Tears began to fall down her cheeks as my own eyes began to line with wetness. Clara's lips trembled, and she gripped the bottom of her tunic so tightly that I could see the whites of her knuckles.

"These interrogations went well into the morning. No culprit was discovered. Guards were ordered to release the remaining prisoners, a warning that if anyone dared to mess with the rightful king of Ehora again, they'd have to answer to the Shadow Lord himself."

As she let out a sob, I felt sick to my stomach, and I struggled to stay present in the conversation.

"When they all left, Declan did not follow. I rushed into the room to find him slumped against the floor. Once I healed him almost to my burnout, he finally opened his eyes. They had returned to their normal shade of green, but I could see the fear and hurt behind them. Right then was when I knew he wasn't the one in control that night."

"Dec," I breathed, a shaky hand covering my mouth.

"He asked me what happened, and Hells"—another sob escaped from her— "I—I...had to explain."

I lifted my arm around her and pulled her trembling body into me. Drawing from my well of dynamis, I summoned all the warm emotions I could think of and pushed them through her. Clara's sharp intake of breath was evidence enough that I'd succeeded.

"Declan made me explain every detail. Every. One. I watched as his body turned pale, as shame and disgust tore through him. I watched him slam his fists into the walls until they were so raw they dripped crimson onto the floor. I rubbed his back as he retched everything he ate for the past year, then held him as he sobbed."

"Hells ..." I breathed.

"I promised him I would do everything I could to fix this. To figure out what had happened. That was when I stumbled on evidence that Alastor must practice blood magic."

"Blood magic?" While reading in the library I had stumbled across a few text that spoke of this dynamis and the horrible things that it was capable of.

"We assumed whatever had happened was a one-time occurrence. However, we were painfully wrong. About a month later, Alastor reported claims of a group of rebels hiding within the city walls. Declan, Liam and Killian did some digging of their own and found it was just a small tavern, a tavern owned by Elysians who did not agree with the man currently sitting on the throne. Declan knew the real reason behind the claim, that the king was disturbed by the lack of support in his own city, and he wanted to prove a point. Obviously, Declan refused."

"I should have known when they allowed him to not do anything. Gods, I should have known." More tears began to fill her eyes again.

"What happened?" I questioned, afraid of the answer.

"That night, Alastor summoned Declan to do his bidding."

The sound of my teeth clenching together rattled inside my head.

"Killian and Liam happened to be on duty that night. They saw him return, covered from head to toe in—in blood."

Hells. My hatred for the king and Alastor was nothing new, but after hearing this…I began to plot my revenge. Declan did not deserve this suffering they had cursed him with. Somehow, I would make them regret what they have done.

"Declan was walking so slowly, gripping a sword. Killian tried to call him, even ran over to him, blocking his path, shaking his shoulders, trying everything to bring him back to the present. Declan used his shadows to fling Killian out of the way, then headed straight towards the cliff."

"No…" My voice was barely audible.

"Declan fell to his knees, bringing the sword out in front of him. Aimed directly over his heart."

Air evaded my lungs, my eyes burning with tears.

"I thank the gods every day that Killian can zephyr. Before Declan slammed the sword into himself, Killian zephyred to him. The force tossed them both over the edge, the sword falling away as they fell off the side. Killian zephyred them both again to diminish the impact of their fall into the ocean. Dec raged against him in the water until they rolled up on the shore and all the fight finally washed out of him."

Declan's apprehensiveness to sit next to me on the cliff suddenly became clearer.

"It took him a few days to finally open up, to stop being upset with all of us…especially Killian. We made him very aware that there was still so much to live for, no matter how much life threatened to break us. We all became so much more than friends that day, we became family, and with that formed an unbreakable bond. We promised each other that no matter how hard life may knock us down, we will always rise back up together. Because together, we are stronger."

Hazel eyes met mine. "Elena, we've only just met, but I can feel that you are struggling with something deep inside. I've felt it every time I've held you. I told you this story because something tells me you may understand what Declan endures. We all fight silent battles every day, whether we admit them or not. The key, however, is that those battles were never meant to be fought alone."

Words evaded me. Every word she said rang true, but the fear of sharing the most vulnerable parts of me was overwhelmingly strong. A fear of all I might lose if I did. "Thank you for trusting me."

"Of course. Maybe one day you'll trust me as well." Clara stood, pulling me up alongside her. On wobbly legs, she helped guide me out of the cell, pausing just short of the door. "Alaric wants to speak with you."

Nerves pinched against my chest. "I don't think it can get any worse than it already is, right?"

CHAPTER 40
ELENA

The tremor in my body continued to quake as Clara and I approached the king's office. Two guards stood watch beside the ornate doors. Their glares were almost as sharp as their swords.

"I wish I could go in there with you," Clara whispered.

Squeezing her hand, I tried my best to give her a reassuring smile, but it only caused her eyes to widen more with concern. Stepping forward, I knocked on the heavy doors.

"Come in."

Fearful I might lose my courage, I wrapped my fingers around the golden handle and opened the door wide.

What I saw inside the room surprised me, my body halting in place as my eyes adjusted to the sight. I had assumed this space would be as dark as the man standing with his back to me but was immediately proven wrong.

A kaleidoscope of colors cast a glow throughout the room from the stained-glass window that Alaric was staring out of. Bookshelves lined the space. Shades of blue covered the textiles and lined the upholstery. On his desk was a vase filled with magenta peonies. Everything about this space was full of life. The only thing that felt out of place was the king.

Alaric swirled his glass of whiskey in his hand before taking a swig and setting it on the windowsill. "You broke your promise to me today, Lady Morrigan. You embarrassed the crown. The Light Phoenix screaming 'no' while trying to stop the punishment of guards didn't exactly paint my decision in a good light."

His voice was low and methodical. As he turned to face me, panic released a flood of dynamis inside my body.

"Did you enjoy my cells, Elena?"

Fear stripped away my voice, and all I could do was shake my head. Dark laughter rumbled inside his chest.

"I didn't think you would. Don't challenge my rule anymore, or that cell will become your permanent residence." His searing gaze burned my forehead, awaiting my answer.

"I understand, Your Majesty."

"Good. Next time, I will not be so lenient. You fail to follow our deal one more time, or step out of line in any way, you will watch your town fall."

Hells. My dynamis surged against my body as his words added pressure against my already constricted chest.

"My son has gone to take care of some business in Vragos. While he is away, you will train with our captains."

Some of the tightness unraveled in my chest. At least he would still allow me that.

"I've also added a few more events that you'll attend with me. We'll have to do some damage control with some of the dignitaries after your little display."

Inwardly, I cringed. The cell sounded more appealing.

"Reports of your behavior during training will be given to me daily, so make sure you are behaving." He drummed his fingers against the solid wood of his desk as he raised an eyebrow, awaiting my submission.

"I understand."

"Excellent. You're dismissed. Nayla will be waiting to begin your training." With a flick of a wrist, he turned back towards the window, ending the conversation.

Shaky legs carried me to the door, until his deep voice halted me.

"Oh, and one more thing." I turned around to see a sly smile spread across his face. "Whatever you think is happening between you and my son needs to end now. Lord Edan and I have arranged for a union between our children. They will be married after the ball at the end of the month."

My heart sank into my stomach as I carried his words with me all the way towards the training ground.

CHAPTER 41
ELENA

The pain in my chest swelled and I began to feel lightheaded as I walked down the corridor that led out to the training ring, which was just outside the kitchen. With each step, I could feel my anxiety building and I paused to lean against the wall to rub the tightness away from my chest. When the pain didn't cease, I decided to cut through the kitchen and grab some water to help calm myself before I fell into a full-on panic attack.

Divine aromas of freshly baked goods invaded my senses as I stepped inside the warm kitchen. Loaves of bread and sweet pastries were scattered across the butcher-block counter. My stomach rumbled at the sight.

A few servants gathered baked goods into small baskets, their glares pinned on mine. Alana stalked out of the pantry carrying a sack of flour. Her eyes met mine and she gave a nod to the open door behind her.

Alana followed me outside a few moments later, apron full of bread and a skin of water.

"Bless the gods, you are wonderful, Alana," I mumbled into the loaf of bread I was devouring.

"Sorry about that, my lady." She nodded back towards the two women inside. "Those two are slippery as eels. Anything said within an inch of their ears goes directly back to Alastor. They're his personal servants."

My lips curled around the loaf of bread as Alana let out a breathy laugh. "Are you alright, my lady?"

She assessed my disheveled appearance as I gulped down water. "Yes, I'm okay, just on my way to meet Nayla for some training."

"If you need more food later, you stop in and see me, alright?"

"Thank you, Alana. I will."

Pulling her into a side embrace, I thanked her once more and made my way out to the training grounds. After talking with Clara about Declan, I needed more than just training for my dynamis. I needed answers. Answers about the secrets they'd been hiding for so long.

If I was to help, I could no longer be left in the dark.

B y the time that I made my way back to the training ring, the other guards had gone, leaving behind Liam, Killian and Nayla. As I got closer, Liam pressed a finger over his lips, his gaze locked on mine. Shortly after, Killian and Nayla appeared behind me. They all huddled in close, wrapping their arms around me.

"Hold on tight, Elena," whispered Killian.

In a flash, my hair twirled around me, and it felt as though I was flying inside of a tunnel of wind. Finally pine needles crunched underneath our boots, and the turbulent wind ceased.

Gigantic pine trees soared above us, and I could hear the sounds of a river rushing only a few feet away. A tent was set up near a small fire pit, and I began to realize that this must be a place they often zephyred to.

My head felt like it was spinning as we all stepped apart from each other. After adjusting my hair back into place, I clutched my stomach, trying to suppress the nausea.

"Was all of that necessary?"

"Yes, little lady. There are a lot of ears and eyes in the castle that shouldn't be privy to what we are about to discuss."

"Sorry, Freckles." Killian chuckled. "The nausea will cease soon. Longer distances stress the body a little more than usual."

"Who put those scars on Declan?" I asked, a little more bluntly than I had intended.

"I think you already know, Lena," Killian said.

I pressed my lips together, trying to force back the rage that was building inside of me. Killian was right, I'd assumed that the king or his advisor were likely responsible. Gods, I had just clung to the hope that I was wrong. "Was this the first time?"

"No," Nayla breathed.

"How long?"

"Too long," they replied, almost in unison.

I tried to erase the image of a much younger Declan displaying the same scars that I had witnessed today. Nayla placed a hand on my shoulder. "Are you okay, Elena?" she muttered.

"Barely," I breathed. "The cruelty of this realm confounds me. How could they do such horrific things to him?"

All three of their heads hung low in silent agreement.

"Ever since my Ascension, I feel like I've been trying to live up to this power the gods decided to bestow upon me. It swirls within me, urging me each day to be good, reminding me of the gods' quest to heal the evil that lies before us. How am I supposed to bring about good, when those men are far darker and more evil than those foul beasts that have threatened the land? If Declan, our most powerful Elysian, can be overpowered, what hope do I have? Honestly, some days I feel like I'm drowning, and I pray to the gods that they just let me fall into darkness."

The admission flooded out of my mouth before I could stop it. Turmoil twisted inside my stomach as I awaited their disappointment.

"I hope you know us well enough by now to trust us. To know you don't have to carry this burden alone," Killian said, giving my shoulder a squeeze.

"It's what friends do," Nayla said, placing her palm on my back and rubbed it soothingly.

"It's what family does," Liam followed. "You're one of us now, Lena. We don't let our family suffer alone ... ever."

Tears welled behind my eyes, and I no longer held the capacity to keep them in.

Over these past years, my father had become my pillar, my support system. However, I'd never fully given in to his help. Guilt over not being to handle every struggle, every fear, made me keep him at a distance, afraid to show too much weakness, too much vulnerability.

Shame had rooted itself deep within me. With each failure, each weakness, a new root dug itself straight into my soul. I was never strong enough, sharp enough, or bold enough.

If I was completely honest with myself, my whole life I'd never felt like I'd been enough of anything.

However, here with my newfound family, I began to see that I had been going about this all wrong. Maybe we didn't always have to be our own strength, or our own anything at all. Why would the gods create a world full of people for us to struggle by ourselves? Perhaps we were not created to ever do life alone in the first place.

"So, what are we going to do to protect our family?" I swallowed as my chest tightened. "And what are we going to do to protect Declan— to make sure that what happened yesterday never happens again?"

Liam's mouth curled up. A smirk danced across Killian's face. Nayla's eyes glimmered with ferocity.

"We train." Liam grinned. "We train you with all we have until you have all of the dynamis of this realm at your fingertips, Light Phoenix."

A mischievous grin spread across my face.

"When do we start?"

They hadn't been joking about the intensity of their training. We started immediately.

After Declan had shared the theory about emotions being the core of our dynamis, the four of them had begun testing out what other dynamis they could get in touch with. Killian had obtained the ability of fire. My eyes grew wide as blazing amber flame danced across his palm and through his fingertips. His emotions had always seemed so calm and collected to me. However, Declan had said that those who obtained this dynamis loved fiercely. It also explained why Eloise had Flame abilities as well.

Nayla had been working with Liam on wielding water, a dynamis we called a Tide. As she manipulated the water like a whip, my mouth gaped wide, then curled into a grin when she slapped Liam against the side of his face with it. Shortly after, he demonstrated his newfound Terran ability by breaking the ground underneath her, causing her to fall flat on her back.

The burst of laughter that came out of my mouth couldn't be quelled. Unfortunately, it sealed my own fate. In one swoop, the ground shifted from under me and a wave of water crashed across my face as I fell. We wiped away the mud from our faces. Only Killian was left pristine.

"Don't even think about it, Liam," Killian growled.

A twinkle shimmered in Liam's eye before he zephyred directly in front of him. With a wiggle of her fingers, Nayla shifted the ground underneath them and splashed them both with another round of water as they fell.

"Hey, whose side are you on?" Liam groaned, rolling off Killian as he swiped more mud from his face.

"Obviously, I'll always be on the Light Phoenix's side."

I gave her a wink as we slapped palms.

"When have you been practicing that?" Killian snorted, finally standing up.

"A man has to have some secrets, right?" Liam rolled his gaze over towards Nayla, waggling his eyebrows at her.

Nayla's tanned skin flushed a rosy red. I stifled my giggle the best I could.

"Alright, your turn, Freckles," Killian said.

Nerves twinged in my stomach as I made my way over to the captain. His golden hair was darkened with mud, but his face shone with excitement. "Let's see if we can get you to zephyr."

Once the words left his mouth, I felt as though my face had turned seven shades of green. A deep laugh bellowed out of him.

"Don't worry, Freckles, once you retch the complete contents of your stomach"—my nose wrinkled as he shrugged— "you won't have to worry about it anymore."

"Oh, boy, sounds like so much fun."

Liam and Nayla both perched up against a tree, watching. Shoving the sleeves of my tunic up on my arms, I bobbed my head, signaling Killian to begin.

A fter excavating the last remnants of my stomach, and the millionth time crashing into the icy river, a frustrated snarl escaped my lips.

For hours, I'd tried to dig deep and find the emotions that would call to my Zephyr dynamis. My first attempts, I'd just ended up launching my Tempest winds, blowing myself backwards into trees, rocks, and the river. Eventually, I was able to make myself zephyr forward, straight into the river, *again*. Water and mud saturated my body, my cheek still swollen and tender from where I had zephyred myself face first into a boulder.

An exasperated scream fled my lips as I dug my fingers into the wet earth beneath me. Palming a rock, I chucked it with all my might into the river in front of me. The act eased the rage building inside me as it splashed into the water.

"Is it safe to come closer, or should I be cautious about you holding any remaining rocks?"

I tossed my head up to meet Killian's gaze and was met with a mischievous smile, one that I couldn't help but return. "You're safe to sit, for now." I patted the ground next to me.

"For your first attempts, you're actually doing quite well, Freckles."

I snorted so loud at his statement, a few birds fled their perches from the trees above.

Killian nudged his shoulder against mine. "In all seriousness, Elena, when I first started, I zephyred myself into the ocean … multiple times."

Folding my arms across my chest, I shook my head at the improbability of that story.

"He speaks the truth, little lady." Liam dropped down on the other side of me. "Declan and I oversaw his training after he joined the guards after his Ascension. Don't think I've ever seen anything flop around so much in the water…well, besides the fish."

"I couldn't swim!" Killian shoved Liam's shoulder behind me.

"Ahh, yes. The flailing arms and gurgling sounds make more sense now."

Giggles bubbled up to the surface, so much that my hand couldn't smother them all. Liam patted my knee. "The point is, Elena, he eventually got the hang of it… floundering and all."

"Yeah, and I learned how to swim." Killian laughed out loud this time.

"Oh, don't act like it was easy for you to learn either, Liam Hart." A dark purr came from behind us. Nayla strolled over to us.

"I—I never said—"

"The memories are flooding back from when we started practicing. Yes, I can see it clearly now—"

"Woman…" he threatened with a growl.

"You zephyred yourself into the side of the cliff so hard that you knocked yourself out." Her sly lips twisted up as Liam's mouth fell open. "I remember having to drag you by your feet towards the ocean and toss you in just to wake you up."

Dark chestnut eyes glared at Nayla, who was biting her lip to contain the mirth. Killian and I were already rolling on the ground with glee as a wave of freezing water splashed over us.

"Liam!" I shrieked.

"Woman! That was supposed to stay between us," he grunted.

Nayla beamed down at me. "Elena needed to know that everyone struggles in the beginning, even you."

He rolled his eyes at Nayla but gave me a pat on my shoulder. "Well, did it help? Are you ready to try again, little lady?"

My shoulders slumped at Liam's words. "Zephyring was my first thought to try because it's the closest to my father's Tempest power, which I already seem to be using. However, each time I try, it feels like there's some missing piece. The more frustrated I become, the more my dynamis fizzles out."

"There lies your problem, Freckles." Killian lifted me up from the ground and placed my palm facing upwards in his. "As you now know, emotions are the force behind our power. The stronger the emotion, the stronger the power."

"Yes, I understand that—"

"Do you?" he interrupted. Killian hadn't used that tone since that day they collected me from my town. The gruffness in his words silenced me. "Just close your eyes, Lena. You wouldn't want Declan to find out you refused our training, would you?" Killian's grin spread wide, and snickers rumbled from beside me.

My lips pinched together, but my glare fizzled away as I did what I was told. Mostly because I didn't want Declan to return and find out he'd been right, I really couldn't take orders. With a harrumph, I slammed my eyes shut.

"Good job, Freckles. Now, I want you to choose one emotion, one single feeling, and hold onto it with everything you have. Pretend you are its captain and it's your young and sassy guard you must put in their place."

Peeking an eyelid open, I saw him smirk. I elbowed him in the gut and closed my eyes once more at the sound of his groan.

"Seriously, Elena, you're in control, you're the boss and only you can tell your dynamis what to do. If you don't believe in it, then it will not believe in you. Remember what Declan taught you in the library. Find that emotion and hold onto it."

I peeked once more as Killian beamed next to me, like he had just given me the key to unlock all the wonders of this kingdom. Hells, if mastering my power was as simple as he'd just made it sound, then there wouldn't be water sloshing between my socks and boots. Closing my eyes once more, I tried to focus, searching for an emotion to hold onto.

The familiar splash of rocks against water arose from behind me, as well as the realization I must have been lost in thought. Amusement grew within me as I watched the stoic captains before me engaged in a battle of "who can skip the rock the farthest."

"You cheated!" Liam snarled.

"No one said we couldn't use our dynamis." Killian shrugged.

They looked ridiculous, arguing like little babes. Nayla was laughing so hard that I was sure she was going to fall off the boulder that she perched upon. The scene before me was heartwarming, as if, for just a small moment in time, we had no weight upon our shoulders. Warmth bloomed in my heart, the feeling spreading throughout me.

Closing my eyelids, I reached for that feeling. It was like I could almost see a bright string of light swaying in front of me. With a deep breath, I wrapped it tightly around me, prepared to hold onto it with everything that I had. I set the end point in my mind. My eyes flung open and I released it all.

Whips of hair assaulted my cheeks as I glided through what felt like time itself, right to the spot I'd intended. Materializing before me were the strong shoulders of two very hard-headed men. All at once, the connection of my dynamis snapped, this time because of my own command.

The gust of wind I'd created by landing tousled their hair, causing a mischievous smirk to spread over my lips. Liam faced me, mouth open. Killian's grin was proud.

Before my courage slipped from me, I dug in deep and pulled on the happy feeling. Another gust of wind flew through me as I released a smidge of Tempest dynamis, launching the two men into the icy river behind them.

A thud and the crackle of leaves behind me alerted me that Nayla had officially fallen off the boulder.

Two sopping wet men emerged from the water. The desire for revenge flickered in their wicked smirks as I squeaked in pure terror. Before I had a chance to zephyr away, thick hands wrapped around my arms, launching me into the river with them.

CHAPTER 42

DECLAN

When I'd arrived in the City of Ash, I'd been given my usual quarters. Sleep had evaded me. All night I'd shifted beneath the covers, lying wide awake reliving the nightmare of yesterday as it pulled the strings of my thoughts. Images of my guards' faces and the terrified look across Elena's face as she brushed her fingertips against mine were branded across my aching heart. Each time they flashed before my eyes, the sear only became more excruciating.

Now, wiping the exhaustion from my face, I tried to focus. The midday sun blazed down upon me, and sweat beaded across my brow. I had a meeting scheduled with Edan's council in an hour. Why he had asked to meet with me separately beforehand had my curiosity piqued.

Footsteps drummed against the smooth, white stone terrace that overlooked the training arena. Like my father, Edan lived a life of luxury and excess, thriving from the coin that he took from the people of his city. Exotic and rare animals were trapped in gold-painted cages sprinkled around his gardens. Extravagantly carved furniture and tapestries made of silks and velvets decorated each room in his villa. Everything was either gilded or adorned in jewels, pristine and polished, just like the marble floor beneath our feet.

"Declan." He nodded, folding his arms over the ledge, mirroring mine. "You know this marriage is going to take place, don't you?"

It appeared my father had gone behind my back and made this deal with Edan, despite my refusal.

"You and I both know what a good alliance it will make, especially considering the state of your father's reputation."

Edan's sneer made my dynamis flare. He'd been after the crown of this kingdom for as long as I could remember. This marriage would be the closest he'd ever been to it, which was exactly why I was going to ensure it would never happen. Especially when the intel the Rebellion had discovered about the Nightshades over the years continued to point back to Vragos.

That was the other reason for being here, to speak with my informant, Brand. A raven had sent word a few days ago that there were new developments in uncovering our mole within the Rebellion. We were so close I could almost taste it.

The crunch of gravel and the murmur of voices below snapped me back into our conversation.

"I'll see you later for the council meeting." I shoved past him as he chuckled under his breath.

"Say hello to my daughter for me."

There was no need to look back. I could feel his smug smile assault me from behind as I stormed my way down to the training arena.

With my dynamis already on edge, the last thing I needed to stumble upon was Adara running her hands through Will's hair. He sat there with pink cheeks and made no attempts to stop her.

Ever since Elena had trusted me with their story that night in the tavern, I itched to unleash my shadows upon him. My fists curled as I thought about what his last words had been to her, the accusations made and the hurt and shame that festered inside her sweet soul because of them.

Clearing my throat, I stalked towards them, whipping my shadows against a crate beside them, causing them to separate immediately. Taking pleasure in their wide-eyed expressions, I passed between them until I came face to face with Will.

"I don't have all day. Show me what you've been working on." My voice was laced with unspoken threat.

Blond waves flopped across his face as his nervous blue eyes shifted to Adara's for permission. She dipped her head, and he made his way to the center of the ring.

Will unleashed his Flame dynamis in searing waves. The flames burst with increased intensity, but it wasn't anything groundbreaking. Adara shifted towards me, caressing my biceps. Recoiling, I stepped to the side, tucking my arms against my chest.

"How the times have changed," she scoffed. "I remember a time when you used to like my hands on you." The smile she gave me was anything but demure.

"That was one time, a very long time ago, Adara. A mistake that lives in the past where it belongs."

She shook her head, turning her gaze back towards Will. Boredom had begun to encroach as Will's flames turned into two flaming ropes of fire.

"Yeah, it's pretty incredible, isn't it," she hummed, observing my startled expression.

"I don't know if 'incredible' is the word I would use."

Ropes of fire twisted and turned as he wrapped them around a few of the practice dummies, scorching the hay within them until they split in the middle.

"You know, it doesn't have to be this hard, Declan. We grew up together, played together just fine. Even once we were older I wasn't too horrible to be around, was I?"

When I allowed myself to shift my glance towards her, her normally impassive face had cracked. It was slight, but there was a wobble to her bottom lip and her fingers twisted the material of her pants.

Guilt washed over me as the realization left my stomach in unease. Adara was just another tool for political manipulation, as I was. Deep down, I knew she was different from her father, something I'd always admired. However, there were several reasons this marriage would never take place. One being the fact that I'd fallen in love with the Light Phoenix.

"No, you weren't that bad to be around, Adara." My words were gentle. "But I will not marry you, and you know why this can never happen."

Hurt flashed through her eyes, but she blinked with silent under-standing.

"I've got to meet with your father and the council. We'll discuss this when you all come for the ball at the end of the month."

With a nod, she dismissed me, and I took my time walking through the villa towards Edan's council room. After this meeting, Brand would be my next stop. Instead of sending a raven with the intel, this time I would meet Warren in person.

Especially now that I had a very important question to ask him.

CHAPTER 43
ELENA

The itchy tulle of my dress suffocated me, encasing me in a violet tomb as I sat in the armchair in my room. Too exhausted to rip it from my body, I instead tore off the long white gloves that went along with it and threw them onto the floor.

Between breakfasts and luncheons with the king, rigorous training of my physical strength and dynamis with the captains, and nights of researching in the library for more information about the Light Phoenix, my candle was almost depleted.

It was becoming harder to mask indifference during these events, especially after all that had happened a week and half ago. I'd learned how truly evil Alaric and Alastor were and how long Declan had been suffering under the curse.

All I wanted to do was sleep, but I needed to meet Nayla in the queen's garden to work on my Terran dynamis. Groaning, I pulled myself out of the chair and peeled off the endless layers of the atrocious dress. As I laced up my boots, my mind stewed over today's luncheon.

Alaric had pushed for updates on my Light Phoenix dynamis. Truthfully, I hadn't asked to train that part of my dynamis because it still terrified me.

Today, I could tell he had finally met his breaking point. If I hadn't produced some showing of progress, I'd feared he would start to become curious. That curiosity could lead him towards discovering what we were really doing. Like controlling multiple forms of elemental dynamis, which was a truth that needed to remain hidden.

To appease the king and perhaps show myself that I still had a sliver of control over it, I'd made my hand glow just as I had in the library. Several guests stood in awe at the sight, but Alaric just growled and walked away. Alastor, on the other hand, seemed to be eerily fascinated.

Chills spread through my back at the thought of him. Every time we met, his gray eyes followed me like snakes studied their prey before they struck. The strange thing about it was that something about him was beginning to feel familiar. Not in the same way that it felt when I was around Declan, but a strong feeling like we had disliked each other for longer than a few weeks. Resentment so strong, it lingered between us like a cobweb we couldn't break free from.

Lacing a knot on the top of my boot, I shook the thoughts from my head. If I was going to access my Terran dynamis today, I needed to be as calm as possible.

L ast night, Nayla had told me to meet her in the garden, underneath the tree of the gods. The wooden door creaked beneath my fingertips as I pressed it open. As always, the aroma of flowers and herbs wafted throughout my senses, each time reminding me of home. Meandering through the maze of flora and trees, I finally spotted Nayla lost in thought sitting on one of the five roots of the gods tree.

So as to not interrupt her thoughts, I lowered myself next to her. Her eyes remained closed as she lifted a stem of lavender to her nose. Inhaling deeply, she sighed, tossing the stem behind her.

"Evening, Light Phoenix." She smiled towards me.

"Good evening, Nayla." I smiled back. "Where were your thoughts wandering just now?"

Her eyes lowered to her palms, and I wondered if maybe I had intruded too much.

"Today is my little sister's birthday," she said. "It's days like this that I'm reminded of the heavy weight of my choice to leave and join the guard."

"I'm so sorry, Nayla. I know my situation is entirely different, but I understand the pain of not being around family."

Producing a weak smile, she rose. "Well, that's why we all have each other, right? Shall we get to training?"

Her face shifted back to calm and collected. I understood—I was no stranger to keeping the darkest parts of you locked away deep down inside. Maybe, with time, I'd finally let my walls fall too.

The wet soil felt cold beneath my fingers. Both of my hands were immersed in the ground, as Nayla had prompted me to.

"This is the best way to connect with your Terran dynamis for the first time. It's how my mother taught me after my Ascension."

Nayla's words faded like the light from her face, her eyes focused on the distance. I knew I should be concentrating on coaxing out my Terran dynamis, but she was obviously having a hard day.

"Your mother...She was also a Terran?"

Though Nayla's ward was up, her solemn nod and blank stare that lingered on a distant memory told me there was a story there. Before I could ask another question, she began to talk.

"She's incredibly powerful, beautiful, and full of compassion. Kind of reminds me of you, Light Phoenix." A flash of warmth flooded her face before it turned somber once more. "I miss her and my sister every hour, every day, every moment. Always." Her voice broke, eyes no longer blank but glossy.

"It wasn't them you were running away from...was it?"

Honey eyes rose from the ground, landing on mine. I waited patiently, removing my fingers from the ground and sitting back on my heels.

"I ran from my father, and the life that he had planned out for me...for all of us." Her shoulders slumped as she let out a long exhale. It was almost as if this was the first time that she had been able to do so. Nayla's hands fidgeted inside her lap. I've never seen her this vulnerable. The guard in front of me was no longer shielded.

"My father—has never been a pleasant man. All my life, I've been a constant disappointment to him, which he made me aware of during every interaction we had. I was too vocal for my own good, not the respectful little lady that he wanted me to be.

"At the first chance he got, he arranged for me to marry a man from the upper class of the City of Ash. My father is a Flame, so he felt strongly that I should marry one as well. He made this arrangement when I was seven. Seven years old, and he already planned to get rid of me." She paused, swallowing deeply before she continued, "Things got worse once my little sister was born. She was everything I was not —beautiful, kind, respectful—and my father swooned over her. Little did he know, behind our closed bedroom door she would release all the hatred she held against the man we called our father. She told me of the terrible acts she had witnessed him do under the guise of 'teaching her the ropes.'

"Together we cried over the way he treated our poor mother, doing horrible things that we couldn't stop no matter how much we wanted to. The walls were closing in as I got closer to my Ascension, because I was to be married shortly after. Things got worse once my dynamis proved to be stronger than my mother's."

"This was all before the first rebellions?" I asked quietly.

"Yes." A weak smile lifted her lips. "I'm old, Lena."

I snorted, and a smirk cracked through her solemn mood.

"I knew I couldn't marry the man my father wanted me to. His vision of my life was not aligned with mine. One day, when intruders masquerading as the rebellion attacked, I knew this was my chance...a way to be free. I told my mom and sister about my plans to escape and begged them to join me. When they wouldn't, I found them a place to hide, and I made a run for it."

"Nayla..." Reaching out, I took her hand and squeezed tight.

"I made it almost to the city gates when I saw the Royal Guard beginning to flood in to help fight. I had every intention of running right past them, that is until I heard the screams. Behind me, a building had fallen, and there were people still trapped inside. Without a thought, I pulled my dynamis, everything I had in me, and I lifted the debris as they fled for safety. It was the first time that I had used that much dynamis, and I drained myself dangerously low, so much so that I passed out.

"When I woke up, I was staring back at Declan, Liam and Killian. They had witnessed what I had done and offered me a position in the Royal Guard on the spot. I accepted, of course, and from that day on I've been here. I write to my mother and sister all the time, but I've never received a response."

Her eyes fluttered shut, my own heart aching over a shared loss of family. Countless letters to my own father sat inside the desk in my room. Letters I hadn't been able to send because of the king's orders. Isolation seemed to be Alaric's favorite tactic. Little did he know, even after cutting us off from our own, we'd found family in each other.

"Declan promised me that one day we would get them out of there to a place where we can all be safe. For now, I'm just waiting for the day that I will get to see them again."

Squeezing my palm, she placed it back into the soil, then picked up the other to do the same. That was my sign that conversation time was over and it was time to refocus on training. Before I did, I added one more thing.

"Thank you, Nayla ... for trusting me with your story. I know that wasn't an easy thing to do."

She rubbed the back of her neck with her palm, rolling it around to release the tension within. "Something about you, Lena, makes it easy for me to talk to you. Perhaps, one day, you'll feel comfortable enough to share all your secrets as well."

I winced. If only she knew the secrets I had locked away.

"My friend, you're not as good at hiding your secrets as you think." She stood. "One day when you're ready, I'll be here to listen."

Before I could respond, she swatted me on the head.

"Ouch!" I laughed. "What was that for?"

"That was for distracting me from your training. Now, let's get back to concentrating."

With a snort and a shake of my head, I saluted. "Yes, Captain."

It took me a while to concentrate on my emotions enough to finally make some progress on my Terran dynamis. I managed to make some cracks within the soil, and even lifted a smaller rock and watched it hover in the air before it plummeted to the ground seconds later.

"Excellent work, Elena." Nayla patted me on the back. "Let's try one more thing before we call it a day."

The sun had started to fall behind the horizon, the sky already painted in an array of warm pinks, violets and oranges. Stretching my arms out wide, I let out a yawn and nodded with approval.

Nayla knelt in the dirt and patted the ground next to her. I mirrored her, sitting back on my heels as I awaited instructions.

"Okay, let's see if you can summon some roots or vines."

"That's possible?" I asked, trying to hide my shock.

With a smirk, she answered. "It is, for some who have powerful dynamis."

Okay then, challenge accepted.

After stretching my neck from side to side, I place my palms on the dirt. Digging my fingers into the ground, I closed my eyes and summoned my emotions, my dynamis.

Terran, Frost and Tide abilities required calm and serene emotions, which was the opposite of me. So, naturally I was struggling with these dynamis the most.

Controlling my breathing was the first step. Stretching my lungs, I inhaled and exhaled four deep, steady breaths. Reaching even further, I searched for the one feeling that had always pulled me out of the dark, that had always helped me find a sense of calm—love.

As painful as it was to remember, I thought of my mother, the way her fingers would brush through my hair as she sang me to sleep. My father's embrace was the next thing I felt. As my dynamis surged beneath my skin, I imagined roots twirling underneath my fingertips, vines slithering out from the ground and curling all around us. With a peek, I noticed the ground around us was still empty, so I dug even deeper into my emotions.

I closed my eyes again. The memory of Declan's face flashed before me, his emerald eyes blazing a hole straight into my soul. All at once, I could feel the softness of his lips as they crashed against my own, and my entire body ignited in furious heat. I could feel my dynamis pulsing everywhere inside of me, rippling against my skin, just waiting to be released.

"Uh…" Nayla cleared her throat. "Elena, your skin is glowing," she whispered, just as the creak of wood arose from behind us.

The roots of the gods' tree began to ripple and sway as smaller roots sprouted from the ground and intertwined themselves around the five solid roots. Silence passed as we both watched the smaller roots create a protective barrier around the larger ones.

"Lena, you should pull back your dynamis."

Nayla's words faded behind me. All I could concentrate on was the demanding call of my dynamis. I could feel the power threading through me, melting into the ground underneath my fingers. When I opened my eyes, my body jolted. Wrapped around my hands and arms were soft green vines, with leaves … and thorns.

"Ouch!" I yipped as a thorn dug into my pointer finger, causing it to bleed.

Before I could wipe it away, the vines took on a life of their own, circling around my wrists. With a forceful tug, the vines slammed my hands back into the ground.

Thousands of voices invaded my mind, everyone talking all at once, a hum of conversation. One voice, however, felt louder than the others, almost like it was trying to summon me. Eyes squeezed shut, I dug my fingers deeper into the soil—

"*Elena!*"

Shocked by the sound, I released my grasp on the soil and crashed onto my backside.

That voice.

It was the same voice I'd heard waking me from every nightmare. The only voice. The voice of the goddess in my Ascension.

As my mind struggled to absorb what had just happened, the vines continued to grow around me and the gods' tree. I opened my glowing palm just as a vine slid between my fingers, and a beautiful bud blossomed into a flower right before our eyes.

"Gods above," Nayla gasped, pressing a kiss to her lips and placing it against the root of the gods' tree behind us. The petals of the flower continued to unfold as we sat silently, in awe over what I had just created.

"Lena," she whispered. "No one has ever done that, not even my mother, and she was...very powerful."

Shaken from my trance, I was able to process her words. "No one has ever done what?"

"No Terran has ever created life, something new from beneath the soil, besides the vines or the roots that they can summon."

Swallowing the anxiety that wedged its way sideways in my throat, I plucked the flower from the vine and gathered the courage to ask the question lingering between the two of us. "What do you think that means, Nayla?"

"It means...you're a very powerful woman."

All the anxious energy leaped out of me in the form of a scoff, in turn causing Nayla to laugh as well.

"So, Lena...what exactly were you thinking about that made you glow?" Her face was alight with mischief.

"That's a secret that will stay locked in a vault forever." I pretended to lock my mouth and throw away the key.

CHAPTER 44

ELENA

I munched away on a delicious muffin as I walked the dimly lit halls of the castle. It was no wonder Eloise was a Flame. She was a bundle of fiery personality and extremely passionate about taking care of others. Like feeding my addiction to baked goods and chocolate.

Eloise had made me swear to stay in the room to rest after I had returned from training with Nayla. She'd told me if I went without rest or sleep for one more night, she would stop covering up the purple underneath my eyes as punishment. Naturally I hadn't followed orders. I'd waited until enough time had passed before making my escape to the library.

Welcomed by the wonderful smell of parchment, I bounced towards the area where I stored the collection of books that Declan had pulled for me. Heaving them onto the table took effort, my arms and body sore from today's training. Just as I snuggled down into my seat, my body jumped at the sound of a sneeze behind me.

"Oh, thank the gods! For once, there will be someone to keep me company while I'm forced to read the thrilling tale of *The Properties of Potions and Elixirs: Volume 12.* You'd think by the twelfth title they'd come up with something a little more original."

Stumbling around the corner of a bookshelf appeared Clara, arms wrapped around several books. They spilled onto the table as she shoveled them out of her arms. Pieces of hair had fallen in front of her face, and I couldn't help but giggle as she blew out a big breath that sent them flying. Clara's head fell forward onto her folded arms on the table as she let out a groan.

"Ugh," she huffed. "I would much rather be reading a book about love, or anything more interesting than this. Alastor has me here every week. Says he requires *extensive* notes on each potion and elixir. I think it's more of a retaliation against me."

"What did you do, Clara?" I placed my hand over my mouth, feigning shock.

Her head rose from beneath her arms, a malevolent grin growing on her face. "Well, I may have accidentally added an extra herb into his daily health tonic that made his tongue swell to the size of a potato. Which may have also been the day he had to deliver a very important speech in front of the king and council."

"You are a vicious woman, Lady Clara. Remind me to never cross you."

"That's probably wise." She smirked, then her lips fell back down into a frown. "Honestly, that man deserves everything he gets, accident or not."

"Agreed."

She got out some parchment and her quill as she began taking notes from the massive book. I opened the red leather book from last night, eager to learn more about different powers within the kingdom, still searching for something to explain the violet dynamis that had erupted between Declan and I. Of course, my thoughts lingered on Declan more than they should have.

"Why hasn't Declan just left?" I whispered.

His captains were aware of the abuse that he had been taking for years from his father and his advisor, so it wasn't a far stretch to believe that his cousin would know as well. Especially since she was also a Healer.

Clara's shoulders tightened as she inhaled a deep breath before glancing my way. "Lena, as much as I would like to share, I wouldn't want to cross my cousin's boundaries more than I already have by telling you about the curse. This story may be one he'd like to tell on his own." She paused, as if choosing her next words carefully.

"He's been living deep in the darkness for a long time. Declan is trapped here, just like I am. However, his father and Alastor have forced him to endure far worse atrocities than I have. There are things that haunt the deepest depths of his soul, but there's still so much beauty inside of it. Dec has always guarded his heart, never opening fully to anyone, even me. Perhaps he's been waiting until he met someone with enough light to help guide him out of the dark." Her hazel eyes twinkled as I let the meaning behind her words settle within me.

"I know that it's been nothing but a whirlwind since your Ascension," she said, covering her palm with mine. "I'm glad that Declan was the one to bring you back here. He needs someone like you, and something tells me that you need someone like him as well."

Lifting her palm from mine, she continued writing down notes from the massive book in front of her, leaving me staring blankly at the words on the page.

Turbulent was the word I would use to describe the interactions between Declan and I. Whenever we were around each other, there was a storm of animosity or euphoria. I supposed there was a fine line between the two. Warmth began to bloom inside of me as my lips curled up into a smirk.

Maybe Clara did have a point. Declan might have been waiting for someone like me, but something deep within me shouted out that I'd been waiting for someone like him as well.

Shoving the thoughts away, I dove back into the pages of text beneath me. I'd been searching for anything that discussed Elysians' dynamis reacting with one another, and I thought I'd finally found something.

There have been some records of combining one's dynamis with another.

Upon further investigation, we have found that these events seem to occur between fated mates...

I paused, rereading the last line aloud to myself.
...seem to occur between fated mates...
...mates...
Gulping down the fear rising within me, I continued reading.

When conducting our research, we have found that mates are often able to pull from one another's dynamis, thus increasing their own. Sometimes, we have witnessed mates using their mate's dynamis in place of their own.

    Unfortunately, there has been a decline of fated mates over the centuries, so we haven't been able to continue our research to prove if our theories are accurate.

A huff of breath escaped my lips as my shoulders relaxed. Fated mates was such an old term. Like the book stated, it was very rare to find couples who were actually mates.

It was once said that the gods themselves selected your perfect match for you to find. As the story went, fated mates found each other through their bond—somehow it guided them on a path towards each other.

Growing up, when girls in my town used to swoon over the stories of mates, I used to roll my eyes. The idea of being bound to someone you had no choice in seemed like a nightmare to me. I believed in true love, one that was created by real connections between two people, not through divine fate. Giggling to myself, I dismissed the silly notion that had arisen in my mind. There was no way that Declan and I could be mates.

As I turned the page, it crinkled. This was one of the oldest books that I had come across, so I was curious if it would include anything about the original Light Phoenix. Not finding what I wanted on the next page, I gently skipped the pages to get nearer to the end of the book. My heart jumped when the image of a Phoenix danced across the page. Unsure what to expect, I sucked in a breath as my eyes roamed over it.

This is the one and only day we were able to witness the majestic dynamis that she possessed, because after the Phoenix rose and released it, she left this world permanently.

Wait.

The Light Phoenix had only used her powers for one day? How was that possible? Unable to control my heart from beginning to race, I kept reading.

Our cities had been battling for control over the realm, and Lord Draven of the City of Shadows was the leading choice to gain that control. His family had been known for centuries to hold the unique dynamis of shadows. It is a power unlike any other in our realm, and still, to this day, no other Elysian has ever shown signs of this dynamis. Many believed that this was a gift from the gods, that it was fate for Draven's family to rule over Ehora.

On this day, a raid was sent into Grinwood, the City of Life. It was later discovered that they were going after a woman who had shown signs of a unique dynamis. There is no real evidence as to what that power was, but it was declared a threat to all Ehora. What proceeded was a massacre like no one had ever witnessed. The woman was found and assassinated, along with others who had stood in the way to protect her.

Hundreds of funeral pyres lit the night that day, but only one burnt the brightest. Through the flames and ashes rose the Light Phoenix. Once flames hit the body of the woman with the mysterious dynamis, she rose up into the sky on massive fiery wings that spread from behind her back. Her body glowed golden and her voice was described to be otherworldly. The Light Phoenix released a sorrowful cry, releasing a powerful white light across the land. The Light Phoenix perished after exerting all of her dynamis, and was later buried beneath the soil for fear of what another pyre might bring.

It wasn't until later that the realm discovered several Elysians, including Lord Draven, had also perished that day. Many witnesses described their deaths almost like their life force was pulled straight from their bodies—one moment they were alive, and in the next dead. Unrest grew throughout the land, and there was a call for a king to be declared immediately to ensure the safety of the land.

Lord Draven had left behind a son, Kage Stallard, who had also inherited the shadow dynamis. It was made known that Lord Kage believed the Light Phoenix was sent to us as a warning of what happens when we allow evil and darkness to sway our minds. He declared the Light Phoenix had rid the land of evil and provided us with the hope of creating a peaceful kingdom.

Supporters of Lord Kage rallied for him and he eventually became the first king of Ehora. Ever since then, Ehora has lived in peace. It was declared that a Stallard shall always remain on the throne. They will bring peace and unite the kingdom, and the Light Phoenix is remembered as the vessel sent by the gods to help them complete this task.

The breath had been knocked out of me while I read, but I couldn't help but laugh out loud at the last line that passed before my eyes.

"... a Stallard shall always remain on the throne. They will bring peace and unite the kingdom."

How fate had been proven catastrophically wrong. I wondered if the gods were shaking their heads at the state the kingdom was in, thanks to Alaric Stallard.

After the shock passed, I reread the passage just to make sure I had read it right the first time. I slouched deeper into the chair, and a heavy sigh escaped from within me.

The original Light Phoenix hadn't even lived long enough to understand the power within her. She had been assassinated for just being different. Shivers ran down my spine at the thought. Would this end up becoming my fate as well?

I ran a hand over the tightness forming in my chest as questions flooded through my mind. Why did people look to me with hope? Had they not read this account of that day? Shouldn't they be fearful of me instead? Or maybe they thought I'd become a weapon and take out the darkness that was shadowing Ehora?

I needed to distract myself before my thoughts turned into an overwhelming fear that I couldn't control. This book seemed too important to place back on the shelf, so I stood and gathered it and a few other books into my arms.

"Everything alright?" Clara's eyes wandered over my worried expression.

"Yes, I just—I'm just a little hungry and tired. I think I'll head back to my room and take a nap."

"You're not coming to the dinner tonight?"

"Oh, Hells," I groaned, "I completely forgot about the dinner tonight. At least you'll be at this one."

"Get a little rest, Lena. Dinner won't be for a few more hours anyway." Her smile warmed me, and some of the worry began to flee.

"See you later, Clara."

I made my way through the double doors of the library and ran right into Alastor Grimshaw. The books clattered to the floor, and I almost toppled with them before hands wrapped around my shoulders and held me steady.

My flesh chilled underneath his palms, and my head filled with the sounds of thousands of horrified screams. My wide eyes locked onto Alastor's. He appeared to be just as fazed. The connection was shattered when a familiar voice from home filled the air next to us.

"Elena?"

Will.

"Everything alright?" he asked, looking between the two of us.

The boy who stood before me seemed quite different than the one I grew up with. His skin looked tanner than I remember, as if he'd spent days in the sun. His normal floppy, blond hair had been combed back and styled. And his clothes looked pristine, not a wrinkle or speck of dirt on them.

Alastor's hands fled from my skin and he stormed down the hallway without so much as a backward glance. Still reeling from what had just happened, I barely noticed that Will had picked up my books and was holding them out towards me.

"It's good to see you again." His words were gentle.

I grabbed the books from him with trembling hands, and then he threw his arms around me. Thrown for a loop, I struggled between wanting to recoil or letting myself relax into something that felt so much like home.

The shock wore off, and I remembered the hurt he'd left me with only two weeks ago. Shoving myself away from his arms, I took two giant steps away.

"What are you doing here?" I asked tersely.

His smile faltered, and he brushed his hand over his mouth before he replied. "After the prince left, Alastor sent a raven to invite all of us to come stay at the castle until the ball."

Of course he did. Hells.

"Where did the prince go?" I asked without thinking.

"Why do you care?" He glared.

"I just—"

Will stepped forward, and my words fell silent as I shifted backwards, leaving me pressed up against the library doors. A sly smirk grew on his face, and all I wanted to do was smack it right off him. "After dinner tonight, I'd like to take you for a walk. There are some things I need to talk with you about."

I pushed him out of my, storming only three steps before his words halted me in my tracks.

"Elena, I want to apologize. I miss you, and I haven't stopped thinking about you since the moment I rode away."

He walked tentatively towards me once more, and for some reason my legs felt like they were stuck in thick mud. Will picked up my hand and placed a chaste kiss upon the top of it. "Please let me apologize tonight, Lena."

Tears pooled underneath my eyes as he walked away like his words hadn't just shifted my world upside down...again.

CHAPTER 45
ELENA

By the time I made it up to my room I had tucked away my feelings, my mask in place once more. This was not the time or place to fall apart. That would have to wait for later tonight when everyone else was asleep.

Eloise was already in my room when I entered, preparing my gown for tonight's dinner. I tossed my books on the table and flung myself down onto the bed.

"Are you alright, sweet girl?" she asked.

"Will's here, and he'll be staying here until the ball."

"Do you want to talk about it?"

A few days ago, Nayla, Clara, and Eloise had joined me in my room while I was getting ready for another of the king's events. After a few glasses of wine, I had opened up about Will and what had happened after the Ascension.

As much as I wanted to share the thoughts whirling inside my head, I couldn't. "No," I breathed. "I'll be alright."

Worry crinkled her delicate features. When I didn't budge, she motioned for me to change out of my clothes and into the dress for this evening.

Surprisingly, my dress for tonight was normal; a simple navy satin dress with short, draped sleeves that left my shoulders bare. Finishing the last braid in my hair, Eloise pulled me into her arms and squeezed tightly. She didn't have to say it. I could feel it in her embrace.

The boost of encouragement I desperately needed to make it through tonight.

***

R elief trickled through my tense muscles when I found the dining hall only partially occupied this evening. The grand table was large enough to fit at least forty or more, but this evening it was only filled halfway.

When I entered, the men at the table rose and dipped their heads. Clara's smile brightened the room as I caught her wink. Unfortunately, being related to the king put her further up the table.

My pulse quickened as Will pulled out the chair next to him. Seeing no other option, I made my way over and took a seat.

A few more guests arrived, and with a snap of the king's fingers, dinner was served.

Struggling to eat from the anxiety that tangled my stomach in knots, I sipped on my wine, taking in all the guests.

Alastor was perched next to Edan, both in deep conversation. Next to Lord Drake was a young woman who shared similar features. The sudden awareness that this was his daughter made my stomach flip, while the feeling of jealousy simmered inside me.

Onyx hair curled in perfect waves over her shoulders. She had a flawless complexion, and a dress in the most vibrant shade of crimson made her amber eyes shimmer. The only thing that tainted her beauty was the bored expression pursing her rosy lips. Even while twirling her fork aimlessly around the vegetables on her plate, she maintained perfect posture.

The scrutiny of my stare must have been felt across the table as she stopped playing with her fork and rolled her eyes up to meet mine.

Sorrow rimmed the edges of her eyes, unlike her father's gaze—Edan's swirled with a haze of displeasure. Our gaze was broken when her father pulled her into his conversation, and my eyes drifted back to the boy beside me.

Will had been staring at me the entire dinner, but that was as far as our interactions went. There were a few moments where I tensed, thinking he was going to speak. Instead, he shoved a piece of bread in his mouth and concealed his words with the rim of his wine goblet.

When the trays of dessert were finally lifted away, I praised the gods for helping me make it through another painful event.

Alaric excused all of us, calling for Clara to follow him, as he needed his nightly elixir. As she walked by, she mouthed an apology. Rising from my chair, I realized the only person left in the hall was Will.

"Walk with me?" He gestured to the terrace behind us.

The dining hall had a wall full of windows, just like the library. The view was towards the flora-covered courtyard, as opposed to the ocean-side view of the library. Glass doors led out to the terrace and down into the courtyard.

Though I knew I should return to my room, a part of me just wanted closure. With a nod, I walked beside him as we stepped out into the crisp night air.

As we made our way down the smooth steps of the terrace, the crunch of the gravel beneath my feet made me shudder. The memory of what had happened in this very courtyard nearly two weeks ago was still fresh in my mind.

A jacket covered my shoulders. I glanced at Will.

"You looked cold." Will placed his hands in his pockets.

"Thank you, that was kind."

"Of course, Lena."

We continued to walk in silence until we reached the fountain near the end of the courtyard. Perching on the back, we had a perfect view of the city below. Thousands of lanterns glimmered in the city below.

Normally a view like this would make me feel peaceful, but all I felt was the thump of my heart in my throat as I waited for Will to speak.

"Lena, I'm so sorry for everything I said in those cells after Ascension. Everything happened so quickly, and when I saw that man … what I had done—" Will's fingers dug into his thighs. I placed my hand over his, and the creases in his forehead began to relax. "Anger took hold of me, and I lashed out to put the blame on anyone but myself. That's something I'll never forgive myself for." Tears lined his eyes as pulled my hand onto his chest, forcing me to face him.

I ripped it away, wrapping my arms around myself, grounding myself to say the words that sat heavily on my chest. "You hurt me when I needed you the most." My voice broke.

His head dropped, the ache of shame filling my body as his emotions wafted into me. With a deep breath I shoved out the emotion, stirring a gentle wind. The last thing I needed was to feel more shame.

"Did you mean what you said? When you told me that you always had to save and protect me?"

"Lena—"

"All this time, did you really feel like I was a burden?" A sob broke free, and I wiped away the tears that escaped.

Will's only response was a heavy sigh, and my sob deepened inside my palms.

Calloused fingers turned my chin back towards him. His hand slid to cup my cheek, thumb tenderly brushing it. "You've never been a burden. I've always loved taking care of you. If you forgive me, give me another chance, I'd like to care of you and our home for the rest of our days."

My mouth went dry. This was a moment where most would swoon. Someone offering their protection and care for the rest of their life seemed the ultimate dream. However, it only made me more depressed.

I wished more than anything that others would stop seeing me as someone fragile and weak, but someone strong and powerful.

I was a soldier in my own personal battle. I rose each day and silently battled a war with my own mind. Even when I broke, I dusted myself off and rose once more.

Killian was right, resilience was the greatest strength. If only others in my life would see it that way as well.

"Edan Drake offered to make me a captain in the Ash Guard after the ball, Lena." He tucked my loose hair behind my head as his smile widened. "I want you to come with me. We would have a place to live, and he told me I could bring my family and anyone else from our town who wanted to come as well."

The air fled from my lungs.

Why was Edan being so generous, and why would he want to help our small town?

"It's such a beautiful city, you would love it. So much art, culture, and even a little library down from the home I would be given. My position comes with a hefty wage. We would have a comfortable life, and you would want for nothing. You would never have to suffer in poverty anymore."

Scowling, I turned my head in disgust. "I don't need *things*, Will. We've both lived without luxuries all our lives and we were just fine."

"Were we, Elena?" His tone was gruff, words clipped.

"All I need in my life is to know the people I love most are safe. At the end of the day, that's all that really matters."

The tension faded from his face as he brushed his lips across my cheek, dangerously close to my lips. "That's all I want too, Lena." His blue eyes bore a hole straight through me. "Let me protect you. Let me keep you safe."

Pulling away, he stood and extended his hand in front of me. "Just think it over. You have time."

Wrapping my palm around his, I let him help me up from the fountain edge.

Nothing but the night breeze passed between us as we made our way back to the terrace and inside the castle. Realizing I still had on his dress jacket, I lifted it from my shoulders, but was paused by his palm.

"Keep it, Elena. I have others, and there's still a chill, even in here."

He gave one more chaste kiss against my cheek and walked in the opposite direction towards his quarters.

Alone, I walked through the dimly lit hallways with only the golden flicker of candlelight and my intrusive thoughts to keep me company.

CHAPTER 46
ELENA

It had been hours, and I was still staring up at the stark white ceiling, trying to escape my spiraling thoughts.

With a frustrated growl, I fisted the sheets and kicked my feet. After my mini-tantrum was over, I realized sleep was obviously not going to happen for me tonight.

Dragging myself out of bed and into some warmer clothes, I decided not to heed Eloise's warning from a few nights before that I should stay in at night.

I'd been sneaking out at night to practice my dynamis in the queen's garden. She had caught me making my way down to the garden one night and scolded me.

I'd heeded her warning for one night, but then had fallen straight back into my routine. The practice was nice, but staring at the stars was the best way for me to clear my mind, and I knew the perfect bench to do it.

Grabbing my thick cloak, I zephyred down to the garden. A whoosh of air shuddered around me as I said a prayer to the gods that my face would not end up slammed against the door. Zephyring through solid objects still made me nervous.

Peeling open my eyes, I sighed in relief to find myself inside the garden walls.

The air was chilly tonight. I could see my breath as little clouds of white swirled in front of me with every exhale. Wrapping my cloak around me, I admired the beautiful scenery.

The lights flickering inside of hanging lanterns illuminated the vibrant garden. At this hour, the only sounds I could hear were from the cicadas and the roar of the waves as they crashed into the shore. For once, my mind was at ease.

As I lifted my head towards the night sky, blanketed with what looked like millions of tiny glistening fireflies, I proceeded to tell them everything that had happened since I had left my hometown.

When I finished, my shoulders sagged as if I had physically removed the weight I had been carrying on my shoulders this entire time. Sitting in silence, enjoying the peace surrounding me, my eyes begin to feel heavy. I made the decision to head back to the castle to sleep.

As I rose, my body jerked back, and I realized my cloak had gotten caught on something next to the bench. I tried giving it a tug, but whatever was attached to my cloak wasn't letting go. With a huff, I squeezed my body through the peony bushes surrounding the bench, then lowered down to the ground to see what was keeping me attached.

With one hand, I reached underneath the bush, feeling around for the root that my cloak was probably hooked on. Cool metal grazed my fingertips, and I jumped back in surprise. Why would there be metal underneath a bush?

I leaned even further down into the ground, my face now flush with the mossy dirt. I had to blink a few times to make sure my tired eyes were seeing what was in front of me. My cloak seemed to be wrapped around a latch for a door.

Why is there a door in the garden?

Since the stubborn cloak refused to detach, I pulled out my dagger and released it with a slice. Curiosity overtook my decision-making abilities, and I cut away the moss to reveal more of the latch.

Digging my heels into the ground for leverage, I attempted to pull the latch. The ground cracked slightly, but not enough. This door hadn't opened in a very long time, and it was now sealed shut with soil and moss.

Crouching down, I began to feel around in the soil, looking for the edges of the door. Just when I was about to toss my hands up in defeat, I felt what must be the corner. A rush of adrenaline began pulsing through me.

I frantically searched for edges with my fingers as I used my dagger cut into the earth to release them. I grabbed the latch and pulled with all my might.

To my surprise, the door released itself from the ground. Sheathing my dagger, I stood and lifted the door all the way open and tossed it backwards into the soil. Wincing at the thud it made, I froze, waiting to see if anyone was alerted. After a few minutes of uneasy silence, I assumed no one was coming.

Below the door was a narrow stone stairway. Darkness loomed beneath, and a chill seeped out from within. Goosebumps rose over my arms and legs.

Beside me was a tree full of hanging lanterns. Standing on my tiptoes, I grabbed the closest one. With my dagger in one hand and the lantern in the other, I made my descent down the stairs.

With each step the air became heavier, mustiness overpowering my senses. I had to pause every so often and take deep breaths to not retch from the pungent smell. Just when I thought these stairs were some cruel torture device that led to nowhere, the lantern light illuminated the stone floor ahead.

Thank gods.

Lifting the lantern, I did a slow spin. Moss-covered walls were lined with bookshelves filled with ancient leatherbound texts, like the one where I had learned about the original Light Phoenix. There was a desk in one corner. Parchment lay on top in a stack, a quill sitting in its inkwell. On the opposite wall a long table held bottles filled with assorted liquids and items. Above the table hung dried herbs and plants, along with several tangled crawler webs. Minus the layers of dust and webs, this place looked like the owner had just stepped out for a quick dinner, then never returned.

My fingers trailed over the books as I walked over to the desk. I lowered myself onto the wooden stool, hoping it would hold my weight. It creaked but held firm.

I riffled through the stack of papers. It appeared to be endless lists of flowers, plants, and herbs. Perhaps this was where the keeper of the garden had their office. There were multiple drawers in the desk, so I pulled out the rectangular drawer first. Inside lay a leather notebook that seemed to be overflowing with loose pieces of parchment. Pushing the drawer closed, I cleared off a space on top of the desk and slid the notebook on top. A leather strip was wrapped around it, holding it together. Once I unraveled it, the notebook exploded, papers flying all over the desk. *Of course.*

Rolling my eyes at my clumsiness, I gathered up the papers while glancing over their contents as I went. These looked like letters. *Interesting.*

Once all papers were collected in a stack, I started reading.

They were letters. No names, just the initials, L and S, penned at the top and the bottom of each letter. At first, nothing seemed out of the ordinary, just conversations between two friends. Until it became something more. As I read, my pulse quickened.

Dear L,

I'm afraid our time has finally run out. We've received word from our sources that he knows what we have been up to these past few months. I know that we're very close to finding a solution to our dynamis problem, but I fear we're running out of time. We've given it a good fight, and I'm confident that others will continue in our place, should anything happen to us both.

Please, protect yourself and your boys. Get out of that place while you can.

Someone has punctured a hole in our defenses, and information is leaking out. We will do everything in our power to snuff out any leads to Oria. Trust no one, L. Eyes are watching.

Once you're all safely hidden, send a raven. May the light always guide you, and the gods surround you.

Until our paths cross again—S

The parchment slipped out of my trembling hands. Dynamis problem? Was there a problem with our dynamis, or was the problem with the discovery that it was rooted in our emotions instead of elements?

What was Oria? If I remembered the old language I'd read about once, the word could be translated to "gods' light." Was this a person, a euphemism, a place?

Intrigue pulled me back to the pieces of parchment littering the dusty desk. I began scanning once more, pulling out information that leapt out at me.

"...they're disappearing at a rapid rate. We need to do something before it's too late, L."

Were they talking about Elysians...or humans?

"...we've noticed as well. It seems after each Ascension ceremony Elysians keep coming out with lesser dynamis."

I'd always thought something wasn't right.

"... he's found a way to suppress dynamis."

Gods. Sweat began to bead on my forehead.

"...we are moving groups of humans out, a few at a time. Your boys have been a tremendous help. We couldn't have done any of this without them. Thank you for sending them our way. Thank the gods we started building so long ago."

Boys? This was the second mention of them. What had these two been building?

"You've done it! I can't believe we've finally figured out a cure. Gods bless us that the first test was successful. I would have never thought to use the gods' tree. I'm beginning to think you were right about there being a connection. Please be careful and make a few more batches so we can test again. This just might be it, L, we might finally be able to turn the tide."

My eyes wandered over the date penned in the corner of the last letter. This one had been sent just before the first one I'd read.

Someone had found a way to suppress our dynamis.

I'd always questioned why those who lived outside of the great cities of Ehora seemed to have lesser dynamis. Even more puzzling was the fact that elders, those who had fled the cities, were also beginning to lose their strength as well. It appeared, however, that these two mysterious rebels had figured out a way to solve that problem.

Something snapped inside of my brain with such force, I slapped my forehead.

Gods. How had I not pieced this together sooner? Will and I, that day of our Ascension, we'd come out of it with dynamis stronger than anyone had seen...especially from those living outside of the cities.

Had we been given something to unleash our powers, something to take away the suppression?

A bead of sweat rolled down my cheek. The walls in the room were closing in on me. I tried my best to control my breathing and my thoughts. The last thing I needed right now was to unleash my dynamis by accident. With all the parchment in the room, it would build to a roaring flame in seconds.

My fingers trailed back over the papers that contained lists of plants and herbs. After a few moments, my brain made the connection. It shocked me so much that my teeth pierced through the flesh of my bottom lip. As I read the words, the taste of copper that filled my tongue became surprisingly appropriate.

"...ginger, rosemary, thyme, hawthorn berries, peonies, blood of an Empath..."

Blood of an Empath?

These weren't just lists for planting, these were recipes, lists of different elixirs. Someone had created a potion to help stop the suppression of dynamis.

The final ingredient was blood.

Meaning they had to use blood magic.

Hells.

G rabbing every piece of parchment I could, I shoved them inside my back pocket. My mind was working faster than my feet, and I stumbled over the stairs I was taking two at a time.

"Damn!" I cursed as my forehead hit the rough stone wall.

Reaching the top, I closed the door behind me. Again, it made a thud. However, instead of silence, this time I heard something else.

"What in the Hells?" shrieked a female voice from behind the peony bush.

"Shh...stay back." A familiar voice hushed the female as heavy footsteps began to make their way towards me. Slowly, I rose, finally meeting the speaker's eyes.

"Freckles?"

"Guilty." I shrugged.

"Lena? For gods' sake, you scared the life out of me!" An extremely out-of-breath and slightly disheveled Clara emerged from behind Killian. Killian's tunic was missing three top buttons, and his hair was ruffled like he had just woken up.

Killian folded his arms over his chest. "What are you doing out here, Lena? Eloise told me you had gone to bed hours ago."

I raised my chin to match his glare. "What exactly were you two doing out here?"

Killian's shoulders fell as Clara ran her fingers through her ravished hair. "We, uhh...we were just... umm."

Unable to suppress the mirth, I watched as Killian stumbled over his words. Eventually, he gave up, running a palm over his flustered face.

"Can you blame me?" He tossed his head towards Clara, whose cheeks flushed.

No, I couldn't blame Killian at all. If Declan were here, I could only imagine what I would be doing right now. The thought instantly heated my cold cheeks, until I remembered why I had rushed up those stairs in the first place.

My palm crashed against my forehead. "Hells, I almost forgot why I was in such a hurry."

Fishing the papers from underneath my tunic, I shoved them towards Clara and Killian. "Our dynamis is being suppressed, but someone else has figured out how to fix it," I whispered. "They used blood magic."

Clara's breath hitched, and Killian rubbed his chin as he thought. We made our way over to the small stone bench, now overflowing with three of us. Clara's eyes wandered over the pages of elixir recipes, and she paused now and then to raise a hand over her mouth. Killian riffled through the letters. With each one, the crease between his brows grew deeper.

Silence lingered. Every so often, Clara and Killian would cast silent looks towards each other, and they would switch papers and continue reading. My hands fidgeted within my lap as I chewed at my already bloody bottom lip. Just when I thought I was about to scream to erase the silence, Killian rose from the bench.

"What is it?" I whispered.

"Where did you find this, Lena?"

"Over there." I pointed at the trapdoor I had discovered earlier.

"Cover it back up, now." The urgency in his tone startled me. "Make sure it looks like it was before. It's important that no one knows that this exists. Understand?"

Swallowing down my fear, I nodded.

"Good. I need to inform Declan. He'll want to know about this immediately."

Flustered, I went back to the trapdoor. Clara followed behind. Scooping soil back around the door, I realized there was no way that we could make it look like it had before.

That was until I remembered my dynamis lesson from earlier with Nayla. I reached for that same emotion I had used before to grow life over the door beneath my fingertips. Just like before, I felt the warmth of my dynamis ripple against my skin and flow through my fingertips into the soil beneath.

"Gods, Lena...you're glowing," Clara breathed.

Opening my eyes, I saw the moss beginning to take root over the door. Moving slowly, I let my dynamis flow until I was confident there was no longer a trace of the door to be seen. I even let it flow over the metal latch, just in case. Before I pulled away, roots began to take shape on top of the door. Twisting and turning, they formed into branches as thick green leaves sprouted on top.

I had to blink to make sure I wasn't dreaming when pale pink peonies began to bloom over the newly created bush. Earlier I'd been able to create a single flower. Tonight, I'd created a whole damn bush. Still in shock, I fell back onto my heels, raising my trembling hands in front of me in awe.

"Lena"—Clara gulped— "I've never seen a Terran do that before."

"Me either." Killian gawked from behind us both.

"Nobody else's entire body glows while they work?" I scoffed, trying to make light of the situation.

"No one else has ever created life, made something grow anew like that, Lena," Killian whispered.

Panic began to flood through me, and I felt my dynamis prickle against my arms. Something about the way everyone had reacted to my Terran dynamis made a million thoughts rush through my head, none of them good.

My chest constricted as I struggled to pull myself out of my downward spiral. A warm palm landed on my back, rubbing circles. Another fell on my shoulder. Warmth began to spread throughout my body as Clara worked her healing magic in more ways than one.

"Breathe, Lena. Deep breaths." Killian spoke calmly.

I was finally able to take a deep breath. My shoulders sagged at the same time as my head. One tear broke free from my restraints. Ashamed of my show of emotion, my weakness, I rubbed it away.

Shaking off their hands, I stepped a few paces away to give myself some space away from them.

"Sorry," I mumbled. If I could use my dynamis to become invisible at this moment, I would have.

Clara rose from where she had been kneeling with me on the ground, dusting off her skirt. Killian grasped her hand in his, then extended the other towards me. With arms tightly wrapped around my body, I eyed his extended hand with hesitation.

"Come on, Elena, take my hand. Let's get you both back inside your rooms, where it's safer." He wiggled his fingers towards me. With a heavy sigh, I stepped towards them, placing my hand inside his. With a tug, Killian pulled us both into his chest and zephyred us into my room.

"Good night, Lena," he whispered, then placed a kiss on Clara's cheek before leaving.

Clara and I slid down into the chairs around the fireplace. Every part of me was laden with exhaustion.

"Lena..." Clara whispered.

"Hmm?" I mumbled, fidgeting with my tunic. I wasn't sure if I was prepared for whatever conversation we were obviously about to have.

"You want to tell me why you're so embarrassed about what happened back there?"

"What?" I feigned ignorance. "You mean being caught in the garden alone?"

Clara pursed her lips. "Elena Morrigan..."

This conversation was going to happen, whether I wanted it or not. Massaging my temples, I tried to muster the words.

There were things that I'd carried with me all my life. Things that I'd tucked away, from Bri, my parents, even from myself. Years I'd been shoving away my darkness, but I was exhausted from trying to hold onto everything myself.

As if Clara could hear the struggle in my mind, she spoke softly.

"In the garden, I could feel the darkness that festers deep within you, Elena. Honey, it's time to release it."

Her eyes pleaded with me to let go. So, I did.

"I suppose the best place to start is at the beginning."

Clara slid her chair closer to mine so that our knees were now touching. "Go ahead, Lena. I'm right here."

My trembling hand enveloped hers and squeezed tightly. Sucking in a deep breath, I began unlocking my past, the source of the endless battles I had within my mind.

"Since I've been small, I've been plagued with vivid dreams. Dreams of wars, battles, loss and pain." I swallowed, struggling to pace my breathing to remain calm.

"Wars here, in Ehora?"

"At first, I thought so. I thought I recognized our kind, our land-scape. However, in each dream I was transported across realms—so many different races and landscapes. There was once even a realm that was entirely made of water. In every battle, we were always fighting against some darkness, something deeply evil." A shiver ran down my spine as images of the enemy flashed in my mind.

"You said 'we.' Who were you with, Lena?"

"In my dreams, there were others, fighting alongside of me, like we were fighting together for a purpose. I could never remember their faces when I awoke. The only part of my dream that was consistent was one voice. She's the one who always pulled me out of my dreams."

"So, these dreams, were they the beginning of your fears? The panic attacks?"

"It wasn't so much the dreams, but the evil that lurked within them. I could never see their faces, as they were always cloaked. However, I could always feel them …smell them. Even now, I feel like the scent is permanently ingrained in my senses. It was what I imagine death smells like—horrid, rotting and full of decay." I shuddered at the memory.

"Though I couldn't see their eyes, I could always feel their piercing, cold gazes on me. Any time I was near them, pain radiated throughout me, along with the most unbearable feeling of hopelessness and despair." Goosebumps spread across my arms. She squeezed my hand tighter, knowing I needed that little push to keep going. "Clara, I know it sounds absurd, but sometimes…"

"Sometimes what, Lena?" she breathed.

"It felt as though they were pulling the life out of me with every dream I had. Like thieves in the night, stealing away my happiness. They attacked every good part about me, going after my very being, until sometimes all that was left when I awoke was fear. Sleeping became something I despised. The idea of being stuck in that darkness the minute I closed my eyes was enough to send my body into a full-blown panic.

"Eventually, that fear spilled over into my waking life. Any time I felt afraid, worried, or like I wasn't doing enough, that feeling of darkness washed over me. That's when I became lost in a battle within my own mind."

"Why do you suppose you dreamt of wars? Have you always been fearful of it?"

"Never. To be honest, Clara, since arriving here I've realized my parents kept many things hidden away from me—to help me, I suppose. I only knew bits and pieces of the past, and we only had vague conversations about the Rebellions. The things I learned most were from talking with the people in my town, or things I stumbled upon in books. The only wars and battles I know are the ones I've witnessed in my dreams."

Warmth spread through our hands, and Clara's healing dynamis worked hard to help me stay calm. "I'm so sorry, Lena. That's not all that burdens you though, is it? I can feel that you're not done sharing yet. There's something far more painful still trapped deep within you."

The truth within her observation radiated through me, cracking the lock that had held my darkest secret for years. My dynamis flared, and it was almost as if my body itself was trying to keep me from spilling my darkness into the world.

Piercing pain radiated in my jaw as I tried to will myself to unclench my teeth. Breathing was becoming increasingly more difficult. Each time my lungs tried to fill with air, it was slammed back down by the heavy weight that pressed against my chest.

Clara pulled me closer, willing her healing dynamis to help once again. Her warmth surrounded my body, allowing a break in my clenched teeth. Rocking back and forth, I struggled to force the words out.

"I—I—" My voice trembled as my teeth clattered together. "Gods I don't think I can do this…"

"Yes, you can, sweet girl. Use that strength you've been building each day. Let it out, honey. Let it all out."

A frustrated growl rumbled, tears now falling like waterfalls as I fought to regain control of my body. When I said these words aloud it would become real, all over again. Shame forced my shoulders down, pushing me further and further down into the darkness. My body tremored uncontrollably.

"Stay with me, Lena." She brushed her hand over my forehead, sweeping the hair from my face. "Sometimes we have to surrender to the dark in order to be healed by the light."

A sob tore through me as I gasped for more air to fill my lungs. "I…I did it…I—"

"You did what, Lena?"

"I k-k-killed her," I sobbed. "Gods, I killed her." Tears streamed down my hot face.

"Who, honey?" she whispered, rubbing my palms with her thumbs, and I felt more of her healing dynamis flood through me.

"My mother."

Clara sucked in a sharp breath.

Something snapped within me the moment the words left my lips. Between sobs, I spilled every detail about that atrocious night. The night that now filled my dreams.

"It was my weakness…my own damn mind paralyzed me, Clara! Fear kept me from saving my mother that night. How pathetic is that? Hells! If I was just normal, she would be right here! She'd still be— alive!"

A faint golden glow hazed over my arms. My dynamis boiled

within me as the feeling of hate burned throughout my body. The hate that I held for myself, the overwhelming disgust I felt when I thought about the panic attack that had stopped me from saving the woman who'd protected me my entire life. She'd saved me even in her last moments, and in the end I couldn't even protect her.

"You want to know what the worst part is?" I sniffled, using my shoulder to wipe away some of the mess I'd made of my face.

Clara nodded, tears falling down her cheeks.

"My father doesn't even know. Not only am I weak, but I'm a damn coward, Clara. I—I—I couldn't even admit that I could have saved her. He sent me to s-s-save her, and I let her die, Clara!

"He came rushing into the house that night and fell to his knees at the sight of us. The sound that erupted from my father is something I hope never fills my ears again. It was like something within him broke that night. All because of my failure! I shattered my father's heart...his soul. I destroyed everything that night."

"Oh, Lena." Clara pulled me into a deep embrace.

"No!" I screamed, shoving my body away. "I don't deserve your pity, Clara. The only thing I deserve is your disgust. What I did is unforgivable."

"Stop!" Clara's yell broke through my haze, catching me off guard. She slammed her body into mine, caging me within her arms. I squirmed and thrashed against her, trying my best to shove away the comfort that I absolutely did not deserve. For such a small thing, Clara was surprisingly strong.

"You're right, Elena, what you did was unforgivable," she whispered, and I was immediately flooded with embarrassment and shame. Her next words floated over my ear, shredding the last of the control I had over my emotions and my dynamis.

"It's unforgivable, Elena, because there is absolutely *nothing* to forgive. No one could control the events of that night except fate. You were there with her, Elena, you gave her peace and calm in those final moments, because she knew she wasn't alone. Nothing about what happened that night is your fault. You need to release that guilt before it consumes you."

Her words created a fissure in my wall, and I broke down. She rocked me back and forth as my body shook. Time passed until I was finally drained of every emotion, leaving me numb inside her arms. My enervated body slumped into Clara's hold.

"I just want to be normal," I breathed. "I don't know how to do this. I don't know what the gods were thinking."

Both of us sat back on our heels on the floor of my room. Sweeping the tangled mess of my hair behind my ears, she used her sleeve to wipe away the tears from my face. Gathering both of my hands within her own, she pinned me with a hard gaze. "I want you to answer me honestly. What does it mean to be normal, Elena?"

"Well, it means that…it means that you're—"

Damn.

Ten minutes ago, I could have answered that question with all the certainty in the world. I would have said, *"Normal is the opposite of me. It's composed, calm, and most of all in control."* However, the more I learned about the struggles this small group of Elysians had endured, I was realizing that wasn't normal at all. No one had complete control over their lives.

"Exactly. There is no right answer to that question, Lena, because there is no normal. Nothing about living, or our existence, is normal. It's messy, complicated…" She sighed. "Sometimes it's so damn painful that some of us feel like they're too tired to even keep on existing in it."

Declan. The pull in my chest throbbed at the thought of the man who was becoming such an important part of my life.

Clara's eyes became glossy and red. "We all fight silent battles every day, whether we admit them or not. What we all need to realize is that those battles were never meant to be fought alone. There may be things that we need to work out within ourselves, such as forgiveness." My shoulders fell under the scrutiny of her stare. "Even then, we don't have to do that on our own."

It had taken me long enough, but I was finally beginning to believe her words.

"Tell me, Lena, can you deny that it feels freeing to finally release the pain that you have been holding within you your entire life? Tell me that you don't find a sense of comfort knowing that you don't have to shoulder your secret alone anymore."

Something had shifted within me tonight. Even though I was still struggling with the guilt and the shame of it all, I did feel like a small part of me had been unlocked. A link of metal had shattered away from the anchor that lived inside of me, the one that fought to hold me down.

Until I confessed to my father, I feared I'd never be fully healed. If I was honest, it might always be inside of me until I learned how to forgive myself. I yearned for the day when I could finally accept myself, broken parts and all.

A silent moment of empathy passed between us. Words evaded me, so instead I wrapped my arms around her. I might never be able to fully thank her for what she'd done for me tonight, but this was a start.

Clara still trembled in my arms, and I leaned back to get a better view of her face. "What's wrong, Clara?" I brushed the hair dampened by tears away from her cheek.

"Forgiveness is hard for me as well. Being stuck in the castle, not being able to help my own mother, or Lenora..." Her voice was meek. "Lena, there are people outside the castle walls at this very moment who are dying. I've tried every elixir, but all they need is a powerful Healer like me. But they will never get that because I'm too much of a coward to challenge Alaric." Another sob hiccupped through her. "I'm so ashamed of myself."

A dangerous combination of sorrow and anger awoke my dynamis once more. I was enraged that this wonderful woman in front of me felt like she was a failure because she couldn't leave the castle to do what she was meant to do...help others. It wasn't right, but I was going to change that. I was going to help Clara get closer to forgiving herself in the way she had helped me tonight.

"Let's go tomorrow," I said. Her eyes widened, and her body went still. "You, me, and Nayla. We'll go in the cover of the night."

"No, Lena. It's too dangerous. If we were caught—no, we can't. It's impossible."

"Nothing is impossible if you have the will to power through it. We can do this, and we will help those people."

"B-but...if Alaric or Alastor catches you, your family, your town—"

"Damn the consequences, Clara," I said in a bold voice I'd never used before, full of confidence and clarity. "It's time we start fighting for what is right and use our fear to push us through instead of holding us back. Tomorrow we take back control."

CHAPTER 47

DECLAN

"Brand thinks the mole is hiding in Grinwood?"

Confusion was etched in Warren's brows when I shrugged my shoulders in response. We ruminated over the intel that Brand had just given us as I paced the squeaky floorboards of the tavern in Atheling where we had agreed to meet.

After spending a few days in Vragos, I had traveled to Oria to make sure the new group of humans we had rescued were safe. Warren had been away with a small group of the Rebellion chasing leads on the Nightshades, so I'd sent a raven for him to meet me and Brand at this tavern after he was done. Lately, they had been one step ahead of us, another reason why it was imperative we found who was leaking our information.

"I'm just having difficulty believing that a mole would come from the city where we have our strongest alliance. Also, everything we've gathered so far has always hinted towards Vragos." I wiped my palm over the scruff of my jaw.

"Maybe the best way to hide is right out in the open," Brand shrugged.

With a frustrated grunt, Warren dropped into a stool next to the bar, threading both hands through his hair. "I'll investigate it. Maybe there's something to this lead. We still have Rebellion members sprinkled throughout each of the cities, so it would be easy for them to hide in the one place we wouldn't think to look."

"Fallon has also been pulling in new recruits and vetting new and old members of Oria. So far, nothing suspicious has been uncovered," I said.

With his head still between his hands, Warren mumbled, "At least that's one bit of good news."

The tavern owner, and fellow Rebellion member, slid us all a pint of ale before heading back into the kitchen. He had closed for the afternoon to give us a chance to speak in private.

"Hey Brand, would you mind giving Warren and I minute alone?"

"Of course, I'll just be outside if you need me." He swiped his ale and exited out the front door, leaving the two of us alone.

Warren took a long drag of ale before setting it down on the bar with enough force to make some of the foam slosh over the side. "How's my daughter?" His voice was low, strained with concern.

I froze.

Even after I had planned for this conversation for three days straight, every word, every counterargument, it didn't matter. In that moment everything went blank, and the words shriveled into dust on my tongue.

"You alright, son?"

I hadn't been prepared for the punch to the gut that I would feel when he called me "son." Normally, hearing it come from him filled me with a sense of pride. Except for today. Today, it left me curled over the bar, trying to extinguish the uneasy feeling of guilt rising within me. Mustering a cough, I pretended to have something stuck inside my throat. I grabbed the ale in front of me and downed the entirety of its contents.

Warren patted my back, and all I could think about was that in a few moments that hand might be wrapped around my neck.

"She's doing well, Warren." I spoke meekly, a tone I never used. If Warren wasn't curious before, he was now. Trying to cover up my panic, I pulled out the stack of letters from Lena that Eloise had taken from her room.

"Here, these are for you. She's been writing to you every day since she's left. I thought you'd like to have them."

He assessed me with narrowed eyes. The stool creaked in the silence as he leaned back and crossed his arms over his broad chest. "She's been with you for two weeks and all you have to tell me is she's doing well, and a handful of letters?"

Hells. This was not going how I had hoped.

"Elena struggled with control of her gift in the beginning. The strength of her dynamis is unlike anything I've ever seen. She's learning how to trust in herself every day. Watching her build that confidence has been enthralling. You've raised an incredible woman, Warren." Licking my lips, I averted my eyes to my empty mug, away from the ice of Warren's glare.

"No," he fumed.

"Warren, I can explain—"

"No!" he shouted, slamming his fist on the counter so hard that his mug rolled off and crashed onto the floor. "I told you to stay away from her, Declan!"

He leaned forward, clawed my tunic and pulled me towards him. My hands wrapped around his wrist as I tried to pull him off, but his fists only constricted more around the fabric.

"You're dangerous! Hells, Declan, you could hurt her at any moment." He freed a hand, clawing it through the scruff of his beard. "If Alastor ever found out—the bastard would use you to hurt her. You know that! Yet you still pursued her."

"I know." Emotion caused my voice to tremble. "But I love her, Warren. None of this was on purpose, and believe me when I say I tried my best to fight it."

Dissatisfaction rumbled within his chest.

"I'm aware of the danger that looms over us, Warren, but I love her despite it. Elena has made me feel alive again. She's given me hope that I'm worthy of happiness. Those alone are more powerful than the dynamis that dwells inside of me. I'll keep on fighting for this kingdom, and for her, because with her by my side I truly believe we have a chance to return the realm back into the light."

Warren shoved me off the stool. His own fell underneath him as he leapt from it and pointed a finger towards me.

"Warren, she's my—"

"You're right," he interrupted, lowering his arm.

My breath hitched as I hoped he was going to allow our relationship, but his features expressed something entirely different.

"You *are* going to protect this kingdom, as will I, because that's our duty. We've followed you, even after everything..." His eyes lowered to my neck, and I rubbed the scar of the curse that seared under his gaze. "You have a duty to lead this Rebellion, and to take care of the long list of responsibilities that fall under that role. From this day forward, my daughter will not be anywhere near that list."

My body stilled. "Warren..."

He turned around and stormed toward the door. Just before setting foot outside, he gripped the edge of the door frame as he turned around once more to face me.

"Do your duty. Protect and train my daughter, but that is all. This thing you think is love ends *now.*"

CHAPTER 48

ELENA

The dark hood of my cloak flapped as I zephyred through the castle. My pulse thrummed, echoing inside my ears as I approached the bridge where Clara and Nayla were already waiting.

So much was at stake for all of us tonight, but so much could be lost if we didn't take this risk. Helping people should always take priority, something those in power had forgotten.

"Do we have everything we need?" Nerves bubbled underneath the surface as I checked over my shoulder one last time.

Clara opened her cloak, showing her satchel full of healing supplies underneath.

"I know you're still working on your zephyring, Clara, so I'll take you with me," Nayla said. "Will you be okay on your own, Light Phoenix?"

"Hopefully. I've been practicing every night."

"Alright then, ladies, let's be swift. Silent as mice and stick to the shadows. We all know what's at stake if we're caught."

Wrapping her arm around Clara, she took off into the night, the gust of her wind swishing the side of my hood. Swallowing down the fear, I followed.

A few moments later, we were outside the city's walls. The farming village was only about a mile away from the capital, so we walked together through the thick, muddy forest that bordered the city walls.

The village consisted of six stone dwellings, each with a thatched roof. Nayla lowered her hood, and, after assessing our surroundings, motioned for us to do the same.

We made our way over to the largest dwelling, and Nayla knocked in a specific pattern. Two slow and three fast taps.

The door creaked open, and a frail woman with red-rimmed eyes peered through. When she saw Nayla's familiar face, the door swung wide and the woman pulled her inside. Clara and I followed, closing the door behind us.

"Thank all five gods," the woman gasped. "I've been praying for a miracle. My b-babes...I fear they may not make it through the night." Her hands covered the sob that broke free. She fell to her knees, showing us all the same sign of respect as they had inside the city.

Clara bent down and placed a hand under her arm to help her up. "Helena, we're here to help. Sorry it took me so long. Please show me to your sweet babes."

Helena swept her ash-blonde hair away from her face and guided us to her children's room. A boy and a girl huddled together, brows sweating and curious black tendrils climbing up the side of their necks.

Their heavy lids opened, and what I saw in their eyes made my breath hitch. Bright golden circles encased the irises of their eyes. The only visual difference between Elysians and humans were those golden rings. Shifting my glance back towards Helena, I saw the same golden glow in her brown eyes.

They were all humans.

Noticing my shock, Helena spoke softly. "The king gives us his grace, my lady, for the food that we produce for the kingdom. However, if he found out we've been plagued by the darkness..."

I nodded in understanding, rubbing her back as I stepped around to the other side of the bed. Clara peeled away the tunics from their tiny bodies. The blackness had spread all the way down their chests, almost like rotted roots growing underneath their skin.

She popped the corks of two vials, giving one to me and the other to Nayla. "When I tell you two, open their mouths and pour the contents into their mouths. Then help me hold them down. This is going to be painful for them."

Worry prickled against the side of my cheek, and I looked to see Helena frozen in terror. I placed my hand in hers and guided it towards her daughter's leg. "They need you. Squeeze their legs and let them know you're here with them."

She nodded absentmindedly and placed her hands around her son's and daughter's ankles.

"Here we go." Clara took a deep steadying breath. "Now!"

We dumped the vials into their parched mouths and held their shoulders down.

Their eyes flung wide open and moans of agony tore out of them as they began to flail on the bed. Clara placed her palms on their chests, and their bodies began to convulse violently.

"Come on, babes, fight for me, loves," she whispered. Her eyes remained sealed shut, the strain on her body evident by the creases on her face.

After a few long, stressful moments the babes' movements began to slow to a roll. Their moans turned to a faint murmur.

Awestruck, I watched the blackness fade away from their bodies until only a few small strands were left behind. Clara's face went pale and she rushed over to the wash basin to release the contents of her stomach.

Helena began sobbing unintelligible words as she scooped her little ones up into her arms and rocked them back and forth.

I helped Clara back onto her feet as Nayla tilted a waterskin into her mouth. Once the color came back to her cheeks, we bid Helena goodbye, because there were still three more houses we had to visit tonight.

Helena rushed over to her small kitchen and gathered a bouquet of lavender. After embracing Clara in a long hug, and taking more vials of elixir for the children, she gave Clara the bouquet. "I know it's not much, my lady."

Clara placed her hand on Helena's shoulder. "It is the most special gift I've ever received, and I will cherish your kindness forever."

Tears welled in my eyes as we made our way out the door.

After four more houses, my eyes were swollen and Clara's bouquet had gotten larger.

"Time to head back, ladies," Nayla whispered, and we all placed our hoods back over our heads.

The mud sloshed between our boots as we walked. Clara's shoulder bumped against mine, and she grasped my hand. "Thank you for convincing me to come tonight. I've never felt more alive or more useful in my entire life. Thank you, Lena." Her voice trembled as she spoke.

Emotion swelled in my throat, blocking the words trying to escape, so I simply squeezed her palm in response.

Trying to change the subject so that we all didn't have swollen eyes in the morning, Nayla began questioning me about my nightly routine in the castle. "Elena, you can't keep sneaking out late at night to practice. It's dangerous."

"I know, I just needed some extra practice, and some time to think."

She sighed heavily. "Alastor has become increasingly suspicious in the past few days. Yesterday, he nearly fired everyone who so much as glanced at him the wrong way. Something has him agitated, and the last time he was this troubled…well, you know what happened."

Indeed. He put a deadly curse on Declan.

Clara murmured besides me, "You need to stay safe, Lena. Will you promise us?"

They both set their gazes on me, pausing for my answer while our feet sank into the mud.

"Yes, I promise."

Smiles began to grow on their lips, until we heard the snap of a branch beside us.

Nayla's hand shot up and she placed a finger over her mouth. More rustles erupted in the darkness, as well as an eerily dark laugh. My muscles tightened as I clutched my dagger.

One by one, black hooded figures in masks circled around us. Nightshades. Tremors shook my body, the memory of the last time I'd seen them flashing through my mind.

Gripping the dagger tighter, I fought against the encroaching fear threatening to freeze me in place just like before. I would not freeze. Whatever came our way, I would fight my fear. No more lives would be lost because of it.

Nayla caught my panicked gaze. "Let's fight our way out of this, ladies."

With a quick nod, the three of us unleashed pure fury.

Bent roots ripped from the ground, wrapped around two of the men and brought them crashing down. Nayla smiled wickedly as she chased them, eager to finish the job.

As I fought off more of them with gusts of wind from my Tempest abilities, I watched with wide eyes as Clara launched icicles towards the men circling her. I'd never seen her use any other dynamis besides her Healing. She was a fury, lashing shard after shard of ice into the flesh of the Nightshades.

A smirk grew across my cheeks, until it was slapped from my face from the man who had invaded my defenses. Disoriented, I blinked to regain focus as I covered the sting with my hand.

He grabbed my neck and slung me back into his broad chest. The Nightshade ripped the dagger from my hand. I used all my strength to thrash against him. His hold crushed my body, and I felt the cool sting of metal as it slid against my neck.

My hair tangled around my face. My hood had shifted when the fighting began. Hot breath brushed against the side of my neck as bile burned the back of my throat.

"Hello, angel."

My entire body went numb. My knees buckled at the sound of the voice behind me. A voice that haunted my memory and my nightmares.

He'd called my mother by the same name mere moments before he'd slit her throat.

"No..." The quiver in my lips shook as much as the rest of my body. Just like that night all those years ago, the air evaded my lungs and I struggled to catch my breath.

Chaos swirled around us as my friends continued to fight off the Nightshades.

Cold lips brushed against the side of my ear and the iron blade dug deeper into my neck, nicking the flesh enough for blood to trickle down from the wound.

"The gods continue to bless us this evening," he purred into my ear. "Three beautiful sirens crossed onto our path."

His teeth bit into the shell of my ear, and I could be silent no longer. "Take your damn hands off me!"

The rumble of his laughter soured the dinner in my stomach. He spun my body in his grip until I was facing his solid chest. One of his meaty palms secured my wrists behind my back, the other slid my dagger inside his belt.

Bastard.

Fiery magic burned and sizzled against my skin, my dynamis filled with just as much fury as me. I'd yet to use my light dynamis—the fear of losing control was too great.

Nayla and Clara were surrounded by three cloaked men. Desperation sank creases of worry into their faces, and I could tell they were reaching the point of burnout.

The man before me tugged my chin, shifting my view back to him. "My men will be very happy tonight." A sly grin formed on his lips. "Especially since we have such a prestigious woman in our grasp, *Light Phoenix.*" Leaning down until we were face to face, he whispered, "I wonder if you'll be just as feisty with me between your luscious thighs?" His deathly grip tightened, locking me in place. "You know what I think, angel? I think I'll have you screaming my name for all to hear."

"Fuck you!" I seethed.

"Oh, don't worry, darling, I plan to."

Searing bolts of dynamis zipped throughout my body. I shut my eyes and thought about Declan, when he'd first taught me to control my power.

"Remember, our dynamis bends to our will. If you don't want it to hurt someone it'll listen...You are in control. You are its captain, it just awaits your command."

"Gods, I hope you're right, Dec," I whispered.

"What did you—"

Before he could finish, bright light flashed between us. The smell of burning flesh overwhelmed my senses.

"SHIT!" he snarled, tossing me backwards.

"This is mine!" I reclaimed my dagger, then kicked his knee and watched in glee as he collapsed onto the muddy forest floor.

Using my moment of freedom, I ran and launched my light dynamis towards the other Nightshades. They howled in pain, shifting their attacks towards me. Dodging their flames, I made my way towards Nayla and Clara.

Side by side, we continued to hold them back.

"I can't hold much longer," Clara panted, her face pale and slick with sweat.

Gathering my remaining dynamis, I prepared myself for one final launch. "Stand behind me," I whispered.

"Lena, no!" Nayla growled.

"Just let me try. It may be our only way out of here."

The tension in my voice made her pause, then she took a deep breath and stepped behind me. Clara followed and I called my humming dynamis.

Love once again became my overpowering emotion. There was a deep, unwavering love for the women behind me and the strength and determination that I'd witnessed from them tonight. No one was going to stop us. We were walking away.

Raising my hands towards the hooded figures, I watched with delight as their eyes filled with terror. I launched a fiery blast of light dynamis and Tempest wind.

White-hot flames blew forward, encompassing the men in a fiery inferno. Their screams filled the air as they ran back into the forest, shedding their cloaks as they tried to stop the flames from searing more flesh.

"How's that for feisty?" I seethed through clenched teeth.

Exhaustion buckled my knees, but Nayla held me upright. "Let's get back to the castle. I feel like I have enough to carry us all back."

We took our time, stopping in the shadows every so often to catch our breaths. Clara still had some dynamis left in her well and used it during our breaks to heal us. It wasn't enough to heal fully, but it was enough to give us the strength we needed to make it back towards the castle.

For safety, Nayla zephyred us all the way back to my room. They'd both stay here until they were fully recovered, then head back to their rooms in the early hours of the morning.

"Nayla, do you think anyone will discover what we did tonight?" I mumbled, fidgeting with my blankets.

"I'll do everything in my power to bury any evidence of it being us. The villagers won't give us away. My only fear is, if it leads back to them, I wouldn't put it past Alaric and Alastor to torture the answers out of them."

Clara's head fell into her hands as her shoulders shook.

I rose from my seat and knelt beside her on the plush rug. As I rubbed her back in soothing circles, Nayla shifted on the couch to do the same.

"You saved lives today, Clara. It was a risk worth taking. One I would take every single day."

She nodded in her hands, but muffled cries rumbled through her fingertips. "What if I saved them, only to sentence them to death?"

The ache in my heart broke wide and I pulled her into my arms. Nayla wrapped her arms around us.

"Clara, I promise to do everything in my power to keep them safe."

CHAPTER 49
ELENA

T he clash of metal against metal filled the morning air as I made my way toward the ring. Liam and Killian were already sparring. I gave them a quick wave to alert them of my presence as I headed for the practice swords.

It had been two days since our escapade outside of the walls. Nayla had been doing her best to bury any mention of it, and so far, we had gone unnoticed.

Gravel crunched behind me, and I inwardly cringed. Will had been joining in my sword training since he arrived at the castle.

Every moment of conversation between the two of us had been filled with all his plans for us in the City of Ash, all the luxuries he'd shower me with, and all the protection he would give me. He talked as if it was a haven. All I saw was a gilded cage.

No matter how long he had watched me train, he still treated me like a frail being who needed to be protected instead of the Light Phoenix that I had become. Declan and the others had always encouraged me to find ways to do things for myself, empowered me to discover my own worth.

His shoulder bumped mine as he sat next to me. "What do you

think?" He pointed to his sword, the pommel encrusted with tiny emeralds.

I scrunched my nose. "It's a bit pretentious for practice, don't you think?"

He simply waved me off, saying something about women not understanding the beauty of a well-made sword.

The lure of luxury had taken hold of him. Each day he was dressed head to toe in fine linen, every outfit covered in gold trim.

"Freckles, did you hear me?" Killian's chuckles broke me out of my thoughts, and I thanked the gods for the reprieve. "Get your ass in the ring, let's practice."

I selected a sword from the bin, then made my way into the ring. Even with all the training with my father, the weight of the sword was still something that I struggled with.

I practiced a few movements while I waited for Liam and Killian to finish their sparring. Each swipe still felt slow and sluggish, and after only a few moves I could already feel an ache blooming in my arm.

"You're getting better, little lady." Liam circled around me to meet my gaze.

Shoving the sword down into the dirt, I folded my arms over my chest. "Stop trying to inflate my ego. Even all five gods can see that I'm not getting any better at this."

With a roll of his eyes, Liam tilted his head towards the training ring. I trotted after him.

Killian dipped his head upon my approach. "You alright?"

"I will be." My eyes shifted to Will admiring his sword in the sunlight. Killian's lips pursed and he took a few steps back to allow me some space.

"Alright, I think you're struggling because of the way that you're gripping your sword," Liam pronounced. "Let's see if we can find you a position that makes it a little easier."

Stepping behind me, he lifted my arm holding the sword. "Let's try a few movements together. Killian, can you spar with Lena so we can work on her posture and hold?"

"Of course."

Killian swiped towards me, while Liam helped guide me to block his attack. Once metal hit metal, I felt the impact vibrate down my arm, wincing at the ache it left in its wake.

"I thought so," Liam huffed. "You're holding the sword too low. It's causing your movements to feel sluggish, and you're taking the full brunt of the impact when the swords collide."

He adjusted my grip and then guided me with the correct movement before releasing me and taking a few steps back. "Alright, little lady, show Killian what you got."

Rolling my head from side to side, I positioned myself in my stance. *Here goes nothing.*

We circled each other for a few moments. I was still trying to muster up the courage to strike. Before I had the chance, Killian advanced towards me. With an extremely uncoordinated swipe, I was able to block, but it threw my feet off balance.

"Focus, Lena," Liam grumbled.

Tossing him a sarcastic salute, I realigned my stance. We began circling each other again before Liam bellowed from the side.

"Your enemies aren't going to dance with you when they fight you, Lena. Get in there!"

Lowering my weapon, I used my other hand to throw an obscene gesture back towards him.

Before I could witness his response, the sound of footsteps thundering towards me pulled me back to the ring. The hum of Killian's sword rang through the air just in enough time for me to lift my sword to barely block his attack. The force of his blade hitting mine sent my ass cascading down into the hard dirt. A growl rumbled in my throat as I massaged my stinging tailbone.

"They're also not going to wait to take a strike while their opponent is distracted." Killian extended out a hand for me to grab.

Slapping it away, I pulled myself up as the two of them snickered. I found my hold, and my glare locked onto Killian's.

"I think the Light Phoenix has finally come out to play!" Liam shouted.

Killian extended his palm towards me, curling his fingers, coaxing me to charge him. The strength in my arm was no comparison to Killian's, but perhaps I could use speed to my advantage.

Digging my toes into the soil, I pushed forward. Killian matched my pace as we raced towards each other, weapons high. Stopping short, Killian raised his sword and braced for impact. Pulling all the weight from my upper body, I grabbed my sword with both hands and leapt towards him. With all my force, I shoved my sword against his.

The sound of the collision rang in my ears as I used my forward motion to turn and sweep around him. Recovering from my first blow, he whipped around as well, but not in enough time to block my next attack. I swung my sword towards his shoulder. As he dodged the blade, I swept my long leg underneath one of his own. He stumbled, arms flailing as he tried to recover. However, it wasn't enough to save him. His heavy, muscled body sent him careening into the dirt, face first. *Ouch.*

A howl of laughter echoed behind me, and I couldn't help the grin that lifted my cheeks. Killian rolled over onto his back, wiping the dirt from his face. I extended my hand towards him. With a snort, he accepted, and I pulled him back up onto two feet.

"Well done, Lena" He gave me a pat on my back.

Before I could ask if he was ready for round two, another hand whipped me around.

"Lena, that was great. But let me show you some moves that will clean up some of those sloppy swipes." Will smiled, like he hadn't just given me a backhanded compliment. Killian's fist clenched as he took a step forward. I pressed my palm against his chest and shook my head.

"I'll be okay," I whispered.

He glared at the boy swinging his fancy sword behind me and then shuffled towards Liam. A little smile twitched against my cheeks as they both crossed their arms over their chests.

Will pulled me into him. With his chest pressed against my back, he placed his sword in my hands. Calloused fingers slid over my arm as he adjusted my grip, eliciting a shiver to ripple over my skin. Unlike before, this shiver felt like my body revolting against his touch. It was as if my dynamis knew how wrong it felt as well.

"Hmm," a familiar deep voice seethed from behind us. "I see while the cat's away, the mice will play."

Shadows rippled over his arms as he glowered at us from the edge of the training ring.

My forehead furrowed, my nose wrinkled in disgust at the way he glared behind me at Will. His hands were balled in fists at his sides, lips curled into a snarl. This was not at all how I'd imagined his return going.

Words stalled on my tongue while I nervously awaited Declan's. Will's arm tightened around my waist in a silent challenge. Declan traced his every move, lingering over the spot where Will's fingers pressed into my hip. When his burning gaze flicked towards mine, my breath hitched as I sucked my lips in between my mouth.

"Welcome back, brother." Killian's words were soft, almost tentative as he approached Declan.

In a flash, he shoved Killian out of the way and zephyred so hard into Will, the force shoved us all into the dirt.

"Hells, Declan! We were just training!" Will huffed as he righted himself back onto two legs.

"You sure that was all you were doing, Wilton?" Declan snarled between clenched teeth. Jealousy flared in his darkened eyes as he ran his fingers through his chestnut hair.

Time seemed to slow down. Liam leaped into the training ring, approaching Declan from behind. Shadows now swirled around Dec's entire body. His face was growing a dark shade of crimson.

"Wh-what is wrong with you?" I stammered, clawing my way back onto my feet.

"What's wrong with *me*?" He laughed sarcastically, taking two steps towards me, shoving Will out of the way.

"Dec," Liam warned.

Declan fumed, reaching out to grab my arm with so much force it caused me to collide into his chest. My body trembled as he gripped my chin to meet his eyes, eyes that were consumed with rage. "My problem, *Wildfire*, is you."

Declan's ward was solidly in place, but I didn't need to access his emotions that way. Every bit of fury and anger he was feeling right now was evident to everyone around.

I licked my dry lips and they parted tentatively as I tried to find the right thing to say to calm him down. His gaze shifted to my lips. Before I could speak, he released his grip on me and shoved his body away from mine.

Pacing back and forth, he ran his palm through his hair, a calming movement to help steady his breaths. My heart ached, and I started moving towards him when an arm blocked my path.

"Liam...let me pass," I begged.

Pained eyes met my own as he lowered his head. When I tried again, he pushed me back. "Sorry, Lena," he breathed.

Fueled by my newfound rage, I stormed in between all of them, gathering my dynamis and pulling it to the surface. Extending my arms, I created an orb of wind between them and launched it at them. It knocked them all off their feet, leaving them gaping up at me from the ground. With a frustrated growl, I let them all have it.

"When you're all done making complete asses out of yourselves, come find me. Then maybe we can get back to doing something worthy of my time."

CHAPTER 50

DECLAN

I was thoroughly fucked, and unfortunately not in the good way.

My feet dangled over the side of the cliff as I stared out into the abyss, watching the tides roll into the shore. Elena was right, I'd been a complete ass. The way Will's fingers had curled into her hip during training had been enough to make me unhinged. These past two weeks had been complete torture for me, and the sight of them together had caused all the frustration within me to finally snap.

Bile rose in my throat as I replayed the events from earlier in my head. I couldn't believe I'd shoved my brother aside in my fit of fury. Not only that, but I'd grabbed Elena by the arm with far too much force, too much anger. What in Hells was wrong with me?

Gods. If I'd left a damn bruise on her, I'd never be able to forgive myself. Clawing my hands into my hair, I rested my elbows onto my thighs while howling my aggression into the wind.

Liam and Killian had thankfully forgiven me, even though I didn't deserve it. They'd brought me down here and coaxed the events of the past two weeks out of me. After hearing the shitstorm of events that had come to pass, they'd allowed me some mercy for my unsavory behavior.

Unfortunately, I couldn't have the same debriefing with my Wildfire as I could with them. There was still too much that she didn't know…that she *couldn't* know until the time was right. How did I even begin to apologize when I was supposed to be ending what was growing between us because of her father?

My mind began to swirl and my chest squeezed against my ribs. With effort, I tried to regulate my breathing before it became anything more. The last thing I needed right now was to have an attack of panic while perched on the side of a very steep cliff. A cliff I was all too familiar with already.

Shaking my head, I refocused on my breathing. That was when I felt the warm heat of a palm on my shoulder and the calming effects of her dynamis running through me. *Clara.*

"I was wondering how long it was going to take you to come find me, seeing as how you're usually the one sent to scold me for all the stupid things I get myself into."

"Uh-huh. You make quite the habit of being a stupid ass sometimes." She crouched down beside me, tossing her legs over the edge of the cliff.

"So, I take it Lena's already told you?"

"Mmhmm."

"And?"

"You're in big trouble." She snickered.

I gave her a playful shove, then rested my head back into my hands. "Yeah, I figured as much."

"Want to tell me what that all was about? I know you know what happened between Will and Elena before she left. What makes you think she would open her heart to him again?"

I sighed deeply into my palms.

"So…that tells me that there's something much deeper at play here."

So much deeper.

Running my palm over my face, I tried to collect my thoughts. It was bad enough talking about it with Liam and Killian, now I'd have to relive it all over again with Clara.

"Your silence is not reassuring, Dec."

Even though a playful smile spread across her face, her eyes told me a different story. There was worry hidden behind them, and I hated that I was the one who'd put it there. I despised that they all had to take care of me, pick me up when I broke apart. Especially when I was the one who was supposed to be protecting them.

"For starters, I had to deal with Drake's daughter for a whole week," I said, rolling my eyes. "Father has secured a marriage between the two of us."

"Oh, Hells." She winced. "How was good old Adara? How did she take the news?"

"She still has feelings for me, but honestly, I think she knows that I'll never love her like she wants me to."

"Well, at least she has more social awareness than her father," Clara scoffed.

"She doesn't seem too hurt. She's resilient and has found affection elsewhere."

Clara's face scrunched, like she'd just eaten something sour. "Who would ever want to be wrapped up with her?"

"Will."

Silence.

More silence.

Then finally a gasp. "Oh, Lena…"

Yeah.

"I know she's over him, but gods…It's going to make her feel…" She paused, fumbling her hands together. "It's going to make her feel used…forgettable. This will hurt her, and that's the last thing she needs right now, Dec. She's been carrying some burdens for a long time, and they're heavy."

My spine straightened as I gnawed on the inside of my cheek. Elena and I both shared the same struggle. I knew she knew the darkness behind my mind, but I kept waiting for her to share what fears made her scream in terror at night. The worries alone were a heavy burden to shoulder, but now it sounded like that wasn't all my little Wildfire had been carrying around with her.

My jaw clenched tight. "That's not the only problem…"

Silence.

"I talked to him, Clara," I whispered. "I told him everything, except the part about us being mates because he didn't let me finish."

"And?"

"He said no," I grunted. "Not just no, but a 'never in his existence and even after that' no."

"Declan—"

"I mean, he's right."

"Dec—"

"I'll probably only end up hurting her, ruin what she's meant to be, endanger all of Ehora—"

"DECLAN!"

"It's for the best," I grumbled. "She deserves so much more than me, Clara. Elena deserves someone who will allow her to shine as bright as all the stars in the sky, as bright as the rays of the sun. I'm the Lord of Shadows. I'll only drag her further into the dark."

Saying the words that had been spinning in my head for days now tore me wide open. My chest burned and it felt as if my heart was going up in flames.

The last thing I wanted to do was let her go, but I'd sacrifice my only chance for happiness if it meant it gave others a chance for survival. I'd sacrifice anything for her, even if it meant my own heart died in the process.

"You know this is the most ridiculous decision you have ever made, right?" Clara snapped.

"It's not—"

"Oh, it's completely fucked up, Declan!" She tossed her hands up in frustration.

"Clara—"

"Don't you dare Clara me! I'm so livid right now, you don't even know."

"I know." My words fell between us, just like my hope for happiness.

"No! You know absolutely nothing, Declan!"

Ouch.

"I had to watch you shatter, break and fall apart when you decided that *you* weren't enough for this world. I watched as you gave up, as you tried to sacrifice your own damn existence for the lives of others." Tears began to roll down her cheeks. I tried to grab her hand to comfort her, but she slapped it away. "Now I'm watching you give up the one thing that might bring you happiness. The one that has already begun to bring you back to life again. I can't... I—I refuse let you destroy yourself again. I won't let you do this."

"It's not my choice—"

"It is."

"But Warren—"

"I don't care."

"Clara..."

She sighed deeply, her fingers digging into her legs. "When has the word no ever stopped you, Dec?" Her eyebrows rose, challenging me to deny her words, which I couldn't. "You have always fought for what's right, fought for those you love. You didn't give up on us... don't give up on her. Change. Your. Damn. Mind."

Two hazel eyes pierced into mine. They were full of a dangerous combination of annoyance and sadness. Without another word, she shifted to her feet and stalked back towards the castle, leaving me alone to fall deep into my spiraling thoughts.

CHAPTER 51

DECLAN

It had been two days. Two long, excruciating days.

I'd yet to come to a decision about whether to end things with Elena or give in to my heart and fight for her with all I had. We were stuck in a painful standstill.

The ball that my father was throwing was at the end of the week, and I still had to help Lena come up with something to display in front of everyone. A display that demonstrated that the king was still in control of the most powerful dynamis in Ehora. A grand show that wiped away doubts about his rule and provided him with a more willing flock of sheep to herd towards attacking the Rebellion. The only problem was that being around Elena, even just for mere moments, was torture.

I'd been dwelling in my shadows, watching her from the sidelines as she trained with my friends...*our* friends.

She took my breath away. Elena had come such a long way since we'd brought her here. Don't get me wrong, I'd always known she had strength within her. However, what I saw now shattered every expectation I'd ever held of her.

In weeks, she'd learned several different forms of dynamis, each one complex on its own. We would never tell her this, because it would make her question herself, but it had taken the rest of us months, years even, to learn what she had mastered in weeks. When Killian and Nayla told me about how she'd created an entire peony bush from nothing, I almost fell out of my chair. Terrans had always been able to manipulate living things, but never had they been able to give them life.

As I watched her produce a small drip of water with Liam's guidance, my heart tugged. Liam had told me she'd been struggling to find peace, to find the calm emotion within her to help let her Tide and Frost dynamis flow. My shoulders fell. I was probably responsible for that particular problem.

If that wasn't enough guilt to add to my shoulders, Killian and Clara had informed me Lena had discovered my mother's secret office in the garden.

I had known my mother spent hours every day in her garden, but I had always assumed she was tending to all the plants and flowers. Instead, she was working hard on creating potions to fight the dynamis suppression. My question was, why hadn't she or my brother told me about it?

Together we had discovered a problem with suppressed dynamis, so why wouldn't they tell me that they'd discovered the cure for it? The things that we could have done with that knowledge that had been lost for the past twenty-three years...

The only conclusion I can come to is that she was trying to protect my brother and I. She knew what this cure could mean, and the less others knew about it the safer it would be.

Thankfully, we had Clara. Ever since Lena had discovered the ingredients of my mother's potion, Clara had been researching ways we could recreate it...blood magic and all. Perhaps this might help me eradicate my blood magic problem as well, severing Alastor's hold over me once and for all.

When I looked back towards Lena, she was drenched from head to toe. Liam's face was so red it looked like he was about to pass out.

Could you die from laughter? With a snort, I shook my head at the thought. *Ah, but what a way to go.*

A splash alerted me, and my body tensed. Elena's mouth gaped open, and if I was seeing correctly from this far away, the tears in her eyes as she took in the sight before her.

Liam was soaked, as was the ground surrounding him. When he tried to take a step forward to congratulate her for finally using her Tide dynamis, he lost his footing and slipped into the mud.

All at once the most radiant sound inhabited my soul. Elena's head was thrown back, both arms wrapped around her body as if to stabilize herself from her own laughter. It was the most captivating sound I'd ever heard.

She helped him right himself back on two legs, and then they both zephyred back to the castle. I was left alone, tucked between my ever-familiar shadows.

Today proved more than ever that Elena would be fine without me. She'd finally allowed herself to let down the walls between her emotions and her dynamis, and I'd never felt so proud of her.

My Wildfire had learned how to burn all on her own. Elena didn't need me, in fact she never really had. Shuffling my feet on the soft soil, I closed my eyes and tried to take a deep breath.

It was time I let my Light Phoenix spread her wings and fly...without me.

Elena

As I sat with a towel drying my soaked hair in front of the fireplace, tears welled up in my eyes.

I couldn't believe that I'd finally been able to calm my emotions enough to use my Tide dynamis. That was a feat that I'd honestly never thought I would be able to achieve.

All my life my emotions had been in control, wild and raging, as they tumbled out of me. Today, I'd been the one who was in control, and I'd never felt more fulfilled in my entire life. Every day, I'd felt more empowered, more alive in my own skin.

Unfortunately, I also had an overwhelming need to share this feeling with the only person who didn't want anything to do with me. The one person who'd promised me that I never had to be afraid to show my feelings. The man who'd unleashed my timid heart, only to push me away.

I was so heated, I swore my hair dried on its own without Eloise's help.

She'd come in earlier to help the seamstress with the fitting for my ball gown. I feared my grumpy demeanor had sent the poor seamstress running for the hills before all the adjustments were made. Eloise had tried her best not to probe about Declan, but had accidentally spilled the beans that he would be the one training me tonight after dinner.

Ever since then, I had been stewing over what I would say when I finally saw him again.

The way he'd treated all of us in the training ring was uncalled for. His words had rattled me, leaving me with a throbbing wound in my heart ever since.

What thoughts had even crossed his mind, and what had altered his feelings towards me so much? Shaking my head, I shoved my face into my towel and screamed. How could you be so full of rage towards a person, but on the other hand need their comfort more than anyone else's in the entire world?

CHAPTER 52
ELENA

Leaning against the wall of the hallway, I regretted the basket of rolls I'd devoured earlier. All of them now felt like boulders inside my stomach, which turned upside down with each step I took towards the ballroom. Towards Declan.

What I'd give to have dynamis that could allow me to time-travel. I could go back to the past and force Declan to stay inside the castle walls. To not leave, to not change his mind about us…about me. With a heavy heart, I pushed open the door and shuffled into the ballroom.

Servants bustled about, setting up the room for the ball tomorrow. By the look of things, the king had spared no expense for this event. Everything dripped in gold, and the light shining through the stained-glass windows made the room come alive with color.

As my eyes roved through the room, my breath hitched at the sight of him. He stood with his back to me, his gaze set on the golden thrones perched at the front of the room.

"Leave us." His stern voice reverberated against the glass windows of the ballroom. The staff scattered towards the exits, leaving Declan and I alone.

As he ran his hand through his already disheveled hair, it pulled the silky black tunic tighter against his muscular body. The memory of it pressing against mine invaded my mind, and my body felt that familiar pull in his direction.

Biting my lip, I struggled to find my anger that I'd been holding onto for days. Until he turned around.

Dark circles had taken root under his eyes, and his chestnut waves were tousled. His lips pressed into a thin line at the sight of me. He folded his arms across his chest. "Took you long enough."

"Seriously, that's the first thing you say to me?

Both arms fell to his sides, fists clenching, and in three long strides he was towering over me. His hot breath scorched my forehead.

"You..." he rasped, as if he struggled to say the words but was forcing himself despite the pain. "You've invaded every crevasse of my mind. I can't think straight around you. You're a distraction."

His words cut me deep, too deep. They tore open the barely healed wound that he had already given me.

Maybe I'd been a fool this entire time, maybe this had always been the plan for me. Now I was feeling everything at all once, all too fast. Scalding heat flooded my body, my dynamis vibrating against my skin like a caged animal begging to be released.

When I glanced down, the familiar golden glow illuminated my skin. Planting my feet firmly into the ground, I raised my trembling hands and shoved the prince. Unfortunately, he only slightly wavered, yet instead of his scowl his face melted into something resembling remorse.

"Was this your plan all along? Hmm?" I seethed, shoving him again. "Thought you could build me up, make me feel strong, independent, powerful...*loved?*"

Verdant eyes widened on my last word, his lips parting slightly.

"All for what exactly?" My palms battered once more against his solid chest as I pushed myself away. "Was it just a challenge to break me? Or to entertain you while I shattered into a million pieces across the floor? Is that what you wanted?" My temper flared, and I knew I was spiraling.

"Fine! You win! I'm broken, okay?" I cringed when the sob tore through me, displaying my failure to hold onto control. "I'm done! I can't take whatever this is anymore …Declan, I'm tired, so tired. This whirlwind of emotions is wrecking me. I'll stop being your distraction. Will has made me an offer, perhaps I'll just take him up on that." The words barely floated across my lips. Tears streamed down my face as I used every bit of strength I had to turn around and escape towards the door. I just wanted to go home.

A strong hand gripped my wrist, pulling me back towards his chest. Once I was slammed against it, both of his arms wrapped against my body and held tight.

Prickly stubble scratched against the side of my cheek as a rough voice warmed my ear. "Wildfire, I never meant to hurt you. You mean everything to me, and I hate that I'm causing you distress." He brushed a featherlight kiss to my neck. "I'm so damn sorry."

What?

He turned me around and tucked my hair tenderly behind my ear. "Allow me to help you find your light, the one that I know burns through you like wildfire and ignites your very soul."

The whiplash of this entire encounter stunned me into silence. Mere moments ago, he'd told me I was a distraction, now he was pleading to help me with my light dynamis.

"There's an emotion that seems to be incredibly powerful for you, Lena. It's helped you accomplish feats with your dynamis that the rest of us have never witnessed."

Thoughts of the peony bush and the twirling roots of the gods' tree flashed before my eyes.

"What is that one emotion that you call to?

The dilemma of whether to be open and vulnerable with the man behind me threw me off balance. The anger within me told me to tell him what he could do with himself. The more levelheaded part of me noticed the pain in his voice and the genuine tone in his apology.

There was more to his change of behavior than he was letting on. Something was eating him alive.

"Love." My voice cracked as I made my decision. His fist covered his lips, tears clouded his emerald eyes. "Dec—"

He lowered his hand. "Hold on tight to that emotion and

command your dynamis. Go on, Elena, show yourself how powerful you truly are."

All at once, every emotion inside of me collided. It was like his words were the key to unlock everything I'd kept sealed within me for so long.

Love. Hopelessness. Frustration. Hate. Anger. Fear. Anxiousness. Happiness. Confusion. Sadness, and so many more. Never did I think it was possible to feel so many emotions at once. It felt like a million embers sparking against the dynamis within me. Everything inside of me ignited, and for once I let it consume me entirely.

Images flashed inside my mind of everything that warmed my soul and kept it kindled all these years. I saw images of me closing my eyes towards the sky, the sun warming my skin and freckles.

Flash.

Now I was dancing with my mom in her garden, her copper hair waving around her like the flames of a fire. Our laughter was so loud, it was like I was there now.

Flash.

I sat on the roof of my home. Darkness surrounded me, but the stars provided me comfort and peace.

Flash.

I watched my mother and father dance together. This moment was the first time that I fully understood the meaning of romantic love. The way they looked lost in the depths of each other's eyes made me yearn to have someone look at me that way one day.

When they caught me watching, their smiles reached their ears as they pulled me into their arms. I'd never felt safer than I had at that moment.

Flash.

The next images flew by my eyes fast, but not too fast for me to feel the impact of each of them. Every person I'd ever loved, cared for, shared a laugh with passed before me. So many familiar faces, even a few new ones. Like a playfully smirking Liam as he splashed me with water, or a mischievous laugh from Clara as we clinked our wine glasses together.

Flash.

The last image was too hard to see, and I fought to lift my eyelids. Searching my mind, I tried to will other memories into existence, but it didn't budge.

Declan's emerald eyes gleamed against the moonlight. It was the memory of the night we defeated the beasts. The night our dynamis had intertwined. It was the night that he was given a glimpse of respect...forgiveness, from the city he loved so deeply.

Bright eyes locked onto mine, their hold so strong I couldn't break away. They were full of gratitude, euphoria, relief...love. With each stride he took towards me, I felt a tug pull deep within my chest. That same feeling I'd felt when our eyes first met. The same ache I felt every time I was around him. It wrapped around me and pulled tight.

Everything went quiet in my mind, and I surrendered to the warmth and fell to my knees. Thoroughly spent, I took in the astounding sight that surrounded me. Tears fell from my eyes, cooling my heated skin.

Darkness engulfed the entire ballroom. The only lights illuminating the room now were millions of tiny, golden spheres of light.

Shining stars in a sea of darkness.

An ethereal image of what I looked like broken apart and scattered across the floor.

They pulsed within the darkness, almost in tune with my heartbeat. As I rose to my feet, I spread my arms and twirled between the tiny stars I'd created.

It reminded me of the first vision I'd seen during my Ascension, except I was awake. This was real, tangible, something I'd created from nothing. I held one of the golden spheres in my palms, and a smile grew on my lips.

"You're astounding, love." Warm knuckles brushed against the side of my cheek, sending shivers down my spine.

Lifting my chin, I was met with the darkened eyes of the man in front of me, void of almost all their verdant green but reflecting the golden light of my stars within them.

"Wildfire, you're glowing."

Sheepishly, I shrugged off his words, as it had become somewhat of a regular occurrence these past few days.

"Look down," he whispered, as his throat bobbed. When I looked down, my breath hitched at the sight.

Every freckle on my body was consumed in a warm golden glow. Every. Single. One.

The mark of my dynamis also hummed with light as well. Instantly, my hands rose to my cheeks and I wondered if I glowed there as well.

"Yes, Wildfire. You're glowing there too." Declan's chest rose and fell with rapid breaths.

I lowered my trembling hands to my pants, squeezing the fabric between my fingers. My heart thrummed against my chest, and I could feel the familiar ache tug inside it as I took two steps back.

Strong arms pulled me back, one wrapped around my waist, the other caressing my back. There was barely any space separating the two of us now.

My lips trembled, and I shook my head. This couldn't happen again, no matter how much I wanted to let him back in. I didn't think I was strong enough to survive another tear in my heart.

With a heavy sigh, my forehead fell against his shoulder, and his arms cinched around me. I placed my shaky hands against his hard chest, trying to block out the feeling of his heartbeat. When I pushed away this time, his arms dropped beside him, letting me free.

"Thank you," I whispered, "for all of this." I gestured at the dazzling night sky I'd created surrounding us.

"That was all you, love." His voice low, pain dripping off each word.

I turned around and made my way towards the doors. The silence was unbearably heavy as I hurried my steps. I had to get away from here before I collapsed under the weight of it all. Grabbing the door, I swung it wide open. No more looking back, it was time to go.

Declan's palm slammed against the door, sealing it shut. Faster than I could think, he spun me around and crashed his lips onto mine. At first, I tried to pull away, but his body caged me in. His thick chest pressed against mine as his fingers dug into the sides of my waist, holding me in place.

This kiss was rough. Intense. Desperate. My knees went weak when his tongue brushed across the seam of my lips, silently begging me to open myself up to him again. To let him in.

So I did. I let myself plummet into the abyss, the unknowns of our future be damned. For once, I was going to savor just this moment.

Our kiss deepened into something passionate, obliterating. My body barely managed to stay upright. Sensing me melting against the door, he lifted my legs up and secured them around his waist.

One of my hands fisted in Declan's chestnut waves, the other twisted around the bottom of his tunic, pulling him closer into me. As I tugged, my body slipped down, causing me to rub against the hard bulge beneath his pants. A guttural growl rumbled against my lips as his palm dug into my thigh, tugging me back up his waist. My thighs clenched around him as his length brushed against my heated core.

Swallowing my surprised moan, he continued to rub against my center, driving me out of my mind. The only thoughts I had at this moment were about Declan and the ways in which I could have more of him.

Sweeping his giant palm through my hair, he tilted my head to the side, peppering kisses down my neck. Down my collarbone, over the top of my chest, he created a delicious trail that my dynamis followed. His hot breath hovered over the sensitive tip of my breast. Even through my tunic, I could feel a devious smile grow, before he covered it with his mouth and sucked.

"Oh, gods..." I gasped.

A delighted rumble hummed from deep within his throat. His lips slammed onto mine again, and we lost ourselves, tangled deep in each other's arms. Every movement was desperate, frantic, passionate. It was as though we both thought that this might be the last time we would be able to do this.

Sealing one more kiss onto my bruised lips, he inched back. The sounds of our breaths filled the silence.

Our eyes locked. Declan's had become almost as black as the room itself.

"Do you trust me, love?" he whispered.

I scoffed, and the space between his eyebrows crinkled.

"Do. You. Trust. Me?"

His words were more forceful this time, squeezing out through clenched teeth. The question rattled inside my mind. *Do I?*

My pulse raced at the same pace as the thoughts that started to flood back into my mind. Once, I had trusted him, but now I wasn't entirely sure.

He kept unraveling the tight threads of myself that I'd been desperately trying to keep hold of all my life. However, right now, with him I felt invincible and safe. Even with all the anger, all the frustration, all the unknowns, I was still grasping onto the hope that he wouldn't ever let me fall.

With a shallow exhale, I met his eyes and nodded. "Yes, sir."

Anticipation began to build as his grip around me tightened. He lowered me to the ground.

Terrified I'd done something wrong, I pulled my teeth between my bottom lip and bit down. He had yet to move away. Both of his hands still created a bruising ache around my hips.

He peered up at the ceiling, as if trying to collect his thoughts. Watching his throat bob up and down, I licked my lips. Never had I thought that something like that could be alluring, but I was about to slowly melt into a puddled mess.

Declan lowered his heated gaze back towards me, his eyes roving up and down my body, looking for any reservations that I might still be holding. When I returned my own fiery gaze, his shoulders eased. An excruciatingly slow smirk spread across his lips.

"Good girl."

His silky voice purred into my ear, shoving all my thoughts out of my head once more. Lips brushed against mine, each kiss more tender than those before.

One hand swirled against the flesh of my stomach before making its way up towards my breast. A thumb caressed the underside of one breast as his other hand fell underneath the top of my leggings. The unexpected intrusion caused me to jump, breaking our kiss for a moment. With his forehead resting against mine, he sighed deeply.

"Trust me, love. Let me make you feel as amazing as you make me feel every day." His words came out in short rasps.

Wrapping my hand around the back of his head, I pulled him into a kiss. With a relieved growl, his hand plunged below my leggings, thumb now rubbing over the sensitive apex between my thighs that had been throbbing with need since I first saw him in this damn room. He stoked the fire within me again, and my entire body flushed with heat as he teased his fingers against the side of my underwear.

"Declan..."

"Tell me to stop," he murmured against my skin.

"Don't stop," I whispered.

A groan ripped through him, and I was blindsided by his large finger dipping inside me, pulsing in and out of the molten core between my thighs. My hips began to writhe uncontrollably against his hand. He added another finger. A cry ripped from my lips, smothered by Declan's mouth as he curled his fingers inside me. With every pulse, the burning fire within me begged to be unleashed. Even my dynamis rippled against the surface of my heated core. Breathing was near impossible.

"Dec...I—"

"Breathe, Lena."

"I—I—"

"Hells," he panted, his slick forehead lying against mine. "You look so beautiful like this, my love."

All thoughts went blank inside my mind, and for once in my life, it felt as though I couldn't think at all.

The pressure within me continued to build, with almost the same intensity as when I unbound my light dynamis earlier. Deft hands worked within me. His thumb continued to add tension where it was needed most. The feeling was so fierce that I feared I might combust if a release from it didn't come soon.

Clutching around Declan's neck, I held on for dear life, sending a prayer to the gods I would survive my undoing. Warm lips brushed against my ear as he whispered one last time.

"Let go for me, love."

Sealing my surrender with a kiss, I careened, seeing stars. Literally and figuratively.

Air around us began to clear its haze as I focused on calming my frantic breaths. Finding my senses once more, I was able to take in the sight around us.

"So. Damn. Stunning," he hummed against my cheek.

Bright, golden spheres appeared around us. One fluttered underneath my nose as a breathless laugh escaped from me. Declan released his grip on me, taking a step back to allow me some space. His fingertips grazed my chin.

"Elena...I—" There was a strain in his voice as he whispered my name.

The blissful smile that had blossomed against my cheeks vanished as he stepped further away. Indecision struck through him, like the chill of the first frost. Tentatively, I raised my hand to comfort him, but he pushed it back down.

"I..." His lips were tight, breathing erratic. "I shouldn't have done that... I'm so sorry. This just can't be, Elena." He paused for one more second, his fingers curling around the edge of the door so hard his knuckles were void of color. "Wildfire, you deserve a beautiful life. With me you'll only find destruction. Live, Elena," With glossy eyes he stormed out the opposite door.

No.

I tore the door wide open.

"DECLAN STALLARD!" My yell echoed through the vacant hallway.

He turned around, eyes reddened with tears streaming down the harsh lines of his chin. That was when I realized his eyes were no longer focused on mine. They had shifted to someone behind me.

Holding my breath, I turned around to come face to face with Will. Blooms of wildflowers dangled in his hand. One glance at my flushed face, swollen lips, and they fell to the floor.

"Will," I breathed, as he stormed off in the opposite direction.

When I whipped around towards Declan, my heart sank to see he had left as well.

Fury burned through me, and a whirlwind of light dynamis scorched through my fingertips. White flames flickered across the hallway as I screamed towards the gods.

Blackened ash replaced the once vibrant petals, and I couldn't help but feel like we were kindred spirits.

CHAPTER 53
ELENA

"Wake, Elena."

"Wake!"

I clutched my racing heart as I tried to soothe myself back to a calm state. The dream had been different this time. It had been darker, colder. No battles, no revisiting of the night of my mother's death. Instead, it was like I was swallowed into a dark void, with no chance of escape.

Screams had echoed against my ears, full of agony, sadness, despair. I almost felt like I might have been trapped there forever until the familiar voice summoned me back to the present. I swept away the hair from my face and eyes as my mind adjusted to the reminder that I was still in the same room that I'd been living in for over a month.

Two nights ago, the man I'd begun to slowly fall in love with had pushed me away...again. Yet here I was hanging on with all I had, because I still had hope. Hope that I could find my way out of the darkness that clouded my light. No longer could I run away from my fears; it was time for me to step up and face them head on.

Luckily, I wouldn't have to do it alone. There was just one person I would have to convince to join me. Declan.

The hurt he'd put me through would not easily be forgiven, but I still felt that he was worth fighting for. So tonight, I would make him sweat a little. Remind him of what he might lose. Remind him that I wouldn't be pushed aside so easily. Make him realize that he wouldn't be able to let me go, because I wouldn't let him.

Smirking to myself, I rose from the bed to take a shower. I'd been burrowing inside my room for the past two days. I hadn't had the willpower to put on a smile for the others after what had transpired in the ballroom. I'd needed to work through my sadness, anger, and confusion before I could wrap my brain around what should happen next.

Yesterday afternoon, I might have secretly told Eloise that I would like some alterations done to my original dress for the ball. There also might have been a few times when I let slip what had happened between Declan and me. It pushed Eloise to get the changes made as soon as possible.

As I dried off my damp hair with a towel, I recalled her words from yesterday.

"Thank gods! That boy has finally met his match in you, Lena. Someone who will go toe to toe with his stubbornness. Someone who will remind him what it means to be happy again. Someone who will fight for those they love.

Tonight, I hoped to do all the above.

Declan

I was a wreck.

I'd hurt her.

She'd trusted me. Opened up to me. Let me...

What am I doing?

My mother would be appalled. I was ashamed to be thankful that she wasn't here to show me that disappointment in person, because it would destroy me more than I already was right now.

I'd valued her opinion of me more than anything in my life, for she was the most amazing soul I'd ever met. Right now, I was more desperate than ever for her unyielding love and support.

Ever since she and my brother had departed from this life, I'd been making a mess of mine. One mistake after another, each one causing someone else in my life pain.

Smoothing my palms down my face, I tried to rub away all the shame, disgust and guilt that dwelled inside of me. So much was weighing down on my shoulders, so many expectations, and everything in me sensed that time was running out. Was I strong enough to hold it all together? Could I make it through all this without sabotaging everything that we'd been working on?

"Thought I might find you here." Liam crouched down beside me on the edge of the cliff, dangling his legs off the edge, matching mine. "How are you holding up, brother?"

I tossed him a pointed expression. He slapped me across the back. "Yeah, I figured that might be the case."

"Everything is a mess." I paused, rubbing my hand over my jaw. "I don't think I can fix it this time, Liam."

Leaning back on his hand, he looked deep in thought as he gazed out into the ocean's waves. "She's stronger than you think, you know?"

I only grunted in response.

"She has her insecurities and struggles, just like we all do. Just like you do." He paused, waiting for me to look at him. "But she keeps meeting every challenge thrown at her. She continues to rise. Every. Damn. Time. You can't keep treating her like some fragile jewel that will break the moment you let her in, Dec. Elena deserves more faith than that."

I sucked my lips between my teeth, nodding in agreement.

"Life has been out of her control for far too long. The little lady deserves to make her own decisions for once."

"You're right, Liam." I lowered my eyes in shame. "I really haven't given her that freedom since day one. I just don't know how to release that control, how to stop the overwhelming need to shield her from those who might hurt her. People like me."

"Again, don't you think it's up to her to decide who she loves?" He deadpanned.

I swallowed deeply, trying not to be shaken by his words. *Damn.*

Could she truly love me? Gods knew that I needed her more than I needed air. That she'd invaded my every thought, every dream. That love was not a strong enough word for the way that I adored her.

Liam cleared his throat. "Dec, I think it's about time you start believing that you're worthy of love, and that you're capable of returning it as well. You deserve to be happy. I believe Elena will be the one to finally show you it's possible."

Climbing to his feet, he extended his hand. After I allowed him to help me up, I embraced him, slapping his back.

"Thank you for always putting up with me, for always reminding me when I'm not thinking straight."

"Anytime, brother." He smirked. "I knew what I was getting into when I was asked to work with the 'willful' prince."

I shoved him in the shoulder, causing him to roar with laughter. His mirth was enough to make me chuckle as well.

"Come on." He motioned towards the castle. "We better get ready. I have a feeling it's going to be an eventful evening."

Me too, brother. Me too.

CHAPTER 54
ELENA

"Lena! All eyes are going to be on you tonight." Clara whistled, and Eloise's grin sparkled just as bright behind me. "I'm going to thoroughly enjoy watching Declan's face when you step into the ballroom. With that dress, you might stop his heart," she snorted. "Good thing I'm a Healer."

My cheeks heated from her appraisal, and the idea of the way I looked influencing anyone, especially Declan. "You really think this will make a difference? Changing Declan's mind doesn't exactly seem like a task that's easily accomplished." A nervous twinge swirled inside the pit of my stomach.

Clara and Eloise exchanged a mischievous smile. "Oh," Clara hummed, "something tells me that tonight, you won't have any problems at all."

They provided me with a lightness I desperately needed. As they went back to work finishing my hair, I snuck a glance at myself in the mirror.

Since the day in the ballroom, my freckles had yet to stop shining, only fading slightly in the following days. I was more comfortable staying out of the spotlight. These were going to do quite the opposite.

However, tonight was about shedding my fears. It was about being bold, giving in to my strength, going after my own happiness. I'd been hiding for far too long, and it was time to fully come into my confidence. Tonight, I would show everyone just how powerful I really was.

"Can I ask you both something? Is this too dangerous a web we're weaving? I can't help but feel selfish for going after happiness, knowing it will have a disastrous effect on everyone else around us. Alaric will not be happy, and I'm terrified of what he and Alastor will do."

Eloise turned me to face her. "Remember what I told you, sometimes we must take risks to be with the ones we love. If you're not willing to fight for that love with all you have, then it's not a love worthy of the chase."

"I'm willing to fight," I breathed.

"I know. That's how I know you both were made for each other." She pulled me into an embrace and whispered, "He's afraid of himself and afraid of hurting you, but he's never stopped loving you."

The prickle of tears pressed against my eyes as she twirled me around the vases of flowers that sat beside my bed. "You see those? Since the first night you arrived, he has been picking fresh flowers for you every day." My eyes widened, and Clara squeezed my hand. Tears began to stir in her eyes as well. "Even when he was away, he told me in his letters which flowers to place in your room each day." Pulling out a folded piece of parchment, she handed it to me. Eloise took a step back and wrapped an arm around Clara, allowing me space to read.

There were flowers to match the color of my eyes, the vibrance of my hair, but it was the ones that touched on parts of my soul that sent the tears sliding down my cheeks.

"Day lilies to light up her day and empower her. Irises to bring her courage and remind her to hold onto hope. Daisies and honeysuckle to stir the happiness and sweetness that dwells within her..."

On and on went the list of all the reasons why these flowers deserved to be in my presence. The parchment crinkled in my hand as

I stared at the blooms inside the vase today. Lavender, forget-me-nots, and delicate pink peonies in full, fluffy bloom.

"Lavender to bring you serenity, forget-me-nots to remind you of his love even from afar, and peonies in full bloom to remind you of your transformation into the stunning woman you have become." Eloise sniffled, and I faced the two sets of glassy eyes behind me.

"He said that?" My voice cracked.

She nodded. "I doubt he intended for me to share." Eloise released a breathy laugh as she wiped away a tear. "But you needed to know he still loves you, he just needs help clearing the fog of his own mind." She leaned back to give my ensemble one final look before pulling me in for a quick embrace. "Ready?"

"I think my cousin needs to be reminded of who makes his heart pulse." Clara held out her hand to help me stand.

"Ready as I'll ever be," I whispered, swallowing down my fear one last time. I placed my arm through Clara's, and we made our way towards the ballroom.

Tonight, I planned to take charge of my destiny, in more ways than one.

Declan

There wasn't enough whiskey in all Ehora to make this night any less difficult.

Tossing back the last remnants in my glass, I motioned to the server for another. The collar of my tunic threatened to deprive me of air until I unhooked the two buttons of my black dress shirt. The simmering heat that had been torching my body since I'd stepped into this ballroom began to cool.

With a refilled glass of courage, I made my way unwillingly back towards the conversation I had needed a reprieve from.

The grand ballroom dripped with gold and lavish linens and table settings. Long tables lined the hall, full of fine meats and fresh fish drizzled in the finest sauces. Trays of sweet rolls and cakes that were iced to perfection sat in the middle of each elaborately decorated table, alongside the thousands of colorful blooms that were cut fresh this from morning my mother's garden.

Wincing at the memory of the state of the garden after so many blooms had been ravaged, I tried to ease my annoyance by reminding myself that I'd spend some time repairing it all tomorrow.

Our kingdom was suffering. So many were struggling to even put food in their mouths. Yet here we were reveling in an opulent ballroom, knowing much of this food would be tossed to the animals the moment the ball ended.

Disgusted by the depravity of it all, I felt the fire flare within me to leave this place behind once and for all and take my place in Oria. Once I knew that Elena would be safe, then I would leave.

"Better now?" my father grumbled beneath his breath.

"Exceedingly," I sneered, lifting the glass to my lips to take another swig.

He rolled his eyes and continued talking with Lord Edan Drake. Clenching my teeth, I tried to control my urge to strangle them both as they continued to talk about Elena like she was some sort of stallion to be broken and trained to do their bidding.

"Yes, I believe with the right motivation her fiery spirit can be tamed." Drake swirled the wine around in his glass. "Give her a week or two with my Adara and Will, and I'll get her on our side."

"I have several ways of making people bend." Adara's gaze fluttered towards mine. Her eyes were still lit with hope that I would eventually change my mind.

If I couldn't have Elena, then I would have no one. Consequences be damned.

The blond boy next to her gave me a glare of death. For a moment I felt a thread of sympathy for Will, having to be stuck this past month with Edan.

Then I was reminded of everything he'd done.

I'd almost torn him apart when I caught him with his tongue practically down Adara's throat last week. I'd tossed him down the stairs after she left. It had only been four steps—he'd survived.

He'd tried to seduce Elena the moment he set foot in the castle. He'd had a choice between the most caring, strong, and enchanting soul in our kingdom, or the life of luxury Edan had promised him. Thankfully for me, he'd chosen wrong.

"She has no need to go to the City of Ash," I growled. "I'm perfectly capable of continuing to train the Light Phoenix here."

Lord Drake shot me a deadly glare, his fingers clenched around his wine goblet. I couldn't help the grin that spread across my face at his displeasure.

"All to be determined after our little demonstration tonight, right, son?" My father leaned over ever so slightly, making sure that I was the only one to hear his words. "Let's hope you don't embarrass us any further. So help me, if you let me down tonight, we will have a conversation you won't like."

The veins in my neck bulged, rage building from deep within me. Wisps of my dynamis rippled shadows across my arms. "Would this conversation happen to take place in a particular dark room you and Alastor are so fond of? No need to feed me false threats when we both know what will really happen."

With another huff, he grabbed the arm of a passing server, demanding she refill his glass of wine. I took another long draw of whiskey, silently full of mirth that I could still ruffle my father's feathers so easily. That was when a chill rolled over me, causing the hair on my neck to stand at attention.

"Careful, boy," Alastor seethed.

The man looked even paler tonight. His light blue eyes seemed darker and more sunken into his skull. As my father stalked over to him, stirring conversations with a few other lords, I couldn't help but take in his appearance as well. I'd noticed that he had been growing weaker as the months passed by, but I'd been too distracted lately to really take in his outward appearance.

The king looked frail, like he had lost a considerable amount of weight. His complexion appeared to be pale as well. I rubbed my chin as an unfamiliar worry for my father wound inside my stomach.

My father used to be kind, thoughtful, and respected by many. Not selfish and full of pride, lusting for more power at every turn.

Ever since Alastor had found a hold over me, a small part of me had begun to question if he might be doing something similar to my father. On darker days, I sometimes wondered if he had even gotten to my brother as well. He might have summoned Keir to get rid of our mother and then himself. I shuddered at the despicable thought, taking another deep swig of my whiskey.

Finishing yet another glass, I began to stalk towards the bar for another until the doors to the ballroom thundered open. Time stood still. My heart stopped dead in my chest.

Every one of my thoughts became consumed by the only distraction that I'd ever let break down my wards. Mesmerized by the living goddess who had just floated in, I barely noticed the rest of the ballroom fall silent.

The glass between my clenched hands began to crack. Thankfully, a server swayed by, replacing my empty cup with a new full one. I stood frozen with a clenched jaw, trying desperately to stop the blood from draining out my head and trailing down towards a less discreet part of my body. Of all nights, this was one where I needed my wits about me, but the way she looked tonight?

I'm doomed. She might very well decimate the shreds of restraint I had left.

My gaze lazily rolled over her soft skin, dusted in starbursts of golden freckles, evidence of her ethereal display of dynamis only two evenings ago permanently ingrained into her skin. Long auburn waves cascaded over her shoulder and down her back. The white dress shimmered underneath the chandeliers filled with thousands of candles that adorned the room. Thin straps wrapped over her delicate shoulders, the neckline plummeting down her body, like a deep chasm between her breasts.

As a dignitary from Atheling shook her hand, she turned, and I could see the back of the dress was almost non-existent. Golden citrine and opal gems decorated the bottom of the dress, making it look like her dress was set aflame. With one scorching look from across the room, my Wildfire lived up to her name, igniting my soul.

It reminded me of every piece of her light that I would be missing if I continued to push her away instead of fighting to hold onto her.

I'd lose her vibrant personality and her brilliant mind. No longer would I witness her compassionate heart and the way she could light up a room with her infectious smile. There would be no one to challenge me the way she had, either. No one understood the darkness of our minds in the way we both did.

I'd been a fool to think I could ever let her go. Even more dense to think that I was saving her from me, when she was the one who had been saving me since we'd met.

Elena was a walking firestorm of inner strength, a storm I wanted to surrender to fully. I knew it wouldn't be easy to ask for forgiveness, I knew I had hurt her severely. I prayed the gods and hoped that for once they would be in my favor.

Now to see if she still burned for me the way I blazed for her.

CHAPTER 55
ELENA

"Breathe, Lena," Clara mumbled under her breath, so hushed that I barely heard her at all.

"They're all staring," I whispered between my trembling lips.

Run. The word kept pounding inside my head. Every instinct told me to kick off these ridiculous heels and leave this place just a distant memory. Reaching for the mantra that often pulled me out of my spiral, I let it repeat in my head, praying the weight of the moment would fade.

I am the light, no darkness can bind me. I have it within me to hold and to guide me.

The tension in my shoulders and back began to release as my eyes fluttered back open.

I can do this. No, I will *do this.*

Not only for myself, but for all of those holding onto the hope that the Light Phoenix would bring them out of the darkness that was decaying the kingdom. Shoulders back, chin tilted up, I let that hope strengthen me, replacing my fear with the confidence to help me make it through the night.

The ballroom murmured back to life, music replacing the silence from a few moments ago.

That was when I felt his gaze, stirring that tug in my chest that kept me connected to the one man I couldn't seem to erase from my mind. His verdant eyes called to me from across the room, beckoning me towards him.

"Come on, Light Phoenix. Let's get this over with so you have the rest of the evening to...*persuade* my cousin." Her pearly whites beamed towards me, as she tugged my arm, setting us on a course towards our hosts for the evening.

Everywhere the candlelight touched glistened with opulence. Even though it was dark outside, the stained-glass windows that depicted the forest landscapes and shorelines of Ehora were brought to life by giant pits of fire outside.

It was unlike anything I had ever seen, and instead of being awed by it, I was overwhelmed with nausea. Mostly due to the sight of the guests from poorer districts of the city with plates piled high with food, while others dressed in fine silks and pearls sneered toward them.

The ache in my heart pulsed. This was probably more food than many of them saw in a week. I knew, because I'd been there as well.

Several days ago, during our last gathering, I had suggested that the king extend an invite to his entire city. Before he was able to reject my idea, several other dignitaries agreed, causing him to send out invites the next day.

Clara relaxed her pace as we approached the circle of powerful people in front of us. Declan's eyes still roved over my body, locking me in an impenetrable gaze.

I held tight onto my ward, trying to not let my feelings spill into the other Empath in the room. However, the physical reaction to his heated gaze seemed to not be as easily contained. Warmth heated my cheeks and flushed down the sides of my neck.

I bit my lip, a dire attempt to distract myself. A low groan murmured from him. I couldn't help the twitch of my lips as Declan drained the whiskey from his glass.

An all-too-familiar voice from home filled my ears, causing my body to freeze. "Looks like you're still capable of knocking men on their asses, Lena. Still damn breathtaking." Will took a deep swig from his own wine glass.

Cloudy blue eyes were full of fire, directed to the man standing across from him, dressed head to toe in black. A man who was currently looking at him like he could kill him with just one snap of his finger.

"Let's dance." Will shoved his wine goblet into Adara's hand and tugged me into the middle of the dance floor.

He twirled me around in a circle, then spun me back hard so I slammed back into his chest. He intertwined his fingers with mine, but his other hand gripped my waist with a bruising grip. Leaning in close, he whispered into my ear. "You look incredible tonight, Elena."

As he pulled away, his eyes assessed my body in a leisurely way that made me feel uncomfortable. His reddened face moved closer to mine, and I could smell the sweet and sour stench of wine upon his breath. "Have you made your decision?" He swayed me back and forth, his grip around me tightening around me in a possessive way that made me worry he might never let go.

Nerves tangled my stomach in knots, but I knew he deserved to hear the truth. "Will…" His eyes widened, and our bodies stilled. "I won't be going back to the City of Ash with you. I'm sorry," I whispered, taking the opportunity to push myself out of his hold.

Will's lip curled as he stepped forward, grasping for me, but was only met with Declan's arm.

"It's my turn to take Lady Elena for a spin around the room," Declan rumbled before he spun us away. "Dare to dance with me, Wildfire?"

Without waiting for a reply, he pulled me closer to his warmth, and I couldn't resist the pull of his gaze. When his fingers brushed against the bare skin of the small of my back, it sparked a burn to kindle down my lower abdomen.

His stubble brushed against my cheek, and my toes curled inside my heels.

"I was a fool," he whispered against my cheek. "You've made me feel alive again. Elena, you've become the reason I wake up in the morning, and you're the last person I think of when I go to sleep. You've become the pulse of my heart, love, and without you I fear it will just stop beating entirely. I'm so sorry for running away. That was the last time I will make that mistake."

"Are you sure?" I arched my brow.

"Well…unless you toss another one of those damn spoons at my forehead again. Only then might I quiver in my boots." A sly grin split his lips as I slapped his shoulder.

Grabbing his collar, I pulled him down until our mouths hovered dangerously close. "Try to run from me again, and I might just use a fork." I used all my restraint to push him back upright before we made a scene in the middle of the dance floor.

Declan's eyes sparkled with mirth as he brought my palm up and pressed his lips against it.

"You have a deal, love."

CHAPTER 56
ELENA

"L et's get this over with, then you and I need to have a long chat."
"Yes, my lady." His hand pressed against the small of my back, and he escorted me towards the powerful men near the dais of the room.

"Now that we are all here"—I motioned between Will and I— "perhaps it's time for the main event? I'm sure we all have more important things to attend to this evening." I feigned boredom as I crossed my arms in front of me.

Delighted, I watched all the feathers I ruffled ripple around the circle. Lord Alastor snarled with disgust. Creases formed between the king's brows, his eyes narrowed in slits. If a look could kill, his just might tonight. Edan rolled his eyes and took a long sip of his wine.

Adara strolled over towards Declan, and my palms curled into tight fists. Placing both hands on his shoulders, she rose on her tiptoes and caressed his cheek with her lips, then whispered against his ear before lowering herself back down and strolling away, giving me a wink as she passed.

Just like Will, she was making a last-ditch effort to hold onto something that was never hers to begin with.

Clara rubbed a soothing hand against my back, and I couldn't help but steal a quick glance in Declan's direction. His eyes were wide, pleading with mine to be unaffected by the display. I silently gestured that I was fine. *Shocked and disgusted...but fine.* His lips twitched ever so slightly, and he tilted his head, giving me a questioning look, as I winced.

Did I say that out loud?

Obviously over our shenanigans, the king bellowed out for the attention of the room. The music silenced, while conversations lulled. He stalked towards the throne and stepped up onto the dais before turning to address the room.

"Tonight, we all will witness history in the making. Yet again, the gods have blessed Ehora and gifted us with two powerful weapons. Warriors of light against the darkness of those who choose to rebel against us." His deep voice boomed against the walls.

Inwardly, I rolled my eyes. Those who rebelled? He wanted to use us against the only group of people in Ehora who were trying to actually help.

Unfortunately, dear king, I have other plans.

A snort burst free beside me, and both Clara and I looked towards Declan inquisitively. A shrug was our only reply as I shifted my focus back to the king.

"These two have become even more powerful than the 'Blessed' among us. One has even obtained a dynamis we have not witnessed for centuries, a dynamis that brought us an era of peace, and I'm here to guarantee that she will bring it to our lands once more."

Cheers and applause thundered within the room's walls. However, the gasps and whispers from those who didn't agree didn't go unheard by my ears. Alastor nodded towards Will, and a space was created around him as he approached the middle of the room.

He rolled his neck in a circle, shaking out his body, preparing it for the dynamis it was about to endure. Will spread his arms wide open and lowered his head, collecting his dynamis from deep within.

Not one sound could be heard, as if we were all holding our breaths with anticipation for what was about to come.

Just as I exhaled, Will's arms combusted in flames.

My jaw dropped as he conjured long strands of fiery whips. He twirled them in circles, slamming them against the marble floors with enough force to make them crackle. His whips blazed over the heads of the crowd, causing guests to shriek and scatter further away.

Suddenly, Will intertwined both ropes of fire for his last party trick of the night. His blue eyes latched onto mine. He stalked towards me, and I could feel my body leaning away from the threat. Just as my head thumped against the chest behind me, Will launched his fiery whips towards me.

Strong arms tugged me backwards just as the whips crackled against the floor. Precisely where my feet had vacated.

As I clawed my way from Declan's hold, my dynamis simmered underneath my skin as rage built inside of me against the person I'd once thought I knew so well. With a devious smirk, he snuffed out his flames and stalked back towards Adara.

"You're next, Light Phoenix," the king summoned.

"Behave yourself, or there will be consequences," Alastor sneered beside me.

Declan's chest rattled with a low growl as he stepped between us, forming a barrier.

"You too, boy," Alastor huffed, before stalking towards the side of the king.

With a shake of my shoulders, the words rolled off me. If I was going to show everyone how truly powerful I was, I was going to need to regain my control.

Just as I began to make my way towards the middle of the room, a voice whispered next to me.

"Show them all. Let them see how powerful you are. Let your light shine, Lena."

My pulse quickened inside my chest. For a whisper, the words were so loud. They felt as though they vibrated inside my head. Turning, I paused, noticing Declan was nowhere near me. Goosebumps pebbled over my skin as I made eye contact with the man still standing amongst the crowd—halfway across the room.

I'm finally losing my ever-loving mind.

"Anytime, Lady Morrigan," the king grumbled from his throne.

Startled by his booming voice, I turned my back to them all. For what I needed to do tonight, I needed to be free of distraction. Silence blanketed the ballroom as my eyelids fluttered shut.

Over this past month, I had come to understand some of the many intricacies of my dynamis. The more confident and comfortable I felt with my emotions, the more vibrantly my dynamis flowed. However, the greatest epiphany I'd had here happened two nights ago when I realized what my strongest emotion was.

Love.

What I had created in that ballroom had taken my breath away, just like it had done the first time I had zephyred or the first time a flame ignited between my fingertips. The same feeling had flowed through me when I grew an entire plant from nothing and splashed Liam with the Tide dynamis I thought I would never be able to achieve. That feeling had consumed my body the night Declan and I had somehow managed to combine our dynamis, creating something spectacularly powerful and beautiful.

Every moment I used my dynamis, I pulled on the emotions necessary to wield it. Inevitably, right before I used my power, love enveloped it, allowing me to do things with my dynamis I never thought I'd be capable of.

I supposed that I shouldn't be surprised that love was my most powerful emotion of all. It was what had kept me going all these years, given me hope, and provided me with the strength I couldn't always find within myself. No matter how difficult my life had been, how far I let myself succumb to the darkness within my mind, I still held onto the faith that love would guide me through it.

The love from those close to me, my family and my small circle of friends. Even the love of a man who had helped me find my true self in more ways than one. For once in my life, I was beginning to love myself.

Fate had taken my life in many directions, but one thing had always remained constant, *love*.

It was a power in itself to show love and in return be loved by others. Sometimes, opening your heart left you vulnerable, but it was a chance that was worth taking.

Somehow, I'd always known deep down in my soul that love was all that really mattered in this life. So, here I stood, full of hope that love would carry me through.

With one last deep breath, I gathered all my emotions, pulling my dynamis to the surface. I could feel the air around me starting to become more turbulent and static.

My long waves lifted from my shoulders and tangled in the wind that surrounded me. As I continued to gather more dynamis, I heard whispers and gasps as my body began to glow a golden shade. The tattoo on my wrist and freckles covering my body pulsed, matching the vibrations of my dynamis within me that waited to be released.

It felt as though fire was consuming my body from the inside out, causing me to wince. Hurried, I wrapped my dynamis in one final emotion—love. Once I did, my dynamis erupted out of me. Blinding white light beamed out of me and over the crowd. Screams echoed the hall, several ducking from fear my light might hurt them, but I knew it wouldn't. I'd learned to bend the light to obey my will. If I wanted it to be peaceful, it would be.

After the shockwave of my dynamis, the candlelight had been snuffed out leaving the ballroom in complete darkness. Closing my eyes once more, I released another wave of my dynamis.

There were no screams this time, just pure, silent awe as they gazed at the constellations of stars above them. Golden bursts of light shimmered in the darkness, and I couldn't help but smile as the crowd innocently reached out to touch them. Some held them close to their bodies, illuminating them against the darkness of the room. It looked almost as though they were holding onto the inner light within them.

I let down my ward and was flooded with pure happiness. The feeling washed over me like a tidal wave, filling my soul completely. A tear slipped down my cheek as those around me let the light into their hearts.

A crackle thundered around the room as lightning ripped across the ceiling. My grip on my dynamis floating around snapped. The beautiful golden stars fizzled out with a pop. The candlelight reignited as the darkness of the room disappeared in front of my eyes.

Next to King Alaric stood Alastor, arms still crackling with lightning as he folded them across his chest. His gaze pinned me from across the room, his lips upturning to a dangerous smile. A shudder rumbled through my bones as he broke his gaze to whisper something into the king's ear.

The king ordered the musicians to play, summoning the room to move on with their evening. Couples filled the floor, sweeping away the last remnants of the events that had just passed.

Once again, I was reminded that I was just a pawn in their malevolent games. Turning on my heel, I stalked out of the doors of the ballroom. I needed fresh air to clear my head before I stepped back into that room.

There was no chance I was going to let them see how they affected me.

CHAPTER 57
ELENA

Damp, salty air whipped against my body the moment I stepped outside. The shock to my system was needed after what had just happened in the ballroom.

Finding a spot by the edge of the cliff, I sat down to enjoy the calming sounds of the ocean before returning to the ball. I hugged my arms across me for warmth, until what felt like a heavy blanket draped over me.

Instead of vibrant green eyes meeting my gaze, I stared at red-rimmed blue ones. Will's golden hair tousled about in the wind, his thick veins bulging from his neck. Scrambling to get away, I pushed myself up and began to toss his jacket back towards him. He grabbed my wrist and shoved me back down to the ground. "Sit down."

"Let me go, Will! There's nothing I want to talk with you about anymore." I tugged against his grip.

"Elena, just—just give me a minute, damn it!" He seethed.

"You had an opportunity to talk with me before you left me. Every chance you took while you were here has resulted in nothing but flashing all of the extravagant things you could buy me or the ways you could keep me locked up in your gilded cage. All those years I wasted, hoping for you to find me interesting and loveable, to find out you've never truly known me at all. I'm sorry, Will, but the time for talking has passed, especially after what you just did earlier." I gestured back towards the castle. "You tried to *hurt* me, Will."

He winced, releasing my wrist so that he could drag both hands through his hair. I began to get up again until he whispered a plea. "Just please give me a minute to explain."

With a huff, I sat back down, my eyes shifted towards the ocean, not the boy sitting next to me.

"I shouldn't have done that. I'm sorry. I just saw the way the prince looked at you, and the way you looked at him. I would never hurt you, Elena, never."

Shaking my head violently, I swiped away the tears escaping my eyes. "But you did! Will, you were my one friend in the realm who I could trust and you hurt me when I needed you the most," my voice strained as I tried to hold in my sob.

"Lena...I'm so sorry. Everything just turned pure chaos!" He snarled, pausing for a moment to calm himself before continuing. "I was angry, worried about my mom and sister, and just felt like I lost all control, you know?"

I scoffed, folding my arms across my chest. "Yeah, I think I know the feeling, Will, seeing as how I was locked up in chains next to you, remember? You could have talked to me, we could have worked through it...together."

He slammed his fists against his legs. "Fuck! I know I messed up, Elena! I've made so many mistakes!" Will's chest heaved, the wind whipping our hair was as turbulent as the harsh words we were throwing at each other. "But...I still love you, Lena!"

My eyes widened as I leaned further away from him in shock. He grabbed my chin as he stood, forcing me to stand as well. Before I knew what was happening, he pulled me towards him and shoved his lips against mine.

A shriek escaped my mouth, only to be swallowed by his own. He wrapped his free hand around the back of my head to hold me in place. I thrashed against him, trying to push him off me.

The hand holding onto my chin released, scooping up my arms

and caging them behind my back. I bit down hard on his bottom lip as the copper taste invaded my mouth. He reared his head back with a snarl.

"That's alright, darling, I've always liked my women with a little bite," he spat.

My mouth gaped open, only for his lips to smother the words. He raged against my tightly clasped lips, trying to rekindle a fire that was no longer there. Disgust swirled around my stomach, and every muscle in my body cringed to escape.

I leaned into his body, partly as a distraction, but mostly so I could use his weight to lift my legs to prepare for an attack. A satisfied growl rippled through him as I pressed against his chest. However, it didn't last long.

I lifted my knee and crashed it into his groin. As he keeled over, I used my other leg to kick his legs out and he fell onto his ass. Will rolled on the ground, cupping his groin as he whimpered.

"Looks like you were right. I *am* still capable of knocking men on their asses." A smirk danced across my face as I looked down to the man at my feet.

"Come on, Elena—you can't actually like him," he snarled. "He doesn't know you like I do, doesn't know how to take care of you like I do. Declan will never love you like I can."

The sharp sting of his words radiated. Squeezing my trembling hands into fists, I planted my feet firmly into the ground before I spoke to Will for the last time.

"Do not act as though you understand the meaning of love, Will." My voice was strong and stern. "Love is being there for someone unconditionally. It doesn't waiver, or falter when life becomes too difficult to handle. When you love someone deeply, you'd give up your entire being to help guide the other out of the darkness and back into the light. It means you'd fight for that person, for every moment until your last breath. True love is an unbreakable bond that can be felt in the deepest depths of your soul. This"—I motioned between the two of us— "this is not love, Will. It never was."

He sighed, dropping his head down. He still cupped his injured groin. I smothered a snicker and wiped a palm across my face, trying my best to wipe away the taste and the memory of what had just occurred.

I started to walk back towards the castle when I paused and looked back over my shoulder towards Will. "Oh, and Will? You were right about one thing. I don't like Declan…I love him."

Will's face turned a deep shade of scarlet. I savored the fury in his face for a few moments before whipping around to crash into a solid body.

Declan

As she swiped the hair away from her face to get a better look at who she'd just crashed into, I tried my best to stifle a smile. Lena was unbearably cute when she was flustered.

Sparkling eyes with swirls of blue and green widened with the realization of who stood before her. A beautiful, rosy flush spread across her cheeks and danced along the smooth curve of her neck.

Her bottom lip sank beneath her teeth, and at that moment, I couldn't decide which of those I desired the most. Was it her dazzling eyes, her soft skin, or the plump bottom lip now buried beneath her teeth? Why choose?

The boy stood up behind her, cupping his groin. I raised a questioning eyebrow towards her.

"Don't ask," she mumbled under her breath, rolling her eyes. Inwardly, I groaned. When would she ever learn what that did to me?

I leaned into the shell of her ear, my lips barely caressing the tip. The breath caught in her throat as a shiver shook her body. It would be unnoticeable to anyone else except me. Since we first met, I'd always noticed the way her body reacted to mine.

"Wildfire, this is a story that you will definitely be telling me soon, in detail." I chuckled darkly, letting my lips brush against the side of her temple. "But not now. Right now, you and I need to talk."

She nodded meekly, hands trembling, quite the opposite of the blazing inferno that had just showed the people of Ehora how powerful she really was.

"Leave," I yelled around her.

Will lowered his hand and rolled his shoulders back while straightening his spine, a challenge stirred by the woman in front of us. Unfortunately, both he and I knew he didn't have a chance in Hells of winning that battle ever again. No matter how fancy his little fire show was tonight, he would never survive the wrath I would bring down upon him if he ever touched her again.

"If you were smart, you would leave us alone now. She may have only bruised that pathetic excuse for a cock between your legs"—my eyes dipped to his pants and back up— "but I, on the other hand, will remove it and feed it to the fish behind you. I'm no fisherman, but I hear they enjoy worms."

Elena's mouth gaped wide open, and I could tell she was struggling not to become consumed by mirth. Even my own lips twitched.

"You wouldn't dare!" he barked, puffing out his chest.

"Look at her one moment longer, and you'll find out just how serious I am." My voice was laced with venom.

He stormed past us both, knocking my shoulder as he passed.

"Careful," I growled. Tracking him closely, I pinned him with my glare until his silhouette disappeared into the castle.

Finally, we were alone.

Silence fell, but I could feel the sizzle of energy electrifying the air, that charged feeling that had always surrounded us whenever we were close. The flush of her skin, and the rapid increase of the pulse in her neck, was evidence enough that she felt it too.

I yearned to drag my knuckles across those rosy cheeks, slide my hands into her thick waves of hair and pull her into an all-consuming kiss. Instead, I took a step back, forcing my hands deep into my pockets.

Tonight, Lena would make her own decisions, her own choices. Life hadn't given her many opportunities to do so, and neither had I. From the very beginning, I'd controlled every situation that involved her. Protecting her had been my driving force, even if it meant protecting her from me.

Two nights ago, I had lost my willpower in the ballroom, giving in to my own needs without giving a second thought to hers. I'd asked her to trust me, then immediately broken it, all because I didn't feel worthy of her or her love. I'd pushed her away because I felt like she deserved better than me. In doing so, I'd hurt her, and I'd have to live with that crushing feeling in the pit of my stomach forever. Forgiveness was not something I expected from her, but gods, the selfish part of me hoped for it.

A delicate hand pressed against my shoulder, and doe eyes stared longingly into mine. "I think I'm going to need to sit down to have this conversation." Lena let out a weak smile.

I nodded, and in one swoop wrapped her in my arms. Her breathy gasp whipped against my shoulder as I zephyred her to the safest spot in the castle. My room.

CHAPTER 58
ELENA

The queasy feeling that rumbled in my stomach every time I zephyred thankfully hadn't appeared tonight, although the feeling of unease fluttered inside of me the moment I realized where Declan had taken me.

"Your room? Really?"

Shrugging his shoulders nonchalantly, he walked over to the bookshelf holding a small bar and made us drinks with his back to me. "It's the most secure room in the castle."

Letting out an exasperated breath, I slumped onto the navy settee in front of the fireplace. "Of course it is," I mumbled, loud enough for my ears only. However, I could tell by his smug smile as he handed me my glass that he had heard as well.

Declan lowered himself into the leather armchair next to me, resting his ankle over his knee. My wandering eyes traced over the way his dress pants tightened against his muscled thighs. They continued to explore up his chest, lingering over the spot of tanned flesh peeking through his tunic that teased me in the most agonizing way.

Declan's gaze was focused intently on his fingers as they circled the rim of his glass.

There was no stopping the blaze that assaulted my cheeks as I imagined those fingers circling over parts of my body. The thoughts spiraling through my mind right now were enough to make even the gods blush.

A seductively slow smile curved on his lips. Instantly, my body was set aflame, my heart pulsing at the same pace as the apex between my clenched thighs. Declan chuckled, taking a long draw of his whiskey. *Hells.*

It was almost like the man could read my mind, and he was enjoying it entirely too much.

With all my strength, I broke free of his gaze, focusing on the ceiling instead, desperately trying to stop my traitorous body from doing anything before we spoke about what this was between us. What it could be.

After taking some much-needed deep breaths, I lowered my head to meet heated emerald eyes. My restraint was so thin now that I felt it begin to buckle under his gaze.

Pull yourself together, Elena, you can do this.

My lips parted to speak. Declan interrupted before I got the chance.

"Hurting you was unforgivable, but I want you to know how deeply sorry I am." He slouched over his knees, elbows resting on his thighs as his hands fidgeted.

"Dec—"

"No, Lena, let me get this off my chest. Please." His voice rasped, as if each word that left his lips was agonizing.

"I've always had a difficult time letting people in, especially after losing two of the most important pieces of my heart." His throat bobbed, holding back the sob threatening to escape. I rubbed my chest to soothe the pressure I felt building. Even with my ward up I could feel the agony within him.

"My mother...my brother"—he paused—"they were my torches in the darkness whenever I lost my way."

I reached across and placed a hand over his knee. He placed his own on top of mine and intertwined our fingers.

"In the way they were my guiding lights, I became their fiercest protector. My life's mission became to make sure no harm would ever pass their way. When I found out they were taken away from me, stolen from this world"—his words were gritted between his teeth as a tear rolled across his face— "I lost hold of my light, and the torch within me dimmed."

I ran my thumb against his fingers, silently comforting him as he spilled the darkest parts of his soul to me.

"Can you...can you come here?" he whispered, falling back deeper into the chair, patting his lap.

The air thickened around us as I tried to decide what to do. This seemed too intimate of a position for us to be in, considering the heaviness of the conversation that we were having, but when I looked at his reddened eyes, I surrendered all worries. The urge to comfort him was by far stronger than the hurt feelings I had been harboring. Right now, we both needed this closeness.

Rising from the velvet settee, I placed my hand on his shoulder, preparing to perch on his knee and swing both of my legs to the side over his.

"No," he breathed, "I want you right here, facing me, Wildfire."

Oh.

Warm hands slid against the bare skin of my lower back as he tugged me forward. His gaze stayed locked on me as his palms slowly lowered to my thighs. Knuckles brushed a heated path along my sensitive skin, sending decadent shivers down my body. He gathered my gown over my knees, allowing me room to straddle his thighs. Once my trembling body was seated, Dec dropped the beaded fabric and pulled me impossibly closer.

We were so close now, that I know he could feel my hardened nipples as they rubbed against his chest. So close that I could feel every heated breath of his on my face. There was nothing I could do to hide the muscles clenching in my thighs. His breath hitched and his forehead fell onto mine. For a moment, the only sounds were the rapid rise and falls of our breaths.

"I lost myself for a long time, Lena. I blame myself for what happened that day. I didn't protect them. After everything that they had done for me, I left them alone. I'm responsible for their deaths. It was all my fault...I couldn't save them..." His words faded to a murmur.

"I vowed that day that no one I cared for would ever be left alone, unprotected." His strained breaths were all too familiar to me. I began to rock with him, trying my best to calm his intrusive thoughts. "Then Alastor—and all those people I—" He choked down a sob, and my arms squeezed tighter. "I hurt them—what if I hurt our friends?

"It killed me to see the hurt in your face these past few days." He sucked his lips between his teeth. "To know that I was the one to cause you distress ripped every one of my heartstrings to shreds. Hells, Lena, what if—what if my hands were the ones that took you away from this world?"

Drawing back from his forehead, I met his gaze. My chest heaved at the blast of emotions that must have slipped past his cracked ward. A chill ran through me, full of despair. Tiny needle pricks attacked my skin from the fear and guilt that was written all over his face.

"The only reason I pushed you away was because I thought that I needed to protect you from myself." He paused as his lashes flickered down. "Lena, I could never live in a world that's not illuminated by your light."

Tears began to fall freely now from my own eyes. Gently, I wiped away the ones escaping from Declan's as I cupped his face with both hands. Reaching deep into my dynamis, I pulled forward the happiest moments I had and lowered my ward to pass them through to Declan.

All the muscles in his jaw began to relax, and the lines in his forehead became less prominent.

"Do you remember what I said in your mother's garden when you first brought me here?" I whispered, tipping my forehead to rest against his again. "I told you once that maybe we were meant to be."

He nodded against my forehead. "The perfect balance of light and dark."

"Since day one, the pull of attraction between our souls has always been strong. No matter how much we pushed away from each other, life seems to find a way to bring us back. We've both trapped ourselves in the darkness for too long, Declan. I believe were meant to be each other's torches. We were meant to guide each other back into the light."

His fingers tightened their hold around my body. I leaned into it willingly, because I knew my next words were going to be difficult.

"I understand your fears, and the weight of the world you carry on your shoulders. I've carried the same guilt with me for a long time as well." I spoke softly.

"Lena, I told you before, you don't ever have to feel ashamed for feeling so deeply," he said, pulling back to hold my chin, forcing me to meet his gaze.

My lashes fluttered closed, because I couldn't look him in the eye when I admitted it. Just as I couldn't when I had told Clara. "I do, Declan. I have a right to feel ashamed." I sniffled. "My feelings were the reason I couldn't save my own mother."

Slowly opening my eyes, I met his own. He stared at me with his dark eyes, so deep a shade of green, it was like I was gazing straight into the lush pine forests of Ehora. There was no judgment waiting inside them, just concern.

"I could have saved her the night she died, Declan," my voice shook.

"Lena—"

"I was there," I interrupted. "I froze, Declan, my physical body paralyzed by the invisible darkness that haunts my mind every day. I let fear consume me, instead of saving my mother. I had a choice, but I wasn't strong enough to take it." He cupped my cheek as my body trembled with guilt. "Enough...I wasn't *enough*, Declan. I never was, and honestly, I probably will never be.

"I pushed you away because I didn't feel like I could ever be enough for you. Sooner or later, you would see that I had been pretending to be shining with light, but in truth I'm just full of darkness."

No longer able to hold the weight of my shame and guilt, I

collapsed into him, my head tucked between his neck and shoulder. Tears cascaded out of me as he rubbed soothing circles on my back.

We sat there in silence for a while. The crackle of the fire and the sniffles between the two of us were the only sounds to break it. Everything felt right in his arms as I felt the tug of the invisible string that connected us together.

"You have always been enough for me." His hushed words warmed my neck. "Perhaps even too much, Wildfire."

I shoved his shoulder, and both of us let out a few breathy laughs. Declan pushed a few strands of hair around my ear, and I hummed as his fingers brushed down my neck and back up over my jaw. Everywhere he touched my body, ignited a tingling sensation against my skin. Pinching my chin between his fingers, he raised my head to meet his stare.

"What happened to your mother was not your fault, Lena," he said. My eyes lowered in shame. "Look at me." His tone deepened. "The fault belongs to the person who took her life."

Unconsciously, my head denied his words, shaking ever so slightly. His grip on my chin became a little tighter.

"Lena, have you ever thought that maybe there was a reason you had a paralyzing attack that night? Perhaps, if you didn't, you would have perished alongside your mother."

He spoke delicately, choosing his words. "The gods and fate have always been a mystery to me, Lena, but maybe they had a plan for us. Maybe we were meant to endure these devastating tragedies to find each other at the right moment. Perhaps we had to unveil the strengths we didn't have the courage to admit we had, by clawing ourselves out of the dark. We need to learn how to forgive ourselves. How can we expect others to do the same if we don't even allow ourselves the same courtesy?"

His words washed over me like cold water, and I shivered. "But I'm broken, Declan." My voice wavered.

"So am I, love. Separate we may be broken, but perhaps together we can make each other whole."

Overwhelmed with the need to be even closer, I let my lips melt into his. Our kiss was tender and raw, full of unspoken devotions and future promises between two souls.

"I heard you don't like me, Elena Morrigan." He smirked against my lips.

"Mmm, yes, that's true," I hummed, earning me a pinch on my thigh.

"There's my fire." His laugh was so infectious, I couldn't help but join in. I sighed deeply, running my fingers over the scruff of his short beard.

"You're right, Declan. I don't like you..." I paused long enough for one of his brows to rise high. "I love you."

He slammed his lips against my own. Our hungry lips devoured each other, starved for the promises deep within them.

"I love you, Elena," he breathed, hovering inches over my lips, "I always will."

He parted my lips with his talented tongue, deepening our kiss further, and I let myself fall away from my thoughts. The hardness of his length rubbed against the thin lace of my underwear, electrifying the fire within my core. Unashamed, I writhed against him, further stoking flames within my already molten center.

"Then show me," I breathed, nervously meeting his hungry stare. Eyes darkened with desire, lids heavy with lust, his hold around me tightened.

"Are you sure, love?"

"Declan, show me how much you love me—I need you, now."

He wrapped his hands underneath my thighs and lifted us both out of the chair. In four long strides, we were in front of his bed, and my heart felt as though it was about to leap out of my chest. As he lowered me to the floor, his eyes roamed over all of me. "Take it off." He ordered.

I sucked in a sharp breath as my eyes widened. No one had ever spoken to me this way, and I was enjoying every damn bit of it.

"While this dress makes you look stunning, Wildfire, for me to properly declare my love to every enchanting inch of that body beneath it, it needs to come off immediately."

"Yes, sir," I hummed, as his eyes blew wide open.

I slowly slid the straps off my shoulders, down my breast and over my wide hips. The elegant dress puddled around my feet, leaving me bare in front of the Shadow Lord. The only barriers left were my underwear and heels.

"*Fucking beautiful*," his breath hitched as he took in the sight. "All night I've imagined what treasures were hidden beneath that slip of a dress. Nothing I imagined compares to the sight before me."

The flush of my cheeks was painfully hot, but not as painful as the surge of energy that spread throughout my entire body from his praise.

"I've always known you had the power to bring any man to their knees, Wildfire." His words were low and husky as he began to unbutton his shirt. "A fearsomely alluring woman in mind, body and soul. Someone as powerful as you, love, deserves to be worshiped. I'll gladly be the first to bow before you."

Every inch of my body began to tremble with anticipation. My eyes were tethered to every one of his movements. Who knew that the act of unbuttoning a shirt or sliding down pants could be so seductive?

We were so close to each other, yet so far away. Unconsciously, my body leaned towards his, pleading with me to do something to relieve the pressure building within. My teeth grazed my bottom lip, and I couldn't help but squeeze my thighs together to help stifle the fever burning between them.

Reverently, I traced my eyes over his body in the way that my fingertips begged to. They roamed over the intricate designs of his dark tattoos, swirling and rippling around each arm and across his chest, over the ripples of his toned abs, down to the article of clothing still acting as a barrier between us.

Wandering lower, my gaze locked on his length, which looked

painfully swollen with need beneath his underwear. Licking my lips, I clamped my thighs tighter.

Declan approached me, lowering to his knees. My dynamis hummed as he brushed his fingertips over my ankles all the way to my thighs. His hands slid against my skin at an excruciatingly slow pace. Those strong hands gripped the tops of my thighs, so dangerously close to where I needed them most.

"Spread your legs." He tapped the sheath of my dagger that was still strapped around it. "As seductive as this looks, I think it may be slightly dangerous to leave on." Tenderly, he kissed the spot where the dagger once was. I jumped at the sound of it clanging against the hard wooden floor. Declan gripped harder around the backs of my thighs, holding me in place.

"The only thing that will be piercing your body tonight will be me, love," he purred, pushing me back towards the bed.

Oh...

Declan's push startled me, causing me to trip over the dress puddled at my feet. Thick arms leapt to right me back on my feet and slammed my center right against his plump lips. The heat of his hot breath against it caused my lacy underwear to dampen further.

"Well, that's one way to get me where you want me, Wildfire." His laugh rumbled as his lips caressed me through the lace barrier. A whimper escaped me as I tentatively pushed up against him, searching for anything to soothe the burn within me.

"No one's ever touched you here, Lena?" His fingers tangled around the lace.

"Just y-you," I whispered.

"That's right, Wildfire. It will always be just me, Elena, because you are mine... forever."

He slid the lace down my legs and tossed it to the side. Picking up each foot, he kissed each ankle as he undid each heel and tossed those aside as well. I now stood completely bare in front of my Shadow Prince.

All of me—my heart, my soul, my body—was now wide open for this man. I was willing to allow my soul to be open to him, but the lingering hint of fear inside of me needed to hear a promise out loud. A promise that from now on, I could trust him and he could trust me.

His fingers brushed over the scar on my arm, and I tried to pull the painful reminder away.

"Who did this?"

"The man who killed my mother and almost killed me." I lowered my head in shame. "He thought me too pathetic to waste his blade on, so he left me with this instead."

"He will die for what he has done, that is a promise, my love."

His lips glided along the scar and up my body until he met my lips. As he pressed a tender kiss to my lips, he wrapped my arms around his back, right over the scars left behind by Alastor's iron-laced whip.

"You never have to hide your scars from me. Though they may have been made in darkness, they are a permanent reminder of how you've healed and continued with your life in spite of it. They're a reminder of your resilience, my love."

I kissed him thoroughly, then pulled back slightly, cupping his chin. An eyebrow quirked as he met my gaze.

"Promise me you'll let me in as well, Declan," I whispered. "If we do this, we do this together. No more secrets, no more doubts. I'm ready to open my heart to you fully, to let you see every inch of darkness and light. If we do this, there will be no more hiding behind the walls we've built for ourselves."

His throat bobbed up and down, and he sucked his lips in between his teeth. Nerves trickled throughout my body and my muscles tightened with the fear that he might turn me down.

He rose to his full height, towering over me. Declan lowered a hand and enveloped mine, placing it right over his rapidly beating heart. "You feel that love?" A sweet smile tugged against his cheeks. "This heart beats for you and you alone. It will continue to beat for you even after life fades from the realm and my body becomes ash in the wind. My love for you is eternal. You are my soulmate, love." He closed the distance between our lips, sealing the promise that I so desperately needed. He pulled back slightly, just enough for me to speak.

"I think I've always known," I whispered. "I was afraid that it would mean I wouldn't have a real choice. That I would be blinded by the bond, and the feelings wouldn't be authentic."

"And what do you think now?" A flicker of worry lit his eyes.

Tracing a path over the hard lines of his abs and up the plane of his chest, my palm covered his rapidly beating heart. Darkened eyes met mine, and my heart pinched at the slight tremble of his lips.

"There is nothing more genuine than this." My fingers smoothed over his heart. "Our souls were meant to find each other. There's no denying my heart only beats this way for you, Declan."

"If we do this"—his voice was low and graveled— "we'll be completing the bond. There will be no going back. Are you sure you wish to be tied to me in such a way, love?"

Grabbing his chin, I brushed my nose against his. "Declan Stallard, you can tie me down in any way you please." A deep groan rumbled in his chest. "I want this bond. I want to know you'll be mine for eternity."

CHAPTER 59
DECLAN

Lena's words sent a million shivers directly to my already aching arousal. I gathered her in my arms and tossed her onto my bed. The sweet sound of her laughter made my cock twitch beneath my underwear, causing me to realize I had yet to remove it.

Crawling over her supple body, I anchored myself on one arm while removing the last barrier between us both with the other. I couldn't help the grin on my face as my gaze danced between my length and her wide eyes while she bit the side of her lip again.

"Don't worry, love. I won't let it hurt you." I chuckled darkly, gently caging her in between my arms. Bringing my lips to the shell of her ear, I whispered softly.

"Once I'm done worshiping your body with my hands…" I brushed my fingertips down her arm, watching her body shiver beneath them.

"… my shadows …"

I summoned my dynamis from within. Dark tendrils of smoke trailed over the fullness of her breasts, down her stomach, against her core and down her legs. Goosebumps pebbled across her body, her face flushed scarlet.

"… and my mouth …"

She whimpered as I took the rosy bud of her breast inside my mouth and sucked. Her hips bucked against me at the sensation. I swirled my tongue around the other, making sure each was shown equal devotion before I continued to savor the rest of her body.

I trailed featherlight kisses down her soft skin and over each glowing freckle that cascaded across it. As I hovered between her legs, I couldn't help but lose myself in the view.

"You're drenched, my love." I caressed her thighs gently, causing them to tremble. "Once I'm done warming you up on the outside, Wildfire, I'll help extinguish that fire burning within," I whispered, blowing a breath over her sensitive, swollen mound.

I couldn't help but enjoy watching her body react. Her hips writhed against my lips, almost sending me over the edge before we even started. I wrapped my arms around her thighs, pulling her flush against my mouth.

She let out a moan so loud that I was pretty sure the entire damn castle heard. It snapped the final tether of restraint I was holding. With each kiss and swirl of my tongue between her thighs, I made silent promises of all the ways I would always protect her. With each lave of my tongue, I showed her how much I adored her and how I would always treat her with tenderness and care.

"Declan—I—I..." she cried, fists tangled in the sheets.

"I know, my love...just breathe. I've got you," I murmured against her.

I deepened my praise, flattening my tongue against her in one long swipe before thrusting it deep within her. Her hips bucked at the unfamiliar intrusion and her thighs crushed against the sides of my head.

"Wildfire..." I chuckled through my squished cheeks. "If you'd like me to finish what I've started, you're going to need to relax your legs before I suffocate down here. Open your legs, love."

"Oh, gods, sorry." She relaxed her trembling thighs slightly.

"I told you, Lena, you never have to be afraid to feel."

Her legs opened and fell to the sides, telling me she trusted me fully. It was almost as if my words were the final key to the lock within her. She was ready to trust me with everything, including her body.

To show my appreciation, I continued to give reverence to my goddess on her altar. Stoking the kindling within her, I added a finger, pulsing back and forth at a steady rhythm. Her toes curled and her hips began to pull away before I pulled her back towards me and placed my hand over her stomach, holding her down. I added another, continuing to build her up higher and higher towards heavens. Her body began to radiate with that familiar golden glow, the one she got when her emotions were overwhelmed by her dynamis.

"I can't...*it's too much*...I—" she gasped in between pants, the heels of her feet digging into the mattress.

"Let go for me, love," I coaxed, lowering my mouth over her sensitive bundle of nerves, grazing with my teeth before I nipped it between them.

It was as if Elena's glow ignited from the spark of her release. A burst of warm light flooded the room, and as it faded, little embers of fiery lights fell around us. She sat up on her elbows, gaping at the sight.

"You're so damn beautiful, Lena," I worked my way up her body to devour her lips. I couldn't hold back any longer. I needed to be inside her now more than ever.

Elena

E verything felt hazy as I trickled back down into my body. Embers of light floated and fell around us, fading out as they hit the mattress. I'd never felt so outside of my body as I had just a few moments ago.

Declan cherished me in ways that my timid self had once been fearful of. I'd never truly felt like my body was desirable. With each tender movement, each caress, Declan praised away the fears I held about my body. Every day, this man continued to unlock the darkest parts of me.

The mattress bent as he rested his arms on either side of my head. His eyes sparkled, reflecting the falling embers. They widened when he looked at me, dragging his teeth over his bottom lip. As if the movement shared a direct energy with my core, I shivered as heat flooded within it again.

"Your eyes, Wildfire, they're also glowing," he whispered, pressing a soft kiss upon my lips. "I've never seen anyone with such a vibrant shade of indigo in their eyes. Lena, it's the most mesmerizing thing that I have ever seen."

I felt his length as it rubbed back and forth against my core, the feeling so intense my eyes squeezed shut.

"Keep those eyes on me, love." He slid deep inside me with one thrust of his hips.

My eyes opened wide as my gasp turned into a moan of pleasure. One of his arms supported my neck, while the other played with my breasts. With each tender roll of his hips, my body felt so incredibly full. Full of warmth, happiness, and pure love. Two shattered souls, mending each other whole.

Our passion fueled a new sensation within my dynamis. Higher and higher we climbed together as I kept my eyes locked on the man filling me with hope. Only a sudden movement made my eyes waver away from his.

Shadows twisted around his arms, working in tandem to caress my body in the most delicious ways. The lights in the room were snuffed out by his shadows, engulfing us in the darkness. A soft golden glow from my skin was the only light illuminating our slickened bodies… until it wasn't.

I could almost hear the hum of our dynamis sing as it called out with an insatiable force. His fingers dug deeper into my thighs as he tried to pull me closer into him.

"Gods, it's never…" Declan panted, his eyes taking on a vibrant violet hue. "It's never been like this Lena. You feel so damn incredible." He groaned, as his rhythm picked up. "I love you."

"Love you too," I cried out in between breaths, and my eyes began to flutter closed.

A low rumble vibrated against my ear. "I said eyes on me, Wildfire."

My eyes flung wide.

"Good girl," he purred, as I watched in awe as his tattoos and shadows began to glow violet.

He rolled his hips against mine, and we continued to ride the waves as the pressure within me built higher and higher. My nails dug into his chest, as I pushed my hips into him.

Declan pulled my knee up to his chest, the angle allowing him deeper. His fingers tightened around my thigh as he thrust so deeply it hit the most sensitive spot inside of me and sent my release crashing through. He continued rocking me through it until he yelled out my name, finding his own.

Bright indigo shadows burst from around both of us, creating swirls of violet, dark shadows and more flecks of golden embers all around us.

Declan fell to the side of me, tenderly curling me into his body. We both sat silently, watching the display of lights, as our breathing settled.

Suddenly, an excruciating burn rippled against my hand, right over my dynamis tattoo and around my wrist. As I winced from the pain, his features mirrored mine.

We both glanced down to our hands. Encircling our wrists was a glowing golden vine etched into our skin. It twisted and swirled around our wrists, both ends wrapping around our original dynamis tattoo. My eyes widened, and Declan let out a low whistle.

"I've heard stories of mates having marks, but I've never seen it for myself. It's beautiful." I whispered.

Declan rolled over to face me, propping his head up with his arm. He grabbed my marked hand within his as his thumb caressed my wrist. "So are you. Thank you for choosing to love me, broken pieces and all." His words wrapped around my heart and soul like a warm hug.

"I love you," I mumbled against his neck. "Thank you for fighting for me, for making me feel worthy. For loving me through all the moments when I don't even have love for myself." Sniffling, I did my best to hold in the tears welling behind my eyes.

"*Always*. I'll fight for you until my final breath passes through my lips, and even after. Nothing will stop me from protecting you with everything I am."

Grabbing his face between my palms, I pulled him in for another deep kiss, and we lost ourselves all over again.

CHAPTER 60
ELENA

Cool, salty air brushed over me as I peeled my eyes open. The sun's rays painted the entire room, and the white curtains around the balcony window danced about in the breeze. I threw my arms over my head, stretching like a cat.

My body had been through muscle aches over the years from all my panic attacks, but this ache was something different. It was a delicate ache, a reminder of all the love that had gone into making it. With a sappy grin, I rolled over to my side in search of the man who put it there.

The side of his bed was cold and empty, and my smile faltered. Had he changed his mind? Did he think this was a mistake? Worry flooded my brain as I clutched the sheets against my chest.

"Morning, love," a deep voice rumbled in front of me.

Standing in nothing but his briefs was Declan. Entranced, I watched every movement he made as the towel caressed over the rest of his body. Never had I been more envious of a damn towel.

A smirk spread across his lips as his eyes locked onto my peeping gaze. Tossing the towel aside, he strode over to me. I could feel my body sinking back into the bed as it trembled with anticipation. He leapt onto the bed and crawled over my body, caging me underneath.

"You're drooling, Wildfire," he whispered into my ear.

Out of reflex, I elbowed him in the gut. He then fell over next to me, laughing so hard his eyes crinkled closed.

Seeing the rare act of this man laughing did unspeakable things to my body and made my heart throb with love. I couldn't help but laugh alongside him as he curled me into his chest. We lay there contentedly as he caressed his fingertips up and down my back. With his other hand, he brushed the hair out of my face and behind my ear, then gripped my chin, lifting my gaze to meet his forest eyes.

"How are you feeling?"

"Sore, but it's a delectable kind of sore." Warmth flooded my cheeks as I bit my bottom lip.

"That's my girl." Declan tenderly kissed my forehead, nipped the tip of my nose, and finally devoured my mouth where he lingered for a while before letting me come up for air. "I made something for you." He rolled off the bed and bounded over to a tray that held several silver lidded platters. He was practically bouncing up and down like a child as he placed the tray in the middle of the ruffled sheets.

"Who are you, and what have you done with my grumpy, brooding Shadow Lord?" Feigning a swoon, I placed a hand against my forehead.

Declan scowled while he placed two of the covered platters on the bed in front of us and poured us each a cup of coffee. He stuck out his tongue at me, which further led me to believe he had lost his mind.

"Careful, my prince. Do that again and I'll find more productive uses for it."

His eyebrows shot up to his forehead before a mischievous smirk spread across his handsome face. "Oh, Wildfire," he purred, "that's a promise I intend to make good on."

We both smiled as the tension between us began to sizzle. Unfortunately, my beast of a stomach decided to growl. I couldn't help but snicker at myself as Declan opened the lid to my breakfast and tossed me a fork. "Suppose we better feed the beast."

"Watch it, Shadow Lord, you just handed me a weapon." I giggled as I twirled the fork between my fingers.

The spread before me was full of eggs, bacon, and a very well-done looking piece of bread. When I looked back up, I was met with Declan's rosy cheeks. Was he blushing?

"You made this by yourself, for me?"

"Of course. I'd do anything for you, Lena. Anything to make you smile."

Gods, I loved this man.

Grabbing the fork, I piled on some eggs and shoveled them into my mouth.

Dear gods! They tasted like they had been marinating in the ocean. He was watching me intently, so I tried my best to not gag as I swallowed it down. After he'd done something so sweet for me, the last thing I wanted to do was hurt his feelings.

A cough made its way up my throat before I could stop it. Seeing me struggle, he reached for the cup of coffee and handed it to me. Without a thought, I knocked back the liquid.

Oh, Hells, it's not coffee!

The thick concoction slid over my tongue and assaulted me with its horrid soil-like taste. It took everything in me to swallow that down, and I felt sick to my stomach.

"It's for, you know..." He cleared his throat, obviously a little uncomfortable. "It helps prevent little Elena's and Declan's from coming to fruition."

I reached over and squeezed his thigh. "Thank you, Dec, for all of this."

He dipped his head as we both clinked our cups together and downed the rest of the vile ingredients.

"It's funny, I used to make these for people in my town all the time, but I never knew how horrible they tasted." I laughed. "I'll definitely have to work on making it more palatable for the future."

"Future indeed." He smirked. Redness flooded my cheeks. "How were the eggs?"

"Amazing," I whispered as I placed another bite into my mouth.

After we finished breakfast, we snuggled back under the covers for a while. Neither of us wanted to leave the comfort of the bed.

"As much as I want to lie here with you all day, all week really"— Declan smirked— "we must meet with Liam, Nayla, Clara and Killian. There's something we would like to tell you."

"I believe I already know," I whispered. "How long have you all been in the Rebellion?"

A smile warmed his lips. Cupping my chin, he pressed a kiss to my temple. "You're a brilliant woman. I shouldn't have kept this from you." Intertwining his fingers with mine, he continued. "There's more to it though. Those letters you found, they were from my mom and one of our allies. We built Oria, the Rebellion City, together. We've been helping humans and Elysians escape the tyranny of my father and the violent acts of the Nightshades."

"Who's in charge of it all?"

He cleared his throat. "A man named Fallon oversees Oria now. He was my brother's best friend. Shamus is our ally in the west in Atheling, and..."

"And you?" I breathed.

He gave a nod. "And your father."

Sitting up quickly, I wrapped the sheets around me. "How long?"

"Warren's been a part of it since we began. He wanted to tell you himself, he just thought you needed time to adapt to your dynamis first. He just wanted to make sure you were safe, Lena."

"He had my entire life to tell me, Declan." I grumbled.

His head dipped, and I knew that he agreed with me, but I started to get the sense that there was a deeper connection between my father and him.

"Thank you for telling me."

"No more secrets. That's a promise I intend to keep."

His lips brushed the top of my shoulder, and I let myself melt backwards into his chest. "Why have you never left?"

The words floated in the air between us before he finally answered. "My mother left me a letter. She begged me to hold on to hope, to keep fighting for my father..." I could feel his jaw clench against my cheek. "She knew that there was still light left in him, and she knew I was the one person who might be able to break through to him. The one who understood the dark and the light, and how to find my way through it."

I turned myself in his arms so that I could face him. "Do you still wish to stay?" I breathed.

With a heavy sigh, he held my head in his hands. "No, love, he's too far gone in the dark. It's time for me to go. We leave tonight."

I embraced him tightly. "Let's get ready then," I mumbled into his neck.

CHAPTER 61
ELENA

Before we even made it out of the door, we were bombarded by a group of captains and one panicked Eloise.

"Clara's gone. We've searched everywhere." Nayla spoke as Killian paced across the floor, threading his fingers through his hair.

"Hells, do you think—?" My wide eyes locked on Nayla. The hand that covered her face was enough of an answer.

"Tell me." Declan approached the two of us.

"We took Clara to heal the small farm community beyond the w-wall." My voice quivered, as the weight of her disappearance lay heavy on my shoulders. "On our way back, we ran into a group of Nightshades."

"Hells!" he shouted, joining Killian in his pacing. "If my father or Alastor discovered this—" His chest rose and fell rapidly. "We need to find her quickly."

Shoving us all out of the door, he gave orders us to stay in pairs. Nayla and Eloise would round up those in the Rebellion inside the walls, then start their journey towards Oria. They argued at first, but Declan shot them down by making a promise to find Clara.

"You two take the east wing of the castle." Liam and Killian nodded as Declan delivered their orders. "Lena and I will take the west, and if we need to we'll make our way down to the dungeon."

That was the last place I wanted to be. I shivered at the thought.

With quick embraces, we parted ways. Grabbing Killian's biceps, I pulled him next to me. "We'll find her, brother, I promise."

His eyes glossed over as he tugged me into his chest. I'd been an only child my entire life, but it just felt right in that moment to tell him that he was more than just a friend to me.

They all were.

Over this past month I'd become so close to these Elysians, I considered them like family, and I wanted him to know he could trust me to find Clara.

"Thank you," he whispered against my forehead, and then released me to catch up with Liam, who had paused ahead to give us a moment.

"I love your compassionate soul," He spoke tenderly as his thumb brushed against my cheek. "Let's find my cousin."

W e'd searched everywhere, and my pulse had become erratic. Declan was doing his best to hide his fear, but the veins strained against his neck. I was about to say something to soothe him when a familiar voice halted my entire body.

The sound wafted through the crack in the door in front of us. Declan placed a finger over his mouth, motioning for me to stay silent as we eased towards the opening. When he peered through the door, his brows furrowed at what he saw, and he held up his fingers to signal just two were in the room.

Will's voice drifted through once more. "So, they want me to join you?"

"Yeah, kid. We need someone like you in our ranks."

The last voice made the blood leave my body, leaving me consumed by both fear and rage. As I thought about our last encounter, all I could think about was barging inside and finishing the job.

Worried about my pale face and rapid breaths, Declan shoved me far enough away from the door that he could whisper to me. "H-he... the m-man ..."

Grasping my face between his palms, he rubbed both thumbs against my cheeks as if trying to coax the blood back into them.

"It's him," I growled.

"Who, love?"

"The man who m-m-murdered my mother." My nails dug into the flesh of my palm as I spoke through gritted teeth. "The Nightshade who tried to kill me and the girls a week ago."

His features shifted, and the hallway began to darken as his shadows ripped free from his body.

"That man is a part of the Rebellion, Lena. Brand has been our spy providing us with intel about the mole." A deep snarl echoed inside my head alongside his words. His lips hadn't moved the entire time.

"Did you just speak to me in my mind?"

His fingers brushed over my closed mouth. I had just done the same. The bond.

"I need to go back in there, Declan. I can't let him see the light of another day."

"Me either."

"Clara?"

"We'll find her, love."

He took my hand, and we made our way back towards the door.

"Ready?" Declan's lips curled into a sinister grin as his shadows swirled around me, tangling with...my own.

"Let's spill some blood, my love."

CHAPTER 62

DECLAN

E lena's shadows blew the doors clear off their hinges. Even though I was consumed with the blood lust for the man inside this room, I couldn't help but swell with pride at the sight of her.

The sounds of guards calling for help rang down the hall, and I knew that we didn't have much time. I cloaked the room with darkness, leaving just the glow of Elena's freckles, the hum of violet over my tattoos and the fierce violet glow within our eyes.

"Nice to see you again, *Brand*."

"Elena, I can explain—" Will pleaded, before Elena used her Tempest winds to blast him against the wall, knocking him out.

Her palms began to glow, and she took a step towards Brand. I smirked as he shifted on his feet, taking two steps back. "Declan, I don't know what you heard, but it's not what you think."

My shadows tossed the small coffee table between us into the wall, and it shattered into pieces. "You're saying my mate lied to me about you?"

His eyes shifted to Elena and she smiled wickedly.

Brand's eyes shrank into slits and his upper lip curled into a snarl. Flames ignited from his fingertips as he set a blast of fiery heat towards both of us. At the same time both of us fired back our dynamis, creating a wall of water that doused his flame.

His mouth gaped wide, but the shock only lasted mere moments before he launched a dagger towards Lena's face. Coiling my shadows around her wrist, I pulled her towards me, but not fast enough to miss the iron blade that sliced through the shell of her ear before it clattered to the floor in the hallway behind us.

"I should have killed you that night!" he seethed, reaching for another dagger, but my shadows beat him to it, slamming it into the wall behind us.

"Which night?" Elena purred. "The one when you killed my mother, or just the other night when you tried to take me in the forest beyond the castle walls?"

A guttural growl tore through my chest at the information my Wildfire had left out.

"Y-you're...that girl on the floor in Lostburrow. All those years ago...that was you, wasn't it?" Brand's chest heaved as shadows wrapped around his body, squeezing him tight.

Elena moved towards me, and I steadied her as she manipulated the shadows around Brand. He thrashed against the shadow bindings, groaning each time Elena constricted them, and his face began to turn a deep scarlet.

When a cry of distress fled from his lips, I wrapped a shadow around his mouth to silence him. "You don't have to do this, love. Taking a life leaves a scar on the soul, no matter how much they may deserve it."

Her brows pinched, creating a wrinkle as she tried to hold in her frustrated tears.

"There are other ways, it's okay," I whispered against her temple, wiping the tears that had fallen.

She lowered her trembling arms. Her shadows receded with them. Brand fell to his knees, gulping for air through his crushed lungs.

The clang of metal and boots of the guards finally filled the doorway.

Five guards began their assault of dynamis, and we both released ours in return. We dodged their dynamis left and right, while eventually knocking out three of them.

Lena suddenly shrieked, and I whipped around to see Brand had risen once more, his hand wrapped firmly around her neck. The dagger now in his other hand rising upwards.

With one hand I blasted turbulent winds towards the remaining guards, with the other I launched my shadows around Brand's neck.

The guards tumbled to the ground, but Brand continued to squeeze the air from Elena's lungs as her feet thrashed in the air.

Time slowed. She mouthed words I'd seen her use before when her anxiety overwhelmed her, just as her entire body came alight with white flame.

Brand's screams tore through the room as I zephyred towards her and wrapped her in my arms. Unlike last time, I felt no sting of ice from her flames. Instead it felt like a calming warmth as I tore her away from Brand.

Residual flames flickered over him as he fell, convulsing on the floor. In a matter of moments his body went still.

Lena trembled uncontrollably. The guards on the floor stilled at the sight, but now scrambled to their feet to stop us.

I lowered my head towards hers and cupped both sides of her face. "We're going to have to fight our way out of here, love."

She nodded solemnly, igniting her palms in icy white flames.

Elena and I used shadows and flames to force our way out of the small room and past the guards. We ran down the hallway into the grand hall, all while dodging blasts of dynamis.

Just as we made it in, Liam and Killian came running in from the opposite direction. Liam blasted shards of ice towards the guards still chasing behind us. Both fell to the ground with a thud.

"Thank the gods." Elena's exasperated voice rasped inside my head.

The reprieve was short lived, as the front entrance of the castle swung wide open and in walked Alastor and my father. Behind them two guards dragged Clara.

Her swollen eyes met mine as she mouthed, "Sorry," then met Lena's eyes to do the same.

Three of the guards who were following us finally made their appearance, and four more stormed in behind us. *Thank all five gods.* They were from the Rebellion.

Lena ignited her palms in white flames, and my shadows burst free. Killian and Liam stepped beside us at the ready.

"Don't make one more move." Alastor's deep voice filled the hall. In a move of dynamis I'd never seen before, he extended his hand, and Clara flew out of the guards' hands and into his grip.

Killian cursed and launched a dagger towards Alastor. To which he zephyred away from just in time.

Damn.

The bastard had figured it out, our secret source of our dynamis. The question is now, how long has he known and which dynamis' has he accessed?

"Stop right there. You know what I can do to her, Declan." Alastor's cruel smile drifted my way. "Let's see to it that she doesn't fall to the same fate."

My shadows stormed in a cloud of rage around me, and I took a step forward. Two hands grabbed my biceps, pulling me back, one Elena's and the other Killian's.

"If you both come with me quietly"—his beady eyes shifted from me to Elena— "I'll make sure Clara remains unharmed."

"No," I growled.

Father stepped forward, the scowl on his face deeper than the wrinkles across his forehead. "She has committed treason, as has the Light Phoenix." My father's glare landed on Elena. "I told you not to break our deal, child. Your punishment is already under way as we burn down that scum of a town you call home."

Elena crashed to her knees with a cry that shredded my heart in two. "No!" she screamed, arms wrapping around her middle as she rocked back and forth.

Clara sobbed in Alastor's hold, while my father's face left me puzzled. Beneath the scowl, I swore I could almost see the gloss of tears forming in his eyes.

Alastor, on the other hand, was drinking Elena's despair like a fine wine. *Bastard.*

"Put her down!" I yelled to him. "This is the last time I'll tell you."

I lowered my voice so only Killian could hear. "When I tell you, I want you to zephyr to Clara and get the Hells out of here."

He shook his head, his eyes shifting from Elena to Clara and back. Worry clouded his eyes, as if the orders I gave were about to shift something within him.

"I've got Lena," I whispered.

Killian's eyes drifted back towards Clara's, and I watched the air flee his chest when her tearstained eyes locked on his. There was no longer any hesitation in the man behind me. He turned to me with a blaze of fury in his glare. "On your signal."

"What is your decision, boy?" Alastor's grip crushed Clara's arm, causing her to scream out in pain.

I slid down on my knees next to Elena and held her in my arms. Her breaths were shallow and her expression had gone numb from shock. "Love, I need you. I know this is hard, but we need to fight the darkness. Fight for your people. Fight for the ones you love."

Her trembling chin lifted, her eyes met mine, and a strange calm settled over her. Behind the despair, something more dangerous ignited. Lena's eyes hardened into a glare to the men behind me.

"Give me your hand. We'll do this together. Let's show them a little something they haven't seen before."

Intertwining our hands, we rose together and readied our stances. I took one last look at Liam and Killian, then the men behind me.

This ended today.

I raised our interlaced hands towards my father and Alastor as Elena's shadows began to darken the hall. My lips twitched at the fear that widened their eyes. "Let's light up the darkness, Wildfire." She nodded, and I whispered to Killian. "Go."

With a flash, he startled Alastor with a punch in the jaw, grabbed Clara and flickered out of the castle just in time to avoid the violet burst of light flowing from our fingertips.

"Hells!" my father bellowed as the blow from our power knocked them both back against the wall with a thundering crash.

The chaos of dynamis unleashed all around us. We dodged each attack, firing back with all our dynamis. None of us held back.

Alastor scrambled to his feet and launched a powerful flurry of lightning bolts towards us. I pulled Elena into my chest and told her to dig deep to create a blast of wind.

The hum of electricity sizzled in the air as the bolts approached.

"Now!"

A turbulent gust of violet light and shadows tore out of us, slamming into Alastor's lightning with such force that it created a wave that knocked everyone in the room to the ground.

My ears were ringing as I came to and noticed Liam towering over us. His arms were waving and his mouth was moving, but I couldn't make out the words.

Below me Elena lay motionless, blood dripping from her nose, but still breathing. *Thank gods.*

"Dec!" My senses slammed back into me all at once, and I jolted at the sound of Liam's deep voice. "We've got to go!"

He helped me up, then I scooped up Lena into my arms. Before we moved, I frantically scoured the room for Alastor or my father, but turned up empty.

"Alastor zephyred them out of here," Liam said, tugging my arm to get me to move.

We made our way past the hallways to the kitchen and out the back door. The stables were nearby, and thankfully our horses were still there when we reached it.

Neither of us bothered with a saddle. It took too much time, and we had to get to Elena's town as fast as we could.

Once seated, Liam lifted Lena up to me and I secured her against my chest. We bolted out of the stables, heading towards Lostburrow.

As the sounds of hooves thundered against the ground, I grasped the reins tighter as a piercing pain struck through my chest. I knew one day this moment would come, they day I'd finally have to leave, but it hurt more than I'd ever imagined.

No matter what darkness had crept in to my home, it was still *my home*. The place where I grew up, the city that I loved, the place where I had made some wonderful memories with the ones I'd loved.

I turned back to take one last look, the castle became smaller and smaller as we galloped away. Glancing down to the beautiful soul lying against me, I realized wherever we were, *she* would always be 'home'.

CHAPTER 63

DECLAN

We rode hard and fast until we made it to the town of Pinepeak, where we had stayed before. That was where I forced Liam to leave for Oria with my horse. He fought me hard, calling me a stubborn ass, but deep down, he knew that we would zephyr faster with just the two of us.

Elena had finally come to during our argument, but still hadn't spoken a word. Her pale face looked exhausted, but determination was written in her actions.

We took turns zephyring in spurts, only stopping for short breaks to replenish our dynamis before launching once more. Night had fallen, and both of our wells of dynamis were drained. It took some convincing, but I finally forced her to pause and sleep for a few hours before we tried again.

Lena lay restless in my arms. She finally rose and walked towards the creek beside us. I followed behind, giving her space to breathe.

Her arms curled around her trembling body, and I ached to surround her with my arms. The sodden ground squelched beneath my boot as I approached her, but she raised her hand, halting me in place.

The moonlight illuminated her haunted face. Even the golden glow from her freckles had dimmed.

"How do you do it?" Her voice was so small, it barely reached my ears. Tremors shook her body as she took a tentative step towards me.

"How do I do what, love?"

A sob broke free and her palm crashed over her mouth before her knees buckled. I leapt forward and pulled her into me, kneeling on the moss-covered forest floor.

"Dec," she sobbed into my shoulder as I rocked her. "How do you rise each day knowing that so many lives have been lost because of your actions, your m-mistakes?"

The mournful cry that spilled out of her broke me entirely. With a deep exhale, I took a moment to find the right words, because truthfully, to rise each day and keep fighting was one of the greatest challenges of my existence. Only once I'd met Elena had I remembered what it was like to feel full of hope, alive with life, with a reason to breathe the air each day.

With one hand, I drew circles on her back. The other held her hand against my heart.

"Did I ever tell you why I call you, Wildfire?" Lifting my hand from her back, I brushed the fallen hair out of her face and tilted her gaze to meet mine. "Wildfires spread rapidly, without any set path or intended direction. They consume everything in their wild, blazing infernos." I paused as her gaze bore into mine.

"From the first moment my eyes met yours, I felt your fire, your spirit, burn a path deep down into my soul. You've destroyed every shard of restraint I have, but I'd let you burn through me time and time again, because just one look in your eyes makes me feel like I'm alive. You give me the strength I need to keep fighting, Elena, you've given me a reason to live."

I paused, her eyes welling with tears.

"Your resilience astounds me, love, but I know that sometimes the darkness feels too much to bear. Those are the days I must fight. The days I search for my torch to guide me back. It hasn't been easy, and it's a weight I'm afraid will always burden our souls."

The tears slid down her cheeks as she nodded.

"I'm here, love, and you'll never have to fight this battle alone anymore. A fire needs oxygen to keep it aflame. Let me be your air, love, let me help you continue to blaze."

Her fingers dug into my back as her arms constricted tighter around me. As she unleashed every bit of despair and anger into my chest, my emotions rippled underneath my skin in the form of my dynamis.

Lena's body began to give off a slight golden glow, and I could tell she was fighting off the same. She sucked in a deep breath as I lowered my head to hers, my lips brushing against her own.

"You are my soulmate. I think I've always been waiting for you to walk into my life. I love you, Wildfire. You've forever branded my soul." I tucked the hair that had fallen in her face behind her ear. My fingers lingered as if trying to commit the feel of it to memory. "Lena, you've pulled me out of the darkness and brought me into the light. I promise with all my heart I'll always do the same for you."

CHAPTER 64
ELENA

A blanket of embers and ash covered the entire town. Screams and shouts rang through the air as wind gusted around where we landed.

Shame curled inside my stomach for taking a few hours' rest before making our way here, but I knew without it Declan and I would have drained our dynamis completely. Then we wouldn't have been able to help anyway.

Without words, we ran into the streets, launching our dynamis at every Nightshade and enemy guard who leapt into our path. As the fighting still erupted all around us, my eyes roved over the bodies that lay lifeless on the ground. Some faces unfamiliar, others I knew like the back of my hand. Fear surged inside me, as I prayed to the gods that the next face I stumbled upon would not be my father's.

As we rounded the corner towards my home, a cloaked Nightshade stepped in front of us and launched a stream of fire towards Declan. Dec dove out of the way just as I conjured a wave of water towards the hooded man.

With the man stunned, Declan took the opportunity to use our combined dynamis and interlocked his hand with mine. The man flew back into the stone wall of the temple behind him and his neck twisted with a snap.

It was hard to not see it as some kind of divine justice. Death by temple wall.

"ELENA!"

A voice that hadn't graced my ears in over a month echoed from down the street. Standing in the road, covered in blood and face blackened in ash, was my father.

Releasing Declan's hand, I sprinted towards him. He met me halfway, and we collapsed to our knees in the dirt beneath us.

"Father," I sobbed.

Tears streamed into his chest where I buried my face. He stroked my hair and pressed a kiss to my temple.

"Sunshine, you're alive." His voice rasped and I squeezed him tighter. "Bless the gods."

Wood crackled and split apart behind us, followed by a thud, the sounds of our town falling apart all around us. I held my father's head between my hands. "Are there still people inside their homes?"

He nodded, and I pulled him to his feet. "We've gotten most to safety, but I was on my way to Ophelia's."

"Let's go."

Declan followed behind us as we fought our way through each corner until we were outside of Ophelia's home. Her two small children were crying outside when we arrived, and Declan scooped them up and moved them further away to safety.

"She must have got the babes out and gone back in for Thomas," my father said.

The crack of wood splintered through the air. We didn't have much time before this entire cabin caved in. Without one more thought I ran into the house, my father and Declan on my heels.

Flames roared inside, and the smoke filled my lungs with an acrid burn. Trapped beneath a fallen beam, Ophelia's body was sprawled out over the floor, arms still wrapped around her husband. The memory of my father holding my mother's lifeless body flashed before my eyes. My dynamis surged within me as I released it straight onto the flames. I would not allow Ophelia and her husband to meet the same fate as my mother.

While I doused the flames with a wave of water, Father's mouth gaped wide. He recovered quickly and gathered a swirling cloud, snuffing out the rest of the fire inside the small cabin.

Declan lifted the beam off Ophelia as fire continued to rage outside. Father scooped her into his arms, and Declan placed Thomas over his shoulder. I followed behind them just as the cabin shuddered and the floorboard underneath my foot caved.

"Gods!" I gasped, clawing at the doorframe, trying to tug my leg free.

A snap crackled above as the entire ceiling began to cave in. Panic invaded my body. I pulled one more time and my leg finally broke free. I tumbled right into Declan's open arms as he zephyred us away just in time to hear the entire building collapse behind us.

"All five gods." Ophelia's raspy voice came from the dirt below me. Dark brown eyes met mine, full of remorse and shame as she mouthed silently, "Thank you."

Two words that meant so much to me. A forgiveness I'd never thought that I would receive.

Grabbing the children, we ran towards the safe haven my father had shouted directions for. The town was silent except for the crackling of embers and wood. Relief trickled through my bones at the knowledge that we wouldn't have to fight anyone else.

That was until a familiar guard stepped onto the road in front of us.

Blood stained the cruel face of the guard who had harassed me the day of the Ascension. When he caught sight of me, his lips curled into a sneer and his hands began to fill with frost.

I let down the children and shoved them behind my father, and Declan lowered Thomas to the ground. Rushing to my side, he interlaced his fingers with mine and a rush of dynamis flooded through me, stealing my breath.

A violet glow shimmered over us, and I could feel the shadows come alive around me. Even when he released my palm, the surge of power still radiated within me.

"One more time, love?"

"One more time."

Our dynamis flew through the air, meeting the guard's icicles and incinerating them into icy dust. He attempted it several more times, but each one was met with failure. The man frantically looked from left to right, searching for backup, but no one was coming.

His panic made the shadows around me swirl and a smirk grow on my face. One look at my face and he bolted. *Coward.*

"He's running, Wildfire." Declan chuckled darkly.

"Not for long, my love."

We launched our dynamis once more, and the guard fell to the ground with a deafening thud.

We carried Ophelia and her family to where the rest of the survivors had huddled together in a makeshift camp. When they were settled, a small group of us went back and used our dynamis to help put out the fires.

Overwhelmed with exhaustion, Declan and I found a quiet spot back at the camp and passed out until my father roused me awake the next day.

"Time to go, Sunshine." His tone was sweet, but he glared at the man beside me.

"Good morning, Warren." Sleep clung to Declan's words, his tone low and graveled.

"Declan." My father's curt tone made me roll my eyes.

With a deep sigh, I rose from the hard ground, stretching the bones in my back into place with a crack.

Some of the horses had been wrangled, as well as a few carts. We would use those to carry those who couldn't walk as we made our way to Oria today. Apparently, Oria had been our neighbor for quite some time.

Hidden within the mountains behind our small town was the Rebellion City.

The sun beat down overhead as we made our way up the winding path between the mountains. Rushing water flooded into my senses, and I peered over the edge of the rocky path to see a creek down below.

At first my father argued to keep going, but then he looked at the sweaty, fatigued faces behind me and conceded. I tended to a few cuts and bruises with the few supplies we had, and Declan used some of his dynamis to heal where he could.

Overcome with thirst, I grabbed my waterskin and made my way down to the creek to fill it. As I approached, a familiar blonde threw open her arms and tackled me to the ground.

"Good to see you too, Bri." My giggle strained under the weight of the priestess.

"Oh, my." She laughed, rolling off me and then helping me up. "My apologies, for not rushing to you earlier, Lena. I've used up my dynamis during the battle, and was passed out in the back of the wagon. I'm so happy to see you safe."

She squeezed me once more as a deep voice cleared their throat behind us.

"Elena, can we talk?" My father looked filled with unease. He threaded one palm through his dark hair while the other fumbled inside his pocket.

"Yes, I think it's time you both told me the truth."

Exchanging a glance with each other, they nodded in unison.

CHAPTER 65
ELENA

"I'm a part of the Light Phoenix bloodline?"

Bri fidgeted with her hands, and my father fiddled with a piece of grass beneath his fingertips, as the sound of the babbling creek next to us filled the silence.

"And you've known this my entire life, and didn't think it was pertinent for me to know?"

The cool stone of my feather necklace rubbed against my fingers, and I paused, realizing this was more of a symbol than I had originally thought. It was a damn declaration of my bloodline.

"So Mother was a part of this bloodline as well?" I asked another question before my father had time to answer the first two.

"Yes." My father smoothed a palm over his chin, then looked around him as if to make sure no one was close enough to hear what he was about to say. "I was sent to watch over your mother. I'm a part of a secret order of protectors of the Light Phoenix bloodline."

My mouth gaped wide as my father continued.

"The first Light Phoenix left behind a daughter. Her existence was kept secret for fear she might one day succumb to the same fate as her mother. Her survival became a top priority, and thus the Guardians of the Light were born." He exhaled, his shoulders relaxing, like he was relieved to finally release the tension of keeping this secret for so long.

"Go on," I mumbled, anxious to know more.

"We were trained as protectors, our identities kept secret as well as our mission. Over the centuries, Guardians were sent to look after the descendants of the bloodline, all awaiting the awakening of another Light Phoenix. They would watch and protect them through their Ascension, and if the descendant did not possess the Phoenix dynamis, then they would train another guardian to one day watch over their heirs. Over the years, one thing was consistent with all the female descendants—they were all given the dynamis of an Empath."

He paused, waiting for me to absorb his words.

"So, my mother...she was really an Empath?" I breathed.

"Yes, she was," Bri said softly next to me.

My mind whirled. "How is that possible? I watched her heal so many people."

"When Queen Lenora discovered the truth of our dynamis, she began testing her theories on me and her sons. I was close with Lenora, because my father was the High Priest, and the King's advisor." She paused, as my lips parted wide. "Your mother had opened up to me about her bloodline in secret, and I began to teach her as well." Her lips tilted upwards from the memory. "Healing came naturally to her."

"Does Declan know?"

She shook her head. "I plan to explain it to him when we get to Oria. The only person who knew of your mother's secret was the queen. That's why she entrusted me with the potions—she hoped that her vision would come true."

"Her vision?" I breathed.

"Two days before her death..." Her eyes began to gloss over, and my father placed his palm over hers. "When I had learned of my parents and my Sían's death, Lenora told me she had been collecting samples from the gods' tree when she began to hear voices."

Air fled my lungs.

"She said a voice spoke to her and told her a light was coming."

"That same day, your mother told me she was pregnant," my father whispered.

"She thought I would be the Light Phoenix."

Both of their eyes met mine as they answered in unison.

"Yes."

A shudder ran through me as my head fell into my palms with a groan. "She hoped the potion would unlock my dynamis enough to let the Light Phoenix dynamis break free," I mumbled through my hands.

"Yes, and I gave the second vial to Will so that you wouldn't have to be alone in your unsuppressed dynamis." Brietta scowled. "A decision I now regret."

Anger boiled to the surface. I had tried to stay calm this entire time, but the hurt of being sheltered from the truth all these years infuriated me. "It still doesn't explain why you didn't tell me. Or why you felt you couldn't trust me with any of this."

"I trusted you, Elena, I just—"

"Then why, Father? Why did you hide this from me my entire life?" I seethed.

"Lena—"

"No!" I shouted. "Don't you dare try to placate me!"

"Elena, you need to breathe." He reached out his hand toward me, to which I shoved away.

"I'm breathing. You don't get to tell me to calm down right now, I have every right to be upset. My entire life has been a facade, and I want to know why."

"You're right, Lena," my father whispered.

"Talk!" I growled.

A small smile tugged at the side of his lips.

"Are you seriously smiling right now?"

My outburst caused a chuckle to exit his lips, to which he slapped a hand over his mouth in effort to smother. I rose to my feet, suddenly overheated with anger.

"No, no...Sunshine, I'm sorry." He chuckled again, raised both hands in defense. "You just remind me so much of your mother right now. She had a fire within her, just like you, Lena. Whenever she thought I was about to do something wrong, she let me have it. Which usually happened about three times a day." He smiled sheepishly at me, as a bit of my fury fizzled out.

"I should have listened to her all those years ago when she told me you were strong enough to handle the truth. Althea always knew you were meant for greatness, Lena, and I should have had more faith in you. For that, I'm so sorry."

He reached out to grab my shaking hands. This time I allowed it. When I met his gaze, his eyes were clouded with tears.

"I've made some irrevocable mistakes, Elena, but everything I did was to protect you both. Everything." He whispered the last word, and a tear slid down his cheek as I choked back a sob.

He pulled me into his arms and we cried until the frustration and the fury melted away. It was one thing to be angry with my father, it was something else entirely to watch the stoic man in front of me fall to pieces as well. Guilt weighed heavy on my chest, once again awakening my dynamis.

As I pulled back to wipe my eyes, something golden flickered between us.

"Elena...what is this?" My father rubbed a rough hand over my now glowing bond on my wrist.

Pulling my hands out of my father's grasp, I opened my mouth to speak when a deep voice behind me beat me to it.

"It's a mating bond, Warren. The one I tried to tell you about a week ago."

Declan's arms wrapped around me, and my teeth crushed against my bottom lip as my father's wild eyes scanned over Declan's wrist as well.

My father tugged me out of the way and grabbed Declan's tunic until they were face to snarling face.

"Warren!" Bri shouted at the same time I yelled at my father.

"I told you to stay away from her!"

"And I told you I loved her!"

"You're dangerous!" my father snarled.

I'd had enough. "So am I!" I seethed, blasting my dynamis towards both, making them fall back on their asses. "Now listen!"

Declan bit his lip to hold in a smirk, while my father's face couldn't decide whether it wanted to be angry or proud.

"I am a grown woman, capable of making my own decisions!" I shouted towards both men. Bri waved her fingers for me to continue. "I love this man, and I know very well what the consequences could be now we're together. There are so many unknowns and fears about what could happen, but you know what? Damn them all!"

Declan and Bri both chuckled into their fists, and my father still sat with his mouth gaping wide.

Taking a calming breath, I tried to quell some of the fury. "Declan makes me a better person, Father. He's helped me learn to love myself and taught me how to find the inner strength that has been hiding within me for so long."

"I can see that," my father breathed.

"I love him because he loves every part of me, broken and all."

Declan's gaze drifted towards me, and the bond tugged inside my chest. "*I love you too.*"

"When you love someone deeply, nothing can stand in your way. Sometimes, it's worth the risk, right, Father?"

His throat bobbed up and down.

"I'm sure that the Guardians of the Light aren't supposed to fall in love with those they're meant to protect, right?"

Declan's brows furrowed. "Who?"

"Later," the three of us said in unison, and his mouth shut tight.

"You're right, Lena. Althea and I took a very big risk, but it's something I will never regret doing, because it gave us you."

Tears welled in my eyes once more. From how much I'd cried this past month, I was surprised there was anything left.

"Sometimes we have to take risks for the ones we love." My father looked towards Declan, who hadn't taken his eyes off me since I began talking. Father's cold expression melted, and a smile cracked through.

He rose to his feet and extended his hand to help Declan up. The air in my chest halted.

Declan wrapped his palm around my father's. Father pulled him up into his arms. "I'm sorry, son. Welcome to the family."

Dec's smile beamed, and even though he tried to fight it, his eyes began to gloss over as well.

"The promise still stands though." My father pulled back, resting his palms on Declan's shoulders. "Anything happens to her, I'll kill you myself. Understood?"

"Yes, sir."

CHAPTER 66

DECLAN

The sun started to set behind the mountains as we approached the opening to Oria.

Hidden between two of the largest mountains of the Umbra Peaks was a small crack, wide enough to fit the horses, but not the carts, so we unloaded those and left them behind.

I took Elena's hand and guided her through the opening. A sting hummed over our bodies, and her nose crinkled before her eyes turned towards mine.

"What was that?" She shivered, rubbing her hands over her arms.

"A powerful ward. It glamours the entrance, and this next one blocks those without the Rebellion mark from passing through." I paused and watched her brows furrow. "Give me your wrist."

"You still haven't learned." She crossed her arms.

A breathy laugh escaped her lips when I rolled my eyes. "Give me your wrist, *please*." I flipped her hand over to show the inside of her wrist and pulled my dynamis to the surface. "This is going to sting a little, Wildfire."

Her eyebrows rose high, and I placed the mark on her wrist. She hissed from the burn of the mark. I removed my hand so that she could see.

The sight caused a sharp intake of her breath, and the sound tugged against the bond, making me ache to be closer.

"It's a phoenix," she breathed.

"You've been giving us all hope, even before you knew it, love." I pressed a tender kiss against her temple and moved her forward through the final ward. "Welcome to the Rebellion, Light Phoenix."

Elena

The sky above was painted in warm hues as the sun set behind the mountain. Everywhere the setting sun touched was gilded by the glow.

Nothing could compare to the stillness of the space surrounding me. The hidden valley of Oria encompassed everything I had imagined the heavens to be.

Lush green foliage and acres of trees heavy with fruit spread across the valley slopes. A waterfall cascaded into a glistening lake below. Homes were carved into the stone walls of the mountain, and some stood tall on their own, probably created from the stone they'd carved away. Lanterns lit each home, as well as the gravel paths. Rows of crops covered a majority of the valley bottom, alongside the riot of wildflowers that lit up every vacant spot.

Nature was majestic, almost transcendent in the way it made me always feel so full of life and light—the soothing trickle of water, the sublime warmth of the sun as it melted across your skin, or the way the soil squished between your toes. A grin spread across Declan's face as he caught my glance.

"Empaths always feel calmer in nature. Especially here."

"It's breathtaking."

"Welcome to Oria," a low, rich voice hummed beside us.

"Fallon." Declan embraced the broad-chested, chocolate-haired man. Stepping aside, he held out an arm towards me. "This is Elena Morrigan, our Light Phoenix."

The man stepped forward and lifted my palm to his lips, giving it a peck. "It's a pleasure to meet the woman who tamed the brooding Lord of Shadows."

A scowl grew over Declan's lips as a deep, hearty laugh burst free beside him.

"I like him." I followed Fallon down the hill to the valley.

"Of course you do," Declan scoffed, lifting me over his shoulder and giving me a swat on my behind before careening down the hill like a wild babe.

When we reached the bottom, he placed me back on two feet and bent over laughing.

"What has gotten into you?" I placed my hand over his forehead to pretend to check for fever. "No fever, maybe it's just the madness."

As I removed my hand, he seized it, pulling me into him, then captured my lips with a mind-altering kiss. His hands threaded through my locks and cupped the back of my head as he devoured every inch of my lips. When he pulled back, my legs were weak and my body trembled with need.

"This place feels more alive with you here." His thumb brushed the side of my of jaw as he held it. "Everything feels more alive with you, love. You've made me see life through a whole different lens, one not clouded and tarnished by my past and my fears. This lens is clear, bright and full of hope."

I leaned into his lips once more, needing him to feel what my words could not express on their own. I gripped his tunic, and we lost ourselves in each other once more.

"Whoa...perhaps we should come back later," Liam said from beside us.

Breaking apart, we laid eyes on the rest of our family, all grinning. Clara whistled low, and I melted into Declan's shoulders to hide the flush of my cheeks.

"Time for dinner, lover boy," Liam jested, earning him a grunt from the man with his arms around me.

"Go get cleaned up, we'll save you a spot at the table." Killian wrapped his arm around Clara and kissed her the top of her head.

We parted ways, and Declan guided us down a gravel path to one of the many rooms carved into the rock. "I don't think I'll ever get used to them being together. Every time I think about it, it's like picturing my brother and sister together." He cringed as I burst into laughter.

"Well, you're just going to have to deal with it, because those two are madly in love."

He shook his head and opened the large wooden door in front of us. The bond in my chest ached as I took in his room.

A whiskey bottle and an array of maps adorned the small table in the corner. Fur pelts covered the bed, and a stack of books lay on the side table, alongside a pair of spectacles.

"You wear glasses?"

A flush blossomed on his cheeks. "Sometimes when the light gets dim, I need them to read. You know"—he prowled towards me, causing the back of my legs to bump against the edge of the bed— "we still have some time before dinner."

I placed a hand over his chest, but it took everything I had in me to push him back. "As much as I would like that, I'm exhausted, dirty, and absolutely ravenous, my love."

He motioned towards a small basin and water pitcher on his desk. "You can use that for now to clean up, but later I'll show you one of my favorite spots for a more … thorough cleansing."

His words sent shivers down my spine, and it was all I could think about as I wiped off the grime and we made our way to dinner.

E ven after everything we'd been through the past few weeks, Oria had brought me a sense of peace.

Here, I was surrounded by everything I loved. Nature, family, Declan. For once, it felt like the dark haze that had haunted me for my entire life had been lifted. Even if it was just for this small moment, I was going to live it.

The hum of laughter skimmed over me as we approached the large wooden table where everyone was seated. Plates of meats, potatoes and vegetables were spread around the table, and everyone was helping each other fill their plates.

Sitting together with the stars as our lights was one of the most calming yet surreal moments of my life. Everyone's smiles wound around my heart like a protective shield, filling in all the cracks and tears that life had torn in it over the years. Every one of them had given me a sense of strength when my own had faltered. I would always be indebted to them for that. They had all saved me in more ways than they would ever know.

Clara filled my cup with another long pour of wine. "Would you like to help me work on Lenora's elixir tomorrow, and one for Declan as well?"

"Of course. Though, I'm just not sure how helpful I'll be."

"Pfft," she scoffed into her cup. "Your father told me all about your brilliant brain and your knowledge of herbs and flowers."

I looked up over my cup just in time to meet my father's gaze. He raised his cup towards me, and I smiled in return.

"He also showed me the largest field of herbs and flowers I've ever seen. I felt like I woke up and stepped into the heavens." She squeezed my biceps with glee. "I can't wait for you to see!"

After dinner, we all helped clean the tables. Declan, Killian and my father had been talking in the corner for a while, and anxiety had begun to curl inside my stomach from their stern expressions. When Killian embraced Declan and their faces shifted to smiles, I finally was able to take a deep breath.

As I wiped down the table with a wet cloth, someone cleared their throat cleared behind me. When I turned, I was surprised to see it was Killian.

"Lena, can we talk?" He rocked nervously on his heels, awaiting my reply. I nodded, and his shoulders relaxed.

"Let's take a seat over there." Killian motioned me over to the center of the city, where the fire pits sat unlit. Lowering himself onto one of the giant logs, he patted the spot next to him. As I sat down, Killian extended his hand and the fire pit ignited in front of us.

"Showoff." I smiled, and he gave me a sheepish grin.

"You looked a little cold."

"Chivalry still exists out here in the Rebellion City." I bumped my shoulder against him as he let out a breathy laugh. Silence lingered for a few moments as I let him gather the courage to say whatever he needed to say.

"Yesterday, your father told you about the Guardians, yes?"

I nodded.

"What he didn't get a chance to tell you was that I was the one he was training to be the next Guardian. When you were born, I was meant to be your protector after Ascension. I'm so sorry I kept the fact that I was your Guardian secret from you. I—I never meant to—"

Interrupting him, I placed my hand over his and squeezed.

"It's okay, Killian, I know everything you all did was to protect me. Your secret didn't hurt me, and honestly, I'm glad to know that I had another pair of eyes watching over me in that damn castle. Honestly, it makes sense now." I laughed. "I was beginning to feel like I couldn't get away from you or Liam. I was thankful when I started to zephyr because I could be stealthier."

A grin spread across his face as he rubbed the back of his neck. "Well, it is a part of my job. Though you didn't make it easy."

"Declan doesn't call me Wildfire for nothing."

Killian ran his hands through his hair. The muscle in my jaw clenched, and I prepared myself for the words that might come out of his mouth. After the past couple of days, I expected the unexpected. Nerves woke my slumbering dynamis, and it prickled like needles against my insides.

"You need to be careful, Lena," he said, his gaze locking to mine. "Now more than ever." Fear rose up my throat, so I swallowed it back down. "I'm serious. You're the last of the bloodline, and the only one in several centuries to have the Light Phoenix dynamis. Our kingdom has been waiting for you for a very long time. This is not the time to be reckless."

I winced at the word "reckless".

A deep sigh came from beside me, followed by a heavy hand on my shoulder. "You're not the problem, Lena. It's everyone else that I'm concerned about. You've had a target pinned on your back since they discovered your dynamis, and now that you've disappeared, they'll be desperate to find you."

Fidgeting uncomfortably, I tried to push down the increasingly sharp pinpricks of my dynamis. This would have been the perfect time to push out these emotions with my Tempest dynamis, but unfortunately, it only worked with others' emotions...not my own.

"Killian, should I leave?" My teeth gnawed against my bottom lip. "Am I putting everyone in this city in danger?"

"We've always lived with the threat of danger, Lena." He winked and my shoulders relaxed a smidge. "It comes with the title Rebellion. Promise me you'll be careful. We cannot lose you. You've become a part of our family." He smiled, then it fell. "Declan can't lose you either, I fear—it would...break him entirely." His eyes misted over as he fought to remain stoic.

"At first, I was upset when Warren told me to remain at the castle until your Ascension ceremony. I couldn't wrap my head around why he didn't want me to come with his family to Lostburrow. After a while, I realized he wanted Dec and Liam to rub off on me a little more." He laughed under his breath. "Liam and Declan grew to be like brothers to me, and it almost shattered me when we almost lost Dec the first time."

A shiver ran down my spine at the thought, and I found myself reaching for Killian's hand again. He held it tightly in mine.

"I haven't seen him this optimistic in a very long time, and we have you to thank for helping him to find that hope again. Promise me you'll be careful, Elena. We need you...*he* needs you."

Now it was me holding back the tears that clouded my eyes.

"Will you promise me?"

"I promise," I whispered.

"Just what exactly are you promising to another man, love?"

A familiar deep voice rumbled from behind me, as I peered over my shoulder to meet two blazing verdant eyes. Declan folded his arms across his chest, but his expression was full of mirth rather than malice.

Killian chuckled, then stood to pat Declan on the shoulder. "I'm glad you two completed the bond." Warmth spread across my cheeks as a gasp escaped my mouth. "You were an insufferable, broody ass without it. A few days ago, this whole situation might have ended with me in the fire." He left with a devious smile and headed back in the direction that Clara had gone earlier.

Declan wrapped his hand around my arm. With two quick tugs, I was off the log and squished up against his solid chest. Butterflies fluttered inside my stomach as his knuckles brushed their way up my arm. He cupped the back of my head, fingers intertwined within my hair.

I licked my lips with anticipation as he swept the hair behind my ear with his other hand. Dec leaned forward, his lips dusting over the sensitive flesh of my ear. Clearing my throat, I managed to whisper a few words. "What should we do now?"

He nipped at the lobe of my ear. "Hmmm," he rumbled against my skin. "There are several things we could do."

Before I could ask just what those things might be, he swung his arms underneath my legs and lifted me off the ground. Declan's lips met mine with a searing kiss, and my entire body vibrated with need.

"Let's get out of here, Wildfire. It's time for me to show you my favorite place in Oria." He waggled his eyebrows, and laughter bubbled out of me. Holding me close, he carried me down a long gravel pathway through a rich orchard of apple trees, until we reached the most enchanting sight I'd ever seen.

CHAPTER 67

ELENA

Moonlight cascaded over the lake, making it sparkle against the darkness of the night. The rush of the waterfall cascading into the pool of water below was a soothing melody to my ears.

Declan's smile warmed the night chill. He kicked off his boots and socks, and I did the same. He guided me to the grotto behind the waterfall. The slate stones beneath us were slick and I tried my best not to slip.

"Let's go for a little swim." He dropped my hand to reach for the bottom of my tunic.

His eyes stayed locked on mine as he lifted my tunic over my arms and then slid my leggings down and tossed them aside. The need to have him close sent my body into tremors as I undressed the strong man before me.

As I slid his belt free, his eyes fluttered closed as I wrapped my hand over his hardened length beneath his pants.

"Careful," he groaned. "You keep doing that and I may have to do other things to you."

"We can swim later." My words were breathless against his neck as I kissed it.

That unleashed his restraint. My world shifted as he lifted me up and then lowered me onto the cool rock. He lifted my hands above my head and ripped off the clothing that remained. In the blink of an eye, we were down to nothing but bare skin between us.

Lips stormed against mine in a wave of passion. His length brushed against my core, and my hips bucked for more. Hot breath warmed my ear as he let out a dark rumble of a laugh. "You need more, love?"

I whimpered. He slid his palm between my thighs, and his fingers traversed through the slickness that awaited.

"Gods," he groaned against my lips as he slid two fingers inside of me. "You're soaked, my love."

Pulsing in and out, he kept stoking the fire within me. He curled his fingers inside of me, his tongue swirling against mine at the same pace. Just when I thought I couldn't wait any longer, his lips traced a line down my neck and I felt his teeth clamp down as I found my release. For a moment my focus hazed. With a sly grin, he pulled his fingers out and licked them clean.

My mouth gaped wide as he captured my lips and thrust himself deep inside of me. Hidden behind the misty veil of water, we lost ourselves in the moment.

Our bodies moved together at a deliciously slow pace. With each roll of my hips and each thrust of his, our bodies spoke the words our voices could not do justice.

His warm hand danced across my neck and over the space between my breasts. My heart thundered underneath his palm as he massaged them. His other thumb tenderly provided the exact amount of attention to the swollen bundle of nerves between my thighs. This man knew his way around my body, anticipating my every need before even I could.

"*More*," I pleaded into his mind as his lips swallowed my whimper. My fingers clawed into the thick muscles of his back as I wrapped my legs tighter around him. Even though we were so close, I felt the need to be impossibly closer.

"Lena," he rasped against my cheek, "I know I've told you this before, but everything about you is absolutely stunning." He thrust harder. My head fell backward into the rock underneath as my back arched up to meet him.

I had never felt so full, so whole, than when we were together like this. I didn't know if I had spoken those words into our minds or not —at this point my reality was in a bit of a haze—but Declan responded.

"I've never felt so damn whole except when I'm here inside you like this, love," he purred against my lips. "Wildfire, you make me feel things I have never felt in my entire existence."

Shifting us, I straddled him. A tender smile grew across his lips at the flush that spread across my neck and cheeks, embarrassment from my inexperience at what to do next.

Declan's hands tightened around my hips as he guided me up and down his length. Everything became more intense at this angle, and my dynamis surged from within. His stubble rubbed against my cheek, his hand gripping the back of my neck as he whispered seductively into my ear.

"That's it, love, ride me. You're in control now. Use me, undo me, wreck me completely. Show me exactly what a powerful woman you really are."

His deep voice thrummed over my sensitive skin, his lips creating a delicious trail down my neck and breasts. My hips began to move, and instantly the fears drifted away. For the first time in my life, I felt like I had complete control. Overwhelmed with emotion, I realized the gift he had just given me. He'd given me the power to make choices, to have a sense of control of something for once in my life, and it had never made me feel more alive.

"You look so good in control, love," he growled. "Now, be a good girl and undo me."

The praise made my cheeks burn. I'd never felt so vulnerable and powerful at the same time. Taking a chance, I embraced that power, increasing my pace as a rush of feelings like no other burst inside of me. My fingers dug into his chest as Declan met my pace, both of us panting as we chased after our highs together. Our dynamis flooded our bodies, illuminating us like glowing stars within the cave.

"Declan," I panted, "I love you." I wrapped my arm around his neck and pulled him into a passionate kiss. Our teeth collided as our lips slammed against each other.

"And I love you. Let go with me," he whispered against my lips.

As he captured my bottom lip between his, I finally let go, screaming his name into the wind. A blinding blast of dynamis fled our bodies, then burst into thousands of tiny little speckles of light. Completely spent, our bodies collapsed onto the ground. We lazed in each other's arms, watching the lights above us glisten.

Declan smirked. "Well, that was mind-altering."

"Life-changing."

"Soul-shattering," he countered, waggling his eyebrows.

The sight caused me to snort, and even though we both should have been catching our breaths, we instead gasped for air from our laughter.

CHAPTER 68
DECLAN

The image of Elena's smooth skin glistening in the moonlight flashed through my mind as I leaned back in my chair in our council room.

"I hadn't realized that our strategy session was so enthralling it could make even the Lord of Shadows break out in smiles," Fallon said from the other side of the table.

The heat of several eyes scalded my face, and I shifted my face back into a stoic calm. Liam and Killian snickered beside me, and Warren's eyes narrowed into slits.

"Right." I spoke sternly. "We now have found our mole. However, Elena made sure to end Brand's life before we left the castle. I am hoping that's where the leak ends, but we should remain cautious just in case."

Several nodded around me, and Fallon shifted in his seat. "Bastard. I vetted that man myself. I should have seen past his calm façade to his slippery soul."

"He fooled us all. I spoke with him the most over the years, and never once questioned anything suspicious."

"Well, now we know he was a part of the Nightshades," Warren grumbled, "and by the way, Edan has seized the castle and taken control while Alaric and Alastor have gone missing, I think it's safe to say our assumptions were right about Edan as well."

"Yes, I believe our next step is to collect as many Rebellion members as we can and bring them here once and for all. It's time we start preparing for battle."

The room fell silent. War was not something any of us wanted, but it was time we all faced the facts—these men weren't going to stop without a fight.

One by one, they nodded agreement, as if they had come to the same conclusion as me.

"It's settled then, Warren and I will begin the preparations and send out teams in the morning."

"How about the elixir?" Warren inquired.

"Clara and Elena began to work on it today. I'll have more information about it by the day's end."

Fallon chimed in, "Finding a way to release the suppression would give us the edge we need. Especially if we end up in battle."

"Let's reconvene at the end of the week," I said. Everyone mumbled agreement and began to shuffle out of the room.

Fallon stopped me on my way out of the door. "It's good to see you smile, Declan. Keir would have been so happy for you." With a pat to my back, he stepped aside to give me some space. "I know it's been difficult these past years, but he would be proud of how you kept fighting through it."

"That means so much to me, Fallon, thank you." My words rasped through the emotion lumped in my throat.

"Your brother was my best friend, and you know I've always thought of you as my little brother as well. You'll always be apart of my family Dec."

"Did Eloise come with you all? I haven't seen her since after your brother..." He swallowed, the rest of the words tugged under by emotion.

"She did. She's been helping new arrivals get set up. You should go find her, it's been a long time. I know you two were close. I'm sure she would love to see a familiar face from happier times."

Fallon grasped my hand in his and pulled me in for another embrace. "It's good to have you home, brother."

Elena

It had been three excruciatingly long days. From sunup to sundown, Clara and I had been working hard on combining the right ingredients to recreate Lenora's elixir and find one that would release Declan from Alastor's curse. Clara thought that the two cures we needed might be more similar than we realized.

Unfortunately, everything we'd tried so far had failed, and the mark of the curse remained on Declan.

"It's sweltering out here." Clara wiped the sweat from her brow.

We woke up early to harvest some more herbs and flowers for more batches of elixirs we were working on. Clara was right, this field was amazing. Rows of every herb and flower as far as the eye could see. It overwhelmed all my senses, reminding me of all the hours I spent working our small garden with my mother. Every smell, sight and petal I touched was wrapped around in a memory of her.

"This should be enough to work for today." I assessed our baskets full of herbs and blooms. "We should head back and get started."

On our way back into town, I glanced to the side to see Nayla chatting with a girl, a little younger than her. I paused, taking in the similar umber skin and long, dark onyx hair. Clara's shoulder bumped against mine as Nayla embraced the girl, both breaking out in tears.

"Is that...?"

"Yes," Clara whispered. "Killian and Liam went out and got her sister last night. Things have gotten bad everywhere since..."

I nodded, knowing what she meant. Since we'd all disappeared.

"Nayla's mother was worried about her safety. So Nayla sent a raven and had her brought to one of our extraction points—safe houses and areas around the kingdom where we can immediately get to people when they need our help."

"Let's give them some privacy," I whispered, and Clara nodded as we both turned to go back to our workstation.

I wasn't prepared for the sight that I stumbled upon, however. Liam, Killian, and Declan all had their bare chests on display as they worked on constructing pieces of furniture under the heat of the sun. I swore all of them must have been modeled after the gods themselves. They shouldn't be allowed to walk around shirtless. Accidents might happen.

They glistened with sweat, and my mouth went dry when I felt the heat of Declan's eyes on me. I didn't even have to see him to feel the weight of his stare.

"You're blushing." The deep timbre of his voice inside my head sent my heart racing. *"The question is...which one of us is making you blush?"* he growled, causing me to jump. Clara eyed me inquisitively.

"Liam," I deadpanned. Declan's hammer collided with his thumb, causing a string of obscenities to fly from his mouth.

"Wildfire, don't make me come over there and show this entire damn city exactly who you belong to."

I gasped, my back straightening from his words. *"You wouldn't dare..."*

At the same time, Warren came around the corner carrying more wood, and following behind him was Brietta carrying a pitcher of water. A devious smile stretched across Declan's face.

"I wouldn't?" he inquired, sliding his thumb inside his mouth to clean away the blood. *"Just to be clear, I'd take you right here, right now in front of everyone... including your father."*

Inhaling my breath too sharply, I choked on my own saliva, causing tears to spring from my eyes. *Oh, gods.*

"Gods cannot save you now. Just me, love. Now, would you like to try that again?"

I nodded silently. *"Only you, always you."*

"That's right, Wildfire, you're mine. Today, tomorrow... forever."

A smirk spread across my face, and fire blossomed straight down to my core. Declan snorted aloud, knowing exactly how he affected me. Hells.

"You're mind-speaking, aren't you?" Clara's face lit up.

"Umm, yes. It's new." I shrugged sheepishly.

"Well, thank all five gods it's in your heads and we don't have to hear it." She tugged my arm. "Come on, Light Phoenix, we've got work to do."

***

"Here, eat this." Clara shoved a strawberry pastry in my face. "You look so pale, Lena. I think we should pause taking blood from you, Bri, and Declan for a few days, let you all replenish."

"No." I stared down at my bandaged fingers and then rubbed the dizziness away from my forehead. "We'll be okay. I just need to remember to eat more."

Clara placed her hands on her hips and shot me with a scowl. She knew we needed Empath blood for the elixirs, but she wasn't happy about the toll it was taking on us. "Alright then, let's test this out one more time."

Blessedly, while everyone had been searching for Clara in the castle, Eloise had snagged her satchel from her room. Inside was Lenora's list of ingredients and notes, Clara's research notebook, as well as samples of bark from the gods' tree.

Clara pulled a piece of the bark on the wooden counter between us, and we both held our breath as she dropped the elixir onto it. The violet liquid sizzled as it contacted the bark.

"Well, that's new." Clara's eyebrows rose.

I swallowed as the darkness that tinged the bark began to fade away. Clara's hand shot over her mouth and she began jumping up and down in excitement. "This is it! We've done it, Lena!"

My heart thundered against my chest as she used her arm to clear a space on our messy workstation and threw her notebook wide open.

"Argh!" she huffed, ruffling through the pages. "I should have made this connection before. Gods, how daft I've been."

"Clara, what are you talking about?"

"Alastor. Fucking Alastor. He had me study different types of elixirs for relaxation, calming, dulling the mind. He said it was to help him sleep, but I think he found a way to use it to curse the land, and maybe it's even part of the curse that has a hold of Declan."

Stunned, I sat on the stool next to her as her fingers ran over the words on the page. "Ah ha!" She rushed over to the herbs, picked a few I couldn't see and crushed them between her fingers before placing them in a bowl and pouring some of our elixir on top.

Once again it sizzled inside, but this time instead of violet, it turned into a deep mahogany.

"He'd often have bandaged fingertips," she breathed. She poured the liquid into a vial and sealed it with a cork as she handed it to me.

"What do you mean?"

"I gave him tonics for warts, remember? I'm beginning to think he was pricking his fingers to use blood magic...and I think that's what's been happening to the land, and maybe even the sickness that spread to those farmers. The kind of curse that he uses on Declan takes a long-drawn-out ritual. It's very similar to Ascension and involves giving your blood back to the soil."

Her fingers scanned over the notes in her book before walked back towards me and extending her palm out. "Give me back Declan's elixir, let me add one thing."

I watched her crush a mixture of herbs, then sprinkled them into the vial. "Let's see if this addition will help."

I was still reeling from all the information about Alastor and the curse when she handed me back the vial, and I squeezed it securely in my hand.

"Let's go find someone to test the elixir for the suppression dynamis on, then you can have Declan try this one."

Before I could speak, she had latched onto my arm and tugged me out the door.

CHAPTER 69
ELENA

"We've done it!" Clara's breaths rang out as we both heaved from exhaustion.

"Seems like we need to bring back training if you two are that breathless after that short jog." Nayla smirked at the sight of us.

"What have you done?" A sweet voice fluttered from the other side of Nayla. Her younger sister came into view and extended her hand meekly towards me. "I'm Zara. It's a pleasure to meet you both."

"You as well," I said, collecting my breath as I shook her hand. "We're glad you came to join us."

"Me too." Her eyes misted as she looked at Nayla, who wrapped her arm over her shoulders.

"So, what did you both do?"

"We think we've made an elixir to stop the suppression of our dynamis." Clara rose to stand beside me. "Now we just need someone to test it."

"I'll do it." Zara extended her hand again.

"No!" Two voices rang out in unison.

One was Nayla's, and the other was from Liam, who now stood behind her. Killian and Declan now towered behind us, and Declan pulled me into his warmth.

"Hello, my love," he whispered against my hair.

"Yes," Zara said firmly. "It's my life, Nayla, and I'm tired of not making any decisions or having any say in it. Just like I didn't have any say when you left." Nayla's shoulders dropped, and Zara gathered her hands into her own. "Let me be useful. I want to have a choice for once."

Liam glanced at Nayla, who turned to me and Clara. "Is it safe? Is there any way something could go wrong?"

"I've been taking a slightly different version for my curse, and though it hasn't worked, I haven't had any side effects," Declan said. "She should be safe."

"Alright, Zara, if this is what you'd truly like to do, I'll allow it." Nayla said, pulling her sister into her side.

Zara's grin grew as bright as the midday sun.

E veryone followed us to the clearing just beyond the city. Declan readied his shadow dynamis just in case we needed a shield. Clara handed Zara the elixir, and we all took a step back as she ingested it.

At first, everything seemed normal. Until a blast of air radiated from all around Zara, so powerful it knocked her to her knees and tossed us all back.

Thanks to Declan's shadows, we all landed softly. Jumping to our feet, Clara and I ran over to help Zara back up.

"How are you feeling?" Clara sounded flustered and full of worry. I helped the other two up on their feet.

"This might sound a little insane, but I feel a little more whole, stable even." Zara admitted with a laugh. "A lot less wobbly, I suppose?"

"Less...wobbly?" Clara's eyebrows rose.

"Well, I've always been a bit of a—"

"Baby deer?" Nayla snickered as she approached us.

"Yes, that's a fair comparison." Zara laughed. "It's hard to explain, but I somehow feel more solid, secure, balanced. Like nothing can make me falter."

Clara pursed her lips, looking over to meet my eyes. I shrugged my shoulders. Clara instructed Zara to test out her dynamis to see if there was any difference.

Zara lifted her hands and the ground beneath us quaked and cracked. Multiple pieces of ground shifted into the sky before she released them and they crashed to the ground.

It left me with goosebumps. My mind whirled with so much excitement that I hadn't even noticed Declan inching closer beside me. He placed his hand on the small of my back as he spoke into my mind. *"Congratulations, love."*

His smile warmed my insides as he pulled me into his chest. *"You've both done an incredible job, and now we have another way to fight back against Alastor and my father."*

"We wouldn't have been able to do any of this without your mother's genius mind. She found all the ingredients and made the first elixir. Queen Lenora basically handed us the keys, we just opened the door."

He nodded. *"True, but you didn't find the recipe, just the ingredients. You and Clara aren't giving yourselves enough credit. What you accomplished is spectacular."* As his lips brushed the top of my head, my body melted into him.

Fallon called out to him from behind and Declan pulled away. I was all too aware of the cold his absence left behind.

I'd fallen so hard for him I didn't think I'd ever reach the bottom.

"Love, you're drooling again." His lips twitched with amusement as we lay in bed.

I shoved him playfully in the shoulder. "You in those glasses, reading a book while bathed in the soft glow of candlelight, has you looking like a late evening snack. My apologies for being slightly ravenous." His lips curled up into a sly grin.

I pulled the vial from the side table and placed it in his palm. His grin faltered.

"I'm sorry. After today, with Nayla's sister...I was just excited to try this one." I reached to take it back.

Fingers closed around the vial as he tenderly rubbed his thumb against my cheek. "I—I just hate watching the disappointment in your eyes every time it doesn't work."

"Declan, this"—I rubbed the reddened curse mark behind his neck — "will never get in the way of me loving you."

He popped the cork off the vial then tilted the contents inside. His nose wrinkled in disgust from the taste as we waited for any effect.

I moved his head forward and ran my fingers over the mark that still lingered, but I couldn't help the haze that began to cloud my eyes. He took off his glasses and set his book aside, then motioned for me to come lie across his chest. As I sniffled against his warmth, he used his dynamis to snuff out the candlelight.

"Are you scared?" he mumbled into my hair.

"I'm not afraid of you, Declan, I'm just worried he's going to take you away from me."

"I'll never let that happen, I promise. Get some rest, love."

With his shadows, he snuffed out the candlelight. I found his lips in the darkness and pressed a kiss on top of them, then allowed my exhausted body to fall asleep wrapped in the safety of his arms.

CHAPTER 70
ELENA

Chills ran through my groggy body as I tried to burrow further underneath the sheets. Disoriented, I reached around, finding no sheets at all.

Panic splashed over me like water, and I was suddenly wide awake. The door was cracked open, letting in the night air from outside. All I had on was a thin nightgown, so the cold cut through me like a knife. Something wasn't right.

"Declan?" I whispered into the dark room.

Silence.

I rose from the bed, grabbed my clothes from the ground and shoved them on. Where had he gone, and why had the door been left open? He would never do that. As I made my way over to the door, I heard a creak from behind me. Swiftly I turned, reaching down for the dagger that wasn't there.

Fuck.

My body slammed against the stone wall of our room and the door was slammed shut. Every part of my body trembled with fear as I remained pinned against the wall. Two hands gripped tightly around my throat, as I tried to claw them off with my own. I couldn't even move my legs, because the intruder had those pinned with his own as well.

Light. I needed to be able to see.

Diving deep into my dynamis, I summoned my it to my hands. Warmth fled from my fingertips until my palms became illuminated in light. All the air left my body when I realized the intruder glaring into my eyes was the Lord of Shadows himself.

"Hello, Elena." A cold, otherworldly voice brushed against my face. The hands around my neck squeezed tighter, eliminating any chance of me screaming for help.

His skin was sickly pale and freezing to the touch. Emerald eyes were replaced with obsidian, empty of life or warmth. Only a void glared back at me.

Fucking Alastor Grimshaw.

He'd summoned the blood curse.

Terror pierced me as my dynamis screamed fully awake. Maybe— maybe I could break him free of this, just like I had almost done in the courtyard that day. I summoned my Flame dynamis and felt my hands begin to blaze against him.

The imposter in front of me grinned.

What the Hells?

Closing my eyes, I pushed my dynamis further. The smell of burning flesh seared my nostrils. He remained unfazed, and his grin spread even wider. I yelled in frustration.

Realization hit me that I was burning the real Declan, even if he was currently trapped inside his own body right now. I called back my dynamis as tears streamed down my face.

With a smirk, Declan leaned forward and licked the tears from my cheeks. I whimpered and squirmed underneath his grip. Nothing about this imposter felt like my love, nothing at all.

"Please ..."

For a mere moment, it almost seemed like his face flinched, like he was trying to break free from the hold the curse held over him. A blink, and it was gone.

"Time to go, Lady Elena," he growled.

He rammed my head into the stone wall behind me, and I fell into darkness.

The splash of waves and a gentle rocking motion woke me from my forced slumber. The only light came from the stars that glistened in the sky and the dim lantern at the front of the boat. My entire body ached as I peeled open my eyes. How long had I been out?

I went to rub my cloudy eyes then realized my hand was not coming when I summoned it. Metal clanked from behind me. How ironic. This whole mess had started with me in iron chains and now it appeared I might meet my end in them as well.

The small rowboat I was in rocked from side to side as it rowed along towards a cove in the distance.

Where was Declan? As if summoned by my words, something thumped against my right side. He lay slumped over the seat, his hands bound with iron as well.

"Declan!" I shouted desperately, using my thighs to try to rouse him.

"That will be no use, child," a low, ominous rattle whispered from behind me. "Master has summoned him into a deep sleep."

With trembling hands, I prayed to the gods that this was all just a dream. There was no way this moment could be real. The voice behind me... *it can't be.*

Piercing pain, cold as ice, seared through my shoulder. A scream ripped from my lips as a black, clawed hand continued to grip me.

No...no...no...gods, no!

The sound of its voice made me convulse with terror. "This is real, child. It's always been real. We have been waiting for you, Elena."

Every part of my skin prickled from its words, but I forced myself to turn around. The urge to know the truth of what lurked behind me was undeniable, no matter how terrifying it was.

Tears streamed down my body, now paralyzed in fear. There was nothing I could do to stop the warm liquid from cascading down my leg.

The image before me had haunted my dreams for as long as I could remember. Behind me sat two large figures in black cloaks that covered their bodies entirely. Just like in my dreams, they had no faces beneath their hoods, only endless voids of darkness.

In unison, they purred in eerie satisfaction over my terror, tilting towards me as if they were trying to absorb every drop of it.

The foul aroma of decay filled the air, making my head swirl with nausea. Still paralyzed by my own anxiety, I fought with my burning lungs to let air in.

It took effort, but I managed to look at the damage the creature behind me had done. My tunic lay in shreds over my shoulder and an angry red scar was seared into my flesh.

My vision began to cloud. My lungs desperately needed air, but fear had compressed them too tightly to absorb any.

Leaning closer towards my shoulder, I noticed something else seared deep into my flesh. I blinked my eyelids to try to adjust my vision. Seared into my flesh was a symbol I'd only seen once while sneaking a glance at the back of Declan's neck. It was small enough to be mistaken for a tattoo, but if eyes lingered for too long, it could be easily recognized. Now, we both had matching scars…and curses.

Well, fuck.

The small boat jolted back and forth as we hit the edge of the shore. Losing my balance, I fell against Declan. Every part of my body felt like it was shutting down as my breaths became ragged. One creature tied up the boat as the other scooped me up into its arms. I felt myself fading. If I didn't breathe soon, I was sure to black out. It carried me up the jagged steps, then dropped me to the rocky ground.

The force of the blow was enough to shock the panic inside of me, allowing me to take a gasp. Only for another familiar voice to make it catch in my throat again.

"Welcome, Lady Elena, so good to have you back."

Double fuck.

The last face that I saw before I passed out was none other than Alastor Grimshaw's.

CHAPTER 71
ELENA

Incessant screams woke me up. All around me was darkness, and I struggled to figure out my surroundings. Where in the Hells was I?

"Declan?"

Another scream rang out.

"Please, love. Answer me. Tell me you're okay."

Nothing but screams answered back.

Every muscle in my body cried out in pain as I tried to move. My arms were free of their shackles. However, sharp thorns tore my flesh, making me realize that they'd been replaced by something else entirely.

A faint glow of light came from above me, and it allowed me to see that I was trapped underneath layers of thorny vines. Black vines twisted around my wrists and ankles, contorted themselves around in my body, securing me in their tomb.

Panic flooded my body. I hated the darkness, and now I was trapped inside of it. Closing my eyes shut, I whispered my mantra to myself.

Meanwhile, I tried to reach for my dynamis, but hollowness was all that I felt. Panic began to take hold of me as I grasped for something that was no longer there.

Screams filled the air again. Each was full of agony and pain. The sound gnawed against my skin, and it almost felt as if the woman's screams were my own. Tears began to well in my eyes for her. I was ashamed that there was nothing I could do to save her from whatever torture she was enduring.

The screams continued for what seemed like hours until something within them changed drastically. As she screamed, her voice became more shrill and high-pitched, almost like a whimper from some sort of...animal.

Silence filled the cold cave that I was being held in, and I strained my neck as high as I could, hoping to catch any hint of a sound that she was still alive.

A howl bellowed from above, sending shivers rippling down my body. I knew that howl, the sound of the beasts that had wreaked havoc on our kingdom. Hot, frustrated tears ran down my cheeks. How could we have missed that Alastor had something to do with these beasts?

Thoughts froze in my mind as a growl emanated from the space above me. Two dark eyes stared back at me as the beast bared its teeth. It tipped its head towards the rocky ceiling as another howl rang from its body.

That was when I saw something that would haunt my memories forever. Below the beast were its thick, matted legs and paws. All except for one leg. A leg that looked very much like an arm...with fingers. *Dear, gods.*

Terror struck me like a knife. He was turning them into these beasts. Someone's mother, brother, sister, child ...they could be one of these foul beasts. The thought made my stomach sour. I only turned my head in just enough time to retch its entire contents.

What kind of depraved Hell have I found myself in?

E very part of my body felt aflame from the rampant torture Alastor had put me through over what I could only assume had been several days. I'd been in and out of consciousness so many times that I'd lost track of time entirely.

When we first began, I hadn't been shocked to see Alastor's face hover before me. There was no surprise when he unleashed his lightning dynamis on me and had his creatures claw their way through my skin. What shocked me was when Will entered the cave and worked alongside Alastor.

Fury screamed inside of me as Alastor ordered him time and time again to seal my wounds with flames. Alastor didn't want me to heal completely, just enough to keep me alive to withstand the next session of torture. The memory of his words sent a tremor of fear throughout my exhausted body.

"You will break for me, Elena, and I won't stop until I find the key to your undoing. When that time comes, you'll hand over your dynamis to me willingly. Until then, you'll feel pain in every part of your body all the way down to your soul. I'm going to make you suffer for all you've taken from me, time and time again."

Those last words still whirled around in my mind. From day one, it had been obvious that Alastor had a strong dislike for me. However, I was perplexed as to why he assumed I'd taken something from him. Whatever atrocities he thought I'd done had certainly fueled his fury.

Even thoughts felt too heavy as my exhausted body slumped against the cold, wet stone I was chained to. Alastor had stepped away, giving me a brief moment of reprieve.

"Love?" I reached out between our faint bond one more time. I've tried to find our connection in every moment that I could, but I felt nothing at all. I couldn't feel my dynamis, but I could somehow still feel a faint tug of the bond. It gave me hope that even if I couldn't talk to him, Declan might still be alive. *"If I survive this...please know that this wasn't your fault, and I will always love you, in this life and the next."* Tears slid down my face when I was met with silence once more.

Begrudgingly, I awaited the searing pain of Will's fire that would no doubt begin soon enough. I had been here for so long that I could barely feel the frigid sea water as it rose and fell against my shins. A heavy sigh passed through my lips when a whisper brushed against my ear. "Elena ..."

The unexpected feeling made my body jolt upward until I was face to face with Will. My lips drew into a thin line as I glowered at him.

"Don't look at me like that." A flicker of hurt flashed through his blue eyes before it fizzled out.

"How else should one look at the person who has been searing the flesh off my bones for gods only knows how long?" Each word scratched like rocks through my sore throat. After days of screams, I was surprised I had any voice left at all. He only grunted in response, folded his arms across his chest and leaned against the rock beside me. "Please, enlighten me on the correct way I should look upon the man who betrayed not only his entire kingdom, but his family and the woman he once claimed to love."

Will huffed, running his palm through his thick blond waves. Not too long ago that simple action would have made my heart palpate. The only reaction it gave me now was nausea.

"Why do you always have to be so—"

"Right?" I snapped.

"No. So—"

"Honest?"

A snarl tore out of him. "So. Damn. Judgmental!" he seethed, his chest rising and falling.

"Is it really being judgmental when it's true?"

My breath hitched as he suddenly invaded my space. His hot, rapid breaths brushed against my temple, and every muscle in my neck tried its best to tilt my head further away.

"You know nothing about my truth!" Will pulled away, releasing a deep breath. "Absolutely nothing."

The harsh lines once present on his face softened, his shoulders fell as his back slumped against the harsh rock. The glisten of a tear caught my eye as it slipped down his cheek, wiped away as he ran a palm over his face. As I bit down on my bottom lip, a twinge of remorse prickled me.

"They took Isabella and my mother." The air vanished from my lungs as he sighed deeply. "After everything that happened at the castle, I was told to abide by their rules or my insolence would be taken out on them both."

"Will—I...I'm so sorry. Where are they now?" I asked tentatively.

The muscle in his jaw clenched. The silence between us became unbearable. "Isabella's here."

"Will—"

"My mother," he interrupted, "she's also here, but ... she's not entirely herself anymore."

Hells.

"I was supposed to coax you into falling for me that night at the ball. When I didn't come through as planned, Alastor turned her into one of those—horrible beasts."

Guilt wrapped around my insides, squeezing so tightly I thought I might faint.

"This isn't your fault."

My eyes clouded with tears as I shifted my chin away to avoid his gaze. He pulled my chin back to face him and didn't let go. "Lena, I can see the guilt and anxiety are reflected all over your face. It's a look I've become very familiar with over the years." A hint of a smile tugged at the corner of his lips, but then slipped back into a frown. "There are several choices I could have made. So many chances to do the right thing, but I was a coward."

"Will, in the end you were just trying to protect your family," I whispered.

"No. Don't be kind to me Lena, I don't deserve it. Protecting my family would have meant doing anything I could to get to them, to save them. It would have meant fighting for the people I loved when they needed me the most." His eyes shot across to meet mine as a chill rippled down my spine. The words sent me back to my speech that I'd given him that night of the ball. "The day you told me that, shame filled every pore of my body. I knew I had let you all down. That was my burden to bear for the rest of my life. Lena, I had choices, but I didn't take them."

My mouth opened wide; however, no words escaped. I just stood there as it opened and closed like a floundering fish.

"It's time I start making the right choices. Time to start fighting to protect those I love," he growled, and in the distance, I heard footsteps entering the cave. "Hang in there a little longer, Lena." His voice was so low it was barely a whisper. "I'm going to help you both get out of here."

I barely had time to wipe the shocked expression from my face before Alastor grabbed my hair and slammed my head against the hard rock. Over and over, my forehead cracked against the hard stone. The metallic taste of blood filled my mouth and my eyes began to swell shut. His relentless attack lasted until I saw stars, my body slumping against the heavy chains.

Falling somewhere between the realm of consciousness and unconsciousness, Alastor's deep voice echoed in my ears. "Elena, I think it's about time we summon your Lord of Shadows, don't you?"

CHAPTER 72

DECLAN

Pain radiated through my body as I struggled to come to. The back of my head throbbed, my eyesight cloudy and blurred. Blood seeped from my wounds and fell to the rock floor beneath me. I attempted to move, but a piercing pain shot through both of my arms and chest.

My fingertips traced the point of a thorn as my eyes adjusted to my surroundings. Thick black roots completely encased my body in thorns. A frustrated growl launched from my chest as I kicked and thrashed against the vines, fighting with all I had to break free.

Elena.

The last time I'd seen her, she was snuggled up against me in our bed. *Damn!* Could she be here—wherever the Hells here was? As I thrashed against my thorny cage, I reached out to her through our bond.

"Lena?"

Silence.

"Love?"

My heartbeat pounded against my ears as I hoped desperately for her response.

"Lena, my love, talk to me!"

That familiar area in my chest started to throb, and instantly I recognized it as our bond. It felt like it was pulling me in the direction of my mate. She had to be close.

"Elena!" I yelled through gritted teeth. My words rattled against the hollow cavern walls before silence fell around me.

"Fuck!" Every effort I made to break free was met by the vines that wrapped around me. They tightened impossibly around my body, slicing deep gashes into my skin. I pulled for my dynamis, but I felt nothing but emptiness. It was almost though my dynamis no longer existed.

"Son, there's no use in resisting. The vines will just continue tightening until they break through the other side."

The air from my lungs vanished. The familiar voice I'd known all my life didn't come from above me—instead the sound rang from right beside me in the cavern.

"Trust me, I know from experience," my father's voice rasped as the crackle of vines filled the air. A grunt, then a stream of curse words flew from his mouth.

"Where. Are. We?" The disdain in my growl was evident as I tried not to make any more movements that could lead the vines to tighten more.

I heard the sharp intake of my father's breath, followed by the crack of bones. The sound of bones breaking was something that I knew far too well.

Screams of agony overloaded my senses. It wasn't just my father I was hearing; a female scream rang through the air as well. A scream I'd heard before. *Elena.*

Rage ignited inside of me. Whoever dared to lay a hand on the love of my life better be prepared to face the judgment of the gods, because they would be meeting their end very soon.

A grunt forced my attention back to the man next to me.

"As far as I'm concerned, you deserve every fucking bit of suffering you're enduring. For once, maybe you might feel a smidgen of what you have been doing to the people of your kingdom," I snarled. "Start. Talking."

Blood boiled within me, my jaw tightening with each moment I waited for my father to open his damn mouth. I needed answers, *anything* that might be able to help me get out of here so that I could save Lena.

"You've been out for days. We're in Alastor's lair." His words were hissed through clenched teeth. There was a time in my life when I might have felt remorse or sympathy for the man next to me. Unfortunately for him, that ship had sailed.

There was only one person I'd burn this entire world for. The one who had wrapped herself tightly around my soul, my guiding torch in the night, my one and only love. Elena.

Another of her screams rattled against the cavern. Once more, I began thrashing against the chain of thorns. The pressure closing in around my chest was so intense, I couldn't tell if it was a result of my overwhelming panic or the vines sinking deeper into me. All I knew was I needed to get to her, *now*.

"Stop!" my father boomed beside me.

"NO!" The vines broke skin around my ankles and arms. "Oh, fuck." A gasp slipped out as the thorns shredded through my open wounds.

"Hells, boy! For once in your damn life, listen to me!"

"I've got to—" My lungs burned from lack of oxygen. Shallow breaths escaped my lips with each wince of pain brought on by the vines. "—save her." Thorns sliced closer and closer to the bone. Pressure began to build behind my eyes, but I had no energy to expend on trying to hold the tears back. Tears mixed with my blood as they rolled down my cheeks.

"Declan—son—"

I stilled at the agony in my father's voice. The way he said "son," dripping with regret, the word burned a hole through my chest into my heart.

"Son." His voice cracked. "You will not be able to help her if you don't breathe."

"You have no right to—"

"Shhhh…breathe, my son."

Everything around me started to become cloudy. I was stronger than this. I had to fight, to pull through. The kingdom, my family, my friends, my love, they were all counting on me. This couldn't end here, not after everything that we'd been through.

"Think of your brother...your mother," he whispered. "They need you to pull through, son."

He was right, everything I did was for them. One deep shallow breath slipped in my lungs. *Good, keep going.* Two, breaths. Three. Four. The tightness in my trembling muscles began to ease before my father spoke again.

"You—you've always been stronger than I ever could be, Declan."

A twinge of remorse swarmed inside my stomach. My father had always despised the fact that my dynamis was more powerful than his. It made him furious that someone like me, who was weakened by anxiety, could be given such a power.

"I'm not talking about your dynamis, Declan. You've always had a strength within you, a power that no gift from the gods could ever replicate. Even as a little boy, I could see it shine through, no matter how hard I tried to break it."

Silence filled the air as I struggled to contain my shock over the conversation we were finally having.

"Even with everything I put you through all these years, things that would break a lesser man, like me, they never once touched you." A sob broke free from my father, my jaw tightened at the sound. "That's what got me into this miserable position in the first place. It's how—" His breaths were becoming shallower.

"Father—"

"No, son, let me finish. I've done nothing to deserve you listening to me, but please allow me to try to atone for the atrocities I've committed all these years. Please, just give me a chance to explain."

"Well"—I winced as the roots tightened at my slip of movement—"it's not like I can really go anywhere, given our current situation."

It was silent for a moment before I heard a muffled laugh from the tomb next to mine. Even the edges of my own lips turned slightly upwards.

"Good point. Well, now that I have your undivided attention, let me get on with it." My father cleared his throat. "This has all been my fault." I would like to say I was shocked by his admission, but sadly, I wasn't. "When Alastor arrived, the kingdom began to fall apart."

"Don't blame the beginning of our downfall on him. That was entirely you, Father. Your lust for power and your intolerance towards the humans is what began this darkness. Alastor just helped spread your hate campaign throughout the kingdom." My words were harsh, but I didn't give a damn. If he wanted to have a heart-to-heart, he was going to be truthful.

A heavy sigh filled the air. "You're right. The desire for dynamis, power...control...had blinded me before Alastor ever set foot in our castle. Alastor is not what we all believed him to be."

"You think?" I snapped.

"I believe he may not even be truly Elysian."

"Stop beating around the bush. What are you saying, Father?"

A frustrated grunt rumbled out of my father. "I'm trying to apologize for unleashing this evil in this kingdom ...for being weak and giving into my desire for power. Alastor has been syphoning my dynamis for centuries."

My brows shot to my hairline.

"He can syphon our dynamis to make it his own, but only after being given consent. If you don't consent, there are other ways he can force it out of you. Mine was the promise of complete control of my entire kingdom, and the promise that our family would continue to be the most powerful Elysians in the land."

"He's responsible for the suppression of dynamis, isn't he?" The words left my lips short and clipped.

"Yes, but it's not just those outside of the cities. I believe that Alastor was the original creator of the blood magic in this land. As you know all too well, that magic has an underlying evil about it."

The scar behind my neck burned against my flesh, as if responding to my father's words.

"Every Ascension, he places another curse upon this land. Each new Elysian who goes through the ceremony leaves with substantially less dynamis as the kingdom darkens and decays."

"Darkens and decays?"

"Have you not noticed that everything in this lair is dead, foul-smelling, and rotted to the core?"

I took a moment to look again at my surroundings. He was right, this place smelled like the breath of ten thousand of those dark beasts. Darkness shrouded every corner. Everywhere I looked screamed death.

"These roots are burrowing their way through the kingdom, killing the land. Poisoning the water in the aqueducts."

My breath caught in my chest, his words striking a chord within me. Could this be why my father had been shutting off the water in different areas of the city?

"Those beasts...those humans and Elysians who have gone missing ..." His voice faded off, allowing me to puzzle together what he hadn't voiced.

"He didn't—" My teeth gnawed against my cheek. "Father, please tell me those beasts are not subjects of our kingdom?" I tried to fight off the wave of nausea.

An audible swallow came from my father. "I could tell you that they aren't, but I'm tired of lying to you, Declan."

The blood beneath my skin boiled. When I finally got my hands on Alastor, I was going to destroy him. Slowly. Painfully. Until he begged for mercy that I would happily deny him.

"I fear, if we do not stop Alastor, our entire kingdom will be consumed entirely by this darkness and the evil that lives inside of it. He's destroying the Kingdom inside and out. You and Elena are the only ones capable of stopping him." A gurgled cough rattled from my father's chest. "Son, I don't think I have much longer."

Every selfish act that he had committed over the years had led this kingdom to where we were now. For a long time, I'd assumed that something was going on with my father, but anger and rage had blinded me, stopping me from confronting him about it. The main reason I'd stayed for so long was to see if he would have a change of heart.

Remorse welled inside my stomach. Perhaps, if I had intervened sooner, we wouldn't have been in this predicament. As I was about to respond to my father for possibly the last time, the sound of a slow clap floated down to us.

"Well done, Alaric. You always did have quite the flair for dramatics," Alastor scoffed. "Now that you're both done with your happy little family reunion, I'd like you both to join me."

With a snap of his fingers, two hooded creatures descended upon us. Black claws extended out of the sleeve of the being that was closest to me. It waved its repulsive hand, and the vines ripped free of my flesh at an excruciatingly painful rate. Both creatures' faces were shielded inside the dark void of their deep hoods, but I could feel their gazes burning my skin.

My father yelled beside me as the creature pulled him out of the ground and wrapped its clawed hands around his arms to hold him upright. It was pressing straight into the broken bone protruding from my father's arm.

"Get your claws away from me!" His words thundered as the creature next to me pulled me to my feet as well. The dark being next to my father growled, digging its claws deeper into his arm, silencing him with pain. The color left in his face dimmed as he tried to endure it silently.

"We don't have all day. Get them up here!" Alastor roared from above.

Claws wrapped tighter around me, and my feet lifted off the ground. The hooded creatures floated us out of the sunken tomb we'd been in.

As soon as my feet touched the ground, my breath hitched at the sight that lay all around me. Thousands of these sunken holes spread throughout the cavern as dark beasts and more of the creatures behind me roved around.

How many others did Alastor have down here?

Alastor stepped directly into my eyeline. A malicious smirk spread across his face. "Welcome to Hells, Declan."

Before I could snap back a response, the creature kicked my legs out from under me, sending me crashing to the rock. Gravel embedded itself into my ripped flesh. I winced as the creature pulled my arms above my head and began to drag me away. A dark rumble of laughter bellowed from Alastor as he stalked ahead of us.

The smell of sea salt and the crash of waves brushed against my senses as the creature continued to drag me. Icy water flooded my back and continued to coat the rest of my body as it was drug through it. A hiss slipped from my father behind me as they wrapped chains around my father's wrist and connected them to the black rock behind him.

Whimpers assaulted my ears, and my gaze landed onto the mangled body chained against the rock in front of me. Only a few specks of her auburn hair showed through the blood that stained it. Pieces of my heart shattered as my eyes rolled over every cut, bruise and burn to her beautiful body. The radiant glow of her freckles had dimmed, and my Wildfire's eyes were swollen shut. The rise and fall of her chest was barely noticeable.

Footsteps splashed behind the rock. The chains behind her sagged and pulled backwards. My eyes followed the chain, which ended in the hands of a familiar Elysian. *Will.*

Rage bubbled and boiled beneath my skin. Though I still couldn't feel my dynamis, the overwhelming need to avenge Lena gave me strength.

The hooded creature was still standing directly behind me. A sadistic grin grew upon my face. I kicked my feet around the creature's, pinned it with my thighs, and bit down hard on its leg. An otherworldly shriek fled from the creature as its thick, foul-smelling blood coated my mouth. While it was distracted, I threw it over my shoulder into the water, holding its head underneath with the weight of my body.

Alastor hissed a command in another dialect at the creature near my father, and in seconds it was on top of me. Its claws dug deep into my shoulders as searing pain peeled at my flesh. The other creature flailed beneath me as I repeatedly jabbed my elbow into the chest of the one latched onto my back. Underneath me, the movements slowed until there was nothing. Twisting my body on top of my other assailant, I slammed its head into the same position beneath the water.

All at once my breath left my body as lightning struck through the both of us. Through the current of fiery light, Alastor's eyes glistened with fury as he unleashed blow after blow of his dynamis.

The roar that exited my body shook the entire lair. It even caused Alastor to stumble, wide-eyed, before he extended his arm to launch his dynamis again. A flash of light—no, fire—flashed before my eyes.

Will stood in front of me, taking the full blow of the lightning strike. With a grunt, he fell to his knees. Alastor stomped towards us both.

"Remember, you can't—" Will paused, trying to settle his breath. "You can't kill him yet."

The glare that Alastor unleashed on Will could have easily burnt a hole. Will regained his footing just for Alastor to send a right hook to his jaw, sending him crashing back down. My lips twitched up at the sight. Even though Will had just shielded me, it didn't erase all the rage I had pent up against him for what he had done to Elena.

"Oh, you think this is all funny?" Alastor glanced at the two dead creatures underneath me. He extended his hand and hissed another command.

A scream filled the cave. I watched in horror as Elena flew across the water straight into his clutch. He wrapped his fingers around her neck, and another scream fled her lips as her feet dangled in the air.

"STOP! Leave her alone. Do your worst to me." I stumbled to my feet and ran towards him. With a flick of his wrist, another bolt of lightning thrashed against me, shoving me backwards. Pain assaulted my body, but I didn't back down. I couldn't, not until I had her safe inside my arms. Shallow breaths rasped from my mouth as I continued to make my way towards him. Blow after blow of his dynamis knocked against my body.

"Son! Stop!" My father's exasperated cries echoed against my ears. Ignoring his pleas, I pushed my body further.

Alastor's eyes began to widen as he took a few steps back. His lips twitched and beads of sweat began to fall down his brow. All at once, his dynamis stopped, halting me dead in my tracks as I paused for a much-needed gasp of air. Alastor's gaze had shifted…onto my father's.

"Let's see who you'll choose." Alastor grinned as fear sliced through my gut as I watched him begin to drain the power out of my father.

My eyes locked on my father's. No words passed between us, just a silent nod and a teary smile. I began my sprint towards Elena, who had already been launched into the air.

No dynamis meant no zephyring. Pushing my body to its limit, I ran with everything I had to catch the woman I loved.

CHAPTER 73
ELENA

S uddenly the air whipped around my face, and a scream ripped through me as I felt weightless as I made a rapid descent.

The gods only knew how our fates would end, and it seemed as though this might be where I met my end.

Faster and faster, I hurtled toward the floor, my heart thrumming so hard against my chest it felt as though it might break through.

"ELENA!"

Declan's yell shattered against my eardrum at the same time as I collided into his solid body. We crashed into the ground and the sound of our bodies crashing against stone filled the cavern.

Declan groaned in agony and forced me to roll off him. The ache in my chest was unbearable. I must have cracked a rib, if not more. Declan's breaths rattled in his chest. *Hells, he must have punctured a lung.*

My swollen eyes barely opened, but it was enough to get a sense of my surroundings.

Declan lay sprawled on the ground, clutching his chest. Both of us were covered in massive amounts of blood and open wounds.

"Don't think his act of valor will save you, Elena." The sound of Alastor's voice made me cringe. A malicious laugh rumbled about the cave as footsteps neared. "I've already taken every last bit of Alaric's dynamis." The king's slumped body dangled from the iron chain around his wrist.

Dec snarled, fighting the pain as he pushed himself onto his feet. I thrust my shoulder under his arm and wrapped my arm around his back to steady us both as we faced Lord Grimshaw.

"You *will* both submit to me." Blackness had almost taken over the white in his eyes, turning them into two pools of darkness. "I will go after your little Rebellion city." My eyes widened. "Yes, I know he's been hiding it from us all these years. I'll take them. Every. Single. One. Each one will die in front of you both, and I won't stop until you both submit to me. The power you hold belongs to me, and I will never stop until it is mine once more."

His words made my mouth become instantly dry. Declan gave my shoulder a squeeze, forcing me out of my spiraling thoughts, reminding me that I was not alone—he was right there beside me, and he always would be.

"Perhaps it's time to show you exactly what I mean," Alastor sneered, stretching out his arm. In a flash, Will dangled from Alastor's hand.

Alastor hissed a string of incoherent words. Declan and I both watched in horror as Will's body began to transform. Dark claws ripped his boots to shreds as thick black fur sprouted over his flesh. He tossed his head back with a scream that chilled my bones as his teeth grew into ivory fangs.

Will turned his body towards us, his blue eyes still full of flame. "Run!"

Alastor's face paled as fire ripped out of every inch of Will's transforming body. The first blast shook the walls of the cavern, sending rocks cascading from the ceiling. I narrowly moved us in time to not get squashed under them. Another blast ripped from Will, met by Alastor's own dynamis. When the two powerful dynamis collided, another blast ricocheted from them.

The force sent all of us crashing to the floor and tore a hole through the side of the cavern. Declan rolled his body on top of me, shielding me from the rocks that crumbled all around us.

Will's howl broke through the sounds of tumbling rocks. *Run.*

He had sacrificed himself so that we could escape, so escape was exactly what we were going to do. Remorse tugged at my heart as I glanced back one last time at Will. With a deep breath, I turned towards Declan and rolled him off me.

"Lena" he grunted, as I somehow found the strength to pull his broken body up and hold him next to me. "You need to make it out of here. Please let me go, love, save yourself."

"No!" I snarled. "I'm never leaving you. We escape together, or we stay here and die together. There's no option in which I'll be leaving you alone."

He tightened his arm around my shoulder. "Alright, let's get out of this Hell, Wildfire."

As we clawed our way through the hole, another growl rang from behind us. We turned our heads just in time to see Will pounce on top of Alastor. A grin lit up my face at the sounds of Alastor's screams.

However, I didn't get to enjoy the moment for long. More growls filled the cavern. Thousands of dark eyes met ours. A whine and a beastly shriek tore my gaze away as Alastor attacked Will with his lightning dynamis.

Three hooded creatures appeared behind the wave of foul beasts that now filled the cavern. The leader of the pack howled, and the horde barreled towards us. Blood pounded inside my ears as I scrambled up the rest of the rocks, pulling Declan in bursts. I gripped the soil on the other side of the hole and pulled us onto it. We both took a moment to inhale the fresh outside air. Wind howled against our broken bodies, and all at once my body jolted with a surge of power.

Declan's eyes caught mine. "Did you feel that too?"

Every inch of my body hummed with my dynamis. The glow of my body was dim, but it was there. Alastor must have used blood magic to curse our dynamis while inside his lair. No wonder we hadn't been able to sense it.

Claws scraped against the rocks behind us. Panic resumed, as well as the familiar pinprick of my dynamis begging to be released from under my skin.

"Love, we've got to zephyr." His eyes shifted to his broken leg and back to mine.

Tears gathered in my eyes as I pulled my crumpled body to its feet and helped Declan do the same. My heart tugged as the pain drained the blood from his handsome face.

He pulled me into his arms as his lips brushed over my temple. "I'll never get tired of the feeling of holding you in my arms, love. When you're in my arms, I know I'm home."

I pressed a kiss to his cheek.

Wind blasted all around us as we zephyred away.

CHAPTER 74

DECLAN

When her lips brushed my cheek, relief warmed my body, and for a moment everything else faded away. That moment, however, became short-lived. Exhaustion weighed heavily on us both, and the hold on our dynamis snapped.

Elena's cry tore a hole through my heart as we fell out of our zephyr.

One branch after another tore at our already mangled bodies. I wound my arms around Elena, trying to shield her from every impact.

We both hit the ground with a sickening thud. More cracks of bone filled the air of the clearing we had slid into. The arm lying underneath Lena throbbed; there was no doubt in my mind that it was either dislocated or broken. Elena curled into me as her breathy whimpers floated to my ears.

She clutched her bleeding thigh with her hand. My jaw clenched at the sight of bones piercing through in multiple spots on her leg and ankle. Elysians might heal faster than humans, but not with this many wounds. At this rate, if we didn't find a Healer soon, we would both bleed out.

With my bruised, but not broken arm, I brushed the tears away from her cheek. She winced as my fingers brushed along the cuts and bruises on her face. I placed my palm flush against her cheek and tried to summon my dynamis to heal her face. It flickered inside me, but settled back into its shallow well.

Elena's mangled body trembled. I could tell she was beginning to panic as her breaths became fewer and more ragged.

"Shhh…deep breaths, love." I pressed a kiss on the top of her head.

"It's not s-s-supposed to be this way," she stuttered between sobs, my thumb brushed against her cheek as I tried to soothe her. "Why would the gods give us such powerful dynamis, let us find each other, become mates, just to have our fates end here? Declan, we've fought the darkness all of our lives, we can't let it finally win."

She had worked alongside a Healer all of her life, she knew as well as I did that there was no recovering from this. "My love"—I held her trembling chin— "no matter what happens today, the darkness will not overcome the light in this kingdom. You've given the kingdom hope, and hope is far more powerful than any dynamis Alastor could steal."

Her bottom lip quivered. Pressure began to build behind my own eyes, my vision becoming cloudy. A howl bellowed, followed by several thousands more. The muscles along my spine froze in place. *They're coming.*

"Dec…I'm so afraid. I don't want to die."

My chest throbbed, but I pulled her closer.

"I can't lose my friends, my family…I—I can't lose you, not when I just found you."

"You will never lose me, love. I told you I would love you forever, and that means even after our bodies turn to ashes in the wind." I managed to smile, trying to wince from the pain that still radiated through my exhausted body. "You can't get rid of me so easily, love. When we meet the gods, we'll do it together."

With the strength I had left, I pressed my lips against hers. Each brush of our lips left an imprint, an unspoken promise of the love that we would bring with us, even after we left this realm. I closed my eyes, trying my best to commit her scent, her taste to memory. Though it might have been one of the gentlest kisses that we had ever shared, it was full of passion. It was one that I will never forget.

Her body jolted, breaking our kiss, at the sound of more howls. They were so much closer now.

"I wish we had more time," she mumbled into my chest.

"Me too, love."

The ground underneath us began to tremble.

"We can't—" Lena swallowed. "We can't let them live, Declan. There are real people inside those beasts, we can't let them continue to be hurt and used by Alastor. We also can't let them hurt the rest of the kingdom. You and I barely were able to kill the three we fought against. Imagine what would happen if there was an attack from all of them at once."

She was right, there was no way we could allow these beasts to live. However, I was unsure how we were going to get rid of them in our current situation.

"I think I know a way to stop them," she whispered. Either I spoke my thoughts into her mind, or she could read the emotion written all over my face. "While in the castle, I—" She licked her lips. "What if we used the rest of our dynamis together? Every. Last. Drop."

"Do you still feel dynamis within you?"

"I feel a little hum, but it feels almost drained completely."

It could work. It had been a powerful blow to the beasts the last time we'd used it. Now that we had completed the bond, our dynamis would be even stronger together. It also might be the only way we could summon our dynamis from our exhausted bodies.

She entwined her fingers in mine and rested our hands on top of my chest. "When I tell you to, I want you to forget about all of the other emotions swirling inside of you and just focus on one. Every time my dynamis was most powerful, I thought about one and only emotion."

"Love?" I hummed against her forehead.

"Yes," she breathed. With just one word, my soul ripped wide open. She sniffled against my chest. "It's time."

Digging down to the depths of my dynamis, I called forth the swell of magic. As the presence of dynamis flooded my body, my muscles convulsed. Both of our exhausted bodies shook as they struggled to contain the dynamis we summoned. Taking one last look at my soulmate next to me, I pulled up every memory, every moment that made me burst wide open with love.

Vibrant light flooded my vision. Elena and I were both dripping in violet, her golden glow surrendered for the purple hue. It felt like my skin was about to erupt with fire. Turbulent wind began to swirl around us, tossing our hair back and forth. Her violet eyes held my gaze, even as our bodies began to hover above the ground.

Her lips mouthed words, but the chaos happening around us was too loud for my ears to hear her. Then, she spoke through our bond. I felt her words all the way down to my soul. They flowed through me like the blood within my veins, like the breath that filled my lungs.

"I'm scared."

"I'll be right by your side. You'll never be alone, love," I whispered into her mind. *"I love you."*

We hovered several feet above the ground now. From above, we could see the beasts spread out over the ground like the shadow of darkness itself. My heart thundered against my chest, beads of sweat dripped down my forehead and neck. I glanced over at Elena. Her head bobbed in a nod. This was it. A solitary tear slid down her cheek as she silently counted us down.

One...

My skin began to tear at the seams.

Two...

Fire engulfed my lungs.

Three.

Blinding violet light burst from inside of us. The force of our dynamis spread miles wide. With immense delight, I watched from above as the horde of beasts fell. Our dynamis washed over them like a wave, and all at once my body felt entirely drained. My view began to blur as we began our rapid descent back towards the ground.

"We did it, my love." Lena's gentle voice caressed my mind.

"I'll see you soon, Wildfire."

Her smile was the last image I saw before our bodies slammed into the ground for the final time.

Excruciating pain was what I had expected. Instead, all that flowed through me now was the feeling of endless love and peace. My eyelids fluttered closed, and the world around me faded away.

CHAPTER 75
ELENA

"*Wake, Elena! Wake!*"

My lashes fluttered as I tried to open my eyes. I struggled to pull myself from my nightmares, just like I had done for the past twenty-three years of my life.

However, something was vastly different about this nightmare. No images played inside my mind, just an endless void of black. Everything felt light, and no matter how much I tried, I couldn't feel the weight of my limbs. It was like my mind was present, but my body wasn't. Panic began to swell in my mind, just as a flash of light swirled in front of me.

A tiny golden orb of light fluttered before me. As it danced around, my eyes followed, and as it moved forward, I followed. With each forward movement, the orb grew, becoming more radiant against the void. I continued to follow the orb as it guided me out of the darkness.

The golden glow eventually grew so big that it was larger than me. It no longer made any more movements, and even though I still struggled to feel my body, a prickling awareness urged me to continue forward. Giving in to the pull, I walked into the light.

A rush of heat flooded my body, and the sudden weight of my

limbs almost took my breath away. The beat of my heart echoed inside my ears, at the same moment a tug pulled against it. A bond... *our* bond. *Declan.*

"Love, open your eyes."

Emotions flooded my body as I opened my heavy lids. I was met with the most hypnotizing view. Chestnut tendrils of hair fell across an enchanting pair of verdant eyes. A shiver rushed down my spine. I could feel a warm palm wrapped around my shoulder, and another cupping my cheek.

Alive.

We were alive. Raw emotion spilled out of me, trickling down my cheeks, as Declan swiped the tears away with his thumb. Leaning forward, he pressed a kiss to my lips. The brush of his lips against mine acted like dynamis inside my soul, rousing me into full awareness. When he pulled back, my eyes were finally able to roam over the environment we now found ourselves in.

Petals brushed my legs as I realized I was lying in a field of endless wildflowers. It felt like Ehora, but more... ethereal.

Pink clouds spotted the blue sky above us, and a warm breeze whistled between the branches of the pine trees surrounding us. A violet haze filtered over everything. Soft material brushed against my fingertips as I glanced down to see my attire had changed to a flowy white dress.

Declan's attire had changed as well. He wore black fitted pants and a black shirt that clung to his arms and the muscles of his chest, unlike the normal flow of a tunic. I was wide-eyed and my mouth slightly agape. He engulfed the sides of my face with his palms, forcing my gaze back to meet him.

"Ready to meet the gods?"

"Wh-what?" One stuttered word was all I was able to muster.

"Come along, you two." A familiar voice fluttered across the breeze.

My entire body stilled as the voice that pulled me out of every nightmare suddenly had a physical form attached to it, one that I'd seen once before, during my Ascension ceremony. The inside of my mouth became dry as I breathlessly forced the words out. "You're her."

A smile spread across her face as wisps of her long, white-blonde hair fluttered in the wind. With a breathy laugh she spoke. "Yes, I'm she." She motioned for us to follow her. Declan wrapped his strong arms around me, pulled me onto my feet and steadied me as I wobbled. "Let's go, you two. We don't have much time together, and we have entirely too much to tell you both before you return." She turned around and continued walking into the woods.

Before we return?

Declan interlaced his fingers in mine, giving them a squeeze of reassurance. Together, we walked hand in hand to whoever awaited us on the other side.

***

The sight before me was nothing that I expected. We had followed the goddess through the forest and into another small clearing where we approached what looked like stone ruins of some sort. A small group of others dressed like Declan and I were sprinkled about the ruins. Some were clad in black like Dec, others in white like me.

So many questions swirled within me as we approached the group, and the goddess motioned for us to take a seat on one of the crumbled stones.

All at once, I felt the heaviness of several eyes on us. I shifted uncomfortably on the stone. Declan rubbed a soothing hand across my thigh.

"Breathe, love. You're safe." His deep voice brushed against the walls of my mind. The rising anxiousness fluttered away.

A knowing smile twitched against the goddess' lips.

Four beings approached from behind, flanking the goddess on both sides. When we'd first approached the stone ruins, my awareness of the sights around me was still adjusting. Now that they were only standing a few feet away from us, there was no doubt the beings in front of us were not Elysian. Declan squeezed my thigh, a quiet acknowledgment that the sight before us was shocking to him as well.

The group of beings stood before us giving us equally assessing stares. The man closest to the goddess towered above me and Declan by almost a full foot. His arms were folded across his chest, making his muscles more clearly defined. Short onyx hair adorned the top of his head, and thick black claw mark tattoos covered the side of his face and neck, matching his black slacks and shirt draped around him. When his violet eyes caught my gaze, he nodded in greeting.

Next to him was a much smaller woman with long, aquamarine hair that stood out against the black of her clothing. She pulled her hair back behind her ear, and I tried to make sense of what I saw. What looked like iridescent fish scales illuminated her rosy cheeks.

When my gaze met her molten amber eyes, she blinked, and both Declan and I jumped where we sat. Her lashes didn't move, only a white film slid back and forth over her eyes. My lips parted as an amused snort fled from her. Realizing my rudeness, I slammed my mouth shut.

"Stop messing with them, Nixie." Another woman snickered from the opposite side of the goddess. My eyes roamed over the points of her white furry ears, down to the feline-shaped citrine irises that were staring right back at me. She elbowed the chuckling man beside her, whose large, pointed ears peeked out through his long white-blonde hair. "Shhhh. Valdarin, they don't remember who you are."

Remember?

The hitch in my breath brought all eyes back on me, including Declan's. I laced my fingers within his, to force my mind to think of that instead of the overwhelming nerves brewing.

"*Wildfire, look at me.*" Declan's low, soothing voice pulled my gaze towards him. "*I'm here, we're together. As overwhelming as this all is, you're not alone, love.*"

"You know, it's rude to have an entire conversation inside your heads while we sit here and watch," the tall being with claw tattoos grumbled. The woman with the aquamarine hair—Nixie, I thought? —elbowed him hard enough to make him grunt with displeasure.

"Don't mind Arthur. Even after all our time together, he still has problems...socializing." Nixie walked towards us with her hand extended. "I, on the other hand, find the whole mind-talking gift romantic. Hi, I'm Nixie."

When our palms met, an overwhelming rush of familiarity prickled throughout my body. It was as if we had done this before. Declan must have had the same feeling, because his eyes widened when she shook his hand. A grin spread across her lips as she returned to her spot. That was when the goddess finally spoke.

"And it's time you know I'm no goddess. My name is Alyth, and behind me are just a few of the Divine. We are the ones you are most familiar with, so we wanted to be here when you returned."

"The Divine?" Declan's brows rose.

He was concerned with their title, but I was more anxious about her insinuation that we already knew these people standing before us. A million flutters rippled inside my stomach.

"We could all stand here and try to explain what is going on right now, but it wouldn't have the same impact as it would if you just told yourselves."

She approached us both, the others following behind. They circled around us, and she placed her hands on our shoulders, guiding us to face one another. The others placed their palms on us as well.

Declan had yet to let go of my hand. "Eyes on me, love."

"As Divine Guardians, we can unveil your mind. We can help you regain your truths. This is very similar to your Ascension on Ehora. Just relax and let your souls do the guiding. Ready?" Alyth asked, and we both nodded, not once breaking our gazes. "Here we go."

CHAPTER 76
ELENA

Ll at once a rush of warmth radiated through my body. The overwhelming feeling of love wrapped itself around my soul and tugged on my heart. It was so all-encompassing, that it felt like it ripped the air straight from my lungs. I tried to keep my eyes open and locked onto Declan's, but they slammed shut.

As soon as they did, I was blinded by a flash of light. Slowly, my eyes began to adjust, and images and memories began to flash in front of my eyes. I watched myself battling dark serpents in a world filled entirely made of water. Nixie was there, and we were surrounded by several others of her kind, all with shimmering tails that moved swiftly through the water.

In another flash of light, I was now helping others hide from the enemy on the other side of a wall. Blasts of metal ricocheted, sending pieces of the walls crumbling to the ground. The people surrounding me had tattoos on their arms as well, but unlike ours they were just a lengthy list of numbers. A blast broke through the walls, and I hurled myself over the frail bodies surrounding me, shielding them from the imminent attack.

The memories continued to flash over and over in front of my eyes. Different worlds, different realms, but in each one we were all battling the same darkness, the same evil as the one we faced on Ehora. Though they might not have been wearing dark hoods, or the sinister face of Alastor Grimshaw, every fiber of my being could feel the darkness radiating off the enemies we were battling.

There were no spoken words in these memories, only emotions. We knew each of the beings surrounding Declan and me. Together, we had all battled against evil in each of these different realms. It wasn't just them I had a strong familiarity with, however.

Shadowing me at every turn on every world was the man who appeared to have stolen my heart more times than I could count. Declan had been by my side for every battle, every triumph and every loss. There wasn't a memory I had that didn't include him.

No matter where we were sent, we'd found each other time and time again.

Love warmed my soul. Our bond tugged me back towards him. Slowly, my awareness of my body became heavier as I fell back into it.

When I opened my eyes, his cheeks were stained with tears, and I could feel cool wetness across my own as well. However, that coolness warmed as I met his eyes once more. They flamed with heat and desire, but most of all an overwhelming amount of love. All of it directed towards me.

A grin spread across his face that made the bond thrum within me. "Well, Wildfire." The deep timbre made me melt into the stone beneath me. "It appears our souls have been intertwined this entire time. We truly are soulmates—"

Before he could say any more, I wrapped my hand around his neck and pulled him into my lips. We got lost in each other for a few moments before someone cleared their throat.

"Sorry." I tossed a sheepish grin to the others. Even Declan's cheeks had a rosy hue to them as he leaned backwards.

"It's not the first time we've had to endure your displays of passion." Alyth grinned.

Now my own cheeks flamed red.

"Alright, alright," Arthur grumbled. "Let's hurry this along. Time is running out before we send them back in."

That was right—Ehora, the planet we were trying to save from evil trying to corrupt it.

"As you now know, our purpose is still the same—guarding worlds and realms as they ascend towards a higher dimension, making sure that evil doesn't corrupt them. Only when there is a threat of a shift of balance are we allowed to intervene. We're supposed to intervene only once as well." Alyth's lashes fluttered downwards, and she fidgeted with the fold of her gown.

"You were the first Light Phoenix, weren't you?" I didn't remember seeing it in my flashbacks, but the more we spoke, the more my memory was returning.

Alyth nodded. "I was given another chance to return, but when I came back as the Light Phoenix, I was blinded by rage. So much hate and distrust had begun to corrupt Ehora, and the night I died, they slaughtered so many of the people I had come to love. In my anger, I wiped out the evil entirely, breaking the one rule we are never meant to overstep."

"Choice," Declan whispered next to me. "You didn't allow them the chance to make a choice to change. To decide to walk towards the light, instead of being pulled under by the darkness."

"Exactly," Alyth breathed. "After I died and returned here, I wasn't allowed to return. In fact, I will not be allowed to intervene at all in the future until I've fully learned from my mistakes." Arthur placed his palm on Alyth's shoulder as a few tears sprinkled down her cheeks.

"This is one of the reasons why you both were sent down in her place," Arthur continued where Alyth had stopped.

"What was the other reason?" I asked.

He brushed his hand through his thick black hair. "We always incarnate in pairs. It's a part of the balance we bring as Divine Guardians."

"The balance between love and wisdom, right?" Declan asked.

"Yes," Valdarin answered this time. "Thus, our outfit selection," he smirked, motioning our clothing. "Some of us are more prone to guidance and wisdom." He pointed to Declan's black outfit. "Others resonate more with the emotions and feelings that bloom from love and peace." This time he motioned towards me. "Both are essential when uplifting others towards the light, and the reason we go together to maintain the balance between good and evil in each place we protect."

Arthur began to speak as soon as Valdarin finished. "I was with Alyth and fell when she fell. Alyth begged to be given a chance to return immediately, but I argued that we needed to wait and give it some time before we returned. I felt there was something bigger plaguing this planet than we had originally thought. However, before we could come to a consensus, Alyth returned to Ehora … and, well, you know what happened after that."

Alyth's cheeks flushed with embarrassment. When Declan and I had made the decision to use our combined power to wipe out the beasts, it had felt like it was necessary to save the ones that we loved. After hearing Alyth, I was beginning to question my choice.

As if reading my thoughts yet again, Declan asked a question to the group. "You said earlier that we're expected to return to Ehora. Explain to me how what Alyth did is any different than what Elena and I just did."

No one answered, so he kept speaking. "The beasts we killed were Elysians and humans. Souls that had been turned into soldiers of evil against their own will. How are we allowed to return, and Alyth cannot?"

"*You* didn't take away their choice." Alyth spoke softly. "The evil one corrupting Ehora did. You both freed them from their suffering—"

"We could have found a way." I sniffled, suddenly overcome with emotion. "We should have found a way to change them back."

Alyth gathered my hands within hers and pulled me into an embrace. "There's no cure for this kind of evil, Elena," she whispered into my hair, pausing to let the words sink in. "They would have been trapped in those beasts forever. You showed them mercy by unraveling their souls from the evil that held them in its clutches." She gave me a squeeze before releasing me. I opened my mouth to speak when Arthur interrupted my thoughts.

"They've found your bodies. We need to hurry this along before we miss our opportunity."

Our bodies? I shivered at the thought. Gods, which one of our friends had had to endure that sight?

"Yes, Arthur's right." Alyth winced. "Alastor must be stopped, and I believe you two are the only ones who can stop him this time."

"Why do you say that?" Declan queried, and from the look on his face, it appeared that this truly must have been something that we hadn't discussed in our prior lives.

"While you were on Ehora, we all tried our best to make sense of why we kept seeing this same type of evil. It's like it keeps following us from place to place. We narrowed it down to where we think it all began. Pyraxia."

An audible hiss, along with a string of curses, fled from Declan's mouth. His reaction was no surprise, because I'd done the same as well. Even though our friends had opened our minds to unveil our memories, it would still take a little time for us to fully remember it all. However, at the mere mention of Pyraxia, memories of the world where I'd first met Declan came into clear view.

It was Declan's original home, as well as our very first mission working together. It was also the first—and would be the last—time we had ever watched an entire world fall into the hands of evil. By fall, I meant everyone, the good and the evil.

Pyraxia no longer existed, and it was the main reason Declan and I fought to guard other worlds from falling under the same blight.

"There are several eerie similarities about the evil that was on Pyraxia." Hairs on the back of my neck rose as memories of the evil on Ehora slid across my skin. I could almost feel the icy touch of the hooded beings, the odor of rot and decay that spewed from them, the beasts and most of all Alastor. The knot that gathered inside my stomach tightened, making me feel suddenly lightheaded.

"It's more than similar. It's exactly the same, and I was too careless to recognize it." The muscles in Declan's jaw ticked. He clawed his hands through his hair.

Placing a hand on his shoulder, I attempted to pull him back from his anxious thoughts. "I was there too, Declan. Hells, I dreamed about their evil, and apparently my past lives. Even I didn't notice it."

His shoulders sagged under my palm. He pulled his hands away from his now rumpled hair.

Suddenly, I remembered something of importance. My eyes roved over the bodies around us until they landed on the one person who I knew could answer my question. Alyth. "You were always there in my dreams, during my Ascension. I thought you couldn't intervene?"

Alyth's lips twisted into a playful smile. "Well, there are always loopholes. We noticed you'd started to dream about your past lives, which never happens." Her smile fell. "All of us began to worry that maybe evil had possibly found a way to stay connected to you both."

Wide-eyed, I turned to face Declan. "You dreamt about our past too?"

His head bobbed silently. "Not to the extent that you did, but still enough to make me feel a constant unease." He frowned. "Maybe they do have some sort of connection to us? We might be the reason Ehora is about to battle one of our greatest evils."

"I heard voices when I touched the gods' tree, and when I bumped into Alastor one day, I heard terrified screams. Do you think maybe that's the connection?"

"I've always felt that the gods' trees had more importance in Ehora, something deeper. When you go back, you should spend more time researching this. Perhaps they're the key to the darkness destroying the realm." Alyth said.

"What about Alastor's connection?"

"That we are still working on, but the fact that when you touched him you heard voices makes me curious just how deep his connection with the two of you goes."

Declan's hands clenched into fists. "It's time, Elena, we need to go back. We need to stop Alastor once and for all. We vowed to never let what happened to Pyraxia happen again."

I cupped the side of his cheek as my thumb gently brushed across it. The muscles in his face loosened and his fists unclenched when I replied. "You're right, it's time to go back and save the people we love. It's time to get rid of him once and for all."

Declan slid an arm around my back, pulling me into his side. "We're ready. What do we need to do now?"

"As you've already figured out, Ehora has a powerful system of magic that derives from one's emotions. It's unlike anything that we've ever witnessed before. Both of you are Empaths, meaning you feel the weight of emotions to far greater extremes than most. Which makes you incredibly powerful"—Alyth paused— "but it also makes it extremely dangerous as well."

"Alastor knows about the true origin of dynamis, doesn't he?" Declan seethed.

"Yes, I'm afraid he does. Anger, fury and hate are incredibly strong emotions that can create an equally devastating dynamis if in the wrong hands. My own display of rage was just a small glimpse of what could happen." Tears streamed down her face, as Nixie stepped next to her and pulled her into an embrace.

"You must work together to control the balance, not just of the world, but within yourselves as well. Together, you'll need to learn how to control your emotions." Arthur's gaze bore into us both as we nodded our heads in a silent vow to do as he said.

Valdarin stepped forward, placing a hand on Declan's shoulder. "You have the choice to go back with a veil over your memories or not. What shall be your decision?"

I was sure we'd done this several times, but the idea of forgetting our memories together all over again turned the contents of my stomach sour. "Forgetting you again is not an option."

Declan's eyes flickered with delight. "It's not an option for me either, love."

"Good, then that's settled." Valdarin snorted. "Now, let's get you back before your grand entrance goes entirely up in flames."

"In flames?" My brow rose.

"Wildfire, you of all people should know how a Phoenix is reborn." Declan smirked.

Fire.

We didn't bury our loved ones, we helped them rise to the gods in the form of ashes on the wind.

"I knew one day your fiery blaze would consume me." He leaned down to give me a kiss. "This time, I'll be coming back with a little fire of my own." As he waggled his eyebrows up and down, the others' laughter filled the air.

Once more they circled around us, hands warming our shoulders. All at once the weight of what we were about to do shifted my mood. With trembling fingers, I clung to the pillar of strength in front of me.

"Time to spread those wings, love," he whispered into my mind. Before I could respond, my vision flooded with a searing, golden light.

CHAPTER 77

KILLIAN

Nothing could have stopped the gaping wound that had torn through me the moment I'd found their lifeless bodies.

We had been searching for Declan and Elena for over a week. Every one of our scouts and spies had been sent out on a massive hunt for them both. I was still torturing myself for not being on guard that night.

The night they'd gone missing, I'd ignored my instincts and decided to let them have some privacy. I'd become too comfortable in Oria, and now I'd lost two of the greatest people I'd ever known because of my lapse in judgment.

A group of us had gotten a lead on Alastor's lair and were making our way to it when we were blown back by a powerful gust of wind and light. Violet light. Liam and Nayla shot me knowing looks, because they had been with me that night when Declan and Elena had combined their powers in the city. Violet light had beamed out of them, both beautiful and devastating as they destroyed the beasts threatening to hurt us.

We'd zephyred immediately to the spot where the blast had been the brightest. However, we were far too late. The sound of Warren's broken yell as he fell to his knees beside Elena still haunted me, as well as the image of Nayla's swollen red eyes and Liam's pale face as he kneeled before our brother. However, the hardest thing to push to the back of my mind was the image of Clara sobbing over their broken bodies in the middle of the field, as she tried over and over to heal them. She pushed her dynamis so far that I had to rip her body off them before she fell to the same fate.

Thick gray clouds now hovered over Oria, covering the stars of the night sky, as if fate was trying to tell us we were drowning in the darkness. The cruel joke being that the only light we would now see was the embers of our beloved friends as they went up in flames on their pyres.

With a solemn sigh, I placed the last layer of branches over Declan and Elena's bodies. "I'm so sorry I failed you," I whispered as pressure built behind my eyes and my emotions swelled within me.

As the Guardian of the Light, I'd been responsible for protecting Lena. As Warren had reminded me several times in these past two days, I'd failed my duty.

"I've failed you both, but I vow to make it up to you. Even if it takes my entire lifetime to do so. Go in peace, my dear friends."

Tears wet my cheeks as I made my way down the ladder from the top of the pyre. Once my feet hit the ground, I swiped the evidence away. On heavy feet, I made my way back to Clara's side where her warm hand interlaced with my own.

Not a sound filled the air except the crackle of the small fire that had been built to light the arrows. Warren's watery eyes met mine and Liam's as he picked up the bow. We joined his side and we each lit our arrows, aiming at the pyre.

Warren's deep voice crackled when he spoke. "May the light always guide you, and the gods surround you." Then he released the flaming arrow into the sky as we launched ours behind him. Sobs and sniffles played a melancholy tune behind us as we watched the shining lights of our kingdom go up in flames.

After a while, many of the city's members retreated to their homes. The few of us closest to Declan and Lena were all that remained. Warren had an arm wrapped around Bri, trying to console her heart-wrenching sobs. The rest of us huddled close, mourning our friends together.

Guilt consumed me, and my dynamis prickled against my skin. With Clara wrapped tightly in my arms, I whispered one final blessing.

An explosion shattered the silence, and a blast of wind knocked us all off our feet.

Liam and I regained our footing, grabbed the nearest quivers and bows, and took aim. Warren and Nayla flanked behind us. We inched closer to the fallen pyre when another explosion halted us in our paths.

Bright light blinded us as it shot straight up into the sky. A deafening cry rang out in the air as I rubbed my eyes to regain my vision.

My breath hitched at the sight before me. It was such a shock that I could no longer hold up the weight of my body, and I crashed to my knees. The others must have joined me, as I heard similar grunts of discomfort as they hit the ground.

"How...It's not p-possible," Warren stuttered, at a loss for words beside me.

Two beings hovered before us, illuminated in golden light. One's gilded wings blazed with a fiery glow, while the other's onyx-feathered wings reflected the light of the fire like a mirror.

A violet hue pulsed around them both as they fluttered to the ground. Both tucked their wings, and with a flash of light they became hidden from sight. Now, all that stood before us was two people we had never imagined we would lay eyes on again.

Declan and Elena.

The clouds cleared away, leaving behind a perfect view of the stars. It was in that moment, I knew the gods had given us another chance.

Tomorrow would be a new day to rid the evil from our land once and for all. Those bright stars shimmering above us were a reminder to keep hope alive. Whatever the darkness decided to throw our way, we will continue to rise against it.

Even death couldn't stop the power of hope.

PRONUNCIATION GUIDE

Lenora: Luh-nor-uh
Keir: K-ear
Eloise: El-o-eez
Ehora: Eh-ror-uh
Elena: Ee-lay-nuh
Declan: Dek-lin
Killian: Kill-ee-an
Liam: Lee-um
Brietta: Bree-et-uh
Warren: War-in
Nayla: Nigh-luh
Alastor: Al-as-ter
Allaric: Uh-lair-ick
Edan: Eh-don
Adara: Uh-dar-uh
Zara: Zar-uh
Fallon- Fal-in
Dynamis: Die-nam-us
Vrine: Ver-een

Atheling: Aeth-ling
Grinwood: Grin-wood
Vragos: Vrah-gos

ACKNOWLEDGMENTS

First and foremost, I would like to thank you for reading my debut novel. Becoming an author was a dream that I thought would always just stay that…a *dream*. By reading this book, you've made it a reality and I will forever be thankful for that.

On that note, there are a few special people that I'd like to thank personally, because there were several times that this book almost never saw the finish line. It's because of their support that this book finally made it to print.

First, I would like to thank my husband Patrick, my real-life 'book-boyfriend' and my forever hero. You've been my torch, guiding me through the dark whenever I've lost my way. *You*, my love, are the main reason this book and my dream to be a writer became real. Thank you for *never* giving up on me and for always believing in me, especially when I had trouble believing in myself. I love you forever and always. Thank you for always loving me, broken pieces and all.

To my son, Hunter, I hope you know how much you inspire me every day. I am so proud of you, and I hope that you continue to chase your dreams every single day. You were always there with a hug when I needed it most. You are a bright light in this world, Hunty, and because of you this world will never be dim.

To my friends and family, your support through this entire process has meant more to me than you will ever know. Every kind word, big hug, or text message made me feel so loved. Thank you for being there for me through all the changes in my life, and loving me through them all.

To my parents—thank you for always being my biggest support-ers, reminding me to have faith in myself, and for always convincing me that there is never a dream too far out of reach. My sister Lyndsay —thank you for always making me laugh and helping me find my balance when you knew I'd reached my breaking point.

To Eleanor, my editor—I'm so thankful that I had you by my side through this journey. Your guidance helped me grow Declan's and Elena's story into everything I'd envisioned it would be and more. You helped me build confidence in myself as a writer and inspired me to keep pushing myself (especially when perfectionism threatened to get in my way.)

To Emily my PA—Thank you for helping me through those hard days and laughing with me when I'm technology challenged! Thank you for continuously boosting my confidence and for always being so understanding! I'm so thankful that our paths crossed, and I gained such a sweet friend in the process.

To my 'Spleens'— (Dahlia, Amaris, Ellie, Pedigo, A.C, Milli, Cyph and Lockwood.) I will forever be grateful for meeting you, loves. You all *saved* me in more ways than one, and this book truly wouldn't have made it into the hands of readers without each one of you. I will always be grateful for the ALL CAPS aggressive support, the laughs, the relentless GIF's, and all the moments in between. You all will *always* have a special spot in my heart. You never gave up on me, even when I gave up on myself. Thank you for always believing. I'm so proud of you all, and glad to have you in my life. Dahlia, I will forever be thankful for you finding my little lost little indie self on social media, and bringing me into the discord. You found me when I needed it the most, and I will forever be thankful for our friendship.

To my "Eastern Loves"— (Thank you LJ Andrews for creating Sigur Havn where I discovered my 'found family' and where you eased my fears of choosing the path to become a writer.) I'm so glad to have been a part of this wonderful community! A huge thank you to a few in particular who have become not only incredible friends but have supported me the entire way through with your endless kind messages, shares, likes and comments. Erin, Jenn, Alisha, Aubrey,

Amy, Hayley and Marci, you all keep me going when I need it most! Thank you for always being so kind.

To my early and late readers, and "Beta Reading Babes"–– thank you so much for reading my book in all of its stages! Vicki, Ellie, Marci—you are all amazing. Vicki, I don't think I can ever thank you enough for *all* the support and love you gave me, especially in those early stages. Thank you for reading multiple drafts and giving me valuable insight every time. I'm honored to know that my book helped make you feel seen. Marci, you read my final version right when I was about to give up entirely. Thank you for giving me not only another eye with editing, but also for making me believe in myself once again and giving me that final push when I truly needed one. Ellie, thank you for taking the time not only to read it, but giving me the much-needed confidence I needed in my darkest of times. All of you helped me continue to follow my passion to write. You made me believe that I was truly an author.

To my bookish buddies and authors pals I've met along the way— I'm so glad that we all met each other. I was nervous about entering into the social media realm, but after meeting you all, I've never been so thankful! Here are a special few that I'd like to thank personally, Cody, Elizabeth R., Sirena, Lance, M.N. Williams, Lydia Grace, November, Danyel, Megan Bowen, Pamela, Diane, Lauren M., and CutenessWolfy. Thank you for always showing this little indie author love and support, and for making the entire process not feel so lonely. Your messages and comments always light up my day, and I'm glad we all have each other to lean on and hype each other up!

To my ARC readers—thank you for taking a chance on me! I hope that you loved it and much as I loved writing it. I will always be thankful for you all wanting to read my debut novel, and I hope you enjoy it so much that you stick around for many more to come!

Finally, to everyone who suffers from any form of mental health, you are meant to do so much in this world. YOU have a purpose. I want to remind you that you are never alone. Keep on reaching out your hand and fighting for your light.

You are more powerful than you can ever imagine.
Don't let the darkness win

ABOUT THE AUTHOR

Amanda Carnahan is an author of fantasy romance and contemporary romance. She's a small-town girl who's always loved getting carried away in stories of love and epic adventures. Amanda thrives on creating stories that help others feel seen, and to feel like they are never alone in this world. When she is not writing, you will more than likely find her reading. When she's not reading, she's snuggling her son and her favorite MC, her husband. She also can be found hanging out with her two fluffy kitties, Whiskers and Shadow. They all enjoy spending time outdoors, whether it's the sunny beaches or the forests, they enjoy all the beauty that California offers.

www.ingramcontent.com/pod-product-compliance
Lightning Source LLC
Chambersburg PA
CBHW020644110726
47901CB00001B/43